"I'm sorry about what happened last night.

"I had no idea my dancing with someone would cause such a problem."

"Yeah, well, this is Montana. Not New York," he said.

His response stabbed at her. "Are you saying dancing causes issues in Montana?"

"A beautiful woman causes issues anywhere," Gage said.

"I'm not that beautiful," she retorted.

Gage looked at her in disbelief. "That's a matter of opinion. Just do me a favor and stay away from the bar the next few days. I don't have the manpower to handle the riots you cause."

"Are you saying this is my fault?"

"I'm saying you underestimated your power," he said.

Lissa felt her frustration build inside her. Her whole body roared with heat. "You're being a jerk. A complete jerk," she told him. She poked her finger again̲͟ ͟ ͟ ͟ ͟ ͟ ͟repeatedly. "If you think I'm s̲ ̲ ̲ ̲ ̲ ̲ ̲ ̲ ̲p being such an idi̲

THE MAVERICK & THE MANHATTANITE

BY
LEANNE BANKS

MILLS &
BOON

First published in Great Britain 2013
by Mills & Boon, an imprint of Harlequin (UK) Limited,
Eton House, 18-24 Paradise Road, Richmond, Surrey TW9 1SR

© Harlequin Books S.A. 2013

Special thanks and acknowledgement to Leanne Banks for her contribution to the Montana Mavericks: Rust Creek Cowboys continuity.

ISBN: 978 0 263 90141 2
ebook ISBN: 978 1 472 00527 4

23-0913

Harlequin (UK) policy is to use papers that are natural, renewable and recyclable products and made from wood grown in sustainable forests. The logging and manufacturing processes conform to the legal environmental regulations of the country of origin.

Printed and bound in Spain
by Blackprint CPI, Barcelona

ROM
Pbk

Leanne Banks is a *New York Times* and *USA TODAY* bestselling author who is surprised every time she realizes how many books she has written. Leanne loves chocolate, the beach and new adventures. To name a few, Leanne has ridden an elephant, stood on an ostrich egg (no, it didn't break), gone parasailing and indoor skydiving. Leanne loves writing romance, because she believes in the power and magic of love. She lives in Virginia with her family and a four-and-a-half-pound Pomeranian named Bijou. Visit her website, www.leannebanks.com.

This book is dedicated to Susan Litman.
Thanks for letting me join the Maverick train again!

Chapter One

My suitcase is packed and I'm ready for my assignment as a lead coordinator for Boot-straps, a charitable organization based in New York City. I'm getting ready to travel from my world to a totally different one. I'm trading subways, theater, high fashion and rush hour crowds for a small town in Montana that's been nearly destroyed by a flood. No more cushy apartment or paved sidewalks for me. I'll be facing mud—a lot of it. I expect I won't find a lot of Wall Street types in a town called Rust Creek. But there will be cowboys—and I've always been curious about cowboys....

— Lissa Roarke

Lissa's roommate, Chelsea, swirled her glass of red wine as she picked up one of the boots from Lissa's suitcase. Chelsea eyed it with disgust. "I can't believe you're actually going to wear something with the label *John Deere*."

"Hey, these are great," Lissa said. "They're weather resistant and the lining is moisture wicking and breathable. They've got removable orthotics, a tempered-steel shank and a rubber outsole."

"But they're ugly," Chelsea said and dropped the boot back into Lissa's open suitcase. She took a deep sip of wine. "I know you're into your job and you want to help people, but are you sure this is a good idea? There must be plenty you can still do here."

"This is a huge opportunity for me. I'll be the lead coordinator. Besides, my rent will be covered and you'll get to rule our little roost," Lissa said, giving her roommate a hug.

"But I'll miss you," Chelsea admitted. "And I've worked so hard to improve your style quotient."

Chelsea worked for a women's fashion magazine and believed one of her missions in life was to help everyone dress with more style and flair. She glanced in Lissa's suitcase again and gave a disapproving sniff. "Couldn't you at least include a Givenchy or Hermès scarf? A Burberry sweater?

Remember what I've told you. Just a few stand-out pieces can really make a difference."

Lissa smothered a chuckle. "Chelsea, I need to be ready to work. I need to give these people a strong impression that I'm there to help them if they're going to take me seriously. They haven't received enough national attention or help. No rock stars are holding concerts for them, and most of their town was practically wiped out, from what I've heard."

Chelsea sighed. "True, I suppose," she said and took another sip of wine. "You're such a good soul. I really will miss you."

"You won't have to share the bathroom," Lissa reminded her.

"Well, when you put it that way," Chelsea said. "Ciao. I'm putting a little prezzie in your suitcase for a time you may need it. Probably tomorrow night," she muttered under her breath. "No peeking."

"You don't need to give me any presents," Lissa said.

"Oh, I do. I have very little conscience, but I can't ignore true north on this one."

While Chelsea moved through the small apartment wearing a morose expression, Lissa double-checked her list and made last-minute preparations for her trip. She was halfnervous and totally excited. Her first assignment as lead coordinator.

She'd never be able to explain it to Chelsea, or her family of high achievers, for that matter, but Lissa had grown weary of life in the city and she was looking forward to being in a totally different environment. Her daily journal entries had grown stale and depressing. Her parents had always cautioned her not to put too much energy into her passion for writing. They thought she should focus on something more practical. Working for Bootstraps had offered her the unique opportunity to help people and also blog about her experiences on their website.

Although she knew her temporary stay in Montana would be challenging, she was looking forward to fresh air, big blue skies and wide-open spaces.

And cowboys. She wouldn't admit it to anyone else, but she'd had a fascination with cowboys for a long time. She wanted to know more about the real kind of cowboy, and apparently Montana was full of them. Lissa felt a twinge of guilt when she thought that Chelsea believed Lissa was being so self-sacrificing by going to Montana.

Lissa closed her eyes and brushed the unwelcome feeling aside. Her first duty was to help the community of Rust Creek Falls, and she was determined to make a difference. Cowboys were just the cherry on top of the assignment.

* * *

In his office, Sheriff Gage Christensen took another sip of coffee as he prowled the small area and listened to Charlene Shelton, a volunteer senior deputy, give her weekly report on how the elderly in his jurisdiction were faring. As soon as he'd begun serving as sheriff, Gage had learned it was a lot easier to appoint a volunteer to check on folks than wait for calls. "I've made all my calls. Everyone is mostly fine. Teresa Gilbert may need a ride to the doctor next week, so we'll need a volunteer driver for that. The only one who didn't answer or call me back was Harry Jones, but you know he's a stubborn one. Always has been. Ever since his wife died last year, he's just gotten worse."

"I'll get Will to check on Harry," he said, speaking of his deputy. "He won't mind."

"I'm still worried about all the people still stuck in trailers since the flood," she clucked. "Winter is coming and I can't believe those cheap trailers will withstand our blizzards."

Gage felt his neck tighten with tension. He didn't disagree with Charlene, but it would take time to put the rural town back together after the flash flood they'd experienced. "We're all working on it, Charlene. In fact, we've got a charity-relief woman coming in from the East. She should arrive this afternoon."

"From the East?" Charlene echoed, clearly enjoying receiving this bit of news. Gage figured she would be burning up the phone wires as soon as they finished the call. "How is someone from the East going to know what to do here? Where's she from?"

Gage hesitated. "New York."

Silence followed. "Well, I suppose they have experience with flooding, but we don't have subways or high-rises."

"I know, but we're not in a position to turn down help. I've been tapping every connection I can find. Some people are responding. Others are already booked. We need to get as much done as possible since winter will hit early."

"Yes, we're in hard times. If only Hunter McGee was still with us," she said.

The mention of the former mayor's name stabbed him. There was never a day that passed that he didn't think about the mayor's death during the storm. Gage blamed himself. His parents had talked him into taking a quick trip to a rodeo out of town and Hunter had agreed to cover for Gage. The flood hit and Hunter had rushed out in response to a call. A tree had fallen on his car and he'd died of a heart attack.

"No one can replace Hunter," Gage said.

"That's true, but we're lucky we have you as sheriff, Gage. You've been working nonstop to help us," Charlene said.

"There's always more to do," he said.

"Well, I'll bring you a pie the next time I come into town. A single man needs a pie every now and then," she said.

Gage looked at the baked goods piled on a table next to the dispatcher's desk. "You don't have to do that, Charlene. We all appreciate the work you do with the calls you make each week."

"Oh, it's nothing," she said. "I can bake a pie in my sleep."

Gage swallowed a sigh. "Thanks for making those calls. Take care, now."

At that moment, he heard the sound of a husky, feminine laugh and wondered who it was. It was a sexy sound that distracted him.

Gage glanced outside his office and saw his twenty-one-year-old deputy, Will Baker, walk into the office with a slim redhead by his side. The woman was a head-snapper with her fiery hair, long legs and confident air.

"Hey, uh, Gage, this is Lissa Roarke, the relief worker you told me to pick up from the airport. She needs someone to show her around town. I can do it."

Gage tore his gaze from the woman's eyes and bit back a smile. He wasn't at all surprised that Will was volunteering to show the pretty New Yorker around. He was practically drooling all over the woman. "That's okay. Vickie," he said, referring to this dispatcher, "needs to leave early, so I'd like you to fill in at the dispatcher desk for a couple hours."

Disappointment shadowed Will's face. "Oh, well, if you need me for anything, Lissa, give me a call. I wrote down my cell number for you. Call me anytime."

"Thank you, Will, and thank you for picking me up from the airport and taking me to the rooming house before bringing me here. You're a much better driver than most of the ones I deal with in the city."

Will stood a little taller. "We take our driving seriously out here."

Gage cleared his throat. "Will, thank you for picking up Miss Roarke. Vickie's waiting, okay." He moved toward the New Yorker and extended his hand. "I'm the sheriff, Gage Christensen. We appreciate your help."

"Please, call me Lissa," she said in a voice that held a hint of a sexy rasp. She returned his handshake. Her hand was small and soft. He had a hard time imagining her smooth, uncallused hand doing hard labor. Her long red hair fell in a mass of curls to her shoulders and he liked the fact that she didn't seem to care about taming it. Maybe she wasn't as high maintenance as he feared. He'd met a few city women and most of them had seemed obsessed with their hair and nails. Her blue eyes glinted with curiosity and intelligence.

"Call me Gage," he said. "Do you need something to eat before I show you around?" He cocked his head toward the table near the dispatcher's desk. "People are always dropping off food for us. It's generous, but if I ate everything they bring in, I'd be as big as a barn. Sometimes I wonder if they're secretly trying to kill me," he joked in a low voice.

Lissa gave a light laugh. "I'm sure they're just showing their appreciation. I'm not hungry, though, because I ate during my layover. I'm anxious to see Rust Creek Falls. I visited Thunder Canyon when one of my cousins got married and it was beautiful."

"I better warn you that Rust Creek is a lot different from Thunder Canyon. Thunder Canyon has a first-class resort and a lot of shops. We have the minimum requirements here. For everything else, we have to head out of town. Things aren't nearly as picturesque since the flood here, either."

"That's okay," she said. "I have some experience with floods myself after living in New York City."

"I can't deny you that. You've had some natural disasters that looked like real messes on the news," he said and led her outside to his patrol car.

"Trust me. They were worse in person," she said and slid into the passenger seat.

Even though he wasn't all that confident that a lady from Manhattan was going to be able to help Rust Creek much, Gage was determined to be gracious. He had a hard time believing this city girl would really understand the needs of a small town. He drove down the street, pointing out the businesses that had mostly survived the flood. "We got lucky that some of our important buildings didn't get hit by the flood. The Masonic Hall," he said, gesturing to the structure as he turned onto North Main Street. "And thank goodness Crawford's General Store dodged that bullet. We get everything from feed to groceries there. And the church is still intact. By the way, the reverend is a good man and he'll be a good resource for you."

"That's good to know," Lissa said. "I'll try to meet him as soon as I can."

Taking a turn, he headed in a different direction. "One of the biggest losses was the elementary school. Teachers are holding classes in their homes. The town just doesn't have the money to rebuild."

"That's terrible," she said, making notes in a small notebook. "I'd like to make that a priority in terms of raising funds."

"This is the flood zone. Most of the houses were lost or damaged on these streets, including my sister's house."

"Can we stop so I can take a look inside the homes?"

"Sure," he said, pulling his car to the side of the road. He took her inside an unlocked house.

"Wow, the door isn't locked. Have you had trouble with looting?" she asked.

"Not so much. People took their valuables when they moved in with family or into the area where most of the trailers are," he said.

She nodded as she stepped inside and looked around. She tapped on the wooden floor with her foot. "This is good," she said as she looked around the bare room. "They've pulled out most of the sources for mold. Furniture, draperies. Even pulled out the dry wall and insulation."

"Some people cooperated and others just took off. We moved out the furniture next door, but the owners haven't touched the drywall."

She bit her lip. "That makes things more challenging, but I have some mold specialists coming in during the next few days. They'll make assessments and start work on our top priority places."

"I was wondering how you were going to get any professionals here since we're in the middle of nowhere. We've taxed our contacts in Thunder Canyon and Kalispell to the max, but those folks need to make a living, too. They can't work for free forever," he said.

She looked at him and nodded. "That's why

I'm here—to fill in those gaps. I remember reading about the trailer village. I've been able to get a few more for the specialists to share since they'll be around for a while. I'm going to have weekly volunteer groups staying at the church. Can you show me more of the damaged areas?"

"Sure," he said as she walked past him to leave the house. Despite her work boots, he noticed she had a nice little wiggle in her walk and she smelled more like a woman than a girl. Her dark and spicy scent was at odds with her fresh face and natural hair. She was more practical than he'd expected, Gage thought. She could be distracting and he didn't need that.

Gage drove out toward several ranches that had been damaged and had lost animals and he noticed Lissa continued to take notes. "Such a shame, but we're here to make it better. It's amazing how this seemed to happen in an instant. When New York flooded, at least we got some notice. Did you have any damage at your ranch?"

"My first floor was pretty much ruined. I lost a lot of personal papers and some photographs. I'm living in a temporary trailer at the moment," he said.

"Oh, I'm so sorry," she said, sympathy sliding through her voice like cool water on hot skin. "That must have been horrible."

Gage thought of the mayor who'd died in the

flood and everything inside him refused her kindness. "I got off easy," he snapped. "Some people lost their lives."

"Yes, of course," she said in an apologetic tone. "I didn't mean to—"

"I think you've probably seen enough to get you started. I'll take you back to the rooming house," he said tersely. As much as Gage wanted help for Rust Creek, he hadn't expected that being around the relief worker would remind him of all he'd been unable to do to help the people stranded by the flood because he'd been out of town. He'd spent every spare minute since the flood trying to help citizens get back on their feet, but the process was slow. Too slow for him.

Lissa climbed the creaky wooden steps to her room, feeling as if someone had taken the wind out of her sails. She'd started out the day filled with hope and determination, and even though the lingering devastation from the flood tugged at her, she'd felt optimistic as the sheriff showed her around.

Of course, it didn't hurt that he was tall and lean with muscles in all the right places, and he walked with a sexy, confident stroll that she suspected could turn into a fast run at the right moment. She liked his deep voice. Everything about him seemed *sure*. He might have his doubts and

regrets about a few things, but Lissa sensed that
Gage was okay in his own skin and didn't waste
time wondering what people thought of him.

At the same time, his brooding gaze suggested
a bit of sadness. She could tell he felt the burden
of helping his community since the flood. She just
wished she hadn't set him off with her sympathy for his own property loss. She should have
known better. Rust Creek Falls had been suffering for months and Gage had a firsthand view of
most of it.

Opening the door to the bedroom that would be
her home for the next month, she glanced at the
comfy-looking bed, chest of drawers, minifridge
and coffeemaker. She was surprised to see a sandwich, chips and water on a tray for her with a note.
"Thought you could use this after your long day.
Let us know how we can help. Melba."

Lissa smiled. The thoughtfulness of Melba
Strickland, the boardinghouse's owner, soothed
her. This never would have happened to her in
Manhattan. That was for sure. She tugged off her
boots and went to the tiny bathroom to wash her
hands and splash her face. All she wanted was to
jump into her pj's, gobble down that sandwich and
hit the sack. She opened her suitcase on the luggage rack and decided she'd unpack some other
time. Digging down into the bottom, she found a

box she couldn't remember packing. She pulled it out and opened it: two bottles of red wine. Lissa laughed. This must have been her roommate's gift.

Shaking her head, she put the box in her suitcase and pulled out her pj's. She didn't need wine. She needed a good night of sleep and the shot of optimism she hoped it would bring.

Gage didn't pull into his dirt driveway until after eleven o'clock. He stopped by the Martins' ranch, where he was helping Bob Martin redo the kitchen floor. The family hoped to be back in the house by Thanksgiving, but it was going to be close. Gage wasn't a certified plumber or electrician, but growing up with his dad had provided him with a lot of practical do-it-yourself knowledge.

He would ask Lissa Roarke if she could send her mold specialists over to the Martins. He thought of her and her long, curly hair and upbeat attitude. Inhaling deeply, he could almost smell her perfume.

Gage scowled at himself. What was he thinking? He'd just met Lissa and he could tell she was city through and through. Not at all his type. He'd dated a couple city girls during his early twenties who'd visited relatives in Rust Creek Falls, and he'd quickly learned that the women didn't have any staying power and needed more amusements than this small town could offer.

Stepping out of his car, he felt a chilly wind sweep through him. He shivered and hustled to the trailer he was living in now. If Gage had devoted himself to repairing his own home, he could have been in it a month ago, but it just didn't seem right to him. Entire families had been uprooted by the flood, so he spent most evenings trying to give those most affected a hand. Even though people were in need, they were more than willing to help their neighbors. That was a fact of life in Rust Creek and it was one of the reasons he'd allowed himself to be talked into running for sheriff.

There may have been times when he'd thought about leaving Montana, but his roots here ran deep. His family and the people were important to him. Ranching was in his blood. Gage stepped inside the trailer and felt the wind shake and rattle through his metal home. Chuckling to himself, he rubbed his hands together before he turned on his coffeemaker. Sometimes he felt like he was living in a tin can. He would get around to fixing his own home after he'd helped more of the families who were suffering.

Gage pulled off his hat and grabbed a pair of pajamas out of one of the few drawers in the trailer. Still cold, he stood over the coffeemaker until the brown liquid made its way to the carafe. Even with the long hours he was pulling he still sometimes had a hard time falling asleep, so he'd started drinking decaf at night. He sure as hell didn't need one more reason to keep him awake.

He poured a cup of the hot coffee then sank onto the sofa that sat across from his television. Turning on the TV, he prepared to lose himself in a ballgame. For a few minutes before he fell asleep, he would think about something besides the way so many of his people were suffering. He watched for several moments before his eyes started to drift closed. He blinked, realizing he was more tired than he'd thought.

Gage brushed his teeth and washed his face, then pulled out the sleep sofa and sank onto the bed. It wasn't the best bed, but it felt good at the moment. He listened to the game with his eyes closed for a few moments then turned off the TV. Sighing, he forced himself not to think about what he had on his plate tomorrow. Instead, a vision of a red-haired woman sneaked into his mind like smoke under a door.

Gage shook his head, willing the image away.

Lissa dragged herself out of bed, started the coffeemaker in the room and stumbled into the shower. It would take a few days for her to get used to the time zone change. It might only be two hours different from New York, and she might be an early riser, but five-thirty a.m. was a little too early for her. Inhaling a cup of coffee, she pulled on a set of long underwear, jeans and a sweater, as she ran through a mental list of what she wanted to accomplish today. Hoping she would succeed after riling the good sheriff, she brushed her teeth and put on a little lip gloss, then headed out of her room.

She smelled the scent of fresh coffee brewing along with something cinnamony baking in the oven and bacon frying. Lissa drooled. She'd planned to grab some yogurt from the local store.

A woman's voice called out to her. "Breakfast is almost ready. Come on in to the kitchen."

Lissa stepped into the warm room, catching sight of Melba Strickland, the eighty-something-year-old owner of the rooming house, removing crispy bacon from a cast iron skillet. "How do you like your eggs, honey?"

"Oh, you don't need to do that," Lissa said, noticing a couple of men at the breakfast table. "I planned to grab a bite on my way to the sheriff's office."

"No need for that when you can eat the best breakfast in town," Melba said, then shot Lissa an assessing glance from behind her glasses. "Besides, you look like you could use a little fattening up, and breakfast is included with your room. Sunny-side up or scrambled?"

"Scrambled, thank you," Lissa said, smiling at the take-charge woman.

"Go ahead and get yourself some coffee," Melba said, nodding toward the coffeemaker with mugs beside it. "There's orange juice, too, if you like. What do you have up your sleeve today?"

"Getting more information about the damage from the flood and trying to get a better feel for the layout of the county. I have a mold specialist coming in tomorrow. I'm hoping that since Montana is usually dry that it won't be the kind of problem we had with Hurricane Sandy."

Melba shook her head. "Trouble is, not everyone was willing to give up their furniture. If I said it once, I said it a hundred times—you have to get all the wet stuff *out* of the house, or you're just asking for more trouble. But I'm an old woman. I don't know anything." Melba plopped the scrambled eggs onto a plate along with a large portion of bacon and a huge cinnamon roll. "There you go. Eat up."

"Oh, that's entirely too—" Lissa stopped at the hard glance Melba threw at her. "Looks delicious. Thank you," she said, wondering if there was a hungry dog close by with whom she could share all the food.

She sat down next to an older man who had cleaned his plate. "Hello. I'm Lissa Roarke."

The man nodded. "Nice to meet you. I'm Gene Strickland, Melba's husband."

"I don't suppose you're still hungry," she said in a low voice.

He shook his head and chuckled. "No chance. But I'll distract her when you're done. You might wanna fix your own plate from now on. Melba thinks women are too skinny these days and she's on a mission to change that."

"Thanks for the tip," Lissa said. She hadn't wanted to offend the rooming house owner the second day she'd arrived in the state.

While Gene drank his coffee, Lissa finished her eggs, a slice of bacon and a few bites of the delicious cinnamon roll. When she could eat no more, she nodded in Gene's direction.

He nodded in return. "Hey Melba, I think we might have a leak in the roof. You want me to fix it?"

Melba frowned. "We don't have a leak in the roof. We better not have a leak in the roof," she said, putting her hands on her hips. "Even if we did, I wouldn't let you go climbing on top of the house at your age. Have you gone crazy? You show me what you're talking about, Gene."

Gene smiled and rose from the table. "I think it's on the northeast side," he said. "Let's take a look."

"Bless you, bless you," Lissa whispered and quickly rose and wrapped the rest of her cinnamon roll to eat later.

Walking out of the rooming house, she felt a hint of moisture in the cold air. She glanced up at the sky. She hadn't checked the weather, but she supposed that with those clouds, anything was possible. Shrugging, she headed down the street to the sheriff's office. The weather wasn't going to stop her today.

As she stepped into the building that housed the sheriff's office, she saw Gage putting on his Stetson and looking as if he were preparing to leave.

"Good morning," she said.

"Mornin'," he said in return. "I just got a call about an accident, so I won't be able to show you around today."

Will immediately piped up. "I can do it," he offered.

"You have to give the home-safety class for the school kids. Remember? You'll be busy all day going to all those different places they're holding class since we lost the school."

Will made a face. "I forgot."

"Good thing I didn't. Those teachers would have been ticked off at both of us if you hadn't shown up," Gage said.

"Well, what are you going to do with Lissa?" Will asked. "You can't just leave her stranded."

Gage sighed. "Maybe I can get Gretchen Paul to cart her around today."

Mildly offended by the word *cart,* Lissa shook

her head. "Oh, I don't want to be any trouble. Perhaps I could rent a car."

Gage and Will glanced at each other. "Not unless you want to go back to the airport and get it," Gage said.

"I don't know. Melba at the rooming house might let Lissa use her car. She might not even charge her," Will said.

"Not a good idea since she doesn't know her way around the country. Will, you need to remember Lissa isn't used to being in a rural place. No telling what might happen if she doesn't have someone to help her," Gage said.

Lissa's stomach knotted at his inference that she couldn't handle the job she was sent to do. "I think you're exaggerating. It's not as if this is Antarctica or outer Mongolia. Most of the roads I'll be driving on will be paved, and Rust Creek Falls isn't known for its violence."

"That may be true, but it's still a lot different than Manhattan and you just got here. You just sit tight. We'll figure out something by this afternoon. I need to head out," Gage said and left her staring after him.

Sit tight? I don't think so, Lissa thought. "Thanks for the tip, Will."

"Hey, maybe you better not do that," Will said. "Gage made a good point. You don't know your way around," he said, a worried look crossing his young face.

"I can read a map," she said, although she would have been much more comfortable with a reliable GPS. "I'll be fine."

Chapter Two

Lissa had been just fine until snow had started to fall and the roads turned slippery. After visiting a mom of three on the list Bootstraps had provided for her who needed new carpet and furniture, Lissa wobbled down the winding side road in Melba's eighteen-year-old Buick. Beggars couldn't be choosers, but Lissa wondered how Melba could possibly use such a vehicle with Montana's treacherous winters.

The snow pelted against the windshield and Lissa gripped the steering wheel so tightly her knuckles were white. The car veered to the center of the road and she immediately pulled it back into her lane. If she could just get to the main road, she thought she would be okay.

Suddenly, a deer appeared in front of her. Her heart jumped and she instinctively slammed on the brakes. The car went into a spin that seemed to go on forever. She struggled to gain control then felt the sickening sensation of the massive Buick tilting toward a ditch.

"No, no, no," she pleaded, willing the car back on the road.

Gravity won and the car slid headfirst into the ditch, stopping with an ugly jerk that yanked her head forward before the seat belt wrenched her back against the seat. It took a few seconds for Lissa to remember to breathe. As she gasped for air, willing her heart to stop pounding, she took inventory of herself, wiggling her shoulders and legs. Everything seemed okay, although the seat belt was holding her so tightly it felt like a vise. Pushing aside the discomfort, she glanced around and tried to figure out how to get out of the ditch. She opened the door to get out, but there wasn't enough room between the side of the ditch for her to open it all the way. Lissa glanced at the other side and grimly noticed that she had succeeded in wedging herself perfectly in the ditch, a feat she wouldn't have been able to accomplish if she'd intentionally tried.

She groaned. Lissa *really* didn't want to call the

sheriff. She could see the scowls and disapproval coming and she couldn't blame him. If she'd followed his advice, she wouldn't be in this mess. Frowning, she realized Gage wasn't the only lawman she could call. Will had given her his number. She could call the deputy and deal with Gage's displeasure another time. She was sick enough at the thought that she'd damaged Melba's car.

Lissa pulled Will's card from her purse and punched in his number. The call went directly to voice mail and she remembered Gage had said something about Will speaking about safety to the elementary children. Lissa reluctantly left a message and decided to wait for him to return the call.

She cut the engine and pulled out her tablet to make notes, but she glanced at the time every other minute. It was just after three o'clock. If Will didn't call soon, she was going to have to call Gage. She couldn't stay out here all night. Who knew how much more snow would fall in this surprise storm? She was already starting to feel trapped.

Her cell finally rang after eighteen minutes. She immediately answered. "Will?"

"Yes, Miss—Lissa," he said. "You said you've had a problem. What can I do for you?"

"Well, I'm in Melba Strickland's car on Route 563," she said and swallowed her pride. "And I'm stuck in a ditch."

Will gave a low whistle. "Are you injured?"

"No," she said. "But I'm going to need some serious help getting out of this ditch."

"Okay, sit tight. We'll take care of you. It may take a few minutes to get there since I'm on the other side of the county."

"Thank you," she said, relief spilling through her. "I really appreciate it."

"It's what I do," Will said. "See you soon."

Lissa slumped back against the seat and took a deep breath. As soon as she got out of this mess, she was going to rent an SUV with the best GPS available. She just hated that she'd let Melba down by wrecking her car.

Twenty-five minutes later, a male voice called to her outside her window. "Will. Thank goodness," she whispered and started the car. She pushed the button to lower the window. "Will?" she called, pleased that the snow had slowed to a slight white drizzle.

"It's Gage," the man said as she craned to see him.

"Oh, great," she muttered to herself.

"I guess you decided not to wait until this afternoon," he said.

"I didn't want to waste time," she said. "I'm going to need a giant can opener to get out."

"Not quite," he said, as he jumped in front of the car. His facial expression no-nonsense, he waved his hand. "Put it in Reverse and don't gun it. Steady pressure," he said.

"Okay," she said and attempted to do what he'd told her. All she did was spin her wheels.

"Okay, now I want you to rock it. Put it in Drive, then Reverse."

She followed his instructions and rocked the car. She was still spinning, but she tried it again and suddenly, the car made several inches backward. "Yay," she cried.

"Good job," Gage said, jumping to the side of the car. "Rock again a couple times then I'm going to give you an extra push.

She followed his instructions. "Reverse," he shouted.

Lissa slammed into Reverse and gunned the pedal while Gage pushed and suddenly she was halfway out of the ditch. "Turn the wheel hard and brake," he said.

The car miraculously didn't slide back into the ditch. Gage tapped on the door. "You ready to get out of there?"

He had no idea, she thought. Lissa released the lock and scrambled from the car so quickly she lost her footing.

"Whoa," Gage said, pulling her to her feet. She felt his brown gaze assessing her and something inside dipped. "You okay?"

She took a deep breath and inhaled the scent of

leather and a hint of cologne. "Of course," she said breathlessly. "I'm just embarrassed and I hate that I probably messed up Melba's car. And I couldn't get out—" She broke off when she realized her words were running together and took another quick breath. "I'm fine."

His lip twitched. "Okay. What I'm gonna do now is pull the car the rest of the way out of the ditch. I tow stuff all the time, so this shouldn't be any different."

Ten minutes later, Gage was pulling the car behind his truck. Lissa sat beside him as he slowly made his way toward the main road.

"I'm sorry I caused you extra trouble," she finally said, glancing at him.

"It happens. It could have been worse," he said with a shrug. "You're lucky you didn't get hurt."

"I really do know how to drive in the snow. I just haven't done as much driving since I've been living in Manhattan," she told him.

"You're just a little rusty. You'll get better with practice. You just might want to take it easy heading out into the snow. We can't be digging you out every day," he said with a chuckle.

"That won't happen," she said a little more sharply than she intended. "I'm not here to cause problems. I'm here to help."

He shot her a quick glance. "Rust Creek Falls

needs that help. You just need to remember you're
in a different place. This isn't Manhattan."

"I know that," she said, crossing her arms over
her chest.

"Then check the weather and take it seriously
the next time you decide to head out into the far
parts of the county," he told her.

He was right. She hated it, but he was right.
"Will do," she muttered.

"Good. Things will go better that way."

They drove the rest of the way in silence.
Gage pulled into the driveway behind the room-
ing house. Because of all the snow on the vehicle,
Lissa wasn't sure how much damage she'd caused.
Hopping out of Gage's truck, she rushed to look
it over and was shocked to only find a few dents.

"Good grief," she said. "I was sure I totaled it."

Gage walked to stand beside her. "Not Melba's
Blue Bomb. It's lasted through floods, blizzards,
bumps, wrecks. Everything."

Lissa shook her head. "Do you think Melba will
be upset about the scrapes and bumps I left on it?"

Gage chuckled. "She'll be hard-pressed to find
'em. Once you tell her about your little bump with
the ditch, she'll be more concerned about your
safety than her car."

Melba waddled toward them from the back of
the house. "Glory be, thank goodness you're alive,"
she said, wrapping her arms around Lissa. "I heard

all about it from Nanette Gilbert. She heard from Sadie Brown. I think one of the teachers told her when she overheard the conversation with Will. I was sure you would end up in the hospital after such a terrible wreck."

Gage covered a chuckle. "It wasn't all that terrible. She just fell into the ditch and couldn't get out. Everything's okay now."

"Well, you can be sure I'm not going to let you drive if there's any chance of snow. If you'd been hurt, I don't know what I'd do. Come on in and let me give you some soup. You can come, too, if you want, Sheriff."

"That's mighty tempting, Melba, but I've got to get back to the office." He glanced at Lissa. "I'm sure she'll take care of you now."

Lissa met his gaze. "Thank you again for getting me out of the ditch."

He touched his hat. "You're welcome."

Gage walked to his car and drove to his office, the whole time thinking about Lissa and the spark in her eyes. He could tell she felt bad about driving into the ditch. He just hoped like hell she wouldn't do the same thing again. When Will had called him with the news, it had given him a jolt. Will had wanted to go after her, but Gage had insisted, and now he was glad he had. Lissa had been well wedged in that ditch.

Lissa's combination of determination and humility got to him. She had a twinge of pride, but it didn't keep her from going after her goals. She made something inside him rumble and burn, and he didn't like it one bit. He didn't have time for any sort of attraction or distraction.

Frowning, he strode into his office building, where a young blonde woman stood. "What can I do for you?" he asked, trying to place her. "You look familiar, but I don't think we've met. I'm Gage Christensen, the sheriff," he said and extended his hand.

She smiled and accepted his grasp. "I'm Jasmine Cates. I'm from Thunder Canyon. I've been helping my brother-in-law Dean with some construction projects here in town."

"Thank you for your help," he said.

"I'm trying to get in touch with someone by the name of Ann Gilbert. Someone brought some of her furniture in for repair, but the phone number they left is disconnected."

Gage felt a shot of loss. "Some people have left town. The flood was too hard on them. Annie Gilbert fell and broke her hip just after the flood. I think she's been staying in Livingston while she gets back on her feet. I can probably find a way to get in touch with her."

"That would be great," Jasmine said, an expression of relief crossing her face. "Her furniture was beautiful. We really want it returned to her."

"Will do," he said. At that moment, Gary Culbert brought in a casserole dish. "What's up, Gary?"

"Edith made some extra chicken potpie and she wanted you to have it. She really appreciated you helping us get our cattle back last week," the thirty-something-year-old man with a cowlick said. He glanced at Jasmine and tipped his ball cap. "There's more than enough to share."

A moment of silent awkwardness passed and Gage finally met Jasmine's gaze. He shrugged. "You want to join me for dinner?"

She bit her lip. "It's a little early, but…"

"It's early for me, too," Gage said.

"Well, you could heat it up in the microwave," Gary said. "This is good stuff. I appreciate you helping us with the cattle, but I was disappointed when Edith insisted I bring you half of what she was baking."

Gage chuckled. "You sure you don't want to tell her I refused her kind offer so you can take it back home with you?"

"She'd skin me alive," Gary said.

"I can come back in an hour or two," Jasmine said, shoving her hands into her coat pockets.

Gage paused a half beat. *Well, hell.* Maybe Jasmine would keep him from thinking about Lissa.

Jasmine didn't talk as fast as Lissa and she didn't make his gut twist into a knot. "Yeah," he said. "That'll work. I'll see you later, then."

For the next two hours, Gage took care of paperwork, answered calls and touched base with Will. It had been a hell of a day. He raked his hand through his hair as Jasmine walked into the office.

"Rough afternoon?" she asked.

He lifted an eyebrow. "Why do you ask?"

"You don't look—" she smiled "—happy."

"Every day is an adventure," he said, rising to his feet. "Are you ready for that chicken potpie?"

"Sounds good to me," she said.

Gage put the potpie in the microwave and heated it. He pulled out two plates and poured himself a cup a coffee. "We have hot chocolate, coffee and cider. What's your pleasure?" he asked.

"Hot chocolate sounds good for tonight. Thank you," she said.

"Have a seat," he said, motioning toward the chair across from his desk. He spooned the chicken potpie onto the plates and set her plate across from him then served himself. "So, how does Rust Creek Falls compare to Thunder Canyon?"

She chuckled. "Rust Creek is a little more rustic, but the people are great. We have a bit more shopping, but the truth is we still do a lot of shopping online."

"It's nice of the folks from Thunder Canyon to

come and help us," he said and took a bite of the potpie. It was delicious, just as Gary had said.

"We're connected in many ways," Jasmine said. "Why wouldn't we help?"

He nodded and continued the conversation and the meal, but he couldn't keep his mind from wandering to thoughts of Lissa. Damn the woman. Images of her red hair and sparkling eyes slid through his mind. Her determination bumped through him. What was going on, he wondered. This was ridiculous.

Finally, both he and Jasmine had finished the potpie, although he couldn't have recalled much about their conversation if asked.

She stood. "This was fun," she said with a sweet smile.

"Yeah. It was," he said, knowing there wouldn't be a repeat. He couldn't mislead a nice girl like Jasmine until he got Lissa out of his head. He extended his hand to Jasmine. "Thanks for all you're doing for us."

She blinked and shook his hand as if she weren't quite sure how to take him. "Um, you're welcome. Maybe I'll see you again?"

"I'm the sheriff," he said. "Everyone sees me at one time or another."

He sensed her immediate withdrawal and wished he wasn't so distracted by Lissa.

She nodded. "Have a nice night."

Fat chance, he thought.

Lissa leaped off her bed in shock as her alarm sounded the next morning. She still hadn't made the adjustment to Mountain Time. Plus it didn't help that she had driven Melba's car into a snowy ditch yesterday. Even more embarrassing was that Gage had rescued her. She didn't want him to view her as incompetent or a pain in the rear. She hadn't helped her case by going out in the snow yesterday, but she was too impatient to wait to be chauffeured. There was too much to be done.

Taking a quick shower, she pulled on her clothes and sneaked down the back steps. Avoiding the temptation of Melba's full breakfast, she scarfed down a granola bar. The temperature was higher than yesterday, but still cold. She blew into the air and saw her own vapor. In Manhattan, she would have worn a hat, gloves and scarf. Today, she wore the same, but it felt more freakin' freezing. The subway was a lot warmer than the great outdoors of Montana.

She made her way to the mayor's office and was surprised to find it open at such an early hour. Stepping inside, she glanced around and saw an elderly woman focused on paperwork. Although Lissa has never seen the woman, she suspected this was Thelma McGee, the mother of the late mayor.

"Good morning. I'm Lissa Roarke," she said, approaching the counter.

The woman looked up from behind her glasses. "Good morning to you. I'm Thelma McGee."

"I'm honored to meet you," Lissa said.

Thelma's eyes softened. "Thank you. You must know about my son."

"I do," Lissa said. "Everyone talks about what a wonderful man he was."

Thelma sighed. "He was," she said. "And I'm just trying to help keep his office running. But it's not easy."

"Everyone appreciates your effort," Lissa said. "I'm here with the Bootstraps organization to help the town get back on track."

"I can't tell you how much we appreciate your help," Thelma said, rising from the computer. "Rust Creek Falls is a bit remote, so it's hard for us to get enough help. Thank you for coming. We all thank you."

Lissa shrugged. "I'm not sure everyone is all that excited about me being here to help."

Thelma lifted her eyebrows and set a cup of coffee on the counter for Lissa. "Are you talking about Gage?"

Lissa felt a rush of heat rise to her cheeks. "I guess you could say that."

"Gage blames himself for everything. He doesn't understand that he doesn't have the power to prevent a flash flood. He's been through a lot. We all have, but he will come around. It just may take a bit longer." Thelma put her hand over Lissa's. "Give him time. Don't pay attention to his crankiness."

Lissa couldn't help but smile. "I'll work on it. I've heard so many good things about you. Now I understand why."

Thelma waved her hand in dismissal. "Don't flatter me. I just want to honor my son."

Lissa's heart twisted at the woman's words and she felt her determination rise inside her even more strongly. She *would* help Rust Creek Falls. She *would* make a difference.

No matter what Gage Christensen thought about her.

Before he'd had his second cup of coffee, Gage saw Lissa Roarke walk through the door of his office. His stomach rolled. He wasn't ready for this.

"Good morning," she said. "I'm glad you're here. I've thought about the day and I would like to do a little more research on the north side of the county. Do you think you could take me? Or should I ask Will?"

Gage's head was spinning. "Whoa, whoa," he said. "Why do you have to talk so fast? Talking fast isn't going to get anything done faster."

"I just want to get things done as quickly as

possible for your town," she said. "They've been waiting a long time."

"True, but unless you have recruits ready today, there's no need to rush," he said.

Frustrated beyond measure, she barely resisted stomping her foot. "Why are you fighting me on this?" she asked. "Is this personal? Do you dislike what I'm trying to do? If I'm the one who's causing a problem for you, then maybe I should just call my boss and ask for a replacement."

"Why are you jumping off a cliff? I just said you talk way too fast. You just need to slow down," he said.

"You haven't done anything but give me a hard time. Maybe you would be happier with someone else heading up this project," she said.

"You just don't understand what you're getting into. Your degrees may work in New York, but they won't do much here," he said.

"How dare you?" she asked. "I'm just trying to help and all you can do is criticize. You act like I personally made it rain here in Rust Creek Falls. I'm calling my boss so he can have someone else come here to help."

Shaking all over, but trying to hide it, Lissa turned and headed for the door. She reached for it, but Gage's hand covered hers.

"Don't," he said in a low voice.

She glanced back at him and he lowered his

head toward her. He pressed his mouth against hers and her head and heart began to spin. She felt a crazy mix of anger, frustration, desperation and attraction, and her knees buckled from the force of the kiss.

Gage gripped her waist and pulled her against him, his breath heavy. Lissa's stomach dipped. She couldn't remember a time she'd felt like this.

Her gaze clung to his for a long moment. Finally, they both took a breath and she stumbled away from him. She took a deep breath, trying to clear her head.

She couldn't take her eyes from his.

He shook his head and exhaled. "I shouldn't have done that," he said and walked away from her.

Lissa's mind swirled. She locked her knees to keep from falling. She forced herself to pull herself together. How was she supposed to deal with all of this? How was she supposed to conquer her attraction to Gage and help the people of Rust Creek Falls? He'd been prickly enough that she'd been able to resist thinking about him all the time, but she knew there was something under Gage's surface that she found way too compelling. It was more than his cowboy boots and his Stetson. She just couldn't ignore the strength he emanated.

She steeled herself against her feelings. She just had to do it. Nothing, not even Gage Christensen, could or should keep her from her goal.

Lissa kept herself occupied at the desk she'd been given at the sheriff's office with plans for repairs for the next day, but thoughts of Gage plagued her. She had never been kissed like that before. She'd never had such powerful feelings before. Lissa was trying to regain control. She tried to tell herself that Gage hadn't shaken her to her bones, but it was hard.

At the end of the day when she went back to her room, she decided to give her cousin, Maggie, a call. Maggie was a lawyer and was working hard to negotiate a release for Arthur Swinton in Thunder Canyon. Although she was swamped, Maggie answered her cell phone. "How is it going, sweetie?" Maggie asked. "I hope you don't feel like I got you shipped to outer Mongolia."

"No. It's not that bad," Lissa said, laughing at Maggie's reference to the rural nature of where she'd been assigned.

"I hope you don't feel like you got pushed into this, but Rust Creek Falls needed some serious help and I thought you could give it," Maggie said.

"It's okay. Besides, you didn't send me—my boss at Bootstraps sent me. You just used your influence to get Bootstraps involved. I'm glad to be the project coordinator for this job. Plus, you know what they say about cowboys. It's all true. I have to say I have never been so thoroughly kissed,"

Lissa said, giving a big sigh over the kiss she'd shared with Gage.

Maggie chuckled. "Well, congratulations on finding your real-life cowboy."

Lissa rolled her eyes. "No congratulations necessary. This cowboy still acts like he can't stand me."

"What? How can that be?" Maggie asked.

"I can't focus on it. I have a job to do," Lissa said.

"Well, I hope your cowboy will help instead of hinder," Maggie said.

"Me, too," Lissa said. "How's the trial going?"

"Well, they don't call it a trial for no reason," Maggie joked.

Lissa laughed. "Seriously, how's it going?"

"We're making progress," Maggie said. "I'm hopeful."

"Spoken like a true lawyer," Lissa said.

"Yeah, well, that's my job," Maggie said.

"And you do it well," Lissa said.

"Thanks," Maggie said. "Take care, cuz. Call me if you need me."

Lissa sank onto her bed at the rooming house. She definitely felt as if she had bitten off more than she could chew. Dragging her tired body to the bathroom, she washed her face and brushed her teeth then fell into bed. Tomorrow would be a better day.

The next morning, Lissa rose early and indulged in Melba's breakfast—with limits. She spooned her own portions onto her plate instead of letting Melba do it. Afterward, she took a brisk walk toward the sheriff's office. What she really wanted was her own wheels, but after her disaster of driving in the snow, she didn't want to cause any more trouble.

Walking into the office, she heard Gage talking on the phone. She took a deep breath and tried to figure out what to do. She didn't want to interrupt, but she wanted to get to work.

A few seconds later, Gage stopped talking. Lissa chewed the inside of her lip and walked toward Gage's office. She peeked inside. "Hiya," she said.

Gage glanced up at her, his expression clearly displeased. "You're up early."

"So are you. We've both got a job to do," she said.

He nodded reluctantly. "True," he said. "I'll get Will in here. He can take you around this morning."

Lissa felt the chill from five feet away. "Thanks," she said.

"He'll be here in a few," he said.

"Okay. I'll wait in the outer office," she said.

He shrugged. "Not necessary. You can get some coffee and sit anywhere you like. I have to check

in with a few people, so I can't give you my undivided attention."

His comment nettled her nerves. "I would never
expect your undivided attention," she told him.
"I'll sit outside until Will arrives, thank you." *And
thank you for being a pain in the butt.*

Chapter Three

Three days later, Gage was still stone-faced when he dealt with Lissa. The good news was that she was getting work done. The mold consultant arrived and conducted evaluations, then taught her how to do the same, which would be more cost-effective as well as a time-saver. She had additional volunteers scheduled to arrive in just a few days.

She shouldn't be giving Gage one more thought, but he was stuck in her mind like a mental burr. She couldn't tell if he was avoiding her because he'd kissed her or because he just couldn't stand her. Neither prospect thrilled her.

Lissa took her regular post-breakfast stroll to the sheriff's office, feeling a little less patient than she had been lately. She usually waited until he'd finished his phone calls, but this time she didn't. She walked right to the door of his office and waved and smiled.

"Good morning, Sheriff," she said in a low voice.

He shot her a considering glance and disconnected his call. "How can I help you, Miss Roarke?"

"I'm actually kind of tired of you helping me. I've respected your advice for several days, but I think I may need to rent an SUV so I won't be such a burden on the sheriff's office," she said.

"You're not a burden," he said. "Will is happy to cart you."

There it was again—the term *cart*. She gritted her teeth. "I'm sure he has other things he needs to do. I'll see if I can get a ride to Livingston to rent a vehicle."

"For my sake and the sake of the entire county, please don't do that," he said, standing.

"I'm not that bad of a driver," she said.

"I have evidence that suggests otherwise," he said in a dry tone.

"I'll have you know that's the only automobile accident I've ever had," she told him.

"Because you usually take cabs or the subway," he said.

"It's not going to snow every day," she argued.

"We'll get some more weather before you know it. Then what will you do?"

"What everyone else does," she said. "Soldier through."

"Sweetheart, trust me on this," he said. "You don't need to be tearing up the back roads of Rust Creek Falls. I don't want to have to rescue you from a ditch or worse."

"One accident and you talk as if I'm completely incompetent," she said. "As if I can't learn how to drive in the snow. You know something, Sheriff Gage Christensen? You are a condescending jerk," she said and walked away.

Fuming all the way back to the rooming house, she climbed the stairs and decided to work from her room today. She could start scheduling the activities of the group of volunteers that would be arriving soon. Sipping hot chocolate, she made calls to the church, where the volunteers would be staying overnight on cots. She double-checked the availability of blankets and linens and was pleased to learn that the community would help prepare some meals for the volunteers.

Lissa contacted the first group of citizens she would be helping. All of them were excited to be receiving assistance. One young mother had been forced to toss all of her children's stuffed animals and favorite comforters due to mold. Lissa added those to the list of things she would do her best to replace.

She skipped lunch, working through it instead, doing her best to avoid thinking about Gage. Oh, how he seemed to know exactly how to upset her and make her feel useless. She would show him. What made it worse was that Gage seemed to be so kind to everyone else. What had she done to make him dislike her so much? *Except for driving into a ditch,* she thought and frowned.

A knock sounded at her bedroom door. "Lissa, this is Melba. You have a visitor."

Curious, Lissa jumped to her feet and swung open the door. "Visitor? Who is it?"

Melba's lip twitched with humor. "Head on down to the front door and you'll find out soon enough."

Lissa followed the older woman down the stairs until Melba stepped aside and waved her hand toward the front door. "Go ahead."

Even more curious now, Lissa opened the door to find Gage standing on the front porch. She stared at him in surprise. "What are you doing here?" she asked.

He gave a wry grin that was somehow too sexy for words. "Now is that any way to greet a guy who brought you flowers?" he asked and presented her with a fistful of flowers he'd hidden behind his back.

Shock and pleasure raced through her. "Wow," she said. "I don't know what to say."

"That's a first," he muttered.

Lissa frowned at him and seriously considered giving back the flowers.

Gage lifted his hands. "Hold on. I'm here to apologize. You're right. I've been acting like a jerk lately."

Lissa dropped her jaw, shocked for the second time.

He sighed. "I haven't been myself since the flood. I shouldn't have—" He cleared his throat. "Kissed you and then taken out my frustration on you. It wasn't fair. If I act like a jerk again, I give you permission to haul off and slug me."

"Oh, I have to confess I've imagined what it would be like to haul off and slug you, but the kiss," she said with a laugh. "The kiss wasn't bad."

He blinked then shot her a smile so charming it took her breath away. "Let's start over. Hi. I'm Sheriff Gage Christensen," he said and extended his hand. "And you are?"

She couldn't resist returning his smile and his handshake. "I'm Lissa Roarke. It's very nice to meet you."

"I'm gonna make sure it's very nice to know you," Gage said.

Lissa felt a funny little twirling sensation in her stomach. "I look forward to that," she said, and she really did.

The next morning, she walked to the sheriff's office and sat at the desk she'd been given in the corner of the front room. She made a list of the calls she planned to make. She was getting excited that the first volunteers would be arriving soon and she could do more than plan. Soon, she would be able to make those promised repairs happen.

A few seconds into her work, a coffee cup and muffin appeared in front of her. She looked up, surprised to find Gage delivering the caffeine and sugar. "Thank you very much. How did I rate this?"

"You're overdue. You rated it before you got here. Though you might not have any room for that muffin if Melba fed you before you left," he said.

"I've learned how to scoot out the back door if I don't want a full country breakfast. Some mornings, it's the most delicious splurge in the world. Other mornings, I don't want that much food."

Gage chuckled. "In my world, I'd love to have that kind of breakfast every day. But maybe not having it's for the best."

Lissa took a big bite of the muffin and chewed on the pastry.

"Looks good," Gage said in approval.

"It is," she said and took another big bite of the muffin.

"Gage," the dispatcher called from across the room. "Harry Leonard's lawn ornaments were stolen again."

Gage groaned. "Somebody needs to give his neighbors' teenage kids something to do. Looks like I may have to be the one. Tell him I'll be right over." He turned back to Lissa. "Let me know if you need anything. Will is escorting a prisoner to Livingston."

"Thanks," she said, trying not to stare too hard at his powerful frame as he left the office. Barely resisting the urge to sigh, she mentally called herself a dork and returned her attention to scheduling repairs.

The dispatcher, Vickie, wandered over to the snack table. "The sheriff is quite the man, isn't he? If I were ten years younger and single, I'd go after him myself. Seems like most of the single girls in town are trying to get his attention. A pretty girl had dinner with him here in the office just the other night."

Lissa felt an unwelcome stab of envy. "He seems so busy all the time. I guess he has to get his companionship when he can."

"Well, I don't know how much companionship is involved. You're right about him being busy. Even though he's on call for the position 24-7, more than one of us wishes he would take a break every now and then. Especially since the flood." The dispatcher shook her head. "He takes it all on himself and can get mighty cranky."

"It must have been hard for him not to be here during the flood."

"Oh, it was," Vickie said. "And losing the mayor... That was a nightmare. The sheriff seems to be sweetening up to you."

Lissa felt a rush of self-consciousness. "I don't think it's personal. I think he values the fact that I'm here to help."

"Hmm. It was nice of him to bring you a little breakfast, though, wasn't it?"

"Yes, it was very nice. But I'm sure he does that kind of thing for everyone. I bet he's done it for you, too," she said.

"Well, maybe if I was slammed with phone calls," Vickie admitted. "But he doesn't look at me the same way he looks at you."

"Up until now, he seemed to look at me like I was a nuisance," Lissa muttered. "I think he's decided I'm determined to help and that's why he's acting nicer."

"You haven't seen the way he looks at you when you're not looking at him. I gotta tell you I think we'd all be happier if the sheriff got a little more—" Vickie broke off and chuckled. "A little more *companionship* on a regular basis. He's a man with needs he's clearly denying. If you can help him out…"

Lissa blinked. Was Vickie suggesting that Lissa take care of his needs? Lissa cleared her throat. "I'm just here to help out with repairs from the flood."

Thank goodness the phone rang, and Lissa was saved from conversation about Gage's needs. She was not, however, saved from a hot image of him, naked and wanting, his eyes burning for her. Lissa felt her body heat all over at the thought. She discreetly fanned herself and decided she could use some cold water.

After a conversation with a very angry Harry Leonard, Gage decided to take a trip to the two neighbors Harry had accused of taking his lawn ornaments. The first was Danielle Hawthorn and her son Buddy. Buddy was fourteen years old and had been involved with some minor looting in the neighborhood. Danielle had two other kids and was raising them by herself since her husband took off three years ago. He'd heard she was working two jobs, so Gage knew she might not be home.

He climbed the steps to the aging house and knocked on the door. Waiting a few seconds, he knocked again. The door opened and Danielle pushed her hair from her face as if she'd just awakened. Her youngest peeked up at him from behind her legs. "Sheriff," she said, her eyes widening in alarm. "Has something happened? Are my kids okay?"

"As far as I know," Gage said. "But you may have a problem. Do you mind if I come inside?"

"No, not at all," she said, opening the door. "Forgive the mess. Tina here is getting over a bad cold."

As if on cue, the little girl sneezed and wiped her nose with the back of her hand.

"That's what tissues are for, sweetie. Go wash your hands real good." She waved her hand toward a chair. "Can I get you some coffee?"

"No. I'm fine, thanks. But I'm a little concerned about Buddy. I got a call from Harry Leonard."

Danielle winced and shook her head. "Oh, no. Not again. I've grounded him too many times to count, but he still finds a way to get together with his friend Jason down the street. They're two peas in a pod and I'm afraid it's turning into a rotten pod. I don't know what to do."

"I have a few suggestions," Gage said. "Seems like Buddy has too much time on his hands, so maybe he could do some volunteering. Does he like any sports? He could help coach some of the elementary kids."

"That's a good idea," she said, then her face fell. "But I'm not always here when he gets home. With my work schedule, I don't know how I could guarantee getting him anywhere after school."

"We might be able to find a way to help you. How about if you talk to Buddy about it?"

Gage visited Jason's family and his parents were similarly appalled. He planned to put Jason in a separate volunteer program. He made a few more visits then headed back to office in the afternoon.

Walking into the office, he saw the dispatcher and Lissa still working at their desks. "Hello, ladies," he said.

"Hi," Vickie said. "I'm headed out in five minutes. It was better than usual today."

"Good," Gage said and turned to Lissa. "How was your day?"

"Good," she said. "I would still benefit from a vehicle."

"As a matter of fact, one of our citizens is willing to donate a truck for your use with the contingency that you don't drive when there's more than a thirty percent chance of snow," he told her.

"I'm grateful for the transportation, but I'm curious how this negotiation took place."

"Harry Leonard has five trucks in his backyard garage and he's willing to let you use one of them, the oldest one."

"Well, Harry sounds like a sweet guy," Lissa said.

"Don't wreck his truck. He'll get cranky," Gage said.

"I'll be careful," she promised, thrilled to have wheels.

"But *no to the snow*," he told her emphatically.

"Unless you give me a snow-driving refresher course," she said.

"No to the snow," he repeated. "But I'll give you a snow driving course. Just don't test your knowledge."

"Thanks," she said with a huge smile that chipped at his heart. "Whew. It's been a long day. What are you doing now?"

Gage frowned. "Paperwork."

"Bummer," she said and shot him a sideways gaze. "Maybe a pretty girl named Jasmine will keep you company for dinner."

He frowned. "Who told you about Jasmine?"

"Vickie," she said. "She seems to know almost everything."

"Jasmine's a nice young girl working with one of the carpenters," he said.

"Uh-huh," she said. "Nice and attractive. I don't want to keep you from her." Lissa rose from her chair and picked up her iPad.

"No one is keeping me from her. I got a casserole and invited her to have dinner because she was trying to find out how to contact a senior citizen."

Lissa met his gaze for a long moment. "You're a good guy," she said.

"Some people say good guys finish last," he said.

"I wouldn't say that, but I'm headed back to the

rooming house," she said. "I have volunteers arriving tomorrow."

"You seem pleased."

"I'm so excited I can't stand it," she admitted. "We can finally start getting something done."

Her enthusiasm burrowed inside him. He smiled. "Yeah, that's good. And we all appreciate it."

"Thanks," she said. "I'm going to make an early night of it, so I'll be ready to greet the volunteers tomorrow. Thank you for getting me some wheels from Harry Leonard."

"My pleasure," Gage said. "But no—"

"Driving in the snow," she finished for him. "That ditch was no fun for me, either."

"It's dark. You want me to walk you back to the rooming house?" he offered because he wanted to extend his time with her.

"I think I'll be okay," she said. "Rust Creek isn't the most crime-ridden place in the world. But thank you for your chivalry."

Gage gave a rough chuckle. "No one's ever accused me of being chivalrous."

"Well, maybe they haven't been watching closely enough."

Gage felt his gut take a hard dip at her statement. He knew that Lissa was struggling with her visit to Rust Creek and he hadn't made it as easy for her as he should have. There was some kind of electricity or something between them that he couldn't quite name. Just looking at her did something to him.

"I'll take that as a compliment. Call me if you need me," he said.

"Thank you," she said. "Good night."

"Good night," he said and wished she was going home with him to his temporary trailer to keep him warm. Crazy, he told himself. All wrong. She was Manhattan. He was Montana. Big difference. The twain would never meet. Right?

The next day Lissa was so busy she could barely remember her name. Her truck was delivered to her, but she barely drove it because she was busy organizing her first group of volunteers. Gage made a surprise visit at the church.

"I'm Sheriff Gage Christensen," he said to the group. "And I want to thank you for what you're doing for Rust Creek Falls. You may not get a mention on the national news, but you'll be heroes in our hearts forever."

Lissa gave him the heart sign with her fingers pinched together, then shuttled her volunteers toward the vehicles that would transport them. She drove the ancient truck Harry Leonard was allowing her to use. It took some getting used to, but she was thankful to have wheels. The day passed in a flurry of work. The volunteers repaired four houses by the end of the day. Lissa was thrilled. She had estimated three houses, so they were ahead of the game.

She worked nonstop from six in the morning until nine at night every day, making sure the volunteers were well fed and got good rest. By the end of the week she was ready for a long night of rest. She gave her volunteers a recognition banquet provided by the local church and stumbled toward her rooming house.

"Want a beer?" Will asked as he met her on the street.

"I'm too old for a beer," she said with a laugh.

"You're not too old for anything," Will said. "You're hot."

She laughed again. "Not tonight. I just want a good night of sleep. But you're a nice guy to say that. You need to pick someone closer to your age," she said. "You're a great guy."

"You calling me a great guy? That almost makes me feel better that you turned me down," Will said.

"Well, it's the truth. You're a great guy. Don't forget that," she said.

Will tipped his hat. "Thank you very much, Miss Roarke. I'll never think of you as old."

"Thank you for saying that, because I sure am feeling my age tonight." Lissa continued to the rooming house and climbed the stairs to her room.

Tonight she pulled out one of those bottles of red wine and took a swig. She took another sip and wasn't the least bit interested in finishing her glass of wine. Instead she stripped and flung herself into a hot shower. She didn't bother drying her hair, which meant it would be a mad mess in the morning.

Putting a towel on her pillow to absorb the moisture from her hair, Lissa climbed into bed and fell asleep almost immediately. The last image that flew through her mind was of Gage. She could almost feel his arms around her as she drifted off.

Lissa dragged herself out of bed and tried to slide past Melba and her big breakfast the next morning. Melba, however, caught her.

"There you are—our sweet heroine. I've been getting calls all week about what a great job your volunteers are doing. You come sit down and let me give you a good breakfast," Melba said.

"Oh, Melba, that's not necessary," Lissa said.

"Of course, it is. You sit down while I fix you a proper breakfast," Melba said.

Soon enough, a huge platter of eggs, bacon, sausage and pancakes was placed before Lissa.

Lissa bit her lip. "Melba, this is wonderful, but I can't eat all this," she whispered.

Melba's gaze softened. "You don't have to eat it all. My dog, Taffy, will eat anything you don't."

Lissa laughed. "Taffy's getting a bonus meal today, but thank you for being so sweet to me."

"You're the one who's doing so much for us. If you need anything at all, you ask me for it," Melba said.

"Thank you, Melba. You're the best," she said and ate the rest of her eggs and bacon. Who could resist bacon?

She finished her breakfast and went out with the volunteers to the next citizens who needed help with their homes. The day went a bit slower, but it was still productive. She dropped by the sheriff's office before she returned to her room.

"It went well today," she said to Gage.

"So I heard," he said in return.

"Not as fast as the first day, but I'm not complaining," she said.

"Neither am I. I keep getting praise—even from Vickie," he said.

"That's good to hear," she said. "But I'm beat."

"Call me if you need me," he said. "It's supposed to snow tomorrow. I don't want you driving."

"Okay, I won't," she said. "But the church van will be leaving in the morning. I hope we won't have trouble on the roads."

"Check in with me every hour or so," he said.

She nodded. "Okay. Hopefully, the weather

won't prevent us from doing our job. I'm determined."

"I like that about you," he said.

She stared at him for a long moment and wished he would take her in his arms and kiss her. It didn't happen.

"Okay," she said. "I'd like to hear back from you in the morning. Sweet dreams," she said and headed for the door.

"Same to you," Gage said.

Yeah, she thought. The good thing about her sleep tonight was that she was so tired she couldn't avoid it. She couldn't help hoping Gage would struggle with his sleep. Wouldn't it be great if he was tortured by thoughts of her? It would only be fair, she thought.

Very fair.

Chapter Four

What an amazing experience. I've already fallen in love with the people of Rust Creek Falls. The former mayor's elderly mother is determined to continue his legacy by working in the mayor's office. It amazes me the sacrifices the citizens have made in order to stay in Rust Creek and rebuild. Sheriff Gage Christensen is clearly determined to give his all to get the community back on its feet. I'm humbled by all that I'm learning about the people here and the volunteers coming to help.

—Lissa Roarke

Lissa couldn't get Thelma McGee out of her mind, so she bought some flowers from the grocery store and took them to Thelma before she was scheduled to go out with the rest of the volunteers for the day's activities.

"Good morning, Mrs. McGee," she said to the gray-haired woman. "I was thinking about you this morning and wanted you to have these flowers."

Thelma widened her eyes in surprise. "For me?"

"Yes," Lissa said. "For you. You've been working hard. I thought these might brighten up your day."

The older woman fumbled with the blooms. "Well, aren't you a sweetheart," she said.

"You're the sweetheart," Lissa said, correcting her.

Mrs. McGee smiled. "I'm so glad you stopped by. I wanted to invite you to dinner this weekend."

Surprised, Lissa blinked. "Um…"

"Don't say no. I don't invite people to dinner all that often, but I promise the food will be good."

"No doubt it will be," Lissa said. "But you don't have to do this for me."

"It's my pleasure," Mrs. McGee said. "You're so full of life. It makes everyone feel good to be around you. We're blessed that you're here to help us."

Humbled by the woman's kind words. "It will

be my pleasure," Lissa said. "When do you want me to come?"

"Sunday night would be fine. Around six o'clock. Thank you for coming. You've been so good for all of us. I know my son would be so grateful," she said, her voice breaking.

Lissa felt the threat of her own tears. She could only imagine how hard it must be to lose a child at any age. Even an adult child. "I'll be at your house on Sunday night. Thank you for the invitation. I'm honored."

The next three days passed in a blur. By the time Sunday night came around, Lissa was beat, but she was determined to meet her obligation for dinner with Thelma McGee. After the volunteers departed at four, she helped the church strip linens and clean. She took a quick shower before she showed up on Mrs. McGee's front porch at five minutes after six. She felt guilty about those extra five minutes.

Thelma opened the door and beamed at her. "Here you are, our angel. Come on in," she said.

Lissa couldn't remember when she'd been called an angel, but she liked it. It made her want to be even more of an angel. "Thank you, Mrs. McGee."

"Please, call me Thelma," she said and led Lissa through the hallway into a den with plump upholstered furniture, soft lamps…and Sheriff Gage Christensen.

He met her gaze with as much surprise as Lissa felt.

"Oh," she said. "Hello."

"Hello to you," he said, holding a glass of something that looked like hard liquor.

"Would you like a cocktail?" Thelma asked. "I gave Gage some whiskey."

"I'm fine," Lissa said, knowing she needed nothing that would make her sleepy. She'd been fighting sleep the entire day.

"Okeydoke," Thelma said. "I'm going to check on my dinner."

Silence followed as she left.

"What are you doing here?" Gage finally asked before he knocked back his whiskey.

"She invited me a few days ago. I tried to refuse, but—"

Gage shook his head. "No one can refuse Thelma. Especially now."

"So what are you doing here?"

"I come every other week. I know she's lonely, and with her son gone…"

He looked at his glass as if he were wishing for more whiskey.

"Well, hey, we repaired some more houses today," she said cheerfully.

"That's good news."

"Another crew is coming next week," she said.

"Gotta give it you, you're pulling in a lot of help. We're really grateful," he said.

"It's what I do," she said. "Just like being a sheriff is what you do."

He paused then nodded and took one last sip from his squat glass. "Yeah."

That one word was just too sexy. If anyone else had said it, it wouldn't have affected her, but when Gage looked at her that certain way and said *yeah,* something inside her quickened and shifted.

Thelma returned with a smile and clasped her hands together. "Dinner is ready."

Grateful for the distraction, Lissa focused her attention on Thelma. "Perfect," she said. "I can't wait."

Lissa did the best acting job she could ever remember. She focused on Thelma and her pot roast and vegetables. She enjoyed the sweet potatoes added to the traditional mixture.

"I cook it all in the oven, covered and at a low temperature for a long time. That's the secret. Low temperature, and don't rush," Thelma said. "Everyone is in such a rush these days, cooking everything in a microwave. If you're not careful, your dinner will taste like cardboard."

Lissa nodded and spared a quick glance at Gage. "I can't deny what you're saying. When I'm in New York, I either heat something up in the microwave or order takeout."

Thelma laughed. "The only takeout we have here is when a friend delivers a meal."

"I get a lot of those," Gage said. "I'm lucky, though. Just like tonight with your pot roast. I'm a charity case."

Thelma laughed again. "You're anything but a charity case. The old women are grateful to you. The young women want a date with you."

"And in between?" Gage asked as he took another bite of pot roast.

"In between, they want you to help with their kids. Tell me I'm wrong," Thelma said.

Gage shook his head. "Can't say you're wrong. You're a smart woman, Mrs. McGee."

"I keep asking you to call me Thelma so I'll feel younger," she said with a coy smile. "Well, I must make a toast," she said, lifting her still-full glass of wine. "To Gage, for working too much to help Rust Creek Falls recover. And to Lissa, for giving us the spark we needed to make our community better. I am so grateful to both of you, just as my son would have been."

Lissa lifted her water glass as Gage lifted his. "Cheers," she said along with him and saw the pain in his eyes.

An hour later, Lissa saw that Mrs. McGee was fading. Lissa covered a yawn. "Oh, my goodness, I'm so tired. You're putting me to shame. Your dinner filled me up and made me want to go to sleep."

Thelma caught her yawn and covered her mouth. "You've been working hard. Having both of you here tonight has been so wonderful."

"Oh, no," Lissa said. "This has been a huge treat for me."

"And for me," Gage added. "I would have had muffins and a burger for dinner if not for this. And trust me, your company was much better than my own."

Thelma sighed. "Well, we're all connected by our love for this community. I'm so grateful for both of you."

"We are grateful for you," Gage said. "Now let us help clean up, or both Lissa and I will be offended."

"Well, now, I wouldn't want to offend you," Thelma said.

Lissa and Gage cleaned up the dishes in a short time, chatting all the time with Mrs. McGee as she sat in a chair in the kitchen. They both said their goodbyes and thank-yous to the lovely woman and walked out the door.

On the porch, she looked up at Gage. "She's a great woman."

"Yeah, and she had a great son," he said, his gaze sad.

"She seemed happy," Lissa said, inhaling the cold night air.

Gage nodded. "I can drive you home," he said.

"It's not that far," she said. "I can walk."

"I'll drive," he insisted and escorted her to his SUV. He opened the door to the passenger side and helped her into her seat then rounded the car to the driver's seat.

He pulled away from the curb.

"How was your day?" she asked.

"Could have been worse. I'm a little concerned about some drug dealers coming into my territory," he said.

"Oh, no," she said, staring at him.

"Plenty of dealers and manufacturers try to move into rural territories, but I've been pretty good about keeping them away. It takes some extra effort. I'll get some help from the state and get them gone."

"That's good. I would have thought drug dealers would be the last thing you would find in Montana," she said.

"Meth users are everywhere. They're like cockroaches. It's my job to stamp them out here, to make it difficult to survive and thrive. So far, I've been successful," he said.

"I'm glad to hear that," she said.

"It's kind of crazy," he said. "More than half of my time is spent on nothing serious. Lawn ornaments and other stuff. I won't tolerate drugs."

"Your community is lucky they have you and

that you have your attitude. You're very protective," she said. "You're an excellent sheriff."

His lips lifted in a slow, sexy smile. "Thanks, Lissa."

Lissa felt a crazy dip in her belly and leaned toward him. "Yes," she said, wanting him to meet her halfway with a kiss that would knock her into next week. "Yes."

A long silence followed. Gage cleared his throat. "Uh, we're here. I can walk you to the front door of the rooming house."

Lissa gaped outside the window of his SUV, surprised to see the rooming house. She tried to gather her wits. "Oh, that's not necessary. Thanks for the ride home," she said and tried to get out of the car. Without unlocking the door first. Finally, she remembered to unlock and push open the door, sliding out onto the ground.

"Good night," she said, determined not to look at him.

"Hey, Lissa," he said.

She couldn't help but turn back around to look at him. "Yes?"

"Thank you for what Bootstraps is doing for us. You're making a big difference," he said.

She gave a slow nod, her mind fighting with her hormones. "You're welcome," she managed, and climbed the steps to the rooming house. She made her way to her room and kicked off her boots.

Totally exasperated, she frowned and scowled at Gage's reaction to her.

Gratitude, she thought. She didn't want gratitude. She wanted passion. Stripping off her clothes, she took a quick shower and pulled on comfy pajamas, cursing Gage all the time. She impulsively poured herself a tiny glass of red wine and took a gulp. Shrugging, she poured the wine down the drain. She wanted cold, cold water instead, and drank some down.

"Could be worse," she said and told herself to get a good night's sleep. "Tomorrow will be ten times better."

She slumped back against her pillow and pulled the covers over her. "When I wake up in the morning, I'm not going to want Gage Christensen. I'm not going to think of Gage Christensen. I'm going to purge him from my system while I sleep."

She kept repeating those words until she fell asleep.

When Lissa awakened in the morning, her first thought was of Gage.

Gage woke up with an uncomfortable jangly sensation inside him. Maybe he should fix his house, so he could make it a home again. The only problem was that he didn't have time. He couldn't see fixing his own house before other people's homes that needed far more work.

He felt grungy and his back was sore. As much as he told himself that the new sofa bed didn't affect his back, he was so wrong. Maybe he was getting old, he thought, as he stumbled to his feet and into the shower. Shoving himself under the shower, he lifted his face to the spray. He would have fallen asleep a lot sooner last night if he hadn't been thinking about Lissa. He didn't want to be thinking about Lissa. He didn't want to be feeling anything for Lissa.

He scowled, focusing on the shower, willing it to clean out his head. He spent some extra moments under the spray then dragged himself out of it and scrubbed himself dry. Gage got dressed and walked out to his car, his mind filled with too many people. The former mayor, his mother and Lissa.

Swearing under his breath, he was determined to extricate his distractions from his head. He turned his favorite country station on super loud and drove toward the office.

He walked inside to find the dispatcher already at her desk. "Mornin', Vickie. How are you?"

"I'm awake and drinking my second cup of coffee, so that's pretty good. How are you?" she asked.

"I've only had one cup, so I better catch up with you," he said with a wink and poured himself a cup. At that moment, Will walked into the office. Gage gave his deputy a nod of greeting.

"I got a call from Danielle," said Vickie. "She said something about her son doing some volunteer work, but said she's going to need some help with transportation."

"Right," he said. "I'm wondering if we can expand the volunteer elder care drivers to anyone else who might need transportation if they have a good reason."

Will snickered. "I don't think Harry Leonard is going to want to transport his juvenile neighbors anywhere except the moon."

Gage swallowed a chuckle. "Can't deny that, but I think we need to keep some of these teens busy before they get into real trouble."

Will sobered. "True. I'm in."

"You're already in over your head," Gage said. "But I appreciate your commitment. I'll put out a request for some volunteers. In the meantime, you and I may be doing some extra carting."

"We've doing a lot of that with Lissa here, at least before Harry loaned her a truck," Will said. "Not that I minded. She's so hot."

Gage felt a trickle of irritation. "Back down, hound dog. You're too young for her, anyway."

Will stiffened his spine and stuck out his chin. "That's a matter of opinion. She seems to respect me."

"Lissa respects everybody," Gage said, growing more irritated by the second.

"She sure does," Vickie said. "But I've noticed more than one man giving her the eye. I wouldn't be surprised if somebody didn't try to snap her up."

Gage frowned. "What do you mean somebody will snap her up? She's too busy for that."

Vickie shrugged. "Everyone has a weak moment and Lissa is a beautiful woman…."

Will cleared his throat. "Well, I'm ready anytime she wants a ride."

Gage ground his teeth. "Step back, deputy," he said and headed for his desk. *What a rotten start to the day.*

"On another subject, I also heard that the Crawfords are spreading rumors about your brother-in-law, Collin," Vickie said in a low voice.

"What do you mean?" he asked, wondering what other bad news he was going to get.

"Those Crawfords are determined that Nate win the post as mayor. They don't think Collin Traub deserves to be mayor, and I'm afraid they may turn this into a dirty race. Everyone should be prepared for it."

Gage sighed. "Thanks for letting me know," he said and made a mental note to talk to Collin. It was always best to be prepared.

A call came in and Gage hit the ground running.

A robbery followed by a fire followed by someone who needed an appendectomy. He also checked by the abandoned house where he'd discovered an illegal drug manufacturer doing business a month ago to make sure no one else had set up shop there. By the end of today he was ready for a trip to Jamaica. But he knew that wouldn't happen. He finally walked back into his office, late. Very late.

The late dispatcher had arrived and was asleep at the desk. Gage couldn't blame the poor guy. Thank goodness there usually weren't many calls at night. Sighing, he walked toward his office.

He heard a soft feminine voice. "Enough for the day," she murmured.

He knew that voice. Lissa. He headed toward her little corner. "How's it going?"

"Long day," she said. "I made a few home visits and a lot of calls. I want to make sure everything is ready for our next group of volunteers."

Gage nodded. "Sounds like you're on top of it.

She rolled her eyes. "That's relative."

He chuckled. "Give me a minute and I'll give you a ride to the rooming house."

She waved her hand. "No need."

"Give me a minute," he told her and went to his office and collected his messages. Thank goodness, nothing was an emergency.

He returned just as Lissa headed out the door.

"Hey," he called, running after her. "Why didn't you wait?"

She glanced back at him. "You've got enough to do. I don't want you to feel like you have to look after me."

"I was just going to drive you back to the rooming house," he said.

She shoved her hands into her pockets. "I can walk. It's not that far or I would use the truck Harry Leonard is letting me use. But actually a couple people invited me to the bar. I thought I might stop there before I headed back to my room."

Surprise rolled through him. "I haven't heard you talk about going to the bar since you've been here."

She shrugged. "I hear change can be good."

He gave a slow nod. "Yeah. I'll take you to the bar," he said, feeling overly protective, but determined not to show it.

"Okay, thanks," she said with a smile.

He helped her into his SUV and drove to the bar, parking in a spot several spots away from the door. Escorting her out of the car, he walked inside the bar with her. Loud country music was playing and the place was filled with the smell of beer and hard liquor. A few couples shuffled around on the tiny dance floor. The smell of tobacco permeated the bar even though patrons were required to smoke outside.

"Is this working for you?" he asked. "Just like a Manhattan bar, right?"

She knitted her brows together. "It's a bit primitive, but it could be worse. I'm going to be here awhile longer, so maybe I should respect the native culture." She glanced up at him and shot him a sassy smile.

His gut took a twist and turn. "If you say so. What would you like to drink?"

"I'm betting they can't make a cosmopolitan or appletini," she said with a sigh.

"I think you're betting right."

"Okay. I'll take vodka and orange juice. That can't be too hard."

Gage tipped his hat. "I'll see what I can do," and he went to the bar. "I'll take a vodka and orange juice and a beer for me."

The bartender gave him a second look. "Vodka and orange juice. I don't think we have any orange juice."

"Do you have any fruit juice?" Gage asked.

The bartender searched his inventory. "We've got some lime."

Gage rubbed his face. "Put in a lot of lime and anything else sweet you have."

"Sweet," the bartender echoed. "We may have some grenadine in the back, for wimps."

"This is for a wimp," Gage said. "A woman wimp."

"Oh," the bartender said. "Why didn't you tell me that from the beginning?" The bartender left, poured the drinks and returned to give them to Gage. "She'll like this," he said.

"What makes you so sure?" he asked.

"Trust me," the bartender said. "I've never had any complaints."

Gage swallowed a sip of his beer and took the drink to Lissa. She accepted it and took a swallow. "Yum," she said. "This is good."

"Take your time," he said.

"Oh, look, it's Jared and Will. They've both been trying to get me to come here. Let's go visit them," she said.

Gage caught sight of the two men she'd mentioned. One was his deputy. The other was the Romeo of Rust Creek Falls. He wondered how in the world Jared Winfree had gotten to Lissa.

Although he didn't respond, he escorted her toward Jared and Will. Both men looked hesitant at his presence.

"Howdy," he said to Jared and Will and took another sip of beer.

"Howdy," Jared said then turned to Lissa. "Are you having a good time?"

She smiled. "I'm working on it. It sure is loud here."

Will nodded. "Yeah, they try to make it feel like a party every night. You wanna dance?"

She blinked. "I think I just want to soak up the atmosphere," she said.

Jared moved closer to her. "I bet you don't have this kind of bar in Manhattan," he said.

Lissa glanced down at the peanut shells on the floor and nodded. "Not that I've seen. But I haven't been to every bar in the city."

Jared slid his arm on the bar behind her back and Gage felt an unwelcome itchy feeling up and down his spine.

"So, how did we get so lucky to have you come to Rust Creek Falls?" he asked.

Lissa looked vaguely uncomfortable. "One of my cousins and I wanted to try to help after the flood. It took a bit of persuading, but my boss finally thought it was a good idea."

Gage cleared his throat. "Where are you from, Jared?"

Jared touched his hat. "I've been in Rust Creek since the flood because the work is here. Before that I've been a rambling kind of man."

"Yeah, so where were you born?" Gage asked.

Jared shrugged. "Doesn't matter where you're born. It's where you've lived that makes you. Right, Lissa?"

"I've lived most of my life in upstate New York and spent the past several years in the city, so I can't comment. I will say that Manhattan is a different world compared to most of the rest of the country," she said.

"Exactly," he said, pointing at her. "Exactly."

Gage found Jared's flirting irritating, but he wasn't going to waste his energy commenting. Instead, he took another long drink of beer.

"So, how do like to spend your spare time?" Jared said, crowding Lissa even more.

She wiggled a little as if she were trying to create some space for herself, but Jared didn't give an inch. "I haven't had a lot of spare time since I got here," Lissa said. "What do you like to do in your spare time?"

"Well, I like this bar and I like pretty, smart girls. You sure I can't talk you into dancing with me?" he asked, leaning in toward her.

It was all Gage could do to keep from jerking Jared out of her range.

Lissa took a deep breath and another sip of her drink. "Like I said, I'm just trying to soak up the atmosphere."

"Let me get you another drink," Jared said and turned toward the bartender.

"Oh, no. I don't need—"

"Sure you do. Every night is Friday night here," Jared said.

"But…"

A young man approached Lissa. "You're the pretty new girl in town. I'm David and I'm here to welcome you to Rust Creek Falls," he said. "Come on and dance with me."

"Oh, no…"

"Now, don't be shy," he said, taking her hand and nearly dragging her onto the dance floor.

Both Jared and Will stared and frowned.

"Who the hell was that?" Will asked.

"Some guy named David who got Lissa on the dance floor," Gage said.

Jared swore under his breath. "Well, that's not gonna happen."

"Whoa," Gage said, but Jared was clearly determined. He stalked onto the dance floor and confronted David.

Gage shook his head, getting a bad feeling in his gut. "This doesn't look good."

"Damn straight," Will said. "How'd this no-name get Lissa to dance with him?"

"Rein it in, cowboy," Gage said. "You're a lawman first."

One second later, Jared took a swing at David. After that, all hell broke loose. Gage soldiered through the crowd, dodging several punches. He found Lissa sitting on the floor, looking dazed and frightened.

"Come on," he said, extending his hand to her.

Taking his hand, she rose. "What in the world—"

"It doesn't take much for some guys to get riled

up. Stay close." He moved through the crowd, again dodging punches. "I'm going to get you to the rooming house, then I'll come back here to settle all this down."

"I can walk by myself," she said.

"Hell, no. You've caused enough trouble. The next thing I know you'll be inciting a riot in the streets."

"I wouldn't incite anything," she complained.

Gage lifted a dark eyebrow. "I think you underestimate your effect on men."

Chapter Five

The next morning, Lissa was extremely reluctant to go to her so-called *command central* at the sheriff's office. She'd heard enough from Melba at breakfast this morning. Everyone was buzzing about the fight at the bar last night. Melba wanted to know which guy Lissa was favoring since several had tried to get her attention. Lissa just asked for more bacon.

After dawdling an extra fifteen minutes, she walked to the sheriff's office and braced herself.

"Well, hello to you Miss Bachelorette," Vickie said.

Lissa winced. "Maybe I should work from the rooming house."

"No, no," Vickie said, moving toward her with a chocolate-chip muffin. "We got extra treats this morning due to you. Don't you go anywhere," she said.

Lissa lifted her hand in refusal. "I just stuffed myself with a breakfast from Melba. I don't know when I'll eat again."

"She's a good cook," Vickie said. "I hear both Gage and Will got socked in the face," she said in a lowered voice. "I can't wait to see if either of them got a black eye."

Lissa bit her lip. "Don't tell me that. I just thought it would be fun to visit the local bar."

Vickie chuckled. "You gave a lot of us a good time."

"But not Gage and Will," she muttered.

"They got a different kind of excitement," Vickie said. "Oh, darn. There's the phone."

The door flung open and Will walked in, wearing a pair of sunglasses. "Hey," he said to Lissa and walked past her.

Lissa winced, wondering what was behind those glasses. "Hi, Will," she said. "How are you?"

"We had to arrest two people last night. We locked the rest of them in a barn for the night," he said.

"I'm so sorry," she said.

"Yeah, it makes for a lot of paperwork," he said and disappeared into his cubicle.

Lissa grabbed a cup of coffee and sat down at her desk. Her concentration nil, she pulled up her list for the day. "Corwin," she said. "I need to call the Corwins to make sure they're ready for repairs."

A moment later, Gage strode through the door, his left cheek red and swollen. He wasn't hiding it. "Hey," he said to Lissa. "Got paperwork."

"Yeah, that's what Will said," she said.

Lissa stared after him, feeling extremely guilty. She hated that she had caused extra work for Gage again. First, falling in a ditch. Second, going to a bar—the only bar in Rust Creek Falls—and starting a fight. Lissa frowned. She wasn't a knockout. How had this happened?

After staying sequestered in his office for several hours, Gage headed out to conduct a patrol and make a few calls. Lissa worked through the day, but was terribly distracted. Finally, at five o'clock, Gage returned to the office. "Hey, Vickie. Give me the most important messages," he said.

"Good news," she said, giving him a couple sheets of paper. "Nothing major."

He flipped through them and nodded. "I'll make some return calls and plan on some visits tomorrow."

"When do you ever get your ranching done?" she asked.

"We have a few people helping out," he said. "I try to handle the morning chores."

"Bet you'd like to sleep late one of these days," she said.

"Yeah," Gage said. "One of these days."

"Well, I'm headed out," she said. "Good night to you and Miss Lissa."

"Good night, Vickie," Lissa called.

Gage echoed her words. Lissa approached him. "I'm sorry about what happened last night. I had no idea my dancing with someone would cause such a problem."

"Yeah, well, this is Montana. Not New York," he said.

His response stabbed at her. "Are you saying dancing causes issues in Montana?"

"A beautiful woman causes issues anywhere," Gage said.

"I'm not that beautiful," she retorted.

Gage looked at her in disbelief. "That's a matter of opinion. Just do me a favor and stay away from the bar for the next few days. I don't have the manpower to handle hot crazy men acting out around you."

"Are you saying this is my fault?"

"I'm saying you underestimated yourself," he said.

She scowled at him. "That's ridiculous. You act as if I can exert control over whoever I encounter."

"Well, here's a news flash. I haven't had to

make arrests at the bar for two months. I don't have time for this, so do me a favor and skip the bar. If you want a martini, I'll buy it for you and deliver it to the rooming house."

Lissa felt her frustration build inside her like a bomb ready to explode. Her whole body roared with heat. "You're being a jerk. A complete jerk," she told him, her voice getting louder with each syllable. She stepped close to him, lifted her chin and poked her finger against his hard chest repeatedly. "If you think I'm so beautiful, why don't you stop being such an idiot and kiss me?"

Complete silence followed, but Lissa didn't break eye contact with Gage. She didn't even blink.

But he did and he took a long breath. "Do you realize you just asked me to kiss you?"

"Well, somebody needs to do something about this insanity," she said.

Gage stared at her for a long moment then began to chuckle. "Darlin', I thought you'd never ask," he said and pulled her against him and took her mouth in a kiss that made the room turn upside down. Her heart hammered against her rib cage, her breath stopped in her throat and her blood raced through her veins like wildfire. The kiss seemed to scream his need and desire for her.

The power of it made her knees weak. She clung to his shoulders, wanting to get closer to him, much closer. Lissa could feel the evidence of his arousal pressed against her. He lifted one of his hands to her jaw, tilting her mouth to give him better access. The move only made her more aroused.

"Oh, Gage," she whispered. "I want you so much." She rubbed herself against him, resenting the clothes between them.

He slid his hand down to one of her breasts and she immediately felt her nipple harden against her bra. She tugged at his jacket and somehow opened it.

He made a growling sound that rumbled through her like the threat of a powerful thunderstorm. There was a sense of inevitability and anticipation that wrapped around them like a cord, drawing tighter and tighter.

Gage pulled back, swearing under his breath, his eyes as dark as midnight. "There's only one way this is going to go tonight, and I'm not making love to you in the office. Come to my place?"

"Yes," she said, because her mouth, her body, her heart wouldn't let her say anything else. So caught up in her feelings for him, she almost walked out the door without her jacket.

"Hey, hold on there," Gage said, grabbing the coat for her. "I don't want you getting chilly on the way."

She laughed. "I don't think there's much chance of that."

Gage locked up the office and escorted her to his SUV. He started the engine and glanced at her. "You sure about this?"

"I've never been more sure," she said.

Groaning, he leaned toward and took her mouth in a long, hot kiss. He pulled back and shook his head. "Can't remember feeling this way," he muttered and drove toward his property.

After a moment of silence, he reached for her hand. "I better warn you my temporary trailer isn't five-star," he told her.

"I'm not worried about the accommodations. I just want the man," she said.

"You know the right thing to say to make a man feel good, Lissa," he said.

She just hoped she knew all the other things that would make him feel good. She wasn't particularly experienced....

Soon enough, he turned onto a dirt road. "I take care of this part of the ranch. My parents handle the other. It's big enough that between being sheriff and doing my chores here I can go weeks without seeing them," he said.

"I imagine they don't like that," she said.

He shrugged. "Everyone knew I would have less time for ranching once I was elected sheriff. I had to be talked into running. It was one of those jobs that chose me."

"Do you wish you hadn't run for office?" she

asked, because he seemed such a natural for the position.

"It's turned into one of those things that seems like it was meant to be. That doesn't mean there aren't tough situations or tough days, but I like being part of the solution." He stopped in front of a trailer and a darkened house.

"I bet you wish you could get back into your house," she said.

"It's not on the agenda at the moment," he said. "There are too many people in worse shape than I am."

"Spoken like a true self-sacrificing community servant," she said and leaned toward him. "But you don't have to sacrifice every moment to the job, do you?"

His eyes lit with arousal. "Not with you around," he muttered and got out of the car. He walked to her side of the vehicle, opened the door and extended his hand. Her stomach dipped as she accepted his strong grip and slid out of the SUV.

She barely took two steps before he swung her up in his arms.

Surprised, she gazed up into his face. "What's this?"

"I just thought you should see that we do things a little different than your Manhattan boys," he said.

"Oh," she said. "Are you saying all the Montana men do this?"

He shot her a mock scolding glance. "Now don't get any ideas."

She shook her head. "Too late. You give me a lot of ideas."

"Just as long as they're about me," he said and set her down when he reached the door.

Leading her into the small trailer, he flipped on a light and turned to her. "I warned you it's not fancy," he told her.

"You also told me you do things different than those Manhattan boys," she said, poking her finger at his chest. "When are you going to show me?"

He grinned. "I think now is good," he said and pulled off his jacket.

Her heart started to hammer when he pulled off her jacket, too. "Come here, darlin'," he said and pulled her into his arms.

He felt so good. All muscle and male, he lowered his mouth to hers in a long, deep kiss that rattled her down to her toes.

He took her by surprise by swinging her into his arms as he walked into a small bedroom. She would never have believed how feminine and desirable that made her feel. Lissa lifted her hands to his face, relishing the slight abrasion of his barely whiskered jaw. Everything about him felt like a *man* to her: the coiled strength of his muscles, his wide shoulders and the way his large hands wrapped around her.

He let her slide down his body, keeping her so close she felt every nuance of him. He kissed her again and she followed her body and mind's instinct, pulling his shirt loose from his jeans. She slid her hands up his bare torso and he sucked in a sharp breath.

"You're making it hard for me to move slow," he said.

"Maybe I don't want you to move slow. I swear I feel like I've been waiting for you to kiss me forever."

"Well, I'm gonna be doing a lot more than kissing you," he said, and pulled her sweater over her head. A half breath later, her bra was gone and he was putting her down on the bed. Following her down, he slid his mouth down her throat to her nipples. Her body felt as if it were on fire. He caressed her until she couldn't remain still any longer.

"Gage," she said, asking, wanting more.

His skin was warm beneath her touch. She skimmed her hands down over his abdomen and unbuttoned his jeans. When she touched him where he was hard and needing her, he swore under his breath.

He took her mouth again and within moments, they pushed each other's clothes away. Her heart raced and she could barely catch her breath. Lissa had never wanted a man so much in her life. Yes, he was incredibly sexy, but he was smart and funny—nearly perfect.

When he caressed her intimately, her mind seemed to stop. "Gage," she pleaded.

"Hold on," he said and pushed her legs apart. His gaze holding hers, he thrust inside her, filling her with him. She clung to him as he moved in a delicious rhythm that made her feel as if everything inside her was tightening with his every stroke. He reached between them and caressed her once again, and Lissa felt herself burst over the edge.

Seconds later, she felt him stiffen and groan as he climaxed.

Lissa knew she would never be the same.

It took Gage fifteen minutes to make the muscles in his legs start working. This little city gal had knocked him sideways. Granted, it had been a while since he'd been with a woman, but he couldn't remember anyone making him this hot and bothered then utterly depleted.

She looked so pretty in his bed with her hair spilled over his pillow, her lips swollen from him kissing her. He looked down at her naked body and felt the urge to take her again. Well, hell, he didn't want her to think he was a complete animal.

Turning his head aside to get a little control, he scrubbed his jaw. "You hungry?" he asked.

Silence followed. "Uh, I hadn't been thinking about food, but now that you mention it I guess I am."

He felt her soft hand on his shoulder and shuddered. She hesitated. "You don't like that?" she asked.

He chuckled then took her hand and pressed it against his mouth. "Too much. It's not gourmet, but how about a grilled cheese sandwich and some soup?"

"Sounds perfect to me," she said, smiling at him.

Gage took one last glance at her tempting naked form and rose from the bed. He pulled a flannel shirt from his drawer and tossed it at her. "Here, cover up. I don't want you getting cold."

"You got me pretty warm without a shirt a few minutes ago," she said in a sexy teasing voice.

"Maybe I'll get you warm again after I feed you. I don't want to be accused of torture," he said.

"If that was torture..." she drawled.

"Put on the shirt, Lissa," he said and pulled on his jeans. "You are too much."

Gage fixed three sandwiches and a can of tomato soup. He offered her a beer, but she asked for water. "Sorry I don't have wine," he said.

"That's okay. You can pick some up for next time," she said with a smile.

"So there's gonna be a next time?" he asked,

liking the idea. At the same time, he knew Lissa was only in town for a short time and he knew he shouldn't get attached to her.

"Do you want to go back to just being friends? No kisses. No touching. No anything," she said, then took a big bite of the sandwich and gave a little moan of approval.

Hell, no, he thought. "You make a good point. I guess we just both need to remember that you're not going to be here forever. So this is temporary."

A shot of vulnerability deepened her eyes for a half second before she looked away. It happened so fast he wondered if he had imagined it. "You're so right," she said, then met his gaze. "This is temporary, so we should make the best of it, shouldn't we?"

Her eyes seemed to challenge him to all sorts of things he'd never imagined. Gage nodded, feeling him sink under her spell. "Yeah, we should."

"So, next time you'll have wine for me, right?" she asked with a smile.

"Sure. White, red or pink?" he asked.

"White," she told him. "Tell me, are you going to take me home tonight or keep me here with you?"

"That's easy," he said. "I'm keeping you here with me."

After a crazy night of lovemaking, Gage and Lissa took a shower together. She dressed in the clothes she'd worn yesterday. He dressed in fresh clothes and they headed for town. "I'll drop you off at the rooming house, okay?"

"That works for me. I have one more day before my next group of volunteers arrive."

"And we'll keep this on the down low, right?"

He felt her gaze on him. "Are you ashamed of being involved with me?"

He glanced at her. "Hell, no. I wanted to protect your reputation."

She widened her eyes. "Hadn't thought of that." She paused for a moment. "I guess if someone's going to ruin my reputation, I'd like it to be you."

"Well, I'm flattered. But if there's a way to protect you, I'll take it," he said.

Again, he felt her admiring gaze on him. "What?" he asked.

"You're pretty amazing," she said.

Her words made him warm and feel good inside. "Not really, but I'll take the compliment," he said.

As Gage stopped next to the rooming house, Lissa leaned toward him and took his mouth in a scorching kiss that reminded him of all they'd done the night before.

"Have a nice day, Sheriff," she said when she finally pulled away.

His whole body on fire, he wondered when he'd be able to rein in his sex drive for her. He needed to get it under control, he thought as he watched her take the steps to the rooming house. When she disappeared inside, he drove to the office and strode into complete quiet. Thank goodness.

He went to his office and began to work on messages and paperwork from the previous day. He heard someone enter the office, but continued working. Moments later, Vickie poked her head in his office with a cup of coffee in her hand.

"I hear the sheriff had a nice visit with our new favorite gal, Lissa Roarke," she said and put the cup of coffee on his desk.

"Wouldn't know," he said.

"Well, everyone else does," she said. "Did you really think Melba would keep it quiet when Lissa didn't come back last night?"

"Like I said," he repeated firmly. "I wouldn't know."

Vickie made a huffing sound of disapproval. "It will go easier if you go ahead and admit that you two are involved. But I can tell you're determined to take the hard way. Good luck."

Gage glanced up after Vickie left. He sure as hell hoped the whole town didn't know about his involvement with Lissa after just one night. How could he protect them both against such public study?

The phone rang, taking his focus from the possibility of the scrutiny. It was another drug call that would consume him for the rest of the day. Gage would do just about anything to keep drugs out of Rust Creek.

Lissa took her time putting on fresh jeans and a sweater. She tiptoed down the back stairs with the intent of sneaking out the back door. Melba's voice stopped her.

"Hey there, darlin'. I hear you've been visiting with Gage," the woman said.

Lissa froze, turning back to meet Melba's gaze. "Maybe a little," she said, not wanting to reveal too much.

Melba folded her hands together. "Well, I must tell you that the whole community of Rust Creek Falls is grateful."

Lissa felt her cheeks flush with heat. "Uh, you're welcome."

"Yes, indeed," Melba said. "We are very thankful. Gage is the best sheriff we've ever had. We want him happy, and it looks like you help keep him that way."

Lissa blinked. "I'm not sure…"

"No need to be sure about anything. We're just glad you're here, making our town better and making Gage happy. Anything I can get for you? I know it's late for breakfast, but I'm happy to make something for you."

"I'm good," she said. "Thanks, Melba."

Lissa scurried out the door into the cold air of near autumn in Montana and prayed the rest of Rust Creek Falls didn't know about her and Gage. She could only hope.

Something told her to take it slow as she walked to the sheriff's office. She entered with a light step. No need to stomp. Heading for her little corner desk, she waved at Vickie, but kept moving. She made it to her desk with no confrontation and took a deep breath.

Seconds later, Vickie stepped in front of her desk. "Hey there, sweetie. I hear you had a nice time last night."

Lissa straightened in her chair. "What makes you say that?"

Vickie blinked. "Well, people are saying that you and Gage…"

"What people?" Lissa asked. "What are they saying? What do they really know?" she asked.

Vickie opened her mouth, but no sound came out. "Uh…"

"Exactly," Lissa said. "Nobody knows anything. This is personal."

Vickie's eyes widened. "Uh…"

"Uh," Lissa said. "Exactly. And I thank you so much for respecting that because you have been a friend to me ever since I arrived in Rust Creek Falls."

Vickie stared at her for a long moment then gave a slow nod. "Okay. I got you, girl," she said.

"Thanks," Lissa said and turned back to her computer screen.

"Here ya go," Vickie said, putting a cup of coffee in front of her. She lowered her voice. "Good luck with that whole privacy thing."

Hours later, Lissa left the office and walked toward the rooming house.

An SUV slowed beside her. The window lowered. "Hey," Gage said. "Want a ride?"

"Am I going away from the inquisitions?" she asked.

"No questions from me," he said and she heard the sound of the doors unlocking.

Lissa opened the door and stepped inside the SUV. "This has been an interesting day."

"Part of your decision to get involved with the local sheriff. Are you sure you want to continue?" he asked.

She reached up to kiss him and chuckled. "How can I resist the most fabulous man I've ever met?"

Chapter Six

They spent the night making love. The next morning, Lissa had to be up early so she could greet her next group of volunteers at the church. Her cell phone alarm went off and she had to drag herself out of a sexual coma. "Oh, please help me," she murmured.

"I'm here for you, darlin'," Gage said, wrapping his arms around her.

"Stop it," she said, snuggling against him.

He chuckled and she loved that sound. It rippled inside her all the way to her heart. "You really want me to stop?" he asked.

She sighed. "Not really. I just need to get going so I can do my job. So I can help Rust Creek."

"Can't argue with that," Gage said. "Although I'd like to keep you here with me all day and all night. I guess I have to kick your gorgeous butt out of bed."

She smiled. "I guess you do."

Lissa and Gage took another joint shower and he got ready before she did. Darn him. This time, at least, she had fresh clothes. She'd decided to pack a set after that first night. While she was getting dressed, he was doing some chores with the horses.

When Gage came back, he fixed some kind of frozen egg biscuit. It wasn't nearly up to par with what Melba would have served, but after their busy night together, Lissa was grateful for anything. She made a mental note to fix breakfast next time.

He helped her into his SUV and they drove into town.

"You go into the office first," he said. "I don't want you taking heat because we're coming in at the same time. It could hurt your reputation."

She did a double take. "My reputation?" she echoed. "I would think it would improve my reputation if people knew you and I were involved."

He gave a slow grin. "Okay, you flatter me. I'm trying to protect you," he said.

"What are they going to say about me? That I've fallen under the sheriff's spell and want to spend every spare minute with him?" she asked.

He groaned. "You're just making it worse. I don't want them to think you're—"

"What? A wild, loose woman?" she asked.

"Well, I don't want anyone calling you—" He broke off. "I don't want to have to punch anyone."

Lissa laughed. "If someone's going to call me a loose woman because I'm involved with you, I'm okay with it. I'll just tell them we're lucky we're together."

He took a deep breath. "You're something else, Lissa," he said. "But go ahead into the office. I'll park the car and come in soon."

"Okay," she said and clutched his coat and pulled him closer. Then she kissed him and she didn't care who was looking.

She pulled back. "There I go, being a tramp. Heaven help me," she said and got out of the car.

"Heaven help *me,*" Gage said just before she closed the door behind her.

Lissa walked out into the cold fresh air and took a long breath. She could face anything if she had Gage. Scary thought that he had such a huge effect on her, but she wasn't going to question it. She was just going to go with it.

She walked into the office to find Vickie on the phone. Lissa waved and smiled then went to get some coffee. A few minutes later, Gage strode into the office. He also waved to Vickie and gave a nod to Lissa.

Lissa worked on her planned itinerary for the day, but she was distracted when still another visitor came through the door. *Grand Central Station?* she wondered.

"Hi, I'm Danielle Hawthorn here with my son Buddy," the woman said. "School's out today and I was hoping Buddy could volunteer with someone."

Gage came out of his office and glanced at the woman. "Danielle," he said.

"Yeah, you mentioned Buddy might be able to volunteer...."

"He can come with us," Lissa said impulsively. "I'm sure we'll have room. If that's okay with you."

"What are you doing?" Danielle asked.

"Flood relief," Lissa said.

"Perfect." She turned to her son. "I'll pick you up at the end of the day. In the meantime, be a good man."

Gage nodded. "We'll see you then," he said, then turned to the gangly teen who looked a bit awkward. "We're glad to have you. Buddy. This is Miss Roarke. She's been helping us repair some of the damage caused by the flood. Do you know anyone who got hit by the flood?"

Buddy nodded. "Lots of my friends. Some of them had to move into trailers."

"Miss Roarke has a crew of volunteers that will be out working today. You just do whatever she tells you," Gage said.

Buddy gave another nod. "Yes, sir."

Lissa extended her hand to the teen. "Buddy, it's nice to meet you and I'm so happy you'll be helping us today. We're leaving in a few minutes from the church parking lot, so we need to get over there right away." She turned to Gage. "Headed out."

"If you need me for anything…"

Lissa smiled. "I'll call you," she said and led Buddy out the door.

At the first house, the team did quite a bit of hammering to replace wooden construction damaged by the flood. A drywall team would finish the job the following day and with any luck, the displaced family would be able to return to their home this week. The crew ate sandwiches in the van. There was enough for Buddy to eat two. In the second house, owned by the Claibornes, the young family had tried to make do despite the damage. Buddy jumped right in to help, removing curtains and upholstered furniture.

Lissa updated the list of replacement items the home would need with the young mother while the children stayed with a neighbor.

"New sofa and at least one upholstered chair. New curtains. How are the curtains in the rest of the house?" she asked the woman.

"I think the ones upstairs are fine. I'm more concerned about the kitchen floor," Mrs. Claiborne said.

"We can take care of that, but it may not be until next week. How are your appliances?"

"My husband, John, saved those by putting them up on some blocks."

"Good for you," Lissa said.

Buddy stepped toward her, holding a musty, moldy, stuffed long-eared bunny. "Miss Roarke, I found this under the sofa," he said, lifting the animal toward her. "What should I do with it?"

"Oh, no," the young mother said. "That's Sara's bunny. We thought the flood washed it away. She's missed it so much. I wish there was some way to save it. I can't tell you how many times she has cried for that bunny."

Buddy looked at the bunny. "Could we wash it?"

"I think it's past saving, unfortunately. Maybe we should add a long-eared bunny to the list?" Lissa asked.

Buddy nodded. "My sister has a little stuffed dog and she screams whenever she can't find it."

Lissa gave him a commiserating smile and squeezed his shoulder. "Sounds like you have a lot of experience with this kind of thing. Thank you for bringing it to my attention."

An hour later, Lissa drove the van back to town. She thanked the crew members for their hard work and promised more tomorrow. They laughed in return. She was glad the townspeople had been so generous about helping with meals. She could rest easy knowing the volunteers would be well fed with a potluck dinner at the church tonight.

"I bet you're tired," she said to Buddy. "We can head back to the sheriff's office. Your mother should be there soon."

"Miss Roarke, would it be okay if we go to Crawford's General Store first? There's something I want to look at," Buddy said.

His request took her by surprise, but she couldn't see anything wrong with it, especially if she went with him. "Of course. I haven't been in the store very much myself except to buy yogurt, so I wouldn't mind a chance to look around in there a little bit."

Walking toward the store, Lissa made conversation with Buddy, asking him about his favorite classes and favorite things to do.

"I like math, but I hate English. I hate writing papers. It's so boring," he said.

"It's good that you like math. Trust me, you'll use it your whole life. But you need to do well in English, too. You'll be writing your whole life, too, one way or another. Even if you're just texting or sending emails. When you grow up and get a job you can't use all those abbreviations like LOL with your coworkers."

"Yeah, that's what my mother says," he said in a glum voice.

Lissa chuckled and opened the door of the General Store. "I'll meet you up front in about five minutes. Okay?"

Buddy nodded and headed toward the back of the store as if he were looking for something specific. Lissa felt as if she were taking a step back in time as she perused the store. Bags of feed and hardware lined shelves and bins, and groceries took the next aisle. Personal care items were arranged on an end cap. Beer and a very few varieties of wine sat in the refrigerated cases. She thought about grabbing a couple cartons of yogurt even though Melba fed her enough breakfast for three people. Recalling the greasy mystery biscuit Gage had offered her this morning, she decided to buy a few cartons along with some fruit.

As she approached the checkout, she saw that Buddy was holding a bag. "What did you buy?" she asked after the clerk rang her purchase.

"A bunny," he said proudly, pulling the stuffed animal from the bag. "It was marked down and I still didn't have enough money, but Mr. Morris said he would cover it for me when I told him why I was buying it."

Lissa's heart swelled with emotion. "Well, if that isn't the nicest thing... I think you should be the one to give the bunny to that little girl."

Buddy shrugged. "I don't know if I can. I've got to go to school tomorrow," he said.

"Maybe we can find someone to give you a ride out there," she said.

"I don't know. I know my mom can't do it. She's working two jobs," he said.

"We'll see," she said as she pushed open the door and walked down the street to the sheriff's office.

She and Buddy walked inside. His mother and Gage looked up as they entered.

"There you are," Danielle said. "I was getting a little worried."

Gage lifted his eyebrows in silent inquiry.

"We did a little shopping. Buddy purchased a stuffed bunny for a little girl whose toy was destroyed in the flood. How's that for being a good man?" she asked.

Danielle dropped her jaw and her eyes grew shiny with tears. "I don't know what to say." She stepped forward and drew her son into her arms. "I'm so proud of you."

"Aw, Mom," he said with a combination of embarrassment and pleasure.

Lissa felt herself tearing up at the sight of the mother and the teen boy. "I think it would be great if he could deliver the bunny personally. Maybe we can work out a time," she said hopefully.

Danielle pulled back and gave a big nod. "We can do that. I'd like to bring Buddy's brother and sister along, too, if you don't mind."

"Mom," Buddy protested.

"This will be a good example for both of them," Danielle insisted. She looked from Gage to Lissa. "I can't thank you enough."

"I need to thank *you*," Lissa said. "Buddy was a hard worker today."

"I can help again sometime if you need me," he said.

"You just said the magic words," Gage said. "I'm sure Miss Roarke will be calling on you." He patted the teen on his shoulder. "Good job today."

"Thanks," Buddy muttered.

Lissa watched them leave with a smile on her face.

Gage led her back to his office. "And for your next miracle, what are you going to do?"

"I didn't do anything," she said. "He really worked hard."

"I'm sure your enthusiasm and praise had nothing to do with it," he said.

She hesitated. "Not that much. He just already had a good heart."

"One step away from detention or forced community service," he said.

"Oh, you're exaggerating," she said. "He's a good kid. You know it. Everyone gets into a little trouble sometime," she said.

"When did you?" he asked.

Lissa gave a sheepish smile. "Well, there was

this one time I landed a borrowed car in a snowy ditch."

"Sounds like an accident," he said.

"And another time there was this little incident in a bar," she said.

"That resulted in multiple arrests," he said sourly. "What about your misspent youth?"

"I skipped school once," she said. "Got caught. I always get caught."

"Get caught doing what?" he returned, sliding his hand down to take hers.

"Got caught drinking a beer in my neighbor's backyard. We lived in a suburb just outside the city. I really couldn't get away with anything," she said, liking the way his fingers felt laced around hers.

"It's a wonder you didn't go wild when you had the chance," he said.

"By then, I didn't want to disappoint them. I wanted them to believe in me." She thought about how her parents had always seemed more proud of her brothers. One was a lawyer, the other worked for a big financial institution. "I guess I still want them to believe in me."

"Don't they?" he asked.

"I don't know. I'm not sure they're all that impressed with my career. I've done some writing along the way and they've always told me not to count on that to make a living."

"You should let me read some of your writing. I bet you're good," he said.

"How would you know that if you haven't read anything I've written?" she asked.

"Because I've watched you. And you're very good at everything you put your energy toward," he said in a sexy voice just before he kissed her. "Shh," he said and kissed her again.

Lissa sighed at the sensation of his lips on hers. It was all she could do not to fling herself at him. Pulling back, she sighed again. "I have some work I have to do tonight."

"Well, damn. I was hoping you would work on me," he said with a wicked grin.

She playfully punched his chest.

"You can stay and have dinner here, can't you?" he suggested.

"Dinner?" she echoed with surprise. "What are we going to eat? Breakfast muffins?"

Gage shook his head. "No. Mrs. Little brought in some lasagna. She said she baked enough for the potluck and had some left over."

"Oh, lasagna," Lissa said, her mouth watering. "I can't remember the last time I ate lasagna."

"I'll take that as a yes. Can't offer you any wine in the sheriff's office, though," he said.

"No problem," she said. "The sheriff already makes me feel a little dizzy."

"Is that so?" he said more than asked and pulled her against him again for another kiss.

Lissa and Gage ate their dinner in his office. He cleared off a corner of his desk and talked about the day. She was amazed by the variety of his tasks throughout the day, let alone each week. She glanced at her watch and saw that an hour had passed. She wondered how it had gone by so quickly.

She helped clear up from the meal. "As much as I would love to stay longer, I've got to coordinate some plans for later in the week."

"I understand," he said and pulled on his coat. "I'll walk you to the rooming house."

"But…" she began then broke off, hesitating to say what was on her mind.

"But what?" he asked, helping her put on her jacket.

"I thought you wanted to keep our relationship on the down low. If people see me spending time with you, then they're going to talk."

"We're okay as long as we don't flaunt it. It's not like I'll be taking you to the bar and dancing with you every night," he said.

"It would be nice to dance with you sometime," she said wistfully.

"I'm not much of a dancer," he said.

"We'll see," she said as he opened the door for her.

They walked slowly down the street, chatting

about anything and everything. When they arrived at the rooming house, she looked up at him. "Better not kiss me," she teased. "We're on the down low."

He shook his head. "You're just determined to cause trouble, aren't you?"

"Who? Me?" she asked, deliberately widening her eyes in mock innocence.

He tugged her toward a huge tree away from the bright porch light from the house and took her mouth in a passionate kiss. Her heart and breath did crazy things in response. When he finally pulled back, she could hardly breathe.

"I think you're the one causing trouble," she said. "And I like it very much."

"Hush," he said, putting his finger to her lips. "We'll just have to finish this trouble some other time. 'Night."

"Good night," she said and wobbled up the porch steps.

Gage decided to stop by the bar before he headed home. He would have much preferred spending his evening with Lissa, but he understood her need to work. She was making things happen in a way he'd never expected. He shouldn't have underestimated her.

He spotted his longtime friend Dallas Traub at

the bar and grabbed the stool next to him. "How's it going?" he asked him.

"As well as it can be. You want a beer?" Dallas asked.

Gage nodded and lifted his finger to the bartender.

"The election for mayor looks like it could get a little interesting," Dallas said.

"Yes. It was so much easier when we had Hunter McGee. I don't know anyone who didn't like him," Gage said, feeling the familiar stab of grief over the former mayor's death.

"Well, it gives people something to talk about," Dallas said and shot him a sideways glance. "Along with that pretty thing from New York who is providing flood relief."

"Yeah. Lissa Roarke is doing a good job. Surprises me how much she's getting done. She has a new set of volunteers rolling in every few days," Gage said.

"I also hear she's spending her extra time with the local sheriff," Dallas said.

Gage rolled his eyes. "Come on, Dallas. You know I don't talk about that kind of thing."

"You may not, but everyone else is," Dallas said and took a gulp from his beer.

"It's nobody's business," Gage said. "We've been keeping things discreet. I don't want people talking about her."

"Too late for that. Sounds like you may have already fallen for her," Dallas said. "Don't get ahead of yourself. Make sure you really get to know her before you get too involved. I sure as hell wish I'd done things differently with my ex-wife. Married her way too fast and it's going to take years to undo the damage."

Gage knew Dallas was recently divorced from his wife and pretty bitter about women in general. "Not every woman is like your ex-wife," Gage said.

"Maybe not," Dallas said. "But you take your time. Don't jump into the frying pan."

Frustration tugged at Gage. "What is this? Trust me, I haven't had any discussions about the future with Lissa," he said. "We both know she's leaving Rust Creek."

"Good. You just keep that in mind. But speaking of women, I heard you had dinner with Jasmine Cates," Dallas said. "How'd that go?"

Gage rolled his eyes. Sometimes he couldn't believe how much people talked about nothing in Rust Creek. He shrugged and took another sip of beer. "She ate a meal at the office with me. Nothing there."

"Hmm," Dallas said. "I spent some time with her, too."

"Really?" Gage said. "I'm glad to hear you're getting out."

Dallas scowled at him.

"Hey, if the shoe fits," Gage said, then changed the subject. "What do you think about those Broncos?"

"It's gonna take more than a star quarterback to pull everything together," Dallas said. "I'd like to see Seattle shake things up."

Gage nodded and took another sip of beer. He'd walked into the bar in a good mood, but talking with Dallas had ruined it for him.

The next morning, just before he left the trailer to do some morning chores, he received a call from his mother. "We haven't seen you in two weeks. Come over for dinner," she said.

Gage raked his hand through his hair. "Aw, Mom, you know how busy I've been. I don't know if I can make dinner tonight, but I'll try to stop by in the next day or two."

His mother gave a big sigh. "I realize you touch base with your father several times a week about ranch business, but I would like to hear from you, too," she said.

Gage felt the guilt screws sinking into his flesh. "I'm sorry, but you know that when I agreed to run for sheriff, my extra time was going to fly out the window. Add in the flood and it's been tough. I'll feel better about things when we see some light at the end of the tunnel. I just wish we could find the funds to get the school rebuilt."

"I know," she said. "But that's a lot of money and a lot of people are hurting these days. Speaking of the flood, though, I hear that volunteer coordinator from New York is very pretty."

Gage felt a twist of dread. He knew where this was headed. "Uh-huh. How's my sister doing?" he asked, trying to derail whatever comments his mother might make about his love life.

"She's fine. In love. But back to that volunteer coordinator. One of my friends told me that you've been seeing her," she said.

"Of course I see her," he said. "Her headquarters is pretty much run from the sheriff's office."

"That's not what I'm saying and you know it," his mother said. "Why is it that I have to hear from a friend that you've started seeing a woman?"

"Probably because you have a life and you're not nearly as gossipy as most of the women in town," Gage said.

"Well, thank you for that," she said. "But I wouldn't be a good mother if I didn't tell you to be careful. You're a good man and most of the single women in Rust Creek would love to be the object of your affection. You should focus on the local girls. This girl is from the city and you know how city people can be. They get bored."

Gage swallowed a sigh. "Thanks, Mom. Glad to know you think I'm boring."

"I didn't say that," his mother said. "I'm just feeling protective."

Gage's heart softened. "That's nice of you, Mom. But you and Dad raised me well and I'm all grown up now. I can take care of myself."

At that, his mother backed down. After a few more moments of small talk, he hung up the phone and groaned. *Why* did people feel the need to give him advice when he hadn't asked for it? He could only hope that no one else would offer commentary on his relationship with Lissa.

Chapter Seven

Lissa worked with her crew of volunteers nearly nonstop for the next three days. Gage barely got to see her for more than fifteen minutes at a time, and although he would pull out his teeth before he'd admit it, he was feeling cranky. Of course, his not seeing Lissa didn't keep people from making comments.

Vickie, the dispatcher, told him to go for it because he "deserved some good lovin'." He got another go-ahead from someone he stopped for speeding. And his deputy, Will, had clearly heard the rumors about Gage and Lissa. Clearly miffed, Will was only speaking to Gage when absolutely necessary.

All this waiting motivated Gage to do a little planning for the next time they got together. He bought wine from the general store—all three kinds. He bought some beer and steaks, along with potatoes, a large can of green beans and some biscuits. Most of what he bought was frozen or canned, so the fresh steaks and potatoes were a stretch for him.

The volunteer crew finally finished a half day of work and left to return home. Lissa walked into the office carrying a bag of something that smelled really good from the deli. "I'm finally done for two days. Barbecue sandwiches for everyone," she said.

"I'm not turning that down," Will said, bounding from his desk.

"Me, either," Vickie said. "Oh, look, you got eight sandwiches. Can I take an extra one home for dinner?"

"Feel free," Lissa said and met Gage's gaze. "Whew. What a crazy busy few days."

"I'll say," he said and accepted one of the sandwiches. "Come on in my office."

"Let me grab a drink first," she said and filled a cup from the water cooler.

She walked into his office and collapsed in the chair across from his desk. Her hair was tousled and her eyes had slight shadows beneath them. "You don't have to kill yourself for this."

"I'm not. I just want to maximize the volunteers when I have them. When they arrive, they want to work longer than I planned for them." She shrugged. "I'm just glad we've had a great combination of skilled and enthusiastic volunteers."

Gage nodded as she took a few bites. "What do you have planned for tonight?" he asked.

She pushed back her hair and smiled. "Besides sleeping?"

"Any chance you'd like to sleep at my place?" he asked.

Her eyes brightened. "How much will I get to sleep at your place?" she asked, leaning forward.

Something about her made him want to eat her up. "I'll let you sleep just as much as you want," he said, and bit into his sandwich.

She gave a low, sexy chuckle. "The trouble is I don't want to sleep when I'm with you. What are you going to feed me for dinner?" she asked.

"Steak and baked potato," he said, feeling a bit proud that he'd already planned the menu.

She widened her eyes. "Really? I didn't know you had anything like that in your kitchen."

"I didn't until last night," he said.

She laughed and the sound made everything inside him feel a little lighter. "Then you've got yourself a date, Sheriff. I'll wrap up some paperwork."

"And take a nap," he told her. They traded bites of their sandwiches with conversation.

"Is that an order?" she asked, tilting her head at a challenging angle.

"A word of encouragement," he said.

"Sort of like the same words you offer people who may end up in jail if they don't follow your encouragement?" she asked.

"You're in no danger of ending up in jail," he promised. "I've just been missing you," he said, surprising himself with the admission.

She blinked then took a slow breath. "I've been missing you, too. I'll try to squeeze in a nap, Sheriff."

"Thanks for the sandwiches," he said and crumpled his wrapper.

She stood and shrugged. "My way of celebrating."

It was all he could do not to pull her into his arms, but Gage knew once he touched her, he wouldn't want to stop. "Later," he said.

"Yeah, later," she said in a husky voice and left his office.

Lissa did as much work as possible then forced herself to lie down for a short time. She was so looking forward to her evening with Gage that she had a hard time settling down. As soon as she fell asleep, however, she heard her cell phone beep.

Lissa dragged her head off the pillow and answered. "Hi," she said.

"You sound dead to the world," Gage said.

She was half awake. His voice made her stomach flip-flop. It was an involuntary response. "I'm awake," she said, propping herself up against her pillow. She took a deep breath and almost slapped herself so she would sound more perky.

"Yeah," he said. "I just wouldn't want you performing surgery or driving a car," he said.

She frowned into the phone. "I don't have to do either, do I?" she asked.

"Good point," he said. "Are you ready? I'm waiting out front of the rooming house," he said.

Yikes. "Sure," she lied. "Give me two minutes. Maybe three," she said as she rose from the bed.

He chuckled. "I'll give you five. Don't trip down the stairs."

"Okay, okay. See you soon," she said and turned off the phone. Racing toward the bathroom, she splashed her face and brushed her teeth. She grabbed her toothbrush, deodorant and moisturizer, then added some clean clothes and cartons of yogurt and an apple from her minifridge to the pile and threw everything into a tote bag and headed out the door. Lissa was one of the few guests with a minifridge in her room. Apparently, the previous guest in her room had needed to refrigerate their medication for a chronic medical condition.

She skidded to a halt at the top of the steps, remembering Gage's words. *Don't trip.* Swearing under her breath, she carefully descended the stairs, running into Melba.

"Well, hi there, darling," Melba said. "Where are you headed?"

Lissa felt a sudden twist of inexplicable embarrassment and guilt. She felt as if her mother had caught her headed out the door for trouble. Where had that come from, she wondered. She was a grown woman. She shouldn't have to explain herself to anyone.

"I'm going out," she said. "A friend invited me to take a break tonight. I'll be back tomorrow."

Melba gave a slow nod. "That sounds like a good friend," the older woman said. "Just don't get into trouble."

"I won't," Lissa said, barely able to keep the laughter from her voice. She was headed straight for trouble. The best kind of trouble.

She scuttled out the front door and down the porch steps to Gage's SUV parked discreetly several yards from the front of the house. She raced into the vehicle and tossed her tote into the backseat. "Whew, that was interesting," she said.

"Mama Melba grill you?" he asked.

She sighed. "It wasn't exactly grilling, but I felt like I was facing both my mom and dad when I was trying to get away with something."

"How'd that work out?" he asked.

"She told me not to get into trouble," she said.

Gage gave a dirty laugh and shifted the card into drive.

The car was nice and cozy and Gage had put low music on the radio. Lissa got so comfortable she drifted to sleep. Sometime later, the SUV hit a bump that awakened her. Lissa glanced at Gage. "How long have I been asleep?"

"Since three minutes after you got in the car," he said.

"Why didn't you wake me up?"

"I want you to get all the rest you can," he said and smiled at her. "I'd like you to stay awake at least for the steak I'm going to cook for you."

"I'm sorry," she said. "I feel like I have sleeping sickness."

"You've been running on adrenaline. You just need a little nap," he said as he pulled in front of his trailer.

"I'm sorry I've been boring," she said.

"You're not boring," he said. "You're pretty whether you're awake or asleep."

His words eased something inside her. "Thanks," she said.

"Just speaking the truth," he said.

He got out of the car and walked to her side of the car to help her out of the door. She was always surprised by his chivalry. Perhaps she'd lived in Manhattan too long, where the men pretty much shoved you out of the cab after a date if they didn't think you were going to put out.

The sky was a dark velvet blanket with bright stars. "It's so beautiful tonight," she said, breathing in the crisp night air.

"Yeah, you are," he said.

She swatted at him. "Stop flattering me," she said.

"Come on inside," he said, leading her inside the trailer. He grabbed the potatoes, washed them and tossed them in the microwave. He put the green beans to warm on the stove and took the steaks out to put on his small gas grill.

"You're so efficient. I don't know what to say," she said.

"I forgot the biscuits. Can you put them in the oven?"

"Sure," she said and returned to the trailer to take care of the bread for dinner. Being with Gage made her feel more energized. After the crew left, Lissa had felt as if she could go into a coma, but Gage brought her back to life. Setting a timer for the biscuits on her cell phone, she went outside to join Gage.

He flipped the steaks. "Biscuits okay?"

"Perfect," she said. "I'm very impressed by this meal. What inspired you?"

"You," he said without hesitation. "I got a little grumpy when I didn't get to spend time with you the past few days. I decided you deserved a good meal, and I was determined to give it to you."

His confession twisted her heart. "That's the nicest thing anyone has ever done for me."

He met her gaze. "You deserve more."

Her heart tripped over itself. "Sheriff, are you trying to get me into trouble?"

He smiled and pulled her against him, taking her mouth in a deep kiss. "I'm doing my best."

Several moments later, everything was ready and Lissa joined Gage for the hearty meal. "Delicious," she told him as she took a bite of steak.

"I aim to please," he said.

Afterward, they went outside and cuddled in the moonlight. "It's so quiet here," she said. "I can't remember being in such a quiet, beautiful place."

"That's our specialty in Montana," he said and looked upward. "That and our wide-open skies."

"It's calming and peaceful," she said.

"A lot different than Manhattan," he said.

"Yes." She took a deep breath. "I hear a song in my head. Perfect for a dance in the Montana moonlight. Would you join me?"

He paused a moment. "You'll have to hum it so I get the beat right," he said.

Seconds later, he pressed one hand against her back and lifted her hand with the other. She hummed under her breath, but he caught on. Soon enough, they were waltzing.

Lissa looked into his face and everything inside her jumped and screamed. She had been waiting for this moment her entire life. Gage was her dream come true.

"You lied," she said breathlessly.

Gage frowned, but didn't miss a step. "What do you mean?"

"You're a great dancer," she said. "The very best."

Gage lifted his head, his throat bared to her as he laughed. "It's the moonlight and the stars fooling you," he said. "They're on my side tonight."

After a night filled with lovemaking and some sleep, Lissa awakened the next morning when she felt Gage rise from the bed. "Hey, is it already time to get up?" she asked, already missing his body next to hers.

"It is for me, sleepyhead. But you can get a few more winks if you like," he said and smiled at her.

"What are you going to do?"

"I've got to ride my horses every now and then to keep them from getting green." Seeing her confused look, he clarified, "That means I would have to do a lot of re-training and conditioning with them. It won't take long," he said and brushed his hand over her hair.

"Can I go with you?"

"You ride?"

"Well, I have," she said. "It's been a while."

"Okay. We can take it slow on the ride, but you better hop out of bed."

She sat up and wiped the sleep from her eyes. "I can move quickly. Just let me splash some water on my face and brush my teeth."

"I can heat up a frozen breakfast biscuit for you," he offered.

"No need," she said, slipping past him to the tiny bathroom. "I brought my own fruit this time. I'll skip your mystery meat, thank you."

"Mystery meat?" he echoed. "What do you mean?"

"Have you read the ingredients on the package?" she asked as she splashed her face. "How many of them can you pronounce?"

"I didn't know you were a health nut," he said.

"I'm not. I just like to be able to pronounce what I'm putting in my body." She brushed her teeth.

"Picky, picky," he teased. "You think those muffins we get at the office are chemical free?"

She didn't argue. She was too busy getting dressed and pulling her hair into a low ponytail. Lissa was excited to go horseback riding. It had been ages since she'd ridden. Within moments, she and Gage tramped to the barn. He saddled up a sweet, aging mare named Sally for her and a gelding named Black for himself.

"I'll lead with Black. He can get a little cantankerous, and I don't want him irritating Sally. You won't have to do much with her. She knows the way and she's got a soft mouth. Let's move along," he said and made a clicking sound.

As they climbed a hill, Lissa marveled at the view. "It's so beautiful and clear. It really does seem like I can see for miles."

"That's what we're known for—wide-open spaces. There's a reason we're called big sky country. A lot different than what you see every day in Manhattan, that's for sure."

"What surprises me is how quiet it is out here. There's always some kind of noise in the city," she said.

"Yeah, people either love it or the isolation eventually drives them crazy. The winters can be pretty harsh here. Add in the lack of accessibility to entertainment and shopping and it's tough to face it on an everyday basis when you're used to having everything within walking distance."

Lissa nodded, wondering if she could see herself living full time in Montana. She honestly hadn't missed New York at all since she'd set foot here. "I haven't gone through a winter here, so I can't really make that call. But it's not like you've got to hitch a wagon to go to town. You can drive."

"As long as you can drive in the snow," he said in a meaningful voice.

She made a face at him. "You're never going to

let me live that down, are you? If I'm such a rotten winter driver, then maybe you should teach me."

"I'll do that," he said, meeting her gaze. "If you're here when it snows again."

His comment stabbed at her. Both of them knew her stay in Montana was only temporary, but she didn't want to think about her time with Gage coming to an end.

After they finished their ride, Gage checked out the rest of the horses and let them into the pasture. "Hmm," he said as he watched for a moment.

"What's the problem?"

"It looks like Damien might be favoring his right side," he said, pointing to a brown horse. "I'll have to check that out later. Let's head back to my place."

Walking back to Gage's trailer, they passed by his house. She paused. "You never showed me your house," she said.

"There's not much to see downstairs. I took out all the upholstered furniture. It's iffy whether I'll need a new floor. I lost the stove and fridge, too."

"Have you filed for any compensation?" she asked.

"Just haven't gotten around to it. The drywall will have to be replaced in one of the rooms. I've already torn out the bad stuff and I ran fans in there like crazy afterward. I'll get to it sometime. Maybe next spring. Why should I get back into my house when there are families still waiting to get back into theirs?"

"Well, why shouldn't you get back into your house?" she asked.

He shrugged. "My house is not a priority," he said. "You take the first shower. I'm going to take care of a few chores."

Staring after Gage, Lissa blinked. He'd sounded almost curt. She admired the sacrifices he was making for the other citizens in his area, but she didn't think he needed to be last in line for repairs. Gage worked his butt off for the community. He could use a little comfort during the few hours he was at home.

Chewing on some possibilities, she took her shower, toweled off and got dressed. When Gage returned, he also took a shower, letting out a shout after a few minutes.

Alarmed, Lissa tapped on the door, carrying her carton of yogurt with her. "What's wrong?"

"Ran out of hot water. It's damn cold," he said.

"Yikes," she said. "Sorry."

Gage stepped from the minuscule bathroom with a towel wrapped around his waist. "No problem. The trailer's stingy with hot water. I'm glad you got yours first."

"Now I feel bad," she said.

"I'll let you make it up to me," he said with a

grin and pressed a quick kiss on her mouth. "Are my lips blue?"

"No," she said with a laugh, admiring his well-muscled body. "You look like you survived the frigid temperature pretty well."

"Sure I did. We need to eat and hit the road. Is that yogurt any good?" he asked.

"Yummy peach," she said. "I've also got blue-berry."

"I like blueberries. I'll give that one a try," he said.

Not that she had offered, Lissa thought, but smiled at the notion that she had influenced him even a tiny bit. He ate two cartons of yogurt and one of her apples.

Apparently Gage liked the food choices suggested for him.

They made it into town and Gage let her off at the rooming house. Lissa prayed she could make it up the back stairway without Melba confronting her. After making it to her room, she breathed a sigh a relief then sank onto the bed. More than anything, she wanted to take a nap. A long nap.

Torn, she dragged herself out of bed. She had fresh volunteers arriving in two days, and she needed to map out a schedule. No rest for the wicked or pure, she thought. And she sure as heck wasn't pure.

Lissa grabbed her iPad and sat in a straight-backed chair. She decided to skip going to head-quarters and focus on working here in her room. Maybe later she could squeeze in a nap.

Just after two o'clock in the afternoon, she'd made dozens of lists and schedules and several appointments and her eyes were drooping, so she took that well-needed nap. She set her alarm for two hours.

Lissa was awakened by an annoying beeping sound. It took her several seconds, but she finally realized the sound was coming from her phone. Oh, wow, she could use some more sleep, she thought. Like maybe twenty-four hours.

That wasn't going to happen, she realized, and stumbled into her bathroom to splash water on her face and brush her teeth. It was her custom-ized routine for waking up when she wanted sleep more than anything.

While she was brushing her teeth, her cell phone rang. She rinsed her mouth then picked up. "Hi," she said.

"Hi. Are you coming back to life?" Gage said.

"I'm doing the best I can," she said.

"Bet you're sore from your morning ride," he said.

She frowned. "Bet you're right. How did you know?"

"Riding uses different muscles. You want to take a break and stay at Melba's tonight?"

"No," she said. "But I do need some more sleep

because more volunteers are coming the day after tomorrow."

"You want me to keep my hands off you?" Gage asked.

"Never," she said.

He chuckled. "I'll pick you up in a few. Look for my car," he said.

"You might want to pick up a couple cartons of yogurt and some fruit," she said.

"Okay," he said. "By the way, I forgot to tell you, but I bought some wine a few days ago."

"You're a great guy," she said.

"Yeah, keep saying that," he said.

Lissa laughed. "You're a great guy. You're a great guy. You're a great—"

"Okay, stop or I'll get sick," he said.

"You're a great—"

Click. Lissa glanced at her phone and saw that Gage had disconnected the call. Even when she was half asleep, he made her feel alive. She grabbed a few items and a change of clothing. She glanced outside her window and saw Gage's SUV parked away from the light cascading over the front lawn.

Her heart skipped a beat and she gathered her belongings in a tote bag then made her way down the back stairway.

"Hey, sweetie," Melba said.

Dumb luck, Lissa thought. "Hi there, Melba," she said and gave the woman a big hug.

"You haven't shown up for breakfast lately," Melba said.

"I know. My schedule has been crazy. My volunteer group just left and a new one is coming in soon."

"Well, everyone is talking about everything you're getting done. You're a marvel. Let me know if there's anything I can do. I'll even let you use my car," the woman said.

"Oh, you're too sweet. Especially after I landed your car in the ditch."

"Bessie's been through more than a little trip in the ditch. And it's all for a good cause," she said. "Taking care of Rust Creek Falls. That's what we're trying to do."

"You're so right," Lissa said.

Melba sighed. "Well, I wish I could do more for you," she said.

"You've already done more than enough. You've given me a second home," Lissa said and hugged the woman again.

"You're a sweet girl," Melba said. "You call me anytime you need me."

Lissa's heart twisted as she headed out the back door and rushed toward Gage's vehicle. She climbed in and took a deep breath. "Hiya. Good to see you."

"Good to see *you*," he said.

"Thanks," she said and sank her head back against the seat.

"I need to let you sleep more tonight," he said.

"Oh, no," she protested. "Keep me awake," she said. "I love the way you keep me awake."

Gage groaned. "You send my good intentions to hell in a handbasket."

Chapter Eight

I'm so excited with the progress we're making in Rust Creek Falls. With new volunteer crews arriving every few days, we get a fresh group of people eager to work and make a difference. The people here are just as fantastic. They are providing meals for the volunteers and many of them are helping their neighbors with damaged homes even while their own homes have been damaged. Even the children are helping! The sheriff continues to work nearly 'round the clock to help everyone get back on their feet. He's an amazing man. I've never met anyone like him and I'm growing more certain, day by day, that I never will again. Sometimes I have to pinch myself that I'm getting to know him on such a deep level.

—Lissa Roarke

Gage savored another night with Lissa, but then the new set of volunteers arrived and she was busy all the time. It gave him an opportunity to stop by his parents' house for a few minutes and catch up on his chores. He checked out his horse, Damien, and decided to call his longtime friend Brooks Smith, the best veterinarian in the area, to come take a look. He'd known Brooks since the two had gone to high school together.

The animal doctor drove in from Livingston about two hours later.

Gage walked outside to meet Brooks. "Thanks for coming," he said, extending his hand. "I would have called your dad, but I hear he's not feeling well lately."

Brooks nodded. "He's not in the best health."

Gage led the way toward the barn. "When are you going to move back to town? It would make sense for you to take over your father's practice, especially if his health is failing."

Brooks frowned. "Try telling my father that. He's not ready to give the practice to me yet. He wants me to be married first," he said in disgust.

"Married?" Gage echoed. "What does being married have to do with taking over your dad's vet practice?"

"He thinks being married adds stability. It's not like I've gone tearing off to Alaska or anywhere else all the time."

Gage shrugged. "True. Maybe he'll come around," he said as they walked into the barn.

"I think he's determined that *I'm* the one who should come around." Brooks shook his head. "Having a wife is a time and energy drain. I don't have time for a wife, let alone a social life right now."

Gage thought about Lissa and how he'd been doing everything he could to avoid a social life until she came to town. "Sometimes a social life finds you even when you're not looking for it."

Brooks glanced at Gage. "Spoken like a man who has a woman on the brain."

Gage didn't like talking about his relationship with Lissa. People offered too many opinions. "I guess it depends on the woman. Some of them don't make it feel like a drain, but I'm no expert, that's for sure."

"I don't know any man who is an expert on women," Brooks said with a laugh. "Now let me take a look at your horse."

Brooks examined Damien and confirmed a mild tendon injury. "Ice and rest. Keep him in the stall.

You can put a gel cast on him then walk him in a few days. I don't recommend an anti-inflammatory in this case because he's more likely to rest the leg if it hurts. Call me if you run into any problems."

"Thanks for coming out," Gage said.

"Anytime," Brooks said as they returned to his truck.

"Good luck with your dad," Gage said.

Brooks gave a rough chuckle. "I'll need it. Take care, now."

Late that afternoon, Gage went into the office and was greeted by Lissa. She was so excited about something that she couldn't keep still. "What happened?" he asked. "Did you win the lottery?"

"In a way," she said. "Someone at Bootstraps has located a furniture store that's going out of business and they've agreed to donate a bunch of furniture to the flood victims in Rust Creek. One of the volunteers from my last crew called and they've raised money to donate new stuffed animals, linens and curtains."

"You're a regular miracle worker," he said, wanting to pick her up and hug her.

"Me?" she said. "It's not me. These are other people making these donations."

"Because you've gotten them all fired up," he said. "That's why your crews are getting twice as much done as you expected and why you're so perfect at what you do."

She stared at him for a half moment. "No one has ever accused me of being perfect," she said.

"Well, you're pretty darn close."

"Thank you," she said. "I could kiss you for that. The reason I'm here a little early tonight is because I'm meeting Buddy and his family out at the Claibornes' house. He's going to give the little girl her bunny. It's last minute, but his mother Danielle has a very hectic schedule. Would you like to go?"

"I'd be honored," he said. "Let me make a few calls and I'll tell Will he's in charge until I get back."

They left for the Claibornes' about thirty minutes later and pulled into the family's driveway with Buddy's family following right after. Gage and Lissa greeted Danielle and her children. Buddy carried a box wrapped in pink paper.

"Is that the bunny?" Lissa asked.

Buddy nodded. "My mom thought the little girl might like it even better if she got to unwrap it."

The small group made their way to the front door and were welcomed inside by Mrs. Claiborne. "Please, come in. Sara, say hello," she said, taking the hand of a young toddler with brown tousled curls looking up with wide blue eyes.

"Hi," Sara whispered then stuck her thumb in her mouth.

"She's a little shy," Mrs. Claiborne said. "Sara,

this young man has brought you a gift. Do you want to open it?"

Sara hesitated then nodded.

Buddy stepped forward and gave the little girl the wrapped gift. "I heard you were missing one of these and saw this. I hope you like it."

Sara plopped down on the floor and tore off the paper. Buddy helped her open the box.

She pulled the bunny from the box and gasped. "Bunny! It's Bunny," she said and hugged the stuffed animal against her.

Lissa's heart squeezed tight and she felt her eyes fill with tears. What Buddy had done was such a small, but powerful example of the generosity she'd seen in all the people of Rust Creek Falls. They'd sacrifice for themselves to make up for someone else's loss.

She felt Gage's arm around her and was so thankful for his strength.

"Buddy, I don't know how to thank you," Mrs. Claiborne said. "You've just made my Sara very happy."

Buddy shoved his hands in his pockets. "It was nothing," he said.

"No, it was something very nice," Mrs. Claiborne insisted. "Sara, tell Buddy thank you."

The little toddler rushed toward him and gave him a hug. "Thank you," she said.

Buddy's face turned red with embarrassment, but anyone could see he was pleased.

"I'm proud of you," Gage said. "You're growing up to be a good man."

"Thank you, Sheriff," he said.

"Well, I guess we should go now," said Buddy's mother, Danielle. "It was nice meeting you. I hope your little Sara will enjoy the bunny."

They said their goodbyes and returned to the driveway.

Danielle stopped and turned to Lissa and Gage. "I can't thank you enough," she said, lifting her hand to her throat. "I was starting to worry, but I can see Buddy's got a solid gold heart. With your help, I'll keep him moving in the right direction."

"Call if you need anything," Gage said. "We've got people volunteering to help with transportation."

"Let me know the next time he's off from school. I'd love for him to keep helping out," Lissa said.

"I'll do that," Danielle said and loaded her family into her car.

Gage opened the passenger door for Lissa and she stepped inside. As soon as she got inside, she burst into tears.

Gage shot her a worried look. "What's wrong?" he asked, taking her hand.

"It just got to me. You can tell Danielle is struggling to keep it all together and they don't have much money. Buddy has to feel the strain. He has a little money in his pocket and what does he do with it? Buys a bunny for some little girl he doesn't even know." She sniffled. "Sorry. It's just one of the sweetest things I've witnessed in a while."

He pulled her into his arms and she allowed herself to sink against him. "Like I said before, you're inspiring everyone to give more than usual."

"I can't take credit for this," she said and took a deep breath. "It's going to be hard for me to leave these people behind. I don't know how I'm going to do it," she said. "I didn't expect to get so attached."

Gage sucked in a quick breath, his eyes giving a stormy glint. "You'll be okay. You'll work it all out, get some perspective and move on."

How could he be so positive about her leaving? she wondered.

"Besides," he said, tipping up her chin with his finger. "You're not gone yet. You're still here. By the time you have to leave, all of us might succeed in driving you crazy." He dropped a kiss on her lips. "Don't think about leaving until it's time to go."

She sank her head against his chest. "If you say so," she said.

"I do."

One day later, Lissa's crew left and she had two days to prepare for the next group. The incoming volunteers had recently increased their numbers, so Lissa was reworking the schedule to accommodate the added volunteers. It was an unusually warm day and she sat in a chair in Gage's front yard. She could feel the heat of the sun on her face.

She sighed with pleasure. These little breaks in between the departures and arrivals of volunteer crews provided her with so many sweet moments with Gage. Every day she spent with him made her want more time with him.

Just up the hill, she could see him walking Damien, helping the horse in his healing process. That was who Gage was—a man determined to help those hurting and in need. Before she'd met him, Lissa would have thought of a sheriff as a tough guy, and Gage was certainly strong. But he was so much more than that. His sense of humor put people at ease even in the worst situations. He cared deeply for the people in Rust Creek Falls and they counted on him in return.

Distracted by her thoughts about Gage, she opened a file on her iPad and began to write about him, what he meant to the people of Rust Creek Falls and what he meant to her. She easily filled the next hour composing her thoughts about him until a shadow fell over her.

"Boo," Gage said and she nearly jumped out of the chair.

She put her hand to her racing heart. "You scared me."

"It was easy. You looked pretty intense. How's the scheduling coming?"

"Pretty good," she said. "I'm not quite done yet."

He picked her up, taking her by surprise, then plopped down on the chair with her in his lap. "You're awfully pretty sitting here in the sun, Miss Lissa."

She snuggled against him. "You're awfully pretty, too," she teased.

He chuckled. "You know a man doesn't like to be described as pretty."

"I think you're tough enough to handle it," she said.

He took her mouth in a kiss that made everything inside her melt. He pulled back just a bit, his eyes dark with arousal. "You look tired. I think you need to go back to bed."

"So, it's nap time?" she asked.

He rose and headed for the trailer. "Maybe later," he said.

They spent the next hour making sweet love. Lissa couldn't believe the combination of feelings he aroused in her. He made her so hungry for him, so crazy with wanting. She couldn't remember feeling safer and...more adored. Yes, adored.

At rest next to him after they'd pushed each

other to the limits then over the edge, her hand on his chest, she felt his heart pounding. The strong, sure beat called to her. She looked at his face and an earthshaking knowledge rocked through her. She was in love with Gage.

"You're staring," he said, his eyes still closed.

"You can't possibly know that," she said. "Your eyes are closed."

"I'm a lawman," he said. "I have eyes in the back of my head and I can see things even when I'm asleep."

"Hmm," she said. "Sounds like Santa Claus."

He let out a chuckle and pulled her on top of him. "You are one sassy woman, Lissa Roarke. A man would have a hard time keeping your mouth shut."

"You didn't want it shut a few moments ago," she told him breathlessly.

"Oh, don't remind me, or I'll have to take you again," he said as if the thought pained him.

"Would that be so bad?"

"No, but I need some sustenance if you're gonna keep wearing me out like this. Come on and fix me a sandwich," he said.

She loved the way he conveniently forgot that he had initiated their lovemaking, but she was too happy to dispute it. Pulling on her clothes, she headed for the tiny kitchen.

"I tell you it's hard to get any work done with

you around," he said after he'd pulled on his jeans
and a shirt.

Work. The word juggled something in her mind
and she panicked. "Oh, no. I left my iPad outside."

"Don't worry. I'm sure it's still there. I'll get it
for you," he said and went outside.

Lissa was surprised to see that Gage had fresh
bread and deli meat and cheese for sandwiches, but
he'd told her he figured if he planned to keep her
barricaded on his ranch, then he'd better be prepared to feed her. And him. It warmed her heart
that he'd planned for their time together. She'd just
finished preparing three sandwiches when her cell
phone rang.

"Lissa Roarke," she said and pointed to the
sandwiches as Gage returned with her tablet.

He nodded and sat down at the table, inhaling
his food as he glanced at her iPad.

"Miss Roarke, this is Virginia Conner," the
woman on the other end of the line said. "We're
just going to need more beds. Five more people
volunteered this morning."

"Well, that's fantastic," Lissa said. "I've got another day to figure this out. I'll call you tomorrow. Okay?"

Excited, she disconnected the call. "I need to
call the minister and a few other women who've
been helping with food. We are getting so many

volunteers there won't be enough cots at the church for them. Isn't this fantastic?"

He smiled at her. "Sure is. That second sandwich is for me, right?" he asked.

Lissa laughed. "Of course it is."

While Lissa made her calls, Gage pushed the screen, thinking he'd play a game to kill some time. Instead of pulling up a game, however, the screen revealed a word document. Curious if this was some of the writing she'd mentioned to him, he scanned the first few sentences.

It didn't take long, however, for him to see that she was writing about him. Uncomfortable, he almost set the device aside, but he couldn't resist this opportunity to see inside her head. She described him as "her beautiful cowboy." Reading the words got under his skin. He shifted in his chair and continued to read. *He is the perfect man, the man I always dreamed I would find. I had begun to think such a man didn't exist until I met Gage.*

Gage raked his fingers through his hair. "Perfect," he muttered. "Nobody's perfect." He sure as hell wasn't. *He is strong, yet gentle and kind, the most honorable man I've ever known.*

Gage shook his head. He couldn't see himself in her description of him. She was writing about a man with a sterling character who had no flaws. Who'd never done anything wrong. The man Lissa wrote about had never failed anyone, and Gage knew he had failed a lot of people when he hadn't been here to help them during the flood.

His gut twisted and he pushed the tablet away from him along with the second sandwich. Lissa was a talented storyteller, no doubt, but she'd fallen for a man who didn't exist.

At that moment, Lissa bounded into the room. "We're covered," she said. "Three people have agreed to allow some of the volunteers to stay in their homes. The people here just keep outdoing themselves."

"Good," Gage said and stood. "Good job. Listen, I've got some more chores to do. I'll be back in a couple hours. Okay?"

"Okay. I'll be here when you get back. I may even take a nap," she said with a wink. She was clearly still so happy that nothing could bother her. Good, he thought, because he had no idea how to handle what he'd just read. No idea at all.

Lissa spent the night with Gage, relishing being so close to him. He made love to her again, but he didn't talk much afterward. She told herself she had just worn out her amazing cowboy. The next day, he let her off at Melba's with a quick kiss.

"We'll talk later," he said. He seemed a little distracted, but he also appeared to be in a hurry to get to the office, so she didn't question him.

Gage had a lot of people counting on him. She felt greedy about their time together because her assignment wasn't going to last forever. She'd decided yesterday, however, to ask her boss to grant her an extension. There was so much more she wanted to do.

The following day, the new crew arrived and since there were more people, there was more for her to do. She popped into the office to find Gage but he was gone. A perfect opportunity to put her plan into action, she seized the moment to chat with Vickie and Will.

"I'm going to ask a huge favor of you and I'm swearing you both to secrecy," she said after she'd persuaded Vickie to join her at Will's desk.

"Are you pregnant?" Vickie asked.

Lissa dropped her jaw and felt her cheeks heat with embarrassment. "Absolutely not."

"That's good to know," Will muttered. "What's this about? I've got work to do."

Lissa had noticed Will had become much less friendly to her since she and Gage had gotten involved. "I really do appreciate your cooperation. Sometime this week, I'm going to try to get the volunteers to fix Gage's house."

Vickie clapped her hands together in approval. "Perfect. He'd never do it on his own."

"You're right. He wouldn't," Will said. "Always puts himself last. What do you need from us?"

"I don't want him to make any unexpected trips home the day that we'll be doing the repairs."

"So, you want us to keep him busy?" Vickie asked.

"No," Lissa said. "I just want you to keep me informed if he decides to go home during the day we're doing repairs."

Vickie glanced at Will. "We should be able to do that. He doesn't sneak home very often, does he?"

Will rolled his eyes. "The sheriff doesn't *sneak* anywhere."

"Okay, then, are you in?"

"Of course," Vickie said.

"Yeah, I'm in," Will said a little more slowly. "He's a lucky guy."

Lissa spent the next several days dodging Gage. She feared he would be able to read her intentions without her saying a word. Avoiding him wasn't as difficult as she'd thought. A part of her was concerned, but she was so focused on renovations she couldn't get too upset.

Nut job, she called herself, but kept going. She didn't know how she and the volunteer group had pulled it off, but fifteen homes were repaired. The church held a banquet for the volunteers the night before they left and Lissa gave a speech, thanking everyone who had contributed. The volunteers would complete a few last-minute projects and leave late tomorrow afternoon.

After the volunteer banquet, Lissa walked toward the rooming house, feeling spent and tired. An SUV pulled alongside her as she walked, and the passenger window was lowered.

"Want a ride?" Gage asked.

"I'm just headed back to the rooming house," she said. "I'm almost there."

"I can give you a ride to my place," he said.

"I won't be much good for you tonight. I'm way past tired."

His gaze gentled. "No pressure," he said. "I'll let you sleep."

She took a deep breath, pulled open the door and climbed into the warm car. "I can't remember when I've been this tired."

"You've been a busy girl," he said.

"I don't have a change of clothes," she warned him.

"You can use one of my shirts," he said. "And I actually have a few extra cartons of yogurt in my fridge."

"Really?" she said, surprised. "I thought you preferred the mystery meat biscuit."

"I like that some days," he said defensively. "But that yogurt and fruit thing is nice, too."

"I can't believe I've had such influence over your eating habits," she said, leaning her head back against the headrest.

"Yeah, well, don't get too arrogant," he said.

"No chance of that," she said and closed her eyes.

Sometime later, she wasn't sure how long, she awakened to the sight of Gage hovering over her. She blinked. "Hi."

"You were snoring," he said.

"Sorry," she said. "I must have been very tired." She glanced around and saw that she was in the bed in his trailer. She leaned back her head, closed her eyes and sighed. "I don't know whether to ask for wine or ice cream."

"Ice cream?" he echoed.

"You don't have any?" she asked,

"I don't know. I might have some chocolate popsicles in the freezer," he said.

Lissa sat up in bed. "That sounds perfect."

He chuckled. "If you say so. Let me check."

He left the room and she closed her eyes again, wishing she weren't so tired. But oh, my goodness, what a week. And the irony was that Gage still didn't know that his home had been repaired. She laughed to herself that she and the workers had been able to pull it off. She couldn't wait to see his face when he realized what had been done. She hoped he would be pleased.

Chapter Nine

Lissa sat up and ate a chocolate sundae popsicle. "I don't want to know how many chemicals are in this," she said as she took a bite. "It's just too good."

"I bought these a few months ago," he said and took a bite of the same kind of popsicle.

"I like that it has several layers. Crunchy on top, then chocolate, then vanilla, then more chocolate." She took another bite. "Yum."

Gage looked at her eating the popsicle and felt unbearably aroused. He had hoped to avoid her, but he couldn't make himself. He wanted her in every possible way, sexually, mentally.... Every way.

"How can I think about eating ice cream when you're in my bed?" he asked.

She took another bite then offered the popsicle to him. "Will this help?" she asked.

He took a bite. "Not really."

She handed him the rest of the popsicle. "I'm ready to toss it and do something else," she said.

He took the popsicle away and returned. Lowering his mouth to hers, he began to remove her clothes. "I've missed you."

"I've missed you, too," she whispered and allowed him to sweep her away.

His sweet lovemaking took her to a different place where it was just Gage and her. She wanted to stay in that amazing place as long as possible, and clung to him as they descended from their sensual high.

"I can't get enough of you," she whispered. "You make me want more and more."

"Same for me," he said, cradling her against him.

"You feel so good," she said, wiggling even closer. "Hold me like this forever."

He didn't respond and Lissa understood. She was asking more than he could give. She was asking more than *she* could give.

The next morning she and Gage awakened. "Can you do me a favor after lunch?" she asked as she pulled him against her.

"What kind of favor?" he asked.

"You don't have to launch a spacecraft," she said.

"Well, that's good. Okay, I'll try. What time?" he asked.

"After lunch? Two-ish," she said.

"Okay. I can do that unless there's an emergency."

"Good," she said.

"What's up?"

"You'll find out at two-ish," she said with a grin.

He frowned in response. "I don't like surprises," he said.

"Hopefully you'll like this one," she said, mentally crossing her fingers.

"We'll see."

"Yeah, we will," she said.

Later that day, Gage received a call from Lissa.

"Hi," she said with breathless excitement in her voice. "It's almost two. Can you meet me at your place?"

"I guess," he said, curious about what she had going on. "Let me make sure Will can cover for me. I can't stay long," he warned.

"That's okay. I just need you for a few minutes," she said and giggled.

He heard a voice in the background. "Hey, where are you, anyway?"

"I'll see you soon," she said and hung up.

Gage shook his head as he rose from his desk. He walked toward Will. "I need to make a quick run back to my place. Can you cover for me? It shouldn't take long."

Will nodded. "No problem," he said. "Take as long as you need."

Vickie looked up from the dispatch desk. "You're going to your house?"

"Yeah," he said, trying to decipher her expression. She had her finger over her mouth as if she was trying to keep a secret.

"Well, have fun," she finally said and smiled.

Gage frowned. "I'll be back soon," he said and headed for his car. During the entire drive to his ranch, Gage racked his brain about what was going on. Lissa was acting too strange. Vickie was, too.

Pulling into his driveway, he started to stop at his trailer. Then he glanced past it to his house. A crowd of people stood in his yard with Lissa standing in front, a big smile stretching from ear to ear.

Gage got a sinking sensation in his gut. She shouldn't have done it, he thought. She shouldn't have gotten the volunteers to spend precious time fixing up his house when other people needed help more than he did.

He got out of his car and the whole group shouted, "Welcome home!"

Lissa rushed toward him. "I know you said you

didn't want it done, but you work so hard for everyone. You don't get very much time off," she said, talking fast. "We just thought that you should have a decent place to stay during the few hours that you're not working." She searched his face. "I hope you'll like it. I hope you're happy."

"I'm sure I'll like it," he said even though he couldn't quite tamp down his resentment. He thought he'd made it perfectly clear that he didn't want his house repaired yet. He wouldn't dare be ungrateful to the volunteers after all the work they'd done.

He took a deep breath and forced a smile. "Introduce me to these fine people and show me what you did."

She smiled and was so excited he would swear she was nearly bouncing. "As all of you know, this is Sheriff Gage Christensen. I hope all of you will introduce yourselves to him. Gage, I'd like you to meet this crew's leader, Tom Samuels."

"Nice to meet you," Gage said. "Thank you for all you've done for Rust Creek Falls and for me."

"We've had a good time," Tom said. "Come inside your house and take a look. As you know, your home was in better condition than most because you got rid of the wet stuff. We took care of the floor, hung some drywall and painted the downstairs. We replaced your linoleum with tile in the kitchen. Your new refrigerator and stove were delivered this morning. We decided we should let you select your own furniture," Tom added with a laugh. "Katie and some of the other ladies took care of your upstairs."

"Upstairs?" he said. "I didn't have any damage upstairs."

A middle-aged woman approached Gage. "Hello, I'm Katie. You didn't have any damage, but we just thought you'd enjoy it more if we dusted and cleaned up a little and washed your linens. It's a real honor to help turn your house back into a home, Sheriff. Everyone we talk to has nothing but praise for you."

A knot of guilt formed in his chest. At the same time, he was overwhelmed by what the volunteers had done for him and everyone else affected by the flood. "I don't know what to say except thank you," he said. "Thank you for this. Thank you for everything you've done for our community. It's people like you that make the world a better place. I think we should all give you a hand," he said and started to clap.

Lissa immediately joined in and the volunteers started clapping, too. It was a unique, joyous moment.

After that, the crowd got into a van and headed back to the church. They needed to pack up so they could begin their journey home. Lissa hung around, waving at the crew as they departed. She turned to him and he could see a bit of anxiety in her eyes.

"You're happy about this, aren't you?" she asked. "I know you said you wanted to be last in line for help, but—"

"You're right," he said. "I did want to be last in line. I don't deserve to get my house fixed when there are families still in need of repairs."

Her face fell. "But this really didn't take very long. The crew worked quickly, and other crews were working on other houses."

"Whatever time they spent on my house should have been spent on someone else's house," he said and sighed. "Thank you, but you shouldn't have." He turned and walked toward his SUV.

Feeling her staring after him, he turned around. "Come on. I'll give you a ride to town."

He helped her into the car and got into his side and started driving. Gage was in no mood for small talk and he sure as hell hoped Lissa would respect his silence. She did until they were about five minutes from town.

"I keep trying to figure out why you're upset about this," she said. "Because you *are* upset."

"I'm not upset," he said, but even Gage could hear the edge in his tone.

"Someone once said to me, it's better to give than to receive, and it's easier, too. I thought it was funny at the time, but I think it may be especially true for you."

He could feel her looking at him, but he focused on driving. Gage was feeling too much right now. Too much he just couldn't explain.

"I won't apologize for helping this happen. It seemed right to me. But I can say I'm sorry you're not happy about it. I really wanted to help make your life better," she said.

Gage hated the crack he heard in her usually peppy voice. "Lissa," he said.

She shook her head. "No. Please don't say any more," she said. "Just let me out at the rooming house."

They were close to town, but not close enough. Those two minutes of silence seemed like they lasted forever. He barely stopped the car before she hopped out. "Lissa," he tried again, not sure what he was going to say.

"'Bye. Hope the rest of your day goes well," she said and walked away.

Gage stared after her, feeling completely empty. How had that happened? How had she burst into his life and made him feel full and alive? And now she'd left him feeling like a jerk.

Well, maybe he was a jerk. What Lissa didn't understand, what nobody seemed to understand, was that Gage was still making up for what happened to Hunter McGee while Gage was out of town. Gage had a feeling he would spend the rest of his life making up for that moment when the mayor died.

Gage could tell that Lissa was avoiding him after the second day that she didn't come into the office. He couldn't blame her. He felt like he'd squashed a butterfly. She had just wanted to do something nice for him, but he just couldn't accept it. It was probably for the best, he told himself. She wouldn't be here forever and he'd already grown far too attached to her. She made his world feel lighter and brighter and he could use that today, he thought, as he checked his watch. This wasn't the first time, nor would it be the last, that he'd drive Thelma McGee to visit her son's grave.

Gage picked up Thelma from the mayor's office. Although every white hair was in place and she was neatly dressed, Thelma seemed a bit more frail today. Trying to keep up her son's tradition of caring for the citizens of Rust Creek Falls was clearly taking a toll on her. Today she carried plastic blue gerbera daisies.

"After that last snow, I feel like I have to go to plastic. Real flowers turn into brown sticks so quickly, even more so when it's cold," she said, as if she felt the need to explain herself as Gage drove toward the cemetery.

"I'm sure Hunter's looking down, glad to see some bright colors on his grave," he said.

Thelma smiled. "Hunter always liked bright colors. When he was a boy, he wanted to paint his room red. At first, I refused. I was afraid he would never go to sleep in such a bright room. Then I gave in and allowed him to paint one wall red. He had such energy. It was hard to refuse him."

Gage nodded. "That's part of the reason he was such a good mayor. That and the fact that he had a vision for Rust Creek Falls."

He turned into the small cemetery and drove to Hunter's grave then helped Thelma out of the car.

"You're very kind to bring me here, Gage," she said.

"I'm glad to be here for you," he said, offering his arm as they took the few steps to the grave. His gut twisting in remorse and guilt, he removed his hat out of respect.

Thelma bowed her head in what Gage suspected was a silent prayer. She bent to place the flowers on the grave.

"Let me do that," he said and took the flowers. He placed them in front of the small headstone.

Thelma pressed her lips together and nodded. "We can leave now."

Gage escorted her back to the car. "I'm so sorry, Thelma. If there was any way I could go back in time and make sure I was here so that Hunter wouldn't have—" He broke off and shook his head.

"Gage, you couldn't have prevented my son's death," she said, looking into his eyes. "You're not thinking this through. Hunter was always in the thick of things. He was a man of the people. Do you really think he would have just stayed at home during a flash flood while people were in danger? You could have had yourself and the whole cavalry, but that wouldn't have been enough for him. He wouldn't be able to sit still if there was a chance he could help or save someone." Thelma put her hand on his arm. "I hate it and I don't understand it, but it was just his time. You're not doing anyone any favors trying to take responsibility for his death. You just need to face the fact that God is more important than you are, and He wanted Hunter with Him in heaven."

Gage was surprised at Thelma's response. She was usually so sweet and mild. He felt as if he was getting a lecture from a teacher. It was the equivalent of a hard mental shake.

"Now, would you please take me to get some wings?" she asked. "I'm hungry and Hunter would definitely approve. He loved wings."

Gage smiled. "It would be my pleasure," he said and drove back to town.

After the meal, Gage drove Thelma home and he returned to the office. He was in no mood to go to his own home tonight. Too many thoughts swimming in his brain.

Walking in the door, he waved to Vickie. She was getting ready to leave for the day. The phone rang and she made a face. "Okay, but this is the last one I'm taking," she muttered and picked up the phone. "Sheriff's office." She paused a long moment. "Oh, no. Not Lissa."

Lightning might as well have struck Gage. He immediately turned to look at Vickie. The dispatcher was furiously taking notes. "They've taken her to the clinic in the next county. They may have to move her to Livingston if she doesn't improve," she repeated. "Unconscious," she whispered, wincing and shaking her head. "What happened?"

She lifted her index finger to Gage. "Unsecured beams. They fell on her. Oh, no," she said. "I'll relay the message."

Gage was already headed out the door. He was pretty sure his heart had stopped when he'd heard Lissa's name. How had this happened? Maybe it wouldn't have if he hadn't been trying to ignore her. He thought the next crew wasn't coming in until tomorrow.

His mind racing, he drove to the clinic. He called ahead for an update but the receptionist wouldn't give him any information because he wasn't a relative. Swearing under his breath, he walked in the door to the clinic. He wasn't going to put up with any bull about not being able to see her. She had come to his town and he was responsible for her as long as she was here.

He approached the receptionist, a sour-looking woman with pointy glasses. "I'm Sheriff Christensen and I'm here to see Lissa Roarke," he said in a firm voice.

She looked him over and not in a nice way. "I'll have to check with the doctor," she said. "I've received several inquiries about her." She walked away and it was all Gage could do not to follow the woman down the hall.

She returned and met his gaze. "The doctor said you can see her in a few minutes. They're still sewing her stitches."

His stomach turned. "Stitches?" he echoed.

"Yes. She'll have quite a few and be black and blue over much of her face and head. But that's all I'm going to say. You'll have to talk to Miss Roarke about her condition. We have policies, you know," she said.

"Then she's conscious?" he asked.

The receptionist frowned. "Yes, she is. That is all I'm going to say. You can take a seat."

Take a seat? Gage had barely been able to sit in his vehicle during the drive over here. He wasn't going to be able to sit until he saw with his own eyes that Lissa was okay.

Eleven minutes and thirty-seven seconds later,

the receptionist waved to him. "You can come back now," she said and led him to an examination room near the end of the hall.

A man and woman dressed in scrubs stood on either side of Lissa, who was flat on her back on a gurney. "We'll have to transfer you to the hospital in Livingston if you don't have someone who can stay with you for the next twenty-four hours," the doctor was saying.

"She can stay with me," Gage said. "I'll look after her."

All three turned to look at him. "Sheriff Gage Christensen," he said, extending his hand to the man who'd been talking when he entered the room.

"Dr. Keller," the man said, returning the handshake. "This is Nurse Benson. Miss Roarke took quite a blow to the head. She was unconscious and will need to be monitored."

Lissa tried to raise up on her elbows. "I'm really much better," she said.

The nurse gently pushed her back down. "You need to keep your head lower to reduce the chance of swelling."

Lissa sighed. "I've got a crew of volunteers arriving tomorrow and I have to brief them and plan—"

"We'll find someone else to cover for you tomorrow and the day after that, if necessary," Gage said to her. It was hard seeing her like this, her face pale except for the bruises already forming, stitches sewn across the gash on her forehead. "If you're sure she can go home, I'll take care of her. Just give me the instructions."

A few minutes later, Gage carefully loaded Lissa into his SUV and put her seat into the recline position.

"I'm really better," she said.

"I'm glad," he said. "But the doctor said you have to rest for a minimum of twenty-four hours. And I know you're going to cooperate, because otherwise you'll have to go to the hospital."

Lissa frowned but didn't argue. "I just don't know what to do about that incoming crew of volunteers," she fretted. "I need to get them pumped up so they can hit the ground running tomorrow."

"Well, you aren't going to be hitting the ground or running for a few days. The doctor said you have to get complete rest, then you can gradually become more active. Gradually," he repeated.

"I don't have time to be gradual," she said in a cranky voice.

"You don't have a choice," he said. "I wish you hadn't gone out to that house by yourself. If I'd been with you, that beam wouldn't have fallen on you."

He felt her gaze on him. "What? Oh, for crying out loud, Gage. Do you think you're responsible for everything? Well, of course you are. Did you hear about that meteorite that went past the earth? You were behind that, weren't you? And that tsunami in the Pacific. What were you thinking? Why didn't you stop that? Along with global warming. Sheesh," she said. "Accidents happen. You see them all the time and you know it's just part of life."

Gage felt a hard twist of discomfort. Lissa sounded an awful lot like Thelma McGee.

"It's my job to take care of my people. How am I supposed to stop being protective?"

"I'm not saying you shouldn't be protective. That's one of the reasons I—" She broke off. "One of the reasons I admire you. But you can't control everything. You can't prevent every accident or natural disaster."

Gage sat with that for a moment. Maybe she and Thelma were right. Maybe he needed to ease off a little bit. "Well, I have to admit, I think I'd have a hard time fighting off a tsunami."

She giggled. "You think?"

It was so good to hear her little laugh. Gage still hadn't let down his guard since he'd seen her. If Lissa wasn't alive somewhere in this world, he didn't know what he would do.

Gage took her to the house. "I'm carrying you," he insisted. "You don't need to take those steps."

"This is ridiculous," she said. "You're going to get a hernia."

He chuckled. "If I do, it will be for a good cause," he said, as he carried her up the flight of stairs to the second floor

"You need to put me down," she said.

"Not until I get you to the bed."

"I need to use the restroom," she said.

"Oh," he said, and set her down at the door to the bathroom. "I'll be here if you need anything."

"I think I can handle this," she said, closing the door in his face.

In a snippy mood, he thought, waiting patiently. A couple moments later, she opened the door. "I would like to walk to the bedroom myself," she told him.

He sighed. "Okay." He followed behind her and when she sat down on the bed, he kneeled down to pull off her boots. He looked up at her to find her looking at him with a soft expression on her face. "I've missed you," she said.

He rose and sat beside her. "I've missed you, too." Reining in the feelings that ripped through him, he leaned forward and brushed a gentle kiss on her cheek. "Let's not waste any more time fighting."

She took a deep breath and let it out. "That sounds good to me."

"I'm glad we agree. Now lie down and don't get up unless I tell you that you can," he said sternly.

Glowering at him, she reclined on the bed. "You don't have to be nasty about it."

"I'm not being nasty, I'm being firm. I'm in charge of you for the next twenty-four hours. That means you have to do what I tell you to do," he said.

"There was a time when you would find another way to keep me busy in your bed," she said with a smile too sexy for a woman with stitches on her head.

"Don't tempt me," he told her and hoped the next twenty-four hours of not making love to her didn't kill him.

Chapter Ten

Gage received no less than twelve offers from people who wanted to help. Three from men who offered to take over sitting with her so he could work. Jared Winfree, who'd caused so much trouble at the bar, even had the nerve to call the office and say he wanted to know where he could take some flowers.

"You can tell him the only flowers he's gonna see are from pushing up daisies if he tries to come anywhere near Lissa," Gage told Vickie heatedly.

"Okay, calm down," she said. "But we're getting a ton of food and we need to do something with it. You want me to bring some by the house?" Vickie asked.

Gage nodded. "Sure. That will be fine. I've been feeding her canned soup, but I think she may be ready for something else soon."

"Okay, now let me talk to Lissa," she said.

"She can't talk," he said. "She's resting." More than likely she was bored out of her mind because he wouldn't let her have either her cell phone or iPad.

"I'll stop by the rooming house and pick up a few things for her. She might like a change of clothes."

"Thanks," he said. "We'll be here."

Lissa would hit the twenty-four hour post-concussion mark in just a few hours, but Gage was going to try to keep her down as long as he could. She'd rested well last night and he'd woken her every three hours just as the doctor had instructed. He'd noticed her touching her forehead as if it hurt, but whenever he asked, she denied it. Instead of arguing, he just gave her a cool cloth.

An hour later, Lissa awakened and a few minutes after that, Vickie knocked at the door. "Come on in," he said to Vickie. "It's nice of you to bring us some food."

"I couldn't subject Lissa to your idea of food after she'd been injured," Vickie said and headed for the kitchen armed with bags and a tote with clothing. Gage relieved her of the bags.

"Let me talk to her," Lissa called from the bedroom. "I'll come downstairs."

"No, you won't," he said, but Lissa was already making her way down the stairs.

"I want to see Vickie," she said.

"Hey there, girl," Vickie said and grimaced. "Oh, my goodness. That beam got you good, didn't it?"

"Is it that bad? I haven't looked today," Lissa said.

"Nothing a ball cap and some makeup won't cover. I brought you a change of clothes and some food. Now sit down before Gage throws a conniption," she said, urging Lissa into a kitchen chair.

"Do you know anything about the new crew? Gage took away my phone," she said in disgust.

"You wouldn't rest if I didn't remove all communication devices and we both know it," he said. "What do you want to drink? I have soda and water."

"Soda," she said, pressing her right eyebrow.

"Oh, look, her head is hurting," Vickie said. "Can she take anything?"

"Not much at the moment," he said. "They told me to give her cool washcloths," he said and dampened a fresh one for her.

"Thank you. It does help," she said then turned to Vickie. "He really has been very gentle."

"Well, I hope so. I'd hate to hear he was being a

cranky pants," Vickie said. "Your new volunteers arrived and the pastor is going to fill in for you the next few days."

"That's nice of him," Lissa said. "Do you know where they're planning to go first tomorrow? Are the lunches prepared for them? And—"

Vickie held up her hand. "I'm sure everything is taken care of. You've got this whole thing running like a well-oiled machine. The local people are coming out of the woodwork asking what they can do."

Lissa smiled. "I know there are good people all over the world, but you guys from Rust Creek Falls keep surprising me."

"Well, we've taken a pretty big shine to you, too. Some of us wouldn't mind if you stayed. Right, Gage?" Vickie hinted.

Gage plastered a confused expression on his face. "Huh?"

"Yeah, huh," Vickie said. "Listen, I've got to go. Will told me to tell you that everything's been pretty quiet if you need to take off another day."

"No. I'll be in tomorrow. I'm taking Lissa to the rooming house and Melba has agreed to look out for her."

"I don't need to have anyone look after me. I'm better," she said.

Vickie leaned toward her and patted her hand.

"Sweetie, you haven't looked in the mirror. You need a little more rest."

Lissa shrugged. "I may look bad, but I feel fine."

"Well, you wouldn't want to scare any of those volunteers," Vickie said and stood.

"Gee, thanks," Lissa said.

"You wouldn't want me to lie," Vickie said with a mischievous grin. "Y'all enjoy the food. That apple cobbler looks to die for. I almost kept it for myself. Bye now."

As soon as Vickie left, Gage dug into the bags of food. "Hey, there's turkey and dressing in here. Beef stew and some rolls and—"

A scream rent the air. Gage whipped around saw that Lissa was no longer sitting in the kitchen. He raced toward the bathroom. Lord, he hoped she hadn't fallen again.

He found her staring in horror into the mirror. "What's wrong?" he asked.

"I look like Frankenstein," she wailed.

He chuckled. "Not really," he said and stepped behind her. "You don't have those weird little bolts sticking out of your neck."

She shot him a sideways glance. "No wonder you've been acting like you're afraid I'll break. Let me see what else Vickie brought. I hope she tucked some concealer in that bag somewhere."

"You don't need to be worrying about how you look. Especially tonight. You need to keep resting."

"My twenty-four hours is up," she said.

"You still need to take things slow. I know it's hard for you, but you've got to be lazy."

"And how would you respond if someone told you to be lazy?"

"The same way you are," he said and gently pulled her against him. "That's why I understand how hard this is for you."

"Thanks for taking care of me. I guess I'm not the best patient."

"Don't worry. You'll be as good as new soon enough," he promised. "Just try not to rush it. Everyone wants you back at full throttle."

After a filling dinner and dessert, Gage returned Lissa's electronic devices to her. She made a few calls and sent several text messages then she took a break. "Everyone's telling me to rest," she said.

"Let's do something we haven't done together before," he said.

She smiled at him. "What would that be?"

"Watch some television," he said.

Lissa punched at him.

Lissa might fight the rest, but Gage noticed she fell asleep on his shoulder halfway through the show they were watching. Gage carried her upstairs and laid her down on the bed.

Her eyelids fluttered open. "Hi," she said.

His heart turned over. She had no idea how pretty she was even with bruises and stitches.

"You don't want to kiss me because I look like Frankenstein," she said.

He lowered his head and took her mouth in a deep caress. "I always want to kiss you, Lissa."

The next day, Gage checked in on Lissa every other hour. By the fourth time he called, she sounded irritated. Chuckling, he hung up the phone and went on patrol to give Will a well-deserved break. On the way back, he filled up his gas tank and spotted Collin Traub doing the same thing. Collin had not only lassoed Gage's sister's heart—he and Willa had been married at the end of July—he had also thrown his hat in the ring as a candidate for mayor of Rust Creek Falls.

Although Gage had voiced his support for Collin, he knew he was supposed to appear more neutral than not. That didn't mean he couldn't warn his future brother-in-law about what he'd heard about the Crawford family. "Hey, man, come here," he called to Collin.

Collin waved then finished filling up his tank and pulled to the side. He strode toward Gage. "How's it going? I know you've been working double time lately. And did I hear the volunteer coordinator from New York got hurt recently?"

"Yeah. She's a pistol, but she was no match for that beam that fell on her," Gage said.

"Ouch," Collin said with a wince. "Will she be okay?"

"If she'll slow down a little bit," Gage grumbled. "But there's another reason I waved you over. As you know, I'm supposed to be neutral on this election, but I thought it was fair for you to know that I'm hearing rumors that the Crawfords are working on a smear campaign on you. Handle that information however you see fit."

Collin nodded with a serious expression and shook Gage's hand. "Thanks. You're a good man."

"I try," Gage said dryly. "Take care, now," he said. "And take care of my sister."

Collin's expression softened. "You know how I feel about your sister," he said.

"Yeah, I know," Gage said, pushing down a twist of irritation. Romance was easy for other folks, but not for him.

Lissa tried to rest, but it was torture when she wanted to be with her volunteer crew. And everyone was so chintzy with the information they provided. "Go rest," they all said. "We're all fine." It was all she could do not to spy.

She'd promised Gage, however, that she would rest, and she was doing her best. He'd taken her back to the rooming house so Melba could check on her every couple of hours, which prevented Lissa from getting into too much trouble.

When she looked at the calendar, she felt sick to her stomach. Her assignment with Bootstraps would be over soon. There was still so much to do. If she were truthful, she couldn't bear the thought of leaving the people of Rust Creek Falls. Even more, she hated the thought of not being close to Gage. He was the most amazing man she'd ever met and she didn't want to lose him.

With that in mind, she wrote a heartfelt email to her supervisor at Bootstraps, pleading for an extension of her time in Rust Creek Falls. She could only hope her supervisor would agree with her.

Just when Lissa was sure she was going stir-crazy from staying inside all day, Melba knocked at her door. "There's a young man who wishes to see you," she said.

"Who would that be?"

"Why, Gage, of course," Melba said.

Lissa slowly went down the stairs to find him at the front door. "Hi," she said. "Nice to see you. What's the occasion?"

"I'm taking you back to my house with me," he said. "Melba took care of you today, but I'll take care of you tonight."

Her heart turned over at the expression in his eyes. How could she leave such an amazing man?

The next morning, Gage took her to the rooming house, but Lissa slapped on some concealer and a ballcap and headed over to the church to meet the volunteers. She knew she probably shouldn't spend the whole day out with them, but she couldn't resist the urge to be with the people who were doing so much for Rust Creek Falls.

She greeted the pastor and his face fell. "Oh, my goodness, Miss Roarke, you must go back to your room and rest," he said. "You're clearly not well yet."

Well, darn, Lissa thought. *So much for rallying the troops.* She needed better concealer.

She went back to her room and moped. How interesting that Gage had never looked at her with horror over her bruises and Frankenstein stitches. Without saying a word, he made her feel beautiful every time he looked at her.

The following day, Lissa went to the general store wearing sunglasses and bought every concealer they carried. Perhaps she should order over the internet. She checked out and the cashier studied her.

"Are you Lissa Roarke, the charity woman from New York?" the cashier asked.

"Yes," Lissa said hesitantly. "I recently had a little accident and I'm trying to conceal the bruises."

"Let me see," the woman said.

Lissa reluctantly lifted her sunglasses and the woman widened her eyes.

"Ouch," she said. "Looks like it was more than a little accident. Yellow for a blue bruise, but the colors will change. After that, green for red bruises. And bangs are your friend."

"How do you know this?" Lissa asked.

The cashier's gaze darkened. "Bad experience. Never to experience again."

"Good for you," Lissa said. "If anything other than a beam hits you in the future, please call me."

The cashier tilted her head. "I'll do that. Good luck with the bruises."

"Thanks," Lissa said and left the general store. That was one more person with whom she felt a bond in Rust Creek Falls. The numbers were racking up.

Lissa did more work on her iPad, but also took a few mininaps. She was surprised how tired she was. Again, at the end of the day, Gage picked her up and took her back to his house.

She felt more energetic than she had felt in days as she walked into his house. "Think you can make love to Frankenstein?" she challenged.

"I've been counting the minutes," he said and carried her up to his bed. He made love to her sweetly and tenderly and she fell asleep in his arms.

Lissa watched her email daily, anxious to get a response from her supervisor giving her more time in Rust Creek Falls. In the meantime, she followed the clerk's instructions and painted the upper half of her face with yellow. Wearing sunglasses, she met the volunteers the next morning.

She saw several people trying to look past her sunglasses, but tried to distract them. When one person was clearly not listening to her, she finally said, "I have bruises. They're ugly. I'm trying to protect you."

"I can deal with it," the man said.

Lissa lifted her sunglasses.

The man winced. "Okay."

"Yeah, give me a break," she said. "How are the repairs going?"

"Good. We would love to be able to place furniture," he said.

"It's coming in the next few days," she said.

The man nodded. "Are you single?"

"Not really," she said, but she appreciated the compliment of being asked.

Lissa visited the different crews by midday and tried to motivate them. She hated how tired she got by midafternoon, but surrendered to her weariness and took a nap. By evening, she was refreshed.

Gage took her to his ranch again. This was becoming a habit. A habit she wanted to continue. They made love again and again throughout the night, though he was utterly gentle with her.

When Lissa awakened the next morning, she was eager to check her email. Surely her supervisor would have made a decision. Hopefully Lissa would be staying another month. She couldn't imagine anything different.

Lissa met with her volunteers and worked with them for a while. By midafternoon, she was pooped and stretched out on her bed at Melba's.

Lissa checked her email again and this time she saw a message from her boss in her inbox. Mentally crossing her fingers, she held her breath and read the email.

Dear Lissa,

We're very impressed with all you have accomplished in Montana. You have far exceeded our expectations and we believe the people of Rust Creek Falls have benefitted greatly from your service there. Because of the progress you've made and also because Bootstraps plans to make a cash donation to the fund for the new school in Rust Creek Falls, we believe it's time to turn our attention and resources to other areas.

That means we will want you to return to New York within the next week as originally planned. Again, thank you for your service in Montana. We look forward to placing you in a position as lead coordinator for another project very soon.

Lissa couldn't believe her eyes. Her supervisor had turned her down flat. She wouldn't even have an extra week. How could she wrap everything up so quickly? How could she leave these people she'd come to love? How could she leave Gage?

Her hands shook with emotion and a knot of misery formed in her throat. What was she going to do?

She was so upset she couldn't imagine talking to anyone, especially Gage. Suddenly the room felt too small so she put on a jacket and took a walk. Her mind swirling with confusion, she tried to think of a solution. Perhaps she could go back to New York and visit Gage occasionally. Even as she considered the possibility, she knew it wouldn't work. She couldn't help wondering if Gage would lose interest if she left. He was so busy. It was a challenge for him to maintain a relationship with her when she was in town let alone when she was on the other side of the country.

She wondered if she should quit her job and start over here in Rust Creek Falls. The trouble was the lack of positions. Plus, she wasn't totally sure Gage would want her to stay. He'd said from the beginning that their relationship was temporary. He'd seemed to accept that fact a lot more easily that she had.

Her cell phone rang, distracting her from her thoughts. She glanced at the caller ID. Gage. She couldn't talk to him. Not yet. She had to figure this out.

Lissa successfully dodged him by going to the church and helping to serve the evening meal for the volunteers. Both they and the pastor were excited with their progress. It was all she could do to hold herself together and praise them for their work and contributions. The pastor hovered over her, encouraging her to go rest. She dragged out the cleanup, but couldn't delay returning to the rooming house after that.

Entering from the back door, she climbed the steps to her room. Thank goodness she'd successfully avoided both Melba and Gage. She opened her door to find Gage sitting in the chair in her room.

She gaped at him in surprise.

"Where the hell have you been, darlin'?" Gage asked. "I've been worried about you."

All her emotions converged on her at once and she burst into tears. "I have terrible news," she said. "Terrible, terrible news."

Immediately on his feet, Gage pulled her into his arms. "Whoa. What's wrong? Did you hear something bad from the doctor? Did you faint or get sick?"

Lissa shook her head. "No, no. Nothing like that." She swallowed hard over her tight throat. "I heard from my boss. I asked her if I could extend my stay here in Rust Creek Falls. She said no," she said, her voice betraying how upset she felt. "I have to leave in a week."

Gage gave a slow nod. He looked away and sighed. "We knew this was coming."

"Yes, but I wanted to stop it," she said. "Or at least delay it."

"I don't like it, either, but we both knew it from the start. Maybe it's for the best," he said. "Not to drag it out and quit while things are good."

She stared at him in surprise. "For the best. How could it possibly be for the best? I've fallen in love with you. I thought you had strong feelings for me. Was I wrong?"

"No," he said, squeezing her arm then backing away. He raked his hand through his hair. "Lissa, I love the way you look at me right now, but what's going to happen if you stick around for a while? I'm not the cowboy hero you think I am. Life is not like an old Western. I'm not perfect. I'm just a man and I'm bound to screw up sometimes. What's going to happen then?"

Confused, she shook her head. "We'll work it out."

"I'll tell you what's going to happen. We won't be working it out. You'll be walking out," he said with grim confidence. "Maybe it's better for us to split while we still have good memories."

Lissa head was spinning from his words. "Is

that all I am to you? A fond memory for your scrapbook?"

Gage rested his hands on his hips and glanced away then back at her. "Listen, you need to know that I saw what you wrote about me. I wasn't snooping. I'd brought your iPad back in the house and you were on the phone. The document came right up." He shook his head. "That man you wrote about. He isn't me. You don't really know me at all."

Anger rushed through her. "Maybe I just know you better than you think you know yourself."

"Lissa—"

The threat of tears too great, she lifted her hands and shook her head. "Stop. I think you've said enough."

Gage sighed and looked at her for a long moment. "I guess I'd better go."

"I guess you'd better," she said.

Chapter Eleven

It was all Lissa could do not to leave town right away. Her heart felt as if it had been ripped from her chest. She felt so deceived. But maybe she had deceived herself. Maybe Gage hadn't felt nearly as strongly about her as she had about him. The realization wounded her in such a way that she knew she'd never completely heal from it.

Wounded or not, she had a job to finish. The volunteers would be here for a few more days and Lissa was determined to maximize the time she had left to help as many residents as possible. Deciding she had fully recovered from her minor concussion, Lissa threw herself into repair work and avoided the sheriff's office. The good thing about hard work was that she was too tired by evening to think about how miserable she was.

The night before the volunteers were to leave town, a thank-you banquet was held for them. Lissa gave her last speech of gratitude and had to tamp down her emotions. It began to hit her hard that she would be leaving in just two days. Blinking back the tears, she gave a special thank-you to the pastor of the church and his congregation for all their assistance.

As she sat down, she noticed some familiar faces standing in the back of the room. Will, the deputy sheriff, nodded toward her. Vickie, the dispatcher waved. Gage helped Thelma McGee into a chair. The sight of Gage made her heart twist so hard she had to look away. What were they doing here? From her peripheral vision, she saw several other citizens she'd met during the past month. What was going on—

The pastor stood in front of the group. "We want to thank the volunteers for traveling from their homes and sleeping on cots, *when* you got to sleep," he added and several people laughed. Everyone knew they spent more time working than sleeping, and everyone was okay with it. "Our community is grateful for your service, and we pray that God will bless you from this experience."

He paused. "There is another person we want to thank and honor tonight, and that is Lissa Roarke."

Lissa stared in shock. She'd had no idea that

she was going to be the focus of the community's gratitude.

"She blew into town like a fast-moving train and inspired everyone around her. With her help, we accomplished much more for people here in Rust Creek who've been hurting and doing without for months. It has been my privilege to work by your side. And now, Mrs. Thelma McGee will make a special presentation," the pastor said.

Gage assisted Thelma to her feet and escorted her to the front of the room. Lissa forced herself not to look at Gage. If she even looked at him, she feared she would burst into tears. Instead she focused on Thelma and noticed that the woman was carrying a box.

"Hello, everyone," Thelma said.

"Hello," several in the crowd said in return.

Thelma smiled. "As most of you know, my son Hunter McGee was mayor for Rust Creek Falls for many years. He was a man devoted to the people and to our future, and we all miss him terribly. After the flood, I think some of us went into shock and we lost something. Something that Hunter always tried to instill in us, and that was hope. Lissa Roarke has not only facilitated repairs for dozens of people, she gave us something more important. Hope. Now I wish I could find a way to make her stay here in Rust Creek Falls, but I know she has to go back to New York."

Thelma opened the box and produced a large

key. "Before you leave, I've been given the honor by the town council to give Lissa Roarke the key to our town, Rust Creek Falls. You've won our hearts, Lissa. We'll never forget you."

Lissa's eyes filled with tears. Walking to the front where Thelma stood, Lissa swallowed hard to gain control, but she didn't know how she was going to do it. She embraced the woman and whispered, "Thank you."

"No," Thelma said and handed Lissa the key. "Thank *you*."

After that, people came to her in a blur, shaking her hand, offering words of gratitude and hugs. She noticed Gage standing behind the crowd, but she couldn't talk to him. She was still too hurt.

More than anything, she wanted to focus on the outpouring of love she was receiving. She wanted to save up the memory of all the wonderful people who thought she had done so much for them, but in truth, she had become so much richer by being with them for the past several weeks.

The crowd finally dwindled and Lissa grabbed her coat to leave. Gage walked toward her, but she put up her hand. "You take care of yourself," she said and quickly walked out the door.

She returned to the rooming house to pack. The day had been so busy she should have fallen asleep, but her mind was too full. Giving up on sleep,

Lissa turned on the light and opened her iPad and began to write.

She wrote about the wonderful people of Rust Creek Falls and how they sacrificed for each other. She wrote about Buddy buying the bunny for the little girl he didn't know. She wrote about the courage she'd seen and the determination to keep going even after the devastation they'd suffered. She wrote about Thelma and her devotion, along with that of Deputy Will. And yes, she also wrote about Gage. How could she not? She wrote for hours, and finally she felt as if she'd expressed at least some of her overwhelming thoughts and feelings about the people of Rust Creek Falls.

After that, it was as if at least part of her was a little more at peace, and she fell asleep for a couple hours. Her subconscious must have known she was leaving even though she was sleeping, because for once she was up before dawn. She made a copy of her revised article, put it into an envelope and ran to the sheriff's office and left it with the evening dispatcher.

Lissa returned to the rooming house and the last big breakfast that Melba would be making for her. She could hardly eat a thing.

"You haven't touched your food," Melba chided her.

"I don't eat as much when I travel," Lissa said. "Nerves, I guess. I appreciate you offering to take me to the airport."

"Well, of course I'll take you," Melba said. "Although all of us wish you were staying."

Lissa just pressed her lips together and remained silent. She didn't know what else could be said at this point, so she went upstairs to close her suitcase. Lissa loaded her luggage into Melba's big Buick and they headed for the airport in Livingston.

"Well, you've got a pretty day for travel," Melba said. "That's a good thing. Have you checked the weather in New York?"

Lissa shook her head, not really in the mood for small talk. But she should be polite. "I haven't," she said. "It's usually pleasant at this time of year, though."

"You'll have all those pretty fall colors from the leaves changing. We get the colors, but we also get the snow."

"That's true. I hadn't even thought about that," she said.

"Well, you've been so busy coordinating all those volunteers," Melba said. "We sure do appreciate you coming to Rust Creek Falls. I know we all hope you'll come back and visit."

Lissa's heart felt sore at the thought. "I don't know," she said. "I'll never forget Rust Creek Falls, but maybe it's best that I keep it as a memory." She thought about what she'd just said and smiled grimly. She sounded like Gage. That couldn't be good.

"You're thinking about a certain cowboy, aren't you?" Melba asked.

"Maybe," Lissa said softly, but remained quiet for the rest of the trip to the airport. Gage was a lost cause. There was nothing she could do. It was a ridiculous situation. She knew they were meant for each other, but Gage just wouldn't admit it.

Gage awoke early and couldn't get back to sleep, so he hauled himself out of bed, thinking he might as well get something done. Of course, maybe the reason he couldn't sleep was that he imagined he was smelling Lissa's sweet scent. He knew he couldn't be. The sheets on the bed had been changed and she hadn't been in his house for over a week. That was the way it was supposed to be, he told himself. That was the way it had to be.

He pulled on his clothes and took care of some early-morning chores. When he returned to the house, he saw a lone carton of yogurt in the fridge. The sight of it made him feel sad. Gage rolled his eyes. A yogurt carton was making him sad? He was losing his mind. Grabbing a frozen biscuit from the freezer, he tossed it in the microwave and told himself that it was time to get back to normal. Lissa Roarke was leaving this afternoon and she wasn't coming back. He'd helped make sure of it.

He drove into town, glancing at Strickland's Boardinghouse. He wondered if Lissa was up eating breakfast. He wondered what she would do before she left town. Gage was pretty sure she wouldn't stop by the office to say goodbye. The thought put him in even more of a dark mood.

Parking his car, he entered the office. Will wasn't there yet, but Vickie was at her desk. "Hey, the night dispatcher left this for you."

"What is it?" Gage asked, curious about the contents of the envelope with his name scrawled across the front of it.

"I don't know," Vickie said. "I'm nosy, but I don't open other people's correspondence."

Gage chuckled. "Okay. Anything I need to address first thing?"

"Nope. Everything's quiet so far," she said.

"Thanks," he said and went to grab a cup of coffee before he went into his office. Shrugging out of his coat, he pulled off his hat and sat down at his desk. He opened the envelope and read the top of the page. *An Essay on True Heroism by Lissa Roarke.* His gut tightened at the title, but he had to read it. He couldn't have torn his gaze from the page if he'd tried.

She wrote about the townspeople and how they sacrificed for each other. She wrote about the children and the teachers who had opened their homes in order to teach classes. She mentioned all sorts of details about the town that proved she had been watching very closely, and not with rose-colored glasses.

The more Gage read, the tighter his chest felt. His throat felt as if were tightening up, too. He rubbed his neck and chest. Lissa had poured her heart and soul into Rust Creek Falls. She'd handed him her heart and soul on a platter.

He continued reading and saw that the subject of the piece had turned to him. He felt a rush of discomfort.

The truth is that Sheriff Gage Christensen is one of the most important foundations of the Rust Creek Falls community. Everyone needs to be able to count on someone, and every-one counts on the sheriff. He shows up for everything from unexpected labor to helping with repairs and arresting a drug manufac-turer trying to hide in the safe haven of his community. He's on call 24-7. He is a man dedicated to his people and his people are grateful for that dedication.

Some people might call the writer of this article biased when it comes to the subject of Gage Christensen, and they would be quite correct. I've had an opportunity to get to know him on a personal level, and he has taken care of me when I needed help. I'd like to end this essay with a thank-you to the cow-boy who stole my heart. I don't want it back.

Overwhelmed by the depth of feeling in her words, Gage leaned back in the chair. Maybe Lissa had more insight than he'd believed. Maybe it wasn't such a bad thing that she thought he was a hero. Maybe she saw past his walls to the man he wanted to be.

How often does a man meet a woman like that? he wondered. How often would a woman like Lissa Roarke come into his life?

The answer hung over him like the blade of a guillotine. *Never,* he realized. He would *never* meet another woman like Lissa. Besides, he wouldn't want *another woman* like Lissa.

He would want Lissa.

The truth slapped him across the face. He'd lost her. Was there any way he could get her back? His mind started spinning. Maybe he could talk to her before she left. Maybe he could convince her.… Maybe.

Gage knew he was going to have to make a strong case for himself after the way he'd told her off. Rising from his desk, he called a friend in the next county who ran a business out of his home. His heart pounding in his chest, he was determined to get out there and back to Rust Creek Falls before Lissa left town.

Gage ran into Will as he headed out the door. "Hey, can you cover for me this morning?"

"Sure," Will said and looked at him with curiousity. "Problem?"

"I'm going to try to fix one before it's too late," Gage said.

Will gave a slow nod. "Is this about Lissa?"

"Yeah," Gage said.

"Good luck," Will said. "If I can't have her, then you're the next best thing."

Too focused to laugh, he headed out the door. He made it to his friend's house and bought the purchase of a lifetime for a man: a diamond ring. After all Gage had put Lissa though, he figured he was going to have to provide physical proof of his feelings for her.

As soon as he got back in his car, his cell rang. It was Will. "What's up?" Gage asked.

"I thought I should let you know that Lissa left early this morning. Melba Strickland took her to the airport. Lissa's flight is this morning."

Gage's stomach sank. "Do you know if she's gone?"

"I don't think so, but I'm not sure. You'd better head straight to Livingston," Will said.

"I'm on my way," Gage said, wondering if he had waited too late and his chance had passed.

At check-in, Lissa was told that her flight was running over an hour late, which only added to her bad mood. She didn't want to be leaving. Now the process was being dragged out even further. Lissa felt as if she were being tortured.

Melba, sweet as always, must have sensed how upset Lissa was and offered to wait with her since there was no need for Lissa to go through security yet. "We can have a cup of coffee or tea," Melba said.

"I don't want to inconvenience you," Lissa said.

"It's no problem," Melba said. "I'm happy to spend some time with you."

Lissa sipped a cup of tea while Melba drank coffee. With each passing moment, Lissa couldn't stop her thoughts of Gage.

She sipped her tea and tapped her foot, but the tea didn't calm her and her foot-tapping did nothing to relieve her of her nervous energy. "You know, Gage said that he and I were destined for failure," she finally said, unable to keep quiet any longer.

"Oh, really," Melba said. "I wonder why he said that."

"He said I was in love with a fantasy man. That I didn't love *him,* the real him," she said, still tapping her foot.

"That doesn't make much sense," Melba said. "You're a grown woman. You should know your mind. It's not as if you're a little girl."

"Exactly," Lissa said. "I'm a grown woman. He kept telling me something was going to go wrong one day and I was going to wake up and be totally disillusioned with him."

"Well, that could happen to any couple," Melba said. "You just have to make the decision you're going to stick together and work it out. I've had to do that with my husband and I've been married to him for over fifty years."

Lissa nodded, still irritated with how Gage had acted toward her the last time they'd talked. She didn't know when she would stop being irritated at him. "You know, now that I think about it, it was like Gage was asking for some kind of guarantee that nothing would ever go wrong between us. As much as I lo—" She broke off and cleared her throat. "As much as I had strong feelings for him, how could we never have an occasion when something would go wrong? It's not possible," she said, feeling herself get more worked up. "*That* is a fantasy. That's an even bigger fantasy. That you'll never have problems?" she scoffed.

Melba took another sip of her coffee. "Very true. Life is full of troubles. It's how you face them that counts."

"You know what?" she said. "I think Gage was scared."

"Really?" Melba said. "Well, you know you're a pretty girl. I wonder if he thought he couldn't keep you interested."

Unable to sit still another moment, Lissa stood. "That's it! That's it," she said. "He let me go because he was afraid of losing me. How ridiculous is that?"

Melba shook her head. "*Men*. Will they ever make sense?"

"Probably not," Lissa said. "But I'm not letting him get away with this. I'm going to confront him with the truth to his face."

Melba stared at her. "What are you going to do?"

"I'm cancelling my flight and I'm going to tell Gage Christensen that he can't fool me. I have him figured out from head to toe. I'm not backing down this time," she said and headed for the counter.

Midway through her conversation with the airline agent, she heard her name being called. By Gage.

"Lissa, Lissa, stop. You can't get on that plane," he yelled as he ran across the airport lobby.

Lissa saw him running toward her and felt as if she were having an out-of-body experience. She was so stunned she couldn't speak.

"You can't leave," he said as he got closer to her. "You'll regret it," he promised. "If not now, then soon. But you will regret it," he said.

The experience reminded her of something out of a movie. A crazy combination of nerves and excitement danced inside her. She didn't know whether to laugh or cry. A laugh bubbled from her throat and she was thankful she wasn't crying.

Gage glanced around and seemed to notice they were drawing a crowd. Based on his expression, he didn't care. He dropped to his knee in front of everyone.

Lissa gasped in surprise.

"I need to apologize for being such an ass," he said. "I know I hurt you and I'm sorry. I never, ever want to hurt you. You're too important to me," he said and took a deep breath. "I love you, Lissa Roarke. You're the best thing that's ever happened to me. I don't care if I have to follow you all the way to New York City. I'm never letting you go again."

Lissa could hardly believe her ears. She'd dreamed of Gage saying these things to her. She was almost afraid to believe it was true.

At that moment, he pulled a jeweler's box out of his pocket and opened it to display a diamond ring.

Her heart felt as if it had stopped in her chest. She shook her head.

His face fell. "You're saying no?"

"No," she said. "I mean…I'm just so surprised. How did this sudden turnaround happen?" she asked.

"It wasn't really sudden," he told her. "I think I've been in love with you since you first walked into my office. I just didn't trust that a sophisticated woman like you could really find happiness with a Rust Creek cowboy like me. But I read your essay this morning and I saw that you really do understand the town—and me." He shook his head. "Maybe *I'm* the one who was stereotyping you."

"Ya think?" she asked, still smarting from how much she'd suffered this past week. He had put her through hell. But the look of desperation on his face made her soften.

"Come on, sweet Lissa. Give this man a break."

She took a deep breath. "I think you'd better get up off that floor and kiss me," she said.

In a flash, he rose from his feet and pulled her into his arms and kissed her until her head was spinning.

She was so caught up in feeling Gage in her arms that she barely noticed the applause from the spectators.

Gage pulled back, his gaze latched on to hers. "Wait. Does that mean yes?"

"Yes, yes, yes," she said. "I'd already cancelled my flight. I just couldn't give you up without a fight."

"The only fighting I'm going to do is for us, not against us," he promised. He scooped her up in his arms and carried her out of the terminal. The crowd cheered behind them.

Epilogue

Gage pulled into the driveway and Lissa felt an overwhelming sense of relief. "I feel like I'm coming home," she said when he stopped his SUV.

Gage held her jaw gently with his hand and kissed her. "That's the way I always want you to feel. Always," he said.

She unlocked the door.

"Wait just a minute, there, city girl," he said and got out of the car and rounded to her side in a quick blur. He picked her up and carried her up the stairs to his house.

"What are you doing?" she asked. "You've done this before. You don't have to do it again."

"Honey, if it makes you happy, I'll be doing it until I can't walk. I just want to keep you happy," he said.

Lissa saw that he still wasn't sure of her. "You need to know that you can count on me. I'm not going to leave you even when things get rough. And they will because that's the way life is, full of ups and downs."

"It's just hard for me to believe that you could give up everything in New York for me," he said and guided her into the house.

"You still don't get it," she said. "You are the man I always wanted but never thought existed. I love you for who you are to everyone. Not just for how you act with me," she said. She stopped in the hallway. "I love you for who you are when no one is around because you're the best man I've ever met. And Gage, I know you're not perfect. You've acted like a jerk to me on more than one occasion."

He blinked. "Me? A jerk?"

She gave him a playful punch. "Yes, you," she said, laughing. "You've admitted it to me and apologized. That's one more reason for me to love you. It takes a wonderful man to admit when he's wrong."

"My only excuse is that falling for you made me crazy. I don't ever want to lose you or disappoint you," he said.

"You're stuck with me," she said. "In good and

bad times. But you may need to give me some winter driving lessons," she said.

"Oh, hell. You're gonna scare me to death if you go out on slippery roads," he said and led her upstairs.

"Then you need to teach me very thoroughly," she said.

"You can be sure I will," he said and started to undress her next to his bed. "I kept dreaming I could smell your perfume," he told her. "I thought I was going nuts. I missed you so much."

"I missed you, too," she said. "I don't want to ever be apart from you, Gage."

"I'll do my best to make that happen," he said and gently put her down on the bed. "I love you and I'm gonna make sure you never forget it."

He kissed her lips then caressed her body and made love to her for the whole afternoon. Lissa was so full of him and his love that she lost track of time. Finally, they came up for air.

A bit of reality slipped in. "I'm going to have to find a job," she said.

"I can support you," he said. "I don't want you to worry about that right now. You'll have enough of an adjustment to make getting through a Montana winter and becoming my wife."

His wife. The words made her dizzy. "I can't wait for it all. You and I are going to have a wonderful life, Gage."

"Honey, you've already made me the happiest man in the world. I can't imagine being any happier."

"Then I'll just have to try a little harder, won't I?" she said, snuggling against him.

"Well, you are a high achiever," he said with a wink. "I think I'd better kiss you again," he said.

"I think you'd better," she said, and knew she had found her true man, and her true home.

* * * * *

There was something about the way Luke was looking at her, the intensity in his eyes that started Julie's heart pounding just a little bit faster again.

"You're always beautiful," he said. "Even the first time I saw you—through the foggy window of your car—you took my breath away."

"Of course, that was before I got out from behind the wheel and you saw me waddle like a penguin behind the belly of a whale," she teased.

"You never waddled," he denied.

"I was eight-and-a-half months pregnant," she reminded him.

"And beautiful."

He brushed his knuckles down her cheek, but it was her knees that went weak.

"And I've been thinking about kissing you since that first day." His words were as seductive as his touch, and the heat in his gaze held her mesmerized as he lowered his head, inching closer and closer until his lips hovered above hers.

A VERY SPECIAL DELIVERY

BY
BRENDA HARLEN

MILLS & BOON

First published in Great Britain 2013
by Mills & Boon, an imprint of Harlequin (UK) Limited,
Eton House, 18-24 Paradise Road, Richmond, Surrey TW9 1SR

© Brenda Harlen 2013

ISBN: 978 0 263 90141 2
ebook ISBN: 978 1 472 00528 1

23-0913

Harlequin (UK) policy is to use papers that are natural, renewable and recyclable products and made from wood grown in sustainable forests. The logging and manufacturing processes conform to the legal environmental regulations of the country of origin.

Printed and bound in Spain
by Blackprint CPI, Barcelona

Brenda Harlen is a former family law attorney turned work-at-home mum and national bestselling author who has written more than twenty books for Mills & Boon®. Her work has been validated by industry awards (including an RWA Golden Heart Award and the *RT Book Reviews* Reviewers' Choice Award) and by the fact that her kids think it's cool that she's "a real author."

Brenda lives in southern Ontario with her husband and two sons. When she isn't at the computer working on her next book, she can probably be found at the arena, watching a hockey game. Keep up-to-date with Brenda on Facebook or send her an email at brendaharlen@yahoo.com.

This book is dedicated to my husband, Neill,
an only child who gained two brothers (in-law)
when we married.

Thanks for being a wonderful husband
and the best father our boys could possibly have. XO

Chapter One

When she woke up the morning of November first staring at water stains on a stippled ceiling, Julie Marlowe wondered if she was having a bad dream. Then she remembered that uncomfortable twinges in her lower back had forced her to take a break on her journey home the day before, and the closest available accommodations had been at the Sleep Tite Motor Inn.

She managed to roll her pregnant body off the sagging mattress and swing her feet over the edge. The bathroom's tile floor was cold beneath her feet, and the trickle of spray that came out of the shower head wasn't much warmer. She washed quickly, then dried herself with the threadbare but clean towels on the rack. She had another long day of travel ahead of her, so she dressed comfortably in a pair of chocolate-colored leggings and a loose tunic-style top. Then she slipped her feet into the cowboy boots she'd bought "just because" when she'd been in Texas.

Seven months earlier, she'd had a lot of reasons for wanting to leave Springfield. But after traveling eight thousand miles through twenty-seven states and sleeping in countless hotel rooms, she was more than ready to go home.

She missed her family, her friends and the comfortable and predictable routines of her life. She even missed her father, despite the fact that he could be more than a little stubborn and overbearing on occasion. The only person she could honestly say that she didn't miss was Elliott Davis Winchester the Third—her former fiancé.

Julie had told her parents that she needed some time and some space to think about her future after ending her engagement. Lucinda and Reginald hadn't understood why she needed to go—and how could she expect that they would when there was so much she hadn't told them?—but they'd been supportive. They'd always been unflinching in their support and unwavering in their love, even when she screwed up.

When she left Springfield, Julie was determined to ensure that she didn't screw up again.

She felt a nudge beneath her rib, and smiled as she rubbed a hand over her belly. "You weren't a mistake, baby," she soothed. "Maybe I didn't plan for you at this point in my life, but I know that you're the best thing that ever happened to me, and I promise to be the best mommy that I can."

The baby kicked again, clearly unconvinced.

Julie couldn't blame her for being skeptical. Truthfully, she had more than a few doubts of her own. She and Elliott had talked about having children and neither wanted to wait too long after the wedding before starting a family, but she hadn't known she was pregnant when she gave him back his ring and left town.

After a quick visit to the doctor confirmed that she was going to have a baby, she wasn't even tempted to change her course. Though she'd known Elliott for two years—and had been engaged to him for six months—she'd suddenly realized that she didn't really know him at all. What she did know was that he wasn't the kind of a man she wanted to marry, and he certainly wasn't the kind of man that she wanted as a father for her baby.

Of course, that didn't change the fact that he *was* the father of her baby, but she hadn't been ready to deal with that reality in the moment. Maybe she'd been running away, but over the past few months she'd accepted that she couldn't run forever. In fact, in her current condition, she couldn't run at all anymore. The best she could manage was a waddle.

And she was ready to waddle home.

Lukas Garrett snagged a tiny box of candy from the orange bowl on the front desk—the remnants of the pile of Halloween candy from the day before—and emptied the contents into his mouth.

Karen, the veterinarian clinic receptionist and office manager, shook her head as he chewed the crunchy candy. "Please tell me that's not your lunch."

He swallowed before dutifully answering, "That's not my lunch."

"Lukas," she chided.

"Really," he assured her. "This is just the appetizer. I've got a sandwich in the fridge."

"PB & J?"

"Just PB today." He reached for another box of candy and had his hand slapped away.

"You need a good woman to take care of you."

It was a familiar refrain and he responded as he usually did. "You're a good woman and you take care of me."

"You need a wife," she clarified.

"Just say the word."

Karen, accustomed to his flirtatious teasing, shook her head.

"Go eat your sandwich," she directed. "As pathetic as it is, I'm sure it has slightly more nutritional value than candy."

"I'm waiting to have lunch after I finish with the morning appointments." He glanced at the clock on the wall, frowned. "I thought for sure Mrs. Cammalleri would be here with Snowball by now."

"She called to reschedule," Karen told him. "She didn't want to leave the house in this weather."

"What weather?" Luke turned to the window, then blinked in surprise at the swirling white flakes that were all that was visible through the glass. "When did it start snowing?"

"About an hour ago," Karen told him. "While you were ensuring that Raphael would never again be controlled by his most basic animal urges."

He moved closer to the window. "Did the forecast call for this?"

She nodded. "Twelve to fifteen inches."

He frowned. "How does global warming result in early season snowstorms?"

"We live in a Snowbelt," she reminded him. "And the current catchphrase is 'climate change.'"

"I'd prefer a climate change that included warm sun and sandy beaches."

"So book a vacation."

"I've been thinking about it," he admitted. And while an island getaway held a certain appeal, he had no desire to go on a holiday alone. Nor was he interested in venturing out solo with the goal of finding an anonymous female someone to share a few days of sun, sand and sex. That kind of thing had lost its appeal for Luke before he'd graduated college.

"Well, another thing you should think about is closing up early," Karen suggested. "Mrs. Cammalleri was your last scheduled appointment and the way the snow's already falling hard and fast, if we don't get out of here soon, we might not get out of here at all."

"The clinic's open until three on Fridays," he reminded her. "So I'll stay until then, but you go ahead."

"Are you sure you don't mind?"

"Of course not. There's no need for both of us to stay, and you've got a longer drive home than I do."

Karen was already tidying up her desk, straightening a pile of files, aligning the stapler with the edge of her desk calendar, putting the pens in the cup.

Luke took advantage of her distraction to snag another box of candy. "If this keeps up, the kids will be building snowmen tomorrow."

"Hard to believe they were trick-or-treating just last night, isn't it?"

"Yeah." He couldn't help but smile as he thought about his almost five-year-old nephews, Quinn and Shane, who had dressed up as SpongeBob and Patrick. Their baby sister, Pippa, was too young to go door-to-door, but even she'd been decked out in a pumpkin costume with a smiling jack-o'-lantern face on the front and a hat with stem and leaves.

His eldest niece—his brother Jackson's twelve-year-old daughter, Ava—had skipped the candy-grabbing ritual in favor of a Halloween party with some friends at the community center. And Jack had chaperoned. Luke wasn't at all surprised that his brother, who had earned quite the reputation as a heartbreaker in his youth, was a slightly overprotective father. The surprising part had been finding out that he was a father at all—especially to the daughter of the woman who had been Luke's best friend since fifth grade.

He was still surprised, and a little annoyed, that Kelly Cooper had managed to keep her weekend rendezvous with Jack a secret for more than twelve years. It was only when she'd moved back to Pinehurst with her daughter at the end of the summer that Luke had learned that his brother was Ava's father and that his designation as "Uncle Luke" was more than an honorary title. He still wasn't sure that he'd completely forgiven her for keeping that secret for so long, but he was genuinely thrilled that Kelly and Jack were together now and making plans for an early December wedding.

"From carving pumpkins to throwing snowballs in the blink of an eye," Karen noted as she turned to retrieve her coat and purse from the cabinet behind her desk—then muttered a curse under her breath as she nearly tripped over Einstein, Luke's seven-month-old beagle puppy.

He'd been one of a litter of eight born to a severely malnourished and exhausted female who had been abandoned on the side of the road. A passerby had found the animal and taken her to the veterinarian clinic. The mother hadn't survived the birth, and Luke had been determined to ensure that her efforts to give life to her pups weren't in vain.

Thankfully, Karen had stepped up to help, and between the two of them, they'd made sure that the puppies were fed and nurtured and loved—and then they'd given them to good homes. But Luke had always known that he would keep one, and Einstein was the one he'd chosen. And he loved the crazy animal, even if he wasn't exactly the genius of his namesake.

When the puppies were first born and required almost constant care, it made sense for them to be at the clinic. Luke also believed it would help with their socialization, getting them accustomed to being around people and other animals, and so he'd continued the practice with Einstein long after his brothers and sisters had gone to other homes. Unfortunately, one of Einstein's favorite places in the clinic was wherever he could find Karen's feet.

"I swear that animal is trying to kill me." But despite the annoyance in her tone, she bent to rub his head, giving him an extra scratch behind his left ear because she knew that was his favorite spot.

"Only if he could love you to death," Luke assured her.

She shook her head as she made her way to the door. "You should go home, too," she said again. "No one's going to come out in this weather."

As it turned out, she was right. Aside from Raphael's owner who came to pick him up, the front door didn't open and the phone didn't ring. So promptly at three o'clock, Luke locked up the clinic and headed out to his truck with Einstein.

Of course, this was the puppy's first exposure to snow, and when he stepped out onto the deck and found himself buried up to his chest in the cold, white fluff, he was not very happy. He whined and jumped, trying desperately to get away from it. And when he couldn't escape it, he decided to attack it. He barked and pranced around, clearly under the impression that he was winning the battle.

Luke couldn't help but chuckle at his antics. The animal would probably play in the snow for hours if he let him, so he finally picked up the pup and carried him to the truck. He sat him on the floor of the passenger side and let the heater blow warm air on him while Luke cleared the thick layer of snow off of his windows.

Luckily he'd found an old hat and a pair of gloves in his office, and he was grateful for both. The unexpected snow-fall might have been fun for Einstein, but driving through it was a completely different story, even with all-wheel drive. The snow had been falling steadily and quickly and the plows hadn't yet been around, so he knew the roads would probably be slick—a fact that was proven when he fishtailed a little as he pulled out of the clinic's driveway and onto the street.

Warm and dry once again, Einstein hopped up onto the passenger seat and pressed his nose against the window, his breath fogging up the glass. When Luke finally turned onto

Terrace Drive, the pup barked excitedly, three quick little yips.
The snow was still falling with no indication that it would let
up anytime soon, and he was as happy as Einstein to know
that they were almost home.

The cold had come after the snow, so the first layer of
flakes had melted on the road, then frozen. Now there was a
dangerous layer of ice beneath everything else, and Luke suspected the tow trucks would be working late into the night.
It would be too easy to slide off the road and into a ditch in
these conditions—as someone had apparently done right in
front of his house.

Julie clenched the steering wheel with both hands and bit
down on her bottom lip to hold back the scream of frustration that threatened to burst from her throat. A quick detour
through Pinehurst to meet with a friend of her brother's from
law school had seemed like a great idea when she'd called
and made the appointment a few hours earlier, but that was
before the snow started.

Still, she'd no intention of being dissuaded by some light
flurries. Except that those light flurries had quickly esca-
lated into an actual blizzard. Weather reports on the radio
had warned people to avoid unnecessary travel. Since Julie
had been on the highway between Syracuse and Pinehurst
at the time and pulling off to the side of the road in order to
be buried in snow didn't seem like a particularly appealing
option, she decided her travel was necessary.

And she'd almost made it. According to her GPS, she was
less than three miles from Jackson Garrett's office—but it
might as well have been thirty. There was no way she could
walk, not in her condition and not in this weather.

Tears of frustration filled her eyes, blurred her vision. She
let her head fall forward, then jolted back again when the horn
sounded. Great—not only had she driven into a ditch, she'd

just drawn attention to the fact by alerting anyone who happened to be passing by. She didn't know if she was more relieved or apprehensive when she realized that no one seemed to be anywhere in the vicinity.

She was sure she'd seen houses not too far back. In fact, she specifically remembered a sprawling ranch-style with a trio of grinning jack-o'-lanterns on the wide front porch, because she'd noted that it wouldn't be too long before those pumpkins were completely blanketed by snow.

She closed her eyes and silently cursed Mother Nature. Okay, maybe she had to accept responsibility for the fact that she'd been driving through a blizzard with no snow tires— but who the heck would have thought that she'd need snow tires on the first day of November?

She felt a spasm in her lower back in conjunction with a ripple of pain that tightened her whole belly. Julie splayed a hand over her tummy, silently trying to reassure her baby that everything was okay. But as the first tears spilled onto her cheeks, she had to admit—if only to herself—that she didn't know if it was. She didn't know how being stuck in a ditch in the middle of nowhere during a freak snowstorm could possibly be "okay."

She drew in a deep breath and tried to get the tears under control. She didn't usually blubber, but the pregnancy hormones running rampant through her system had been seriously messing with her emotional equilibrium. Wiping the trails of moisture from her cheeks, she tried to look on the bright side.

She knew she wasn't lost. She wasn't exactly sure where she was, but she'd followed the directions of her GPS so she wasn't actually in the middle of nowhere. She was in Pinehurst, New York. An even brighter side was found when she pulled her cell phone out of her purse and confirmed that her battery was charged and she had a signal. Further proof that she wasn't in the middle of nowhere.

Confident that she would be able to get some roadside assistance, Julie leaned over to open the glove box to get the number and gasped as pain ripped across her back. Gritting her teeth, she blew out a slow, unsteady breath and prayed that it was just a spasm. That the jolt of sliding into the ditch had pulled a muscle in her back.

On the other hand, it could be a sign that she was in labor. And right now, that was *not* a scenario she wanted to consider.

"Please, baby—" she rubbed a hand over her belly "—don't do this now. You've got a couple more weeks to hang out right where you are, and I'm not even close to being ready for you yet."

Moving more carefully this time, she reached for the folio that contained her vehicle ownership and warranty information and—most important—her automobile association card. Hopefully there wasn't any damage to her car and as soon as it was pulled out of the ditch, she could be on her way again.

Except that when she dialed the toll-free number on the card, she got a recorded message informing her that all of the operators were currently busy assisting other customers and to please hold the line if she wanted to maintain her call priority. She disconnected. It would probably be easier—and quicker—for her to find the number of a local company and make a direct call. Or maybe, if she was really lucky, a Good Samaritan with a big truck conveniently equipped with tow cables would drive down this road and stop to help.

A flash of color caught the corner of her eye and she turned her head to see a truck drive past, then pull into a driveway she hadn't even noticed was less than ten feet from where she was stranded. The vehicle stopped, the driver's side door opened and then a gust of wind swirled the thick snow around, obliterating her view.

She thought she heard something that sounded like a dog barking, but the sound quickly faded away.

Then there was a knock on her window, and her heart leaped into her throat. Not thirty seconds earlier, she'd been praying that a Good Samaritan would come to her rescue, and now someone was at her door. But how was she supposed to know if he had stopped to offer help—or if his intentions were less honorable?

Her breath was coming faster now, and the windows were fogging up, making it even harder to see. All she could tell was that he was tall, broad-shouldered and wearing a dark cap on his head. He was big. The road was mostly deserted. She was helpless.

No, she wasn't. She had her cell phone. She held it up, to show him that she was in contact with the outside world, then rolled down her window a few inches. A gust of cold air blasted through the scant opening, making her gasp.

"Are you okay, ma'am?"

Ma'am? The unexpectedness of the formal address in combination with the evident concern in his tone reassured her, at least a little. She lifted her gaze to his face, and her heart jolted again. But this time she knew the physiological response had nothing to do with fear—it was a sign of purely female appreciation for a truly spectacular male.

The knit cap was tugged low on his forehead so she couldn't see what color his hair was, but below dark brows, his eyes were the exact same shade of blue-green as the aquamarine gemstone ring her parents had given to her for her twenty-first birthday. His nose was just a little off-center, his cheekbones sharp, his jaw square. He had a strong face, undeniably masculine and incredibly handsome. His voice was low and soothing, and when he spoke again, she found her gaze riveted on the movement of his lips.

"Ma'am?" he said again.

"I'm okay. I'm just waiting for a tow truck."

He frowned. "I'm not sure how long you'll have to wait. I managed to squeeze through just as the police were putting up barriers to restrict access to Main Street."

"What does that mean?"

"It means that the primary road through town is shut down."

She sighed. "Any chance you have tow cables in your truck?"

He shook his head. "Sorry."

She gasped as another stab of pain slashed through her.

"You *are* hurt," he decided. "Let me call an ambulance."

She shook her head. "I'm not hurt. I think...I'm in labor."

Chapter Two

"Labor? As in having a baby?" Luke couldn't quite get his head around what she was saying. Not until he noticed that her hand was splayed on her belly.

Her very round belly.

How had he *not* noticed that she was pregnant?

Probably because his most immediate concern, when he'd spotted the vehicle in the ditch, was that the driver might be injured, maybe even unconscious. He hadn't given a passing thought to the driver's gender. And then, when she'd rolled down the window, he'd been absolutely spellbound by her wide and wary blue-gray eyes.

But now, with his attention focused on the bump beneath her shirt, the words that had seemed undecipherable suddenly made sense. "You're pregnant."

Her brows lifted in response to his not-so-astute observation. "Yes, I'm pregnant," she confirmed.

She was also a pretty young thing—emphasis on the

young. Early twenties, he guessed, with clear, flawless skin, high cheekbones, a patrician nose and lips that were surprisingly full and temptingly shaped.

He felt the subtle buzz through his veins, acknowledged it. He'd experienced the stir of attraction often enough in the past to recognize it for what it was—and to know that, under the circumstances, it was completely inappropriate.

Young, beautiful *and pregnant,* he reminded himself.

"Actually, I don't think it is labor," she said now. "I'm probably just overreacting to the situation."

But he wasn't quite ready to disregard the possibility. "When are you due?"

"November fifteenth."

Only two weeks ahead of schedule. He remembered his sister-in-law, Georgia, telling him that she'd been two weeks early with Pippa, so the timing didn't seem to be any real cause for concern. Of course, Georgia had also been in the hospital. The fact that this woman was stuck in a ditch and nowhere near a medical facility might be a bit of an issue.

He took a moment to clear his head and organize his thoughts, and saw her wince again.

"Are you having contractions?"

"No," she said quickly, and just a little desperately. "Just… twinges."

Apparently she didn't want to be in labor any more than he wanted her to be in labor, but that didn't mean she wasn't.

"I think I should call 911 to try to get an ambulance out here and get you to the hospital."

"It's probably just false labor."

"Have you been through this before?"

"No," she admitted. "This is my first. But I've read a ton of books on pregnancy and childbirth, and I'm pretty sure what I'm experiencing are just Braxton Hicks contractions."

He wasn't convinced, but he also wasn't going to waste

any more time arguing with her. Not with the snow blowing around the way it was and the condition of the roads rapidly getting worse. He pulled out his phone and dialed.

"911. Please state the nature of your emergency."

He recognized the dispatcher's voice immediately, and his lips instinctively curved as he recalled a long-ago summer when he and the emergency operator had been, at least for a little while, more than friends. "Hey, Yolanda, it's Luke Garrett. I was wondering if you could send an ambulance out to my place."

"What happened?" The clinical detachment in her tone gave way to concern. "Are you hurt?"

"No, it's not me. I'm with a young woman—"

He glanced at her, his brows raised in silent question.

"Julie Marlowe," she told him.

"—whose car went into the ditch beside my house."

"Is she injured?"

"She says no, but she's pregnant, two weeks from her due date and experiencing what might be contractions."

"Twinges," the expectant mother reminded him through the window.

"She insists that they're twinges," Luke said, if only to reassure her that he was listening. "But they're sharp enough that she gasps for breath when they come."

"Can I talk to her?"

He tapped on the window, and Julie lowered the glass a few more inches to take the device from him. Because she was inside the car with the window still mostly closed, he could only decipher snippets of their conversation, but he got the impression that Yolanda was asking more detailed questions about the progress of her pregnancy, possible complications and if there were any other indications of labor.

A few minutes later, Julie passed the phone back to him.

"If I thought I could get an ambulance through to you, I'd

be sending one," Yolanda told Luke. "But the police have completely shut down Main Street in both directions."

"But emergency vehicles should be able to get through."

"If they weren't all out on other calls," she agreed. "And the reality is that an expectant mother with no injuries in the early stages of labor, as Julie seems to think she might be, is not an emergency."

"What if the situation changes?"

"If the situation changes, call me back. Maybe by then the roads will be plowed and reopened and we can get her to the hospital."

"You don't sound too optimistic," he noted.

"The storm dumped a lot of snow fast and there's no sign that it's going to stop any time soon. The roads are a mess and emergency crews are tapped."

He bit back a sigh of frustration. "What if the baby doesn't want to wait that long?"

"Then you'll handle it," she said, and quickly gave him some basic instructions. "And don't worry—I reassured the expectant mom that Doctor Garrett has done this countless times before."

"Please tell me you're joking."

"I'm not." There was no hint of apology in her tone. "The woman needed reassurance, and I gave it to her."

And although her statement was technically true, she'd neglected to mention that the majority of the births he'd been involved with had been canine or feline in nature. He had absolutely no experience bringing human babies into the world.

Luke stared at Julie, who gasped as another contraction hit her. "You better get an ambulance here as soon as possible."

Julie was still mulling over the information the dispatcher had given her when she saw her Good Samaritan—who was apparently also a doctor—tuck his phone back into the pocket of his jacket.

"Let's get you up to the house where it's warm and dry."

She wished that staying in the car was a viable option. She was more than a little uneasy about going into a stranger's home, but her feet and her hands were already numb and she had to clench her teeth together to keep them from chattering. She took some comfort from the fact that the emergency operator knew her name and location.

She rolled up the window—no point in letting the inside of the car fill up with snow—and unlocked the door.

As soon as she did, he opened it for her, then offered his other hand to help her out. He must have noticed the iciness of her fingers even through his gloves, because before she'd stepped onto the ground, he'd taken them off his hands and put them on hers. They were toasty warm inside, and she nearly whimpered with gratitude.

He walked sideways up the side of the ditch, holding on to both of her hands to help her do the same. Unfortunately the boots that she'd so happily put on her feet when she set out that morning had smooth leather soles, not exactly conducive to gaining traction on a snowy incline. She slipped a few times and no doubt would have fallen if not for his support. When she finally made it to level ground, he picked her up—scooping her off her feet as if she weighed nothing—and carried her to the passenger side of his truck. She was too startled to protest, and all too conscious of the extra twenty-nine pounds that she was carrying—and now *he* was carrying. But when he settled her gently on the seat, he didn't even seem winded.

He drove up the laneway, parked beside the house. When he inserted his key into the lock, she heard a cacophony of excited barking from the other side of the door.

"You have dogs?"

"Just one." Her rescuer shook his head as the frantic yips continued. "We just got home. I let him out of the truck at the end of the driveway when I saw your vehicle, and he raced ahead to the house to come in through the doggy door, as he always does. And every day when I put my key in the lock, he acts as if it's been days rather than minutes since he last saw me."

"They don't have much of a concept of time, do they?"

"Except for dinnertime," he noted dryly. "He never forgets that one."

He opened the door and gestured for her to enter. But before Julie could take a step forward, there was a tri-colored whirlwind of fur and energy weaving between her feet.

"Einstein, sit."

The dog immediately plopped his butt on the snow-covered porch right beside her boots and looked up with shiny, dark eyes, and his master scooped him up to give her a clear path through the door.

"Oh, he's just a little guy. And absolutely the cutest thing I've ever seen."

"He's cute," the doctor agreed. "And he hasn't met anyone he doesn't immediately love, but sometimes he's too stubborn for his own good."

She slipped her boots off inside the door, and when he put the puppy down again, it immediately attacked her toes with an enthusiastic tongue and gentle nips of his little teeth.

"Einstein, no!"

The pup dropped his head and looked up, his eyes filled with so much hurt and remorse, Julie couldn't help but laugh.

The doctor looked at her with a slightly embarrassed shrug. "He's got some kind of foot fetish. I'm not having a lot of luck in trying to curb it."

"No worries, my feet are too numb to feel much, anyway."

"Come on." He took her arm and guided her down the hall

and into what she guessed was a family room. The floor was a dark glossy hardwood and the walls were painted a rich hunter-green, set off by the wide white trim and cove moldings. There was a chocolate leather sectional and a matching armchair facing a gorgeous stone fireplace flanked by tall, narrow windows. The lamps on the mission-style side tables were already illuminated, but as he stepped through the wide, arched doorway, he hit another switch on the wall and flames came to life in the firebox.

"You should warm up quickly in here," he told her. "I converted to gas a few years ago. As much as I love the smell of a real wood fire, I prefer the convenience of having heat and flame at the flick of a switch."

"You have a beautiful home," Julie told him. And, it seemed to her, a big home, making her wonder if he had a wife and kids to help fill it. She hadn't seen a ring on his finger, but she knew that didn't prove anything.

"I like it," he said easily.

She moved closer to the fireplace, drawn by the flickering flames and the tempting warmth. "Do you live here alone?"

"Me and Daphne and Einstein," he clarified.

She was reassured by this revelation that she wouldn't actually be alone with a stranger. "Daphne's your...wife?"

"No."

He responded quickly—so quickly she couldn't help but smile. The immediate and predictable denial was that of a perennial bachelor with absolutely no desire to change his status.

"Daphne's a three-year-old blue Burmese, and not very sociable. Unlike Einstein, you'll only see her if she decides you're worthy of her presence."

Which meant that they *were* alone—except for a cat and a dog. But he was a doctor, and the emergency operator had vouched for him, and she had to stop being wary of everyone just because her experience with Elliott had caused her to doubt her own judgment. "It's a big house for one man and two pets," she noted.

"Believe me, it felt a lot smaller when I had to share it with two brothers."

"You grew up here?"

He nodded. "Born and raised and lived my whole life in Pinehurst, in this house. Well, I wasn't actually born in this house—my mother wanted to do things more traditionally and give birth in the hospital."

"That was my plan, too," she admitted.

"Sliding into a ditch and going into labor during an unexpected snowstorm was a spur-of-the-moment decision?" he teased.

"I'm not in labor," she said again. "My baby isn't due for another two weeks and first babies are almost never early."

"Almost isn't the same as never," he told her, and pushed the oversize leather chair closer to the fire so that she could sit down.

When she lowered herself into the seat, he sat cross-legged on the floor facing her and lifted her feet into his lap. "Your feet are like ice," he noted.

She was startled by the boldness of the move and felt as if she should protest—but only until he started to rub her toes between his hands, then she closed her eyes and nearly moaned with pleasure.

In fact, she probably did make some kind of noise, because Einstein bounded over, eager to play with her feet, too. But one sharp look from his master had him curling up on the rug in front of the fire.

"Don't you own winter boots or a proper coat?" the doctor asked her.

"Of course I do, but it wasn't snowing when I started out this morning."

"Started out from where?"

"Cleveland," she admitted.

"Then you obviously did a lot of driving today."

"About seven hours."

"Heading back to Boston?"

She eyed him warily. "What makes you think I'm going to Boston?"

"I saw the Massachusetts plates on your car, and there's just a hint of a Boston accent in your voice."

"I wasn't planning on going any further than Pinehurst today," she said, deliberately not confirming nor denying his assumption. Then, because she'd rather be asking questions than answering them, she said, "Is Luke short for Lukas?"

"It is." He set down the first foot and picked up the second one.

"I've been researching baby names," Julie told him. "Lukas means bringer of light."

And she thought the name suited him, not just because he'd rescued her—bringing her hope if not necessarily light—but because it was strong and masculine.

"Have you narrowed down your choices?"

She nodded.

"Any hints?"

She shook her head, then gasped when the pain ripped through her again.

Luke released her foot and laid his hands on the curve of her belly. She tried to remember everything she'd read about Braxton Hicks and how to distinguish those false contractions from real labor, but in the moment, she was lucky she remembered to breathe through the pain.

After what seemed like forever, the tightness across her belly finally eased.

"Twinge?" Though his tone was deliberately light, she saw the concern in his eyes.

"Yeah." She drew in a deep breath, released it slowly.

"I'm going to put the puppy in the laundry room, just so that he's out of the way in case things start to happen." Then he took the dog away, returning a few minutes later with an armful of blankets and towels and a plastic bin filled with medical supplies. He covered the leather chaise with a thick flannel sheet, then folded a blanket over the foot of it.

"Is there anyone you should call?" the doctor asked. "Anyone who's going to worry about where you are?"

She shook her head. Her parents wouldn't know that she'd been caught in this storm because they hadn't known about her intention to detour through the Snowbelt on her way home.

"Husband? Boyfriend?" he prompted.

"No." She could see the direction he was going with his questions, and she was almost grateful when her body spasmed with pain again. It was easier to focus on the contraction—whether false or real—than on the reasons why her relationship with her baby's father had fallen apart.

She was gripping the armrests of the chair, but noticed that he was looking at his watch, counting the seconds. She panted softly and tried to think of something—anything—but the pain that ripped through her. The books she'd read talked about focal points, how to use a picture or some other item to evoke pleasant memories and a feeling of peace. Right now all she had was Luke Garrett, but his warm gaze and steady tone—proof of his presence and reassurance that she wasn't entirely alone—somehow made the pain bearable.

"Ninety seconds," he said. "And I'd guess less than five minutes since the last one."

"It doesn't look like my baby's going to wait for a hospital, does it?"

"I'd say not," he agreed. "Did you take prenatal classes?"

"No."

"Your doctor didn't recommend it?"

"I've been traveling a lot over the past few months, so I didn't have a chance."

"Traveling where?"

"Pretty much everywhere."

"Work or pleasure?"

"Both."

She knew it sounded as if she was being evasive, and maybe she was, but it wasn't in her nature to share personal information with someone she didn't know and whom she probably wouldn't ever see again when the roads were finally cleared and her car was pulled out of the ditch.

"I'm just making conversation," he told her. "I thought it might take your mind off of the contractions."

"I was counting on an epidural to do that," she admitted.

His lips curved. "Well, it's good that you have a sense of humor, because an epidural isn't really an option right now."

She liked his smile. It was warm and genuine, and it made her think that everything was going to be okay. "I knew it was too much to hope that you rented a spare bedroom to a local anesthesiologist."

He took her hand, linked their fingers together and gave hers a reassuring squeeze.

"I'm scared," she admitted.

"You're doing great."

"I don't just mean about giving birth," she told him. "I mean about being a parent."

"Let's concentrate on the giving birth part for now," he suggested.

She sucked in another breath and gritted her teeth so that she didn't embarrass herself by whimpering. Or screaming. The pain was unlike anything she'd ever experienced, and she knew it would continue to worsen before it got better.

"Breathe," Luke said, and she realized that she wasn't

doing so. She released the air she was holding in her lungs in short, shallow pants. "That's it."

"Okay," she said when the contraction had finally eased.

"Two minutes," he announced, not very happily.

She could understand his concern. Her contractions—and she knew now that they were definitely contractions—were coming harder and faster. The idea of giving birth outside of a hospital was absolutely terrifying, but somehow, with Luke beside her, she felt confident that she would get through it. More importantly, she felt that her baby would get through it.

"Should I get undressed now?"

It wasn't the first time he'd had a woman say those words to him, but it was the first time they'd come at Luke completely out of the blue.

And apparently Julie realized that her casual statement might be misinterpreted, because her cheeks flooded with color. "So that you can examine me," she clarified.

Examine her. Right. She was an expectant mother and he was the doctor who was helping to deliver her baby. Of course she would expect him to examine her.

He mentally recalled the brief instructions he'd been given by the 911 operator. Thankfully the human birthing process wasn't very different from that of other mammals, but Luke felt more than a little guilty that Julie was offering to strip down for him because she thought he was an MD.

It should have been simple enough to think like a doctor. But he couldn't forget the quick punch of desire he'd felt when his eyes had first locked with hers. Before he'd realized that she was eight and a half months pregnant. Still, the fact that she was about to give birth didn't make her any less attractive, although he would have hoped that this tangible evidence of her involvement with another man should have cooled his ardor.

But the combination of her beauty and spirit appealed to something in him. She'd found herself in a tough situation, but she was dealing with it. Sure, she was scared. Under the circumstances, who wouldn't be? But she'd demonstrated a willingness to face that fear head-on, and he had to respect that courage and determination. And when he looked into those blue-gray eyes, he wanted to take up his sword to fight all of her battles for her. Not that she would appreciate his efforts—most women preferred to fight their own battles nowadays, but the desire to honor and protect was deeply ingrained in his DNA.

He wasn't interested in anything beyond that, though. Sure, he liked women and enjoyed their company, but he wasn't looking to tie himself to any one woman for the long term. His brothers had both lucked out and found partners with whom they wanted to share the rest of their lives, and he was happy for them, but he didn't see himself as the marrying kind. Certainly he'd never met a woman who made him think in terms of forever.

Which was just one more reason that he had no business thinking about Julie Marlowe at all. She might be beautiful and sexy but she was also on the verge of becoming a mother—no way would she be interested in a fling, and no way was he interested in anything else.

So he gave her privacy to strip down—and his plush robe to wrap around herself. He was trying to think about this situation as a doctor would—clinically and impartially. But how was he supposed to be impartial when she had those beautiful winter-sky eyes and those sweetly curved lips, sexy shoulders and sexy feet? And despite the baby bump, she had some very appealing curves, too.

When he returned to the family room, he was relieved to see that she was wearing the robe he'd left for her so she wasn't entirely naked beneath the thin sheet she'd pulled up over herself. But she still looked vulnerable and scared, and every last shred of objectivity flew out the window.

She was panting—blowing out short puffs of air that warned him he'd missed another contraction. "I thought I had a pretty good threshold for pain," she told him. "I was wrong."

He knelt at the end of the chaise, and felt perspiration beginning to bead on his brow. She was the one trying to push a baby out of her body, and he was sweating at the thought of watching her do it. But when he folded back the sheet and saw the top of the baby's head, everything else was forgotten.

"The baby's already crowning," he told her.

"Does that mean I can start to push?"

"Whenever you're ready."

He talked her through the contractions, telling her when to push and when to pant, trying to ensure that her body was able to adjust to each stage and rest when possible.

Of course, it was called labor for a reason, and although it was progressing quickly, he knew it wasn't painless. Her hands were fisted in the sheet, and he covered one with his own, gave it a reassuring squeeze. "It won't be too much longer now."

"Promise?"

He looked up and saw that her stormy eyes were filled with tears and worry. "I promise."

As she pushed through the next contraction, the head slowly emerged. The soft, indignant cry that accompanied the baby's emergence from the birth canal confirmed that its lungs were working just fine.

"You're doing great," he told Julie. "Just—"

He didn't even have a chance to finish his sentence before the baby slid completely out and into his hands.

Chapter Three

Luke stared in awe at the wet, wrinkled infant that was somehow the most beautiful creature he'd ever seen. And when the baby looked at him with big blue eyes wide with innocence and wonder, he fell just a little bit in love with the little guy.

He wiped the baby's face carefully with a clean, soft towel to ensure that his nose and mouth were clear of fluid. Then he wrapped him, still attached by the cord, in a blanket and laid him on his mother's chest.

"And there he is," he told her.

Julie blinked, as if startled by this statement. *"He?"*

"You have a beautiful, healthy baby boy," he confirmed. "Born at 4:58 pm on November first."

"A boy," she echoed softly, her lips curving just a little. "My baby boy."

Tears filled her eyes, then spilled onto her cheeks. She wiped at them impatiently with the back of her hand.

"I'm sorry. I'm not usually so emotional."

"It's been an emotional day," Luke said, feeling a little choked up himself.

It took her a few minutes to get her tears under control before she spoke again, and when she did, she surprised him by saying, "I thought he'd be a girl. I *wanted* a girl." After a moment she continued. "I don't even feel guilty admitting it now. Because looking down at him, I know that I couldn't possibly love him any more if he had been a she. All that matters is that he's mine."

"Why did you want a girl?" he asked curiously.

"I guess I thought it would be easier to raise a girl, since I was once one myself. I don't know anything about little boys. Or big boys." She glanced up at him and offered a wry smile. "And personal experience has proven that I don't understand the male gender at all."

"Are you disappointed that he's a he?"

She shook her head. "No. I'm not disappointed at all. He's...perfect."

"That he is."

"I never expected to feel so much. I look at him, and my heart practically overflows with love." But she managed to lift her gaze from the baby to look at Luke now. "Thank you, Dr. Garrett."

He didn't know how to respond to her gratitude, especially when he felt as if *he* should be thanking *her*. Because in his entire life, he had honestly never experienced anything more incredible than helping to bring Julie's beautiful baby boy into the world.

What he'd told her earlier was true—the hard part was all hers. And he couldn't help but be awed by the strength and determination and courage she'd shown in face of the challenge. He felt honored and privileged to have been a part of the experience, to have been the very first person to hold the brand-new life in his hands.

By the time he'd cut the cord and delivered the placenta, Julie had put the baby to her breast and was already nursing. And Luke finally let himself exhale a silent sigh of relief.

He tidied up, gathering the used sheets and towels, then left mother and child alone while he stepped away to call Yolanda to let her know that an ambulance was no longer a priority. She offered hearty congratulations and a smug "I knew you could handle one little baby" then signed off to deal with other matters.

After putting a load of laundry in the washing machine, Luke fed Einstein, then realized that his stomach was growling, too. And if he was hungry, he imagined that Julie was even more so. He put some soup on the stove to heat, then peeked into the family room again.

"How are you feeling now?"

"Exhausted," she admitted. "And ecstatic. I don't know how I can ever repay you for everything you've done."

"I'm just glad I was here to help."

She smiled at that. "And if an ambulance could have got through the storm, you would have shipped me off to the hospital in a heartbeat."

"Absolutely," he agreed without hesitation.

"Since I am still here, there is something I wanted to ask you."

"Sure."

"What do you think of the name Caden?" She looked at him expectantly, trying to gauge his reaction.

"What does it mean?" he asked.

"Fighter or battle."

He nodded. "I like it."

She smiled down at the baby before lifting her eyes to

meet his again. "Then let me formally introduce you to Caden Lukas Marlowe."

She saw surprise flicker in his eyes, then pleasure. He offered his finger to the baby, and Caden wrapped his tiny fist around it, holding on tight. "That's a lot of name for such a little guy," he noted.

"You don't mind the 'Lukas' part?"

"Why would I mind?"

She shrugged. "I wanted him to have a small part of the man who helped bring him into the world. I know we probably won't ever see you again after we leave Pinehurst, but I don't want to forget—and I don't want Caden to forget—everything you've done."

"You're not planning to go anywhere just yet, are you?"

"Not just yet," she assured him. "But I figured you'd want to get us out of here as soon as the roads are clear."

Of course, she couldn't go anywhere until her car was pulled out of the ditch and any necessary repairs were made, but she didn't expect her Good Samaritan to put them up for the duration.

He shrugged. "As you noted, it's a big house for one person and two pets."

She wasn't entirely sure what he was suggesting. Was he really offering to let them stay with him? And even if he was, she could hardly stay in the home of a man she'd just met. No matter that she already felt more comfortable with him than with the man she'd planned to marry.

Before she could ask, she heard the sound of footsteps stomping on the porch. Despite the fact that the roads were still closed, Lukas didn't seem at all surprised to have a visitor—or that the visitor, after a brisk knock, proceeded to open the door and walk right into the house.

Einstein had been released from the laundry room and cautiously introduced to the baby. Since then, he hadn't left Julie's side. But he obviously heard the stomping, too, because he raced across the room and down the hall to the foyer, barking and dancing the whole way.

The sharp barks startled the baby, and Caden responded with an indignant wail of his own. Julie murmured reassuringly and snuggled him closer to her chest, and by the time the visitor had made his way down the hall to the family room, he was settled again.

"This is a friend of mine," Lukas told her, gesturing to the tall, dark-haired man beside him. "Cameron Turcotte." Then to Cameron he said, "This is Julie Marlowe and Caden."

"Are the roads clear now?" Julie asked him. She assumed that they must be if he was able to get through, although she couldn't begin to fathom why he would have chosen to visit a friend in the middle of a snowstorm.

"The plows are out in full force, but it's going to take a while," he told her. "Main Street is technically still shut down, but I knew the officer posted at the barricade and told him that I had to get through to deal with a medical emergency."

"Are you a doctor, too?" Julie asked him.

Cameron's brows lifted. "Too?"

"Yolanda wanted to reassure Julie that she was in capable hands with Doctor Garrett," Lukas told his friend.

The other man chuckled.

"Why do I feel as if I'm missing something?" Julie asked warily.

"The only thing that matters is that you and your baby are okay," Cameron said. "And since I was on my way home from the hospital, Luke asked if I could stop by to check on both of you. With your permission, of course."

She looked questioningly at Lukas. "I don't understand. You said everything was okay. Is something—"

"Nothing's wrong," he said, answering her question before

she could finish asking it. "But you may have misunderstood my qualifications."

She frowned. "What do you mean?"

"I'm a DVM, not an MD," he told her.

It only took her a few seconds to decipher the acronym, and when she did, her jaw dropped.

"My baby was delivered by a *vet*?"

Lukas nodded.

Julie was stunned.

And mortified.

Dr. Garrett wasn't a qualified medical doctor—he was an animal doctor.

She drew in a deep breath and tried to accept the reality of the situation. And the truth was, neither of them had had any other choice. She'd been stranded in his house in a blizzard with no one else around to help. Her options had been simple: accept his assistance or try to deliver her baby on her own. And, in his defense, he hadn't claimed to be a doctor—it was the 911 operator who had offered that information.

And she'd grasped at it with both hands. It wasn't how she'd wanted to deliver her baby but knowing that she had no chance of getting to a hospital, she'd considered herself lucky that her car had gone into the ditch by a doctor's house. Proving once again that she had a tendency to see what she wanted to see.

"I didn't intend to deceive you," Lukas said to her now. "But you seemed to find comfort in believing that I was a medical doctor, and I didn't want to cause you undue stress by correcting that impression."

And she'd willingly stripped out of her clothes because a doctor—especially an obstetrician—was accustomed to his patients doing that. Glancing at the veterinarian who had delivered her baby, she didn't doubt that he was accustomed to women stripping for him, too, although probably not in a clinical setting.

"So." She cleared her throat. "How many babies have you delivered?"

"One," he admitted.

"And it looks to me like he did a pretty good job for a first-timer," Cameron—*Doctor* Turcotte—commented.

"But I think we'd both feel better if Cameron checked Caden over, just to make sure I didn't miscount his toes or something."

She could smile at that, because she'd already counted his fingers and toes herself.

"And you might want some numbers—weight and length, for example—to put in his baby book," Cameron said.

"I guess 'tiny' is somewhat vague," she admitted, relinquishing the swaddled infant to the doctor.

He measured Caden's length and the circumference of his head, then he used a kitchen scale to weigh the baby.

"Not as tiny as I thought," he said, handing the infant back to his mother. "Just about seven and a half pounds and twenty inches. A pretty good size for thirty-eight weeks. You obviously took good care of yourself throughout your pregnancy."

"I tried to exercise regularly and eat healthy," she said, then felt compelled to confess, "but I sometimes gave in to insatiable cravings for French fries and gravy."

"Well, I don't think those French fries and gravy did any harm to you or your baby," Cameron assured her.

He opened a backpack she hadn't seen him carry in. "Newborn diapers and wipes," he said, pulling out a bunch of sample packs. "Some receiving blankets and baby gowns."

"Thank you," Julie said. "I've got a few outfits and sleepers in the trunk of my car, just because I wandered through a baby store the other day, but I didn't think I'd be needing diapers just yet."

"Well, there should be enough here to hold you for a couple of days, until you can get out—or send Luke out—to stock up on supplies." Then he said to his friend, "You did a good job—for someone who doesn't specialize in obstetrics."

Lukas narrowed his gaze in response to Cameron's grin, but he only said, "Julie did all the work."

"Knowing you, I don't doubt that's true," the doctor teased. "Now I'm going to get home to my wife and kids, while I still can. If the storm doesn't blow over, you might be snowed in for the whole weekend," he warned Julie. "But if you have any questions or concerns, please call."

"I'm sorry."

They were Luke's first words to Julie when he returned to the family room after seeing Cameron to the door.

"I'm not," she told him. "I'm grateful."

He sat down across from her. "You're not even a little bit mad?"

She shook her head. "I'm a little embarrassed. Okay, more than a little," she admitted. "But the truth is, I couldn't have done it without out you."

"It was an incredible experience for me, too."

"Could you do one more thing for me, though?"

"What's that?"

"Not tell anyone that you got me naked within an hour of meeting me."

"Not even my brothers?"

"No one," she said firmly.

He chuckled. "Okay, I won't tell anyone. But speaking of telling—was there anyone you wanted to call? Or have you already posted newborn photos from your phone on Facebook or Twitter?"

She shook her head. "I don't do the social media thing."

His brows lifted. "Do you do the telephone thing?"

"Of course, but I don't think any of my friends or family is expecting to hear any news about a baby just yet."

"He's only a couple weeks ahead of his due date," Lukas reminded her.

Which was true. It was also true that no one was expecting any birth announcement because no one had known that she was pregnant. Not even her parents, because it wasn't the type of news Julie wanted to tell them over the phone. She'd wanted to talk to her mother in person, to share her joy—and her fears—with the one person she was sure would understand everything she was feeling. But she'd been traveling for work for the past seven months and hadn't had a chance to go home. In fact, no one aside from her boss at The Grayson Gallery knew, and it wasn't Evangeline's voice that Julie wanted to hear right now—it was her mother's.

But more than she wanted to hear Lucinda's voice, she wanted to see her, to feel the warmth of her arms around her. Julie wondered at the irony of the realization that never had she more craved the comfort of her own mother than after becoming a mother herself.

"I guess I need to figure out a way to get home."

"You're not going anywhere until this storm passes," Lukas pointed out to her.

Watching the snow swirl outside the window, she couldn't dispute the point.

She'd hoped to be home before the weekend. She'd only taken this detour through Pinehurst to discuss some issues with the lawyer her brother had recommended. Of course, she hadn't admitted to Daniel that she was the one in need of legal advice, because he would have demanded to know what the issues were and insisted that he could handle whatever needed to be handled.

Instead, she'd told him that she had a friend in New York State—because she hadn't been too far away at the time and heading in that direction, suddenly aware that she couldn't go home until she had answers to some of the questions that had plagued her over the past several months—who was looking for a family law attorney and wondered if he had any contacts in the area.

"I guess you're stuck with us for a little bit longer, then," Julie finally said to Lukas.

"It's a big enough house that we won't be tripping over one another," he assured her.

"When the snow stops, I'll have my car towed and make arrangements for someone to come and get me."

"I already called Bruce Conacher—he owns the local garage and offers roadside assistance—to tell him that your car was in the ditch. He's put you on the list but warned me that there are at least a dozen vehicles ahead of yours."

"I'm not sure if that makes me feel better or worse—knowing that I wasn't the only one who slid off the road in that storm."

"You definitely weren't the only one," he assured her. "And I'm sure there will be more before the night is over. But on the bright side, the storm hasn't knocked out the power lines."

She shuddered at the thought.

"It's past dinnertime," he pointed out. "Are you hungry?"

"Starving," she admitted.

"How does soup and a grilled cheese sandwich sound?"

"It sounds wonderful," she said.

Luke headed back to the kitchen where he'd left the soup simmering. He ladled it into bowls, then flipped the grilled cheese out of the frying pan and onto the cutting board. He sliced each sandwich neatly in half, then transferred them to the plates he had ready. He carried the soup and sandwiches to the table, then went to the drawer for cutlery.

"It smells delicious," Julie said, coming into the room with Caden carefully tucked in the crook of one arm.

"Of course it does—you're starving," he reminded her.

She smiled at that, drawing his attention to the sweet curve of her lips.

He felt his blood pulse in his veins and silently cursed his body for suddenly waking up at the most inappropriate time. Because yes, he was in the company of a beautiful woman, but that beautiful woman had just given birth. Not to mention the fact that she was in his home only because there was a blizzard raging outside. There were a lot of reasons his libido should be in deep hibernation, a lot of reasons that feeling any hint of attraction to Julie Marlowe was wrong.

But after six months of self-imposed celibacy, his hormones apparently didn't care to be reasoned with. Not that he'd made a conscious decision to give up sex—he just hadn't met anyone that he wanted to be with. At least not longer than one night, and he was tired of that scene. He was looking for more than a casual hookup.

He could blame his brothers for that. Until recently, he hadn't wanted anything more than the casual relationships he'd always enjoyed with amiable members of the opposite sex. And then he'd started spending time with Matt and Georgia, and Jack and Kelly, and he'd realized that he envied what each of them had found. He'd even had moments when he found himself thinking that he'd like to share his life with someone who mattered, someone who would be there through the trials and tribulations.

But he figured those moments were just a phase. And the unexpected feelings stirred up by Julie Marlowe had to be another anomaly.

She was simply a stranger who had been stranded in a snowstorm. He'd opened up his home to her because it was what anyone would have done. And he'd helped deliver her baby because circumstances had given him no choice. The fact that his body was suddenly noticing that the new mom was, in fact, a very hot mama, only proved to Luke that no good deed went unpunished.

She moved toward the closest chair, and he pulled it away from the table for her. As she lowered herself onto the seat, he caught just a glimpse of shadowy cleavage in the deep V of the robe she wore before the lights flickered. Once. Twice.

Then everything went dark.

He heard Julie suck in a breath. Einstein, who had positioned himself at his master's feet as he was in the habit of doing whenever there was food in the vicinity, whimpered. Beyond that, there was no sound.

No hum of the refrigerator, no low rumbling drone of the furnace. Nothing.

And the silence was almost as unnerving as the darkness.

"So much for the power holding out," he commented, deliberately keeping his tone casual.

Thankfully, he had an emergency flashlight plugged into one of the outlets in the hall. It ran on rechargeable batteries and automatically turned on when the power went out, so the house wasn't completely pitch black. But it was pretty close.

While he waited for his eyes to adjust to the darkness, he reached for Julie's free hand, found it curled into a fist on top of the table. He covered it with his own, squeezed gently.

He heard the distant howl of the wind outside, a sound even more ominous than the silence. Julie heard it, too, and shivered.

"I've got some candles by the stove," he told her. "I'm just going to get them so we can find our food."

He found half a dozen utility candles in the drawer, set a couple of them in their metal cups on the counter and lit the wicks. The scratch of the head against the rough paper was loud in a room suddenly void of all other sound. He lit a couple more and carried them to the table.

They were purely functional—a little bit of illumination so that they could see what they were eating. And yet, there was something about dining over candlelight—even if the meal was nothing more than soup and sandwiches and the lighting was necessity rather than mood—that infused the scene with a romantic ambiance he did not want to be feeling. But somehow the simple dishes and everyday glassware looked elegant in candlelight. And when he glanced across the table, he couldn't help but notice that Julie looked even more beautiful.

"Dig in before it gets cold," he advised.

She dipped her spoon into the bowl, and brought it up to her mouth. Before her lips parted to sample the soup, they curved upward and her gaze shifted to him. "Chicken and Stars?"

"So?" he said, just a little defensively.

"So it's an unusual choice for a grown man," she said.

"It's my niece's favorite."

"How old is your niece?"

"I have two nieces," he told her. "Two nieces and two nephews. Matt's daughter, Pippa, is only a baby. Jack's daughter, Ava, is twelve going on twenty."

Her brows drew together, creating a slight furrow between them. "Is Jack short for Jackson?"

"Yeah," he admitted. "Why?"

"Your brother is Jackson Garrett?"

Now it was his turn to frown. "You know Jack?"

"Actually, he's the reason I came to Pinehurst," she admitted.

Luke carefully set his spoon down in his bowl, the few mouthfuls he'd consumed settling like a lead weight in the pit of his stomach. "Please tell me that he isn't the father of your baby."

Chapter Four

"What?" Julie lifted her head to look at him, her blue-gray eyes wide. "No. Oh, my God, no! I've never even met the man."

Luke exhaled a long, slow breath. "Okay," he finally said. "So why were you coming to Pinehurst for a man you've never met?"

"Because my brother, Daniel, knows him. They went to law school together." She picked up half of her sandwich, nibbled on the corner. "Why would you ask if your brother was the father of my baby?"

"Because it was only a few months ago that I found out Ava—the niece who likes Chicken and Stars soup—was Jack's daughter."

"She's twelve and you only met her a few months ago?"

"No—I've actually known her since she was a baby," he clarified. "But I didn't know that my brother was her father."

"I'm having a little trouble following," she admitted.

"Ava's mother, Kelly, was one of my best friends growing up. When she was in college, she had a fling with some guy and got pregnant, but she never told me who that guy was."

Julie's gaze dropped to her bowl again. "She must have had her reasons."

"She had reasons," he acknowledged. "But I'm not sure anything can justify that kind of deception."

"Is your brother still as upset about it as you are?"

His smile was wry. "Is it that obvious?"

"There was a bit of an edge to your tone."

"I was—maybe still am—upset," he admitted. "I was the first person she told when she found out she was pregnant, because I was her best friend. When Ava was born, Kelly asked me to be the godfather, but she never told me that her baby was actually my niece."

"And you didn't even suspect the connection?"

"No, I didn't suspect anything. Because I didn't know that Jack and Kelly had been involved, however briefly."

"So why didn't your brother guess that the child she was carrying might be his?"

"Because he didn't know she was pregnant. Kelly made me promise not to tell anyone," he confided. "I thought she'd met someone when she was away to school, fallen for the wrong guy and ended up pregnant. So I promised, because I never suspected that her baby was my brother's baby."

"Why didn't she tell him that she was pregnant?" Julie asked curiously.

"I guess she was planning to tell him, but by the time she knew about the baby, he was engaged to someone else."

She winced. "That would hurt."

"Yeah." He could acknowledge that fact without accepting it as justification.

"How did his wife react to the news that he had a child with someone else?"

"She never knew. They were divorced more than five years ago," he told her. "And now Jack and Kelly are engaged."

"Apparently your brother has forgiven her for keeping their child a secret."

"It took him a while, but he did. And Ava is thrilled that she's finally going to have a mother *and* a father."

"In a perfect world, every child would have two parents who loved him or her and one another," she said.

Which told him absolutely nothing about her situation. Where was Caden's father? Was he part of their lives? Luke didn't think so, considering that she hadn't wanted to contact anyone to let them know that she was in labor, or even later to share the news that she'd had her baby.

"I feel fortunate that I grew up in that kind of home," he said, in the hope that offering information to Julie would encourage her to reciprocate.

But all she said was, "That is lucky."

And then, in what seemed an obvious attempt to change the topic of conversation, "How long do you think the power will be out?"

Or maybe she was genuinely worried. He heard the concern in her voice and wished he could reassure her, but he didn't want to give her false hope. "I don't know. I think it depends on what caused the outage."

"So it could be a while," she acknowledged.

"It could," he agreed. "But we've got the fireplace and lots of blankets, candles and flashlights, and a pantry full of canned goods. I promise—you might be bored, but you won't freeze, get lost in the halls or starve."

Her lips curved. "If nothing else, today has proven to me that there's no point in worrying about things I can't control."

He could tell that she was trying to stay upbeat, but he didn't blame her for being concerned. She was a first-time mother with a brand-new baby, trapped in a stranger's house without any power in the middle of a snowstorm.

"Speaking of starving," she said. "I think this little guy's getting hungry."

By the flickering light of the candles, he could see that the baby was opening and closing his mouth and starting to squirm a little despite being snugly swaddled in one of the receiving blankets Cameron had brought from the hospital.

"Just hold on a second," Luke said, and went down the hall to retrieve the emergency flashlight.

He came back with the light and guided Julie the short distance back to the family room.

"While you're taking care of Caden, I'll get some blankets and pillows," he told her.

"Okay."

It didn't take him more than a few minutes to gather what they would need, but he took some time to putter around upstairs, giving the new mom time to finish feeding her baby. He didn't know a lot about the nursing process. Matt's wife, Georgia, had only recently weaned Pippa, and while she'd been pretty casual about the whole thing, Lukas had always averted his gaze if he was around when she was breastfeeding the baby. Not that he was uncomfortable with the act of a mother nursing her child—he just didn't think he should be looking at his brother's wife's breasts.

Of course, the whole train of thought was one that should definitely—and quickly—be derailed. Because now he was thinking about Julie's breasts. And since there was no family connection between them, and therefore no intrinsic moral conflict, he couldn't seem to shift his thoughts in a different direction.

He changed out of his jeans and shirt and into a pair of pajama pants and a long-sleeved thermal shirt. Bedtime usually meant just stripping down to his boxers and crawling beneath the sheets of his king-size bed, but he didn't want to be too far away from Julie and Caden in case either of them needed anything through the night. Not to mention that it would probably get a little chilly in his bedroom if the power stayed out through the night.

He remembered that Julie was still wearing the robe he'd given to her earlier, and while it had served the purpose of providing some cover during the childbirth process, he didn't think she would be very comfortable sleeping in it. He rummaged through his drawers until he found a pair of sweatpants with a drawstring waist and a flannel shirt with buttons that ran all the way down the front so that it would be easier for her to—

Trying *not* to think about that, he reminded himself sternly.

Instead, he turned his attention to the storm. He could hear the wind howling outside and the brush of icy snowflakes battering against the windows. If it didn't stop snowing soon, it would take him forever to clear his driveway. And if the power stayed out, it would take even longer because his snowblower required an electric start.

The starter on the gas fireplace was electric, too, so he was grateful he'd turned it on when they'd first come in from the storm. The fire would keep the family room toasty warm, which wouldn't just make it more comfortable to sleep through the night but was absolutely essential for the newborn.

He gathered up the clothes for Julie—adding a thick pair of socks to the pile—and the blankets and pillows and carted everything down the stairs. Having lived in this house his whole life, he wasn't worried about missing a step or bumping into a wall, but he was worried about Einstein getting tangled up in his feet. However, the dog was conspicuously absent as Luke made his way down the stairs, causing him to wonder where the pint-size canine had disappeared to and what mischief he might be getting into.

He found the puppy curled up beside the sofa, close to Julie and Caden.

She was obviously exhausted after her busy—and traumatic—day, and she'd fallen asleep with the baby still nursing. The sight caused an unmistakable stirring in his groin, and Luke chastised himself for the inappropriate reaction. She was a stranger, in his home and at his mercy because of the storm. She'd just given birth to a baby, and he was ogling her as if she was a centerfold.

Except that he had never seen anything as beautiful as the sight of the baby's tiny mouth suckling at his mother's breast. The tiny knitted cap that Cameron had brought from the hospital had fallen off Caden's head, revealing the wisps of soft dark hair that covered his scalp. His tiny little hand was curled into a fist and resting against his mother's pale, smooth skin.

Luke tiptoed closer to set the bundle of clothes beside her on the couch. As he neared, Einstein lifted his head, his tail thumping quietly against the floor.

"Good boy," he whispered, patting the dog's head.

Then he unfolded one of the blankets and gently laid it over the lower half of her body, careful not to cover the baby. The little guy looked up at him, those big blue eyes wide and completely unconcerned. His mother didn't even stir.

Luke took another blanket and a pillow for himself and settled into a chair nearby, prepared for a very long night.

When Julie awoke in the morning, she found the bundle of clothes Lukas had left for her on the sofa. Though she had more than a few changes of clothes in the suitcases in the trunk of her car, she didn't want to trudge through the snow to retrieve them while wearing nothing more than her host's robe, so she gratefully donned the borrowed shirt and sweats.

He'd also put a few toiletries out on the counter of the powder room: hairbrush, new toothbrush and a tube of toothpaste, all of which she put to good use.

Her first clue that the power had been restored was that the light in the powder room came on when she automatically hit the switch. Her second was the tantalizing aroma of bacon that wafted from the kitchen as she made her way down the hall. Though her grumbling stomach urged her to follow the scent, she knew she needed to take care of her baby's hunger first. Because she had no doubt that Caden would be hungry, too.

She'd lost count of how many times he'd woken her in the night, his avid little mouth instinctively seeking her breast and the sustenance it provided. And while he never seemed to nurse for extended periods of time, he nursed frequently. The books she'd read offered reassurance that this was normal, but reading about it and living it were two entirely different scenarios. She understood now why new mothers were always exhausted—feeding a newborn was pretty much a full-time job.

Of course, she also realized that she wasn't really feeding him yet, and that the frequent nursing sessions were necessary to help her milk come in. Throughout her pregnancy, she'd gone back and forth on the breast versus bottle issue but, in the end, she was persuaded by all the benefits found in breast milk—not to mention the simplicity of the method.

"Something smells delicious," she told Lukas when she finally made her way into the kitchen.

"Hopefully better than the bread and jam you would have got if the power had still been out," he told her.

"Right now, even that sounds good," she told him.

"How do bacon, eggs and toast sound?"

"Even better."

"How are you doing this morning?"

"I'm a little sore," she admitted. "And tired."

"I don't imagine you got much sleep with Caden waking you up every couple of hours."

She winced at that. "Obviously he woke you up, too."

He shrugged. "I'm a light sleeper. Thankfully, I don't need a lot of sleep, so I feel pretty good. Of course, being able to make my morning pot of coffee helped a little."

"I gave up coffee six months ago," she admitted, just a little wistfully.

"So what can I get for you?" Lukas asked. "Juice? Milk?"

"Juice is great," she said, noting that there were already two glasses poured and at the table.

He gestured for her to help herself, then pointed to the carton of eggs on the counter. "Scrambled or fried?"

"Whichever is easier."

"Which do you prefer?"

"I like both," she assured him.

He shook his head as he cracked eggs into a bowl. "You're a pleaser, aren't you? The type of person who says yes even when she wants to say no, who goes out of her way to avoid conflicts or disagreements."

She laughed. "No one's ever accused me of that before," she told him. "But I do try not to be difficult—at least not until I've known someone more than twenty-four hours."

"So how do you like your eggs?" he prompted.

"Benedict," she told him.

He chuckled. "Okay. But since I don't have hollandaise sauce, what's your second choice?"

"Scrambled," she decided.

"That wasn't so hard now, was it?" He added a splash of milk to the bowl, then a sprinkle of salt and pepper and began to whisk the eggs.

"I'll let you know after I've tried the eggs."

He grinned as he poured the mixture into the frying pan.

"My brother and sister-in-law are going to stop by later today, as soon as Matt finishes clearing his driveway."

She moved closer to the window. "I can't believe it's still snowing out there."

"It's just light flurries now," he noted. "Nothing like what we had yesterday."

"Everything looks so pretty, covered in a pristine blanket of snow."

"Take a look out the back," he suggested. "It's not quite so pristine out there."

She carried Caden to the window at the back of the room, noted that the snow there had been thoroughly—almost desperately—trampled. And then she spotted the culprit. Einstein, Lukas's puppy, was racing around as if being chased by the hounds of hell. He had his nose down and was using it like a shovel to tunnel through the cold white stuff and then, when he'd pushed enough to form a mound, he'd attack it.

She chuckled. "What is he doing?"

"I have no idea," Lukas admitted. "*He* has no idea."

"It's his first snow," she guessed.

"Yeah. He's been out there for half an hour and every few minutes, he spins in a circle and barks at it."

"Pets are a lot like kids, aren't they?" she mused. "They give you a fresh perspective on things we so often take for granted."

"Some of them," he agreed. "Daphne's perspective is neither sociable nor very sunny."

She laughed again. "Considering I haven't seen more of her than a flick of her tail, I can't disagree with that."

"She ventured downstairs last night to sleep by the fire, but I'm sure it wasn't for company but only warmth."

"It was warm," Julie agreed. "I even threw the blanket off a couple of times in the night."

"I thought about turning the fire off, but until the power came back on, I was reluctant to lose our only source of heat."

"I really can't thank you enough," she said. "When I think about what could have happened if you hadn't come home and found me in the ditch last night—"

"There's no reason to think about anything like that," Lukas told her.

"Well, I'm grateful. I don't know anyone else who would have done everything that you've done—for me and Caden."

"If the people you know would have left a laboring mother trapped in a ditch, you need to meet new people."

She managed to smile at that. "Okay—most of my friends would have opened their doors under those circumstances, but I don't know that their hospitality would have outlasted the storm."

"Are you suggesting that I should throw you out into a snow bank now?"

"Well, maybe you could wait until after you've fed me breakfast," she suggested.

He set a plate in front of her, then reached for Caden.

Julie transferred the baby to him without any protest or hesitation. After all, this man had helped bring her son into the world. And even if that hadn't been her choice at the time, she couldn't fault his competence—and she couldn't forget the expression of awe and wonder on his face as he'd gazed down at her newborn baby. Or the sense of absolute rightness that she'd felt in the moment that he'd placed the tiny, naked body in her arms so that he could cut the cord.

It was as if that act had somehow forged a bond between them—two strangers brought together by circumstances neither of them could ever have foreseen.

"He really is tiny, isn't he?" Lukas said, settling the sleeping baby into the crook of his arm. "I'll bet he doesn't weigh half as much as Einstein."

"You wouldn't say he was tiny if you'd had to push him out of your body," Julie told him, and dug into her eggs.

He winced at the thought as he picked up his own plate to take it to the table. "You're probably right about that."

She nibbled at a slice of crisp bacon and hummed with pleasure as the salty, smoky flavor flooded her taste buds. "Why is it that the foods that are so bad for you always taste so good?"

"I never really thought about it," he said, scooping up a forkful of eggs.

"You wouldn't."

"What's that supposed to mean?"

"You're a guy. You don't have to count calories or worry about fat content or carbs."

He shrugged as he chewed. "I pretty much eat what I want to eat."

"For the past several months, I have, too," she admitted. "I figured a pregnant woman should be allowed some latitude. Of course, I'll probably regret it when those extra ten pounds keep me in maternity clothes for another couple of months."

"You don't look as if you're carrying ten extra pounds," he told her.

"Right now it's more like twenty."

"Then you were too skinny before."

She picked up another slice of bacon. "No one ever accused me of being skinny, either," she assured him.

He studied her from across the table for a minute before he asked, "Why would you want to be?"

It wasn't a question anyone had ever asked her before. All of her friends—everyone she knew—wanted to be thinner, prettier, richer. It was every American woman's dream. Wasn't it?

"I've never understood why women obsess so much about their bodies," Lukas continued.

"Yeah, because men never judge us on the basis of our appearance," she said dryly.

He didn't deny it. "A pretty face and an appealing figure usually catch our attention," he admitted. "But men are simple creatures. We're not looking for perfection—we're just looking for a woman who's willing to get naked with us."

Her brows lifted. "Really?"

"Pretty much."

"I'll be sure to share that insight with my friends when we're sweating through Zumba classes."

He grinned. "We also like women who aren't afraid to shake their stuff."

Julie couldn't help smiling at the predictably male response. And as she finished her breakfast, she found herself marveling over the fact that she'd known Lukas for such a short period of time but somehow felt comfortable and at ease with him.

At home in Springfield, she knew a lot of people through her job at The Grayson Gallery and through her association with Elliot. As a result, she felt as if she had a certain image to uphold. She would never pop out for a quart of milk unless her hair was neat and her makeup immaculate. She rarely wore blue jeans and the only gym shoes she owned were exclusively for use in the gym.

Now she was wearing borrowed clothes that didn't fit, her hair was in a haphazard ponytail and her face was bare of makeup. And maybe it was because Lukas had held her hand as she sweated through labor and childbirth, but he seemed unaffected by the absence of mascara on her lashes and he honestly didn't seem to care who she was. He'd come to her aid simply because that was the kind of man he was, with no ulterior motive or hidden agenda. It wasn't just a surprising but a liberating revelation.

As was the fact that when he talked to her, he actually

seemed to listen to what she was saying—even if they were having a nonsensical conversation about carb counting or Zumba classes. He was charming and funny and genuine, and she'd never known anyone quite like him.

And whenever he smiled at her, she felt a subtle clenching low in her belly that made her just a little bit uneasy. Not because she worried that he would do or say anything inappropriate, but because she was worried that her response to him was inappropriate.

The last time she'd had sex was probably the night that Caden was conceived. In the eight and half months since then, she'd hardly thought about it—she certainly hadn't missed it. So why was she thinking about it now?

Was this flood of hormones through her system simply a side effect of the birth experience? Or was it connected to the sexy man who had rescued her from a blizzard and delivered her baby?

If she'd met Lukas Garrett in a different time and place—and if she wasn't the new mother of a beautiful baby boy—she would probably strike up a conversation, flirt with him a little, see if there was any evidence that the sizzle she felt was reciprocated.

But it wasn't a different time or place, and Caden was her priority. She didn't have the leisure or the energy for any kind of romantic complications.

As she pushed away from the table to carry her empty plate to the sink, she couldn't help but feel just a little bit disappointed by the fact.

Chapter Five

The window by the sink overlooked the driveway, and as she glanced outside, she realized that she'd been so focused on the snow earlier she hadn't noticed that it was cleared.

"How did you have time to shovel your driveway already?" she asked.

"I didn't. Jon Quinlan came by first thing this morning with his plow."

"Is he a neighbor?"

"Not exactly."

It was an evasive response from a man who had impressed her as being anything but, and it piqued her curiosity. "Then what is he—exactly?"

"He owns a landscaping and yard maintenance company."

"So why didn't you just say that you hire someone to clear it?"

"Because I didn't hire him," he admitted. "And he won't let me pay him."

"He must not have a very successful business if he works for free." She returned to the table and took the baby again.

"That's what I keep telling him, but Jon thinks he owes me. His daughter has a poodle-mix named Sparky. A few years back, Sparky had a hernia, but Jon had just been laid off from his job and didn't have the money for the surgery."

"But you did the surgery, anyway," she guessed.

He lifted one shoulder. "I couldn't let the animal suffer."

And in that moment, she realized it was true. Someone else might have turned the man away, but Lukas Garrett couldn't. It simply wasn't in him to do nothing when he could help. She also realized that he wasn't comfortable talking about what he'd done because he didn't think it was a big deal.

So instead of commenting on his generosity, she asked, "What kind of pet does Mrs. Kurchik have?"

He was visibly startled by her question—so she tapped a finger to the label that advertised "Mrs. Kurchik's Peach Jam" on the jar.

He shrugged again. "An aging basset hound and a battle-scarred tabby cat."

"The joys of living and working in a small town?"

"Pinehurst isn't nearly as small as it used to be, but the population growth hasn't affected the sense of community," he told her.

Before she could comment further, she heard something that sounded like a thud from behind the door to the laundry room. "What was that?"

"Einstein," he admitted. "He can come in and out through the doggy door, but I closed the inside door so that he doesn't race in and track snow through the house."

She frowned as another thump sounded. "Is he...knocking?"

He laughed. "Maybe he does think that's what he's doing. It's certainly a better explanation than that he likes to bang his head against the door." He pushed away from the table. "I'd better go dry his paws and let him in before he gives himself brain damage—if it's not already too late."

While Lukas was dealing with the dog, Julie decided to give her parents a call. She bypassed the handset on the table for her cell phone. Not just because she didn't want her host to incur long-distance charges for the call but because she didn't know how to explain a stranger's name and number showing up on her parents' call display. It was easier all around to call from her cell, as she was in the habit of doing.

When she heard her mother's voice on the other end of the line, her throat tightened and her eyes filled with tears.

"Hello?" Lucinda said again when Julie was unable to respond. Then, confirming that her mother had checked the display, "Julie—is that you?"

She cleared her throat. "Yes, it's me. Hi, Mom."

"Is everything okay?"

"Of course," she said. "I think the connection just cut out for a second."

"I'm so pleased to hear from you. I was going to call from the car on the way to the airport, but I wasn't sure of your schedule."

"You're going to the airport?"

"We're on our way to Melbourne." Lucinda practically sang out the announcement. "Your dad booked the tickets for our thirty-fifth anniversary."

Julie wondered for a minute if she'd somehow overlooked the milestone because of everything going on in her own life, but she knew that she hadn't. "Your anniversary isn't until the end of the month."

"But Reg wanted us to be there for our anniversary," her mother explained. "To celebrate thirty-five years together at the place we met."

Julie knew the story, of course. Her mother had been an

American student studying in Melbourne, her father had been on vacation after his first year of law school, and they'd met at a café near Brighton Beach.

"We always said we would go back some day, but we never did. After we got married, we got so busy with other things. Your father was building his career, and I was focused on raising four children."

"You sound really excited about this," Julie said, wishing that she could share her mother's enthusiasm. For the past several months, she'd been looking forward to going home. Now her return was almost imminent, but her parents weren't even going to be there. And she was more than a little apprehensive about the prospect of returning to Massachusetts—and facing Elliott—while they were away.

"We both are," Lucinda told her. "It's been a long time since we've been on vacation together, just the two of us."

"Then it's definitely long overdue," she agreed with false cheerfulness. "When will you be home?"

"December seventh."

"You're going for more than a month?"

"Thirty-five days—one for each year we've been together."

Which, Julie had to admit, was an incredibly romantic gesture on her father's part. And it was incredibly selfish of her to be upset because her parents were leaving the country rather than hanging around at home to welcome the grandchild they didn't know they had.

"That's…wonderful," she finally said.

"You'll be home by then, too, won't you?" Lucinda asked her.

"I'll be home by then," Julie promised, gently tracing the curve of her baby's cheek with her fingertip. "With a surprise for you."

"For me?" Lucinda sounded delighted.

"For both you and Dad."

"I can't wait," her mother said. "Although honestly, it's enough to know that you're finally coming home. We've missed you, baby."

She felt the sting of tears in the back of her eyes. "I've missed you, too. All of you."

"You're doing okay, though?" Lucinda prompted.

"I'm doing better than okay," Julie assured her. "I needed the time away, to figure some things out, but I'm looking forward to coming home." And it was true, even if the thought of seeing her former fiancé tied her stomach into knots.

"Where are you now?"

"In Upstate New York."

"I saw on the news that there's a big storm moving in that direction. You make sure you keep an eye on it," her mother advised.

Julie had to smile. "I'll do that."

"Oh, your father's tapping his watch," Lucinda said regretfully. "I have to run."

"Okay. Give my love to Dad. And have a fabulous time."

After Einstein was dry, Lukas carried him into the kitchen to ensure that he didn't try to jump all over their guests. Except that when he opened the laundry room door, he found Julie's chair was empty and both mother and son were gone.

His heart gave a little jolt—an instinctive response that he didn't want to think about too deeply—but settled again when he heard her voice in the family room. At first he thought she was talking to Caden, but as he finished tidying up the dishes from breakfast—not an easy task with the dog tucked under his arm—he realized that she was on the phone. Though he wasn't trying to listen to her conversation, he couldn't help but hear bits and pieces of it. She sounded cheerful and upbeat, so he was surprised—and distressed—to enter the family room after she'd ended the call and see tears on her cheeks.

From the time they were kids, his brothers had always teased him about his protective instincts. He never liked to see anyone or anything hurting. It was one of the reasons he'd become a vet—to help heal injured creatures. It still broke his heart when he couldn't save one of them, and it still brought him to his knees whenever he saw a woman in tears.

"Julie?" He crouched down beside the sofa, setting Einstein on the floor by his feet. "Is everything okay?"

She wiped at the wet streaks on her cheeks, but the tears continued to fall. "I'm sorry."

"Don't apologize," he said. "Just tell me what I can do to help."

She offered a wobbly smile but shook her head. "Nothing. I'm just being a big baby."

Which he didn't believe for a minute. "Do you want to tell me about the phone call?"

"My mom," she admitted. "I guess, now that I'm a mom, too, I really wanted to hear her voice and to tell her that I would be home in a few days. I haven't seen them in a while—my fault, because I was working out of town—and I just found out that she and my dad are going to Australia for a month."

He frowned. "They couldn't postpone their trip to see you and meet their new grandson?"

"They probably could—and they would."

"But?" he prompted.

"But it's their thirty-fifth anniversary and the trip was a surprise for my mom from my dad, a journey back to the place they first met."

"You didn't tell them that you had the baby, did you?"

"No," she admitted.

"Will there be anyone else at home when you get there?"

She shook her head. "My youngest brother, Ethan, is at school in Washington. He won't be home until Christmas break. Daniel lives in Boston and Kevin in New Haven."

"Are you going to tell them about Caden?"

"I can't tell them before I tell my parents," she said matter-of-factly.

"What about…" He wanted to ask about Caden's father, but he let the words fade away. He was undeniably curious, but he had no right to ask. They had been brought together by circumstances beyond anyone's control, and he didn't want to make her uncomfortable by pressing for information she didn't want to give.

She looked up at him, waiting for him to finish his question. She seemed to tense, as if she anticipated what he was going to ask and didn't want to answer. But instead he only said, "What do your brothers do?"

"Daniel's a corporate attorney, Kevin's the producer of a talk radio station and Ethan is still trying to figure out what he wants to be when he grows up."

"How old is he?"

"Twenty-seven," she admitted.

"You're the youngest."

"Is that a statement or a question?"

"It's a guess," he admitted. "But you don't look like you're even close to thirty."

"I'm the youngest," she confirmed, but didn't actually tell him how old she was.

"And the only girl."

She nodded.

"How was that—growing up with three older brothers?"

"Most of the time it was great," she said, then one corner of her mouth quirked upward in a half smile. "Except when it wasn't."

Being one of three brothers himself, he knew what she meant.

"Any of them married? Kids?"

"Just Kevin. He and Brooke recently celebrated their second anniversary, and they're expecting their first child in March."

"So Caden is the first grandchild for your parents?"

She nodded.

He frowned. "That's a pretty big milestone for most people."

She just nodded again.

He sensed that there was something she wasn't telling him, something she didn't want to tell him. And although he knew it wasn't any of his business—after all, they were only strangers whose paths would never have crossed if not for an unexpected snowstorm—he couldn't help but comment. "I know Caden came a couple of weeks early, but I wouldn't have thought they'd make plans to go anywhere when you were so close to your due date."

She finally lifted her gaze to meet his. "They wouldn't have—if they'd known I was pregnant."

He couldn't quite get his head around what she was saying. "Are you telling me that you managed to keep your pregnancy a secret from your family for the better part of nine months?"

"I didn't intend to keep it a secret," she admitted. "I wanted to tell them. But when I first left town, I didn't know I was pregnant."

"When did you know?"

"A few days later. And then, I didn't know *how* to tell them. It didn't seem like the kind of news I should share over the phone, and I was sure I would see them soon. But my job kept me so busy, I never had a chance to go home."

"You haven't been home in nine months?"

"Actually, it's more like seven months—since April," she admitted.

"And that kind of extended absence isn't unusual?"

"It was an extraordinary career opportunity," she explained. "As an art curator at The Grayson Gallery, I was invited to travel to select galleries around the United States with Evangeline Grayson's private collection of impressionist and post-impressionist art."

"Has it been that long since you've seen Caden's father, too?" Luke asked.

"Caden doesn't have a father," she said coolly.

His brows lifted. "I might not have any kids of my own, but I'm pretty sure I understand the basics of reproduction."

"Then you know that donating sperm doesn't make a man a father."

He didn't believe that her child had been conceived through intrauterine insemination. She seemed too young to have chosen that route—and too defensive. Which suggested that the story of Caden's father was a little more complicated than she wanted him to know.

And while he had a lot more questions, he accepted that she had no obligation to tell him anything. He also suspected that if he pushed for answers, she might lie, and he'd rather wait until she trusted him enough to tell him the truth.

So all he said was, "I just got a message from Bruce. He's towed your car, but he won't have a chance to look at it until Monday at the earliest."

"Monday?" she echoed, obviously disappointed.

He shrugged. "He's going to be busy the rest of the day hauling cars out of ditches, and he doesn't work on Sundays."

"I guess I should make some kind of arrangements, then."

"Arrangements for what?" he asked.

"Transportation to a hotel."

"We don't have a hotel in Pinehurst," he told her. "There are a few bed-and-breakfasts, and one roadside motel on the outskirts of town, but no hotel."

She frowned at that. "I guess I could try the motel."

"Why would you want to try somewhere else when there's plenty of room for both you and Caden here?"

She was shaking her head even before he finished speaking.

"Why not?" he challenged.

"Because we've imposed on you too much already."

"It's not an imposition."

"How is having a stranger and her newborn baby in your home *not* an imposition?"

"Because I want you to stay," he told her honestly. "At least until the weather clears and your car is fixed."

He didn't need to point out that there was no one waiting for her at home, as her response confirmed.

"I feel like I should decline your invitation, but considering that my options are extremely limited right now, I'll say thank you instead."

"You're welcome. I made up the bed in the first room at the top of the stairs," he told her. "It has a private en-suite bathroom, so you don't have to worry about sharing one."

"Does it have a shower?"

"As a matter of fact, it does."

"Because I would really appreciate being able to... Oh, no."

"What's wrong?"

"My suitcases are in the trunk of my car, and my car's on its way to Bruce's Body Shop."

"Your suitcases are already upstairs in the spare bedroom."

"They are?"

He shrugged. "You mentioned that you'd been travelling, so I figured you'd have some essentials with you. I got your luggage out of the trunk this morning."

"Thank you," she said sincerely. "After a shower and some clean clothes, I just might feel human again."

The guest room was bathed in natural light that poured through the pair of tall narrow windows. The double bed was covered in a beautiful sage-green comforter in a rich suede-like fabric. The dressers had strong but simple lines and were made of light-colored wood, and—as promised—her suitcases were on top of the blanket chest at the foot of the bed. The overall effect of the room was both warm and welcoming, and Julie wanted nothing as much as she wanted to fall into the bed and sleep for several hours.

Actually, that wasn't entirely true. As much as she wanted sleep, she wanted a shower even more. She opened the biggest suitcase and found her robe, then dug around for the toiletry bag with her shampoo, body wash and feminine hygiene products. Thankfully, she'd thought to stock up a few weeks earlier, because she wouldn't want to have to ask Lukas to make a trip to the pharmacy for her. On the other hand, the man had willingly stepped in to deliver her baby, so there probably wasn't much that fazed him.

The en-suite bathroom not only had a glass-walled shower with an adjustable showerhead but a separate soaker tub. For just a few seconds, Julie imagined herself sinking into a tub filled to the rim with frothy, scented bubbles, but she didn't want to chance taking a bath without checking with a doctor first. She also didn't want to leave Lukas with Caden for too long. Her host seemed comfortable and easy with the baby and she appreciated his willingness to help with him, but her son was her responsibility and a quick shower would have to suffice.

The towels on the rack were the same sage color as the spread in the bedroom, and thick and fluffy. There were apothecary jars filled with cotton swabs and cotton balls on the granite countertop and an assortment of decorative soaps in a basket on the apron of the tub.

She reached into the shower to turn on the faucet, then quickly stripped out of her clothes. When she stepped under the spray, the warm, pulsing water felt so good she nearly whimpered with relief. She poured a handful of body wash into her hand, then slicked it over her skin. She'd always figured that they called it *labor* because it wasn't a walk in the park, but she hadn't expected it to be such sweaty work. In retrospect, however, she was grateful that the process had gone so smoothly.

Since she'd learned of her pregnancy, Julie had been focused on doing everything she could to take care of herself and her unborn child. Everything she'd done over the past eight months had been with the goal of giving birth to a healthy baby.

Of course, she hadn't planned to give birth on a stranger's family-room couch, but when the only alternative was the frigid interior of a ditched car, it was undoubtedly the better option.

She'd thought about the birthing process a lot in recent months, but she'd always imagined herself in a brightly lit and sterile hospital room with a team of doctors and nurses around her. She'd never considered a home birth. That was fine for other people, if they chose, but not for her. She wanted to be in a hospital with medical personnel and pain-numbing drugs and emergency equipment in case of any complications.

It had been scary, the realization that there were none of those supports available when she went into labor, and she was sincerely thankful that there had been no problems. She was even more thankful that Lukas had been there to deliver her baby. Yeah, the realization that he was a veterinarian and not a medical doctor had thrown her for a minute, but in the end, all that really mattered was that he'd helped bring Caden into the world, because there was no way she could have done it without him.

It wasn't just that he'd been there to catch the baby—his calm demeanor and patient reassurance had alleviated a lot of her doubts and fears so that the process wasn't quite as terrifying as it might otherwise have been. She hadn't planned on having anyone in the delivery room with her and had resigned herself to going through the process alone.

In the end, however, she didn't feel as if she'd been alone at all. Lukas Garrett might have been a stranger, but he'd been there for her. And now, after everything they'd shared, she really felt as if he was a friend—someone she could count on.

Trust didn't come easily to her, especially not since the incident with Elliot, but she trusted Lukas. Of course, she'd had no choice but to trust him when she was in the middle of labor. She couldn't get to the hospital and her baby refused to wait to be born. But with every look, every word and every touch, he'd been compassionate and gentle and reassuring. And when she'd finally pushed her baby out into the world, she'd been grateful not just that someone was there to receive him, but that it was Lukas.

She squirted shampoo into her hand, scrubbed it through her hair. Through the whole childbirth experience, she'd been so preoccupied with the process and trying not to panic that she hadn't thought about anything else. She'd barely even noticed her rescuer's impressive physical attributes—but she hadn't been nearly as preoccupied this morning.

A brand-new mother probably shouldn't be aware of the incredible sexiness of a well-built man, but she was still a woman, and Lukas Garrett was definitely a man. A man who made her blood hum and her skin tingle, and those were very definite warning signs that Julie should keep a safe distance from him.

She'd been hurt by Elliott. Not just by his actions and his words, but by the realization that she hadn't known her fiancé nearly as well as she'd thought she did. She'd seen only what she wanted to see, and she'd made the wrong choice. Again.

Her father—a baseball aficionado—was fond of the expression "three strikes and you're out." So after Julie's third strike in the romance department, she'd accepted that it was time to walk off the field. That was it—she was finished with dating and done with men.

Travelling across the country with Evangeline's collection, she'd had more than a few handsome men cross her path. But none of them had made her feel anything. She chatted, she flirted—it was part of the job, after all, to be sociable—but she didn't feel anything. In fact, she'd been certain that she wouldn't ever feel anything again, that what Elliott had done had left her numb inside.

She wasn't feeling numb now.

She knew that her body was flooded with hormones as a result of the pregnancy and childbirth processes. It was entirely possible that her physiological response had absolutely nothing to do with Lukas Garrett personally and everything to do with the fact that she had an overabundance of estrogen and progesterone zinging through her system that wanted to rendezvous with the testosterone in his.

Except that she hadn't had the same reaction to Cameron Turcotte. The other man was arguably just as handsome as the veterinarian, but her pulse hadn't even fluttered when he'd walked into the room. Of course, he'd also worn a wide gold band on the third finger of his left hand, so maybe her hormones weren't completely indiscriminate, after all. Or maybe it was the emotional connection that had been forged through the sharing of the childbirth experience with Lukas that was stirring her up inside.

Whatever the reason, it was a complication she didn't need or want. Thankfully, this awareness or attraction or whatever she was feeling wouldn't be an issue for long. As soon as Bruce checked over her car and deemed it road-worthy, she would be on her way back to Springfield and would probably never see Lukas Garrett again.

With that thought, she flicked off the tap and reached for a towel. Every inch of her skin felt hypersensitive, almost achy, as she rubbed the thick terry cloth over her body. It had been a long time since anyone had touched her—since she'd even thought about a man's hands on her. But she was thinking about it now. And wanting.

Muttering an oath of frustration, she wrapped the robe around herself and knotted the belt at her waist. Her hair was dripping wet, and she'd forgotten to get her hair dryer out of the suitcase, so she strode back into the bedroom to retrieve it—and let out a startled gasp.

Chapter Six

Luke didn't realize Julie had finished in the shower until he heard her gasp.

"Sorry." His apology was immediate and sincere. "I didn't hear the water shut off, and I didn't expect you to finish in the shower so quickly." Which was true, even if it didn't begin to explain his presence in her bedroom.

She tugged on the lapel of her robe, no doubt to close the open V that he couldn't help but notice dipped low between her breasts. "What are you doing in here?"

"I found something in the attic that I thought you could use."

She glanced at Caden, lying on his back in the middle of the bed, as if to reassure herself that he hadn't been abandoned or neglected. "What is it?"

"Come and have a look," he invited, and stepped aside so that she could see.

Her gaze shifted, her eyes went wide. "Oh. Wow."

Her instinctive response obliterated any lingering doubts about his impulsive gesture.

She took one step forward, then another. She knelt beside the cherry wood cradle, her lips curving as she ran a hand over the smooth, glossy wood. "This is…beautiful."

"It's old," he admitted.

"Timeless," she whispered, almost reverently. Then looked up at him. "Was it yours?"

He nodded. "But it was Jack's before it was mine, and Matt's before that."

She trailed a finger down one of the spindles. "I've never seen anything like it."

"It was handmade by Rob Turcotte—Cam's father. He was a really good friend of my dad's—and an incredibly talented carpenter. He made it as a gift to my parents when my mom was expecting Matt."

Luke was babbling, but he couldn't seem to stop himself. Because he hoped that conversation would help focus his attention on something—*anything*—but the sexy curves of the woman in front of him.

He knew that he should look away, but he seemed to be suffering a momentary disconnect between his eyes and his brain. Or maybe he was simply a red-blooded man facing a beautiful, mostly naked woman. Looking at her now, he never would have guessed that she'd given birth just about eighteen hours earlier.

Her skin was rosy from the shower, and droplets of water glistened on her skin. The short silky robe belted at her waist did nothing to hide her distinctly feminine shape, and the hem skimmed just above her knees, drawing attention to her long, sexy legs.

His gaze skimmed upward again, and he couldn't help but notice that her wet hair tumbled over her shoulders, dripping onto her robe so that there were wet patches on the fabric just above her breasts. And when he realized that the nipples of those breasts were taut beneath the silky fabric, his mouth went completely dry and the blood in his head started to quickly migrate south.

He took a deliberate step back, a tactical retreat.

She cleared her throat, then gestured to the suitcases at the end of the bed. "I forgot my, um, hair dryer."

He nodded. "Clothes," he said, his voice sounding strangled. "You might want some clothes, too."

Her cheeks flushed prettily. "Yeah."

"I'll get out of your way," he said, and hurried out of the room.

After Julie's hair was dried and she was dressed in a pair of yoga pants and a tunic-style top, she fed Caden again before carrying him back downstairs to the family room. Apparently Lukas had found more than a cradle in the attic, because he was now in the process of putting together something that looked like a playpen.

"This doesn't have any sentimental value," he said, when she entered the room. "It's just old. And it probably doesn't comply with current safety guidelines, but since Caden isn't rolling around yet, it should suffice if you want to put him down for a few minutes without having to worry about Einstein climbing over him."

She eyed the structure dubiously as she settled back on the sofa. Although Lukas's puppy had actually shown incredible restraint around the baby so far, she wasn't convinced that the well-spaced spindles would keep him out. "Are you sure Einstein can't squeeze through those bars?"

"I'm sure," Lukas said. "He's tried three times already and he keeps getting his head stuck."

"Oh, the poor thing." She rubbed behind the puppy's ears,

and his whole back end wagged happily in response to the attention.

"The 'poor thing' should have learned after the first try," Lukas grumbled.

"Isn't perseverance a virtue?"

"What you think of as perseverance others might consider stubbornness or stupidity," he said, with a stern look at the puppy.

Einstein, obviously sensing his master's disapproval, dropped his head and looked up at him with sad eyes.

Julie had to bite down on her lip to hold back a smile. "I think he's a lot smarter than you give him credit for."

Before he could respond to that, the back door slammed, and she heard a female voice say, "Snowsuits and boots off." The command was followed by the rustle of outerwear being shed and the thump of boots hitting the floor, then footsteps pounded.

Lukas winced. "It sounds like Matt may have brought the whole family," he warned.

She was afraid to ask what "the whole family" entailed, but the first part of the answer was apparent when two dark-haired boys raced into the room. They were similarly dressed in jeans and hooded sweatshirts, one red and the other blue, and Einstein raced to greet them, dancing around their legs.

"Where is he?" The one in red pushed ahead. "I wanna see him."

"Me, too," his brother chimed in.

Lukas stood in front of Julie—a human barrier between the new mom and the eager twins—and held up his hands. "Slow down, boys."

"But we wanna see the baby," red shirt entreated. "We don't have a boy baby at our house."

"We just gots a girl," blue shirt said.

"You *have* a girl," an authoritative female voice said from the doorway.

The boy in red tilted his head to peek around Lukas. "Her name's Pippa," he told Julie. "She's our sister."

"And who are you?" she asked him.

Now that the boys weren't barreling full-speed ahead, Lukas stepped aside so that they could talk to Julie—and see the baby.

"I'm Quinn." He nudged his brother closer. "This is Shane."

"And I'm their mother." The other woman set an overflowing laundry basket on the floor beside the sofa. "Georgia."

Her smile was warm and genuine, and Julie found herself responding easily. "Julie Marlowe. And this is Caden."

"Oh—he's absolutely gorgeous," Georgia said, crouching down for a closer look.

"Speaking of gorgeous—where is Pippa?" Lukas asked.

Georgia slapped a hand to her forehead. "I knew I was forgetting something."

Julie actually felt her heart skip a beat. Had she really—

Then the boys giggled.

"You didn't forget her," Quinn assured his mother. "She's with Daddy."

"We gots a new daddy," Shane told Julie. "'Cuz our first daddy went to heaven."

Julie didn't have a clue how to respond to that, so she was relieved when Georgia spoke up.

"There are some more things in the van," she told Lukas. "And the boys insisted on bringing Finn and Fred, too, so I'm sure Matt would appreciate a hand."

"I've got two I can lend him," he said, and headed out to do that.

"Who are Finn and Fred?" Julie wondered.

"Our puppies!" Quinn announced.

"From the same litter as Einstein," Georgia elaborated.

"The local softhearted vet was stuck with eight orphaned puppies, and somehow convinced his brother to take two of them."

"What's a orphan?" Shane wanted to know.

"*An* orphan is someone who doesn't have a mommy or a daddy," his mother explained.

"How was he born if he didn't have a mommy?"

Georgia forced a smile. "Can we save this conversation for home? We came here to meet Julie and her baby, remember?"

Shane nodded. "He's even smaller than Pippa."

"She was about the same size as Caden when she was born," Georgia told him. "Although it's probably hard to remember that now."

"I never heard of the name Caden," Quinn told Julie. "But we gotsa Cain in our kinnergarden class."

"He eats glue," Shane informed her solemnly.

Julie had to chuckle at that. "Well, hopefully I'll teach Caden not to do that before it's time for him to go to school."

The boys crowded closer to get a better view of the baby. Caden looked back at them, his big blue eyes wide. For a whole minute, neither of the twins moved, they just watched intently.

Finally Quinn's gaze shifted to Julie. "Does he do *anything*?"

"Not really," she admitted. "Right now, he eats a lot and sleeps a lot."

"Does he poop a lot, too?" the boy wanted to know. "'Cuz Pippa does."

Julie found herself laughing again. "Well, he hasn't done a lot of that yet, but he was only born yesterday."

She saw movement in the doorway, and glanced over just as Lukas walked back in. Two seconds later, she realized that it wasn't Lukas, after all, but a man who looked so much like him, he had to be his brother. And the baby on his hip—an adorable little girl dressed in pink overalls with tiny pink sneakers on her feet—had to be Pippa.

"There's my girl," Georgia said.

Pippa smiled widely, showing four tiny pearly white teeth, and held her arms out to her mother.

"She is gorgeous," Julie said.

"That's because she looks just like her mama," Matt said, touching a hand to his wife's shoulder.

"Another unbiased opinion," she said dryly.

He just grinned. "I'm Matt," he said, offering his hand to Julie. "The *real* Dr. Garrett."

"Not that he has much more experience than Lukas when it comes to delivering babies," Georgia said.

"I did an obstetrics rotation in med school," he pointed out.

"How many years ago was that?" his wife challenged.

"More than I'm willing to admit."

"Well, according to Dr. Turcotte, Lukas did just fine," Julie told him.

"Lukas had the easy part," Matt told her.

"I'm not sure how easy it was to keep me from going into full-scale panic when I realized I wasn't going to make it to the hospital to have my baby," she admitted. "But he did it."

"Those Garretts know how to get what they want," Georgia told her.

"That we do." Her husband's admission was accompanied by a quick grin.

"I wanna play outside," Quinn said. "In the snow."

"Me, too," Shane said.

"That sounds like a terrific idea," their mother agreed. "Especially if Daddy and Uncle Lukas go with you."

Both boys turned to Matt. "Yeah, Daddy. *Pleeease.*"

He looked at Georgia, his brows lifted. "Trying to get rid of me?"

"Just so that Julie and I can share labor stories and talk about babies and breasts and—"

"I'll go play with the boys," he said.

"Yay!" They raced out of the room with as much energy and enthusiasm as they'd raced into it.

Matt dropped a kiss on the top of his wife's head and walked out of the room.

"I'm so sorry," Georgia apologized when they were gone. "I really tried to entice the boys to stay at home with Ava—Jack and Kelly's daughter—but even though they absolutely adore their cousin, they didn't want any part of that today."

"I'm glad you brought them," Julie assured her. "They're fabulous kids."

"Most days," Georgia acknowledged with a weary smile.

"And Matt—does he always do what you tell him to?"

"Usually." The other woman grinned. "Of course, it helps that it's usually what he wants to do, anyway. And he loves spending time with the kids—it gives him an excuse to act like a kid himself."

"Do you mind if I ask you another question?"

"Ask away."

"How did you manage two of them? I feel as if I didn't sleep at all last night, and Caden's only one baby."

"I wasn't on my own when the twins were born. Their dad worked a lot of long hours, but it seriously helped me get through the day just knowing that I could pass one or both of them off to him when he got home. So if you have any kind of support network, I would strongly recommend you utilize it."

"I'll keep that in mind," Julie said.

She was relieved that Georgia hadn't asked about Caden's father. She didn't want to lie but she didn't know any of these people well enough to tell them the truth. Still, she knew that she needed to tell someone, which made her think again about the appointment she'd missed with Jackson Garrett.

Since her reasons for wanting to consult with a lawyer hadn't changed, she should reschedule that appointment. Except now that her brother's friend was also the brother of the man who had delivered her baby, the situation was a little more complicated, making her doubt whether she should confide in him or find different legal counsel.

"Another thing to keep in mind is that it will get easier," Georgia told her. "It will take a while, but you and Caden will establish rhythms and routines, you'll start to anticipate his needs and adjust your schedule accordingly."

"Fingers crossed," Julie said.

"And when things get really crazy and you want to outscream your screaming baby, just try to remember that incredible feeling of love and joy that filled your heart when he was first placed in your arms."

"I still feel that," Julie admitted. "Every time I look at him."

"Savor it," Georgia advised.

"What aren't you telling me?"

The other woman hesitated, then shrugged. "Pippa went through a colicky stage, which was pretty much pure hell for about three months."

Julie looked at the smiling, cooing baby. "Neither of you looks any the worse for wear."

"Not now," Georgia agreed.

"You have a beautiful family."

"I'm a lucky woman—although it took me a while to get settled here in Pinehurst and realize how very lucky."

"You're not from here?"

Georgia shook her head. "I moved from New York City last February."

"That's a major change—not with respect to geography so much as lifestyle, I would think."

"You'd be right. But I needed to make a major change.

Phillip, my first husband, passed away when I was pregnant with Pippa, and I found it more than a little overwhelming to be on my own with two toddlers and another baby on the way. So when my mother invited me to move in with her, it seemed like a perfect solution." She smiled wryly. "And it was until four months later when she moved to Montana."

"Why Montana?"

"She fell in love with a cowboy." Georgia smiled. "Which was great for her but a little unsettling for me, since I'd moved here to be closer to her. And then Matt moved in next door to me."

"That's how you met?"

She nodded. "And three months later, we got married."

"Fast work," Julie mused.

"On his part or mine?"

"I guess you'd have to tell me."

Georgia chuckled. "I wasn't looking for happily-ever-after. I wasn't even looking for a relationship. I had my hands more than full enough with three kids, but Matt found a way to be there, to fit in, to be everything I never knew I needed. How could I not fall head over heels in love?"

Julie didn't envy the other woman her happiness. Georgia had obviously traveled a difficult road to get to where she was at. But she did wonder what it would be like to fall head over heels in love and to know, as Georgia obviously did, that she was loved the same way in return.

Julie had never experienced that depth of emotion. She'd had intense crushes and serious infatuations, all of which had eventually faded or fizzled. She'd thought she was in love with Elliott—she never would have agreed to marry him otherwise—but she also would never have described herself as head over heels. Their affection for one another had grown over time, a result of common goals and shared interests. Which, in retrospect, seemed more like the foundation for a

strong business partnership than a successful marriage. And
then even that foundation had crumbled.

"Of course, the Garrett men are all charmers," Georgia
continued. "Which might explain why Luke is the only one
in Pinehurst who's still single. Is your baby's father in the
picture?"

The question came at her so unexpectedly, Julie found herself shaking her head before she realized it.

"Good."

"Why is that good?" she asked curiously.

"Because of the vibes in the air between my brother-in-
law and you."

"I think you're misinterpreting something."

"Am I?" the other woman mused.

She felt her cheeks flush. "I don't even know him."

"You don't have to know a man to be attracted to him,"
Georgia said matter-of-factly.

"I suppose not," she agreed.

"But I didn't mean to make you uncomfortable."

"You didn't. I'm not," Julie said. "I'm...confused."

Georgia smiled. "Yeah, I remember that feeling, too."

Julie didn't know what to say to that, so she was grateful that the other woman didn't seem to expect a response.

"But I didn't come over here to play matchmaker, only to
bring a few things that you might be able to use for Caden."

"It looks like more than a few things," Julie noted, relieved
by the change of topic.

"I had twins," Georgia reminded her. "Which means that
I had to have two of everything, including infant car seats.
I'm still using one for Pippa, but you're more than welcome
to the other one. The base secures into your vehicle, and the
carrier pops in and out, which is great for carting a baby
around or even just as a place for him to sit while you're
doing something else.

"When the twins were babies, I used to put them in their car seats on the floor in the bathroom while I was in the shower, because I was absolutely paranoid that something would happen if I didn't have my eyes on them every single minute."

Julie smiled at that. "Glad to know it's not just me."

"It's not just you. In fact, it's probably most new mothers."

"I just feel so completely unprepared. I thought I'd have more time to get ready. My own fault for listening to a friend who assured me that first babies never come early."

"They are more often late than early, but each baby comes in his own time," Georgia told her.

"It would have been nice if Caden had waited to come until after the storm had passed."

"But now you have an interesting story to tell when he asks about when and how he was born."

Julie would never forget the circumstances of her son's birth—or the connection that she now felt to the man who had helped deliver him. "There is that," she agreed.

"Mommy!" Clomping footsteps came through the kitchen, then a snow-covered bundle appeared in the doorway. Wrapped up as he was in the bulky snowsuit with a red hat pulled down to his eyes and a matching scarf wrapped around his throat, Julie couldn't tell if it was Quinn or Shane. But if she had to guess, she would say Quinn, since he seemed to be the more talkative and outgoing of the two brothers.

"Uncle Luke sent me in to get a carrot," he announced.

Georgia rose to her feet. "A carrot?"

"We made a snowman!"

"You look like a snowman," his mother told him.

The child giggled. "Shane 'n me made angels in the snow, too."

"Well, you're dripping all over Uncle Lukas's floor," Georgia chided. "So come back to the kitchen while I find you a carrot."

Since Caden was asleep again, Julie set him down in the playpen and followed them to the other room. "I think I want to see this snowman."

"It's out there." Quinn pointed a red, snow-covered mitten toward the back window.

Julie had made her share of snowmen as a kid, but even with the help of her older brothers, she'd never managed to put together anything of the scope or scale that the twins, along with their new daddy and uncle, had assembled.

It was a larger-than-life creation, with arms that reached up to the sky. There were mittens on its hands, a striped scarf around its throat, and a matching knitted hat on its head. The eyes were probably dark stones but they looked like coal and the mouth was made up of smaller stones curved into a lop-sided but undeniably happy grin.

But as impressive as the snowman was, it was Lukas, wrestling in the snow with his shy nephew, who captivated her.

Georgia joined her at the window.

"Isn't he awesome?" the little boy said.

Yes, he is, Julie thought, before she tore her attention from the flesh-and-blood man and shifted it to the one made of snow.

"I almost expect him to start dancing," she told Quinn.

"You'd need a magic hat for that," Georgia advised.

"Do we have a magic hat?" he asked hopefully.

"Nope. Just a carrot," the boy's mother said, and handed him the vegetable.

When Frosty's nose was in position, Matt decided that the boys' hard work had earned them big cups of hot chocolate with lots of marshmallows on top. Of course, this suggestion sent them racing back into the house to beg their mother to make it, which warned Luke that his brother wanted to talk to him without the twins overhearing their conversation.

A suspicion that was confirmed when Matt said, "So what's her story?"

There was no point in pretending he didn't know who the "her" was that his brother was asking about. "I don't know many of the details," he admitted. "She tends to skirt around personal questions."

And though his brother probably wasn't concerned with her financial status, Luke suspected that Julie came from a family with money. The car Bruce had towed out of the ditch was a late-model Audi A6 that he knew, from a trip to last year's auto show, was worth a pretty penny. The watch on her wrist was also pretty—and costly—and her clothes were likely designer. He wasn't familiar enough with any specific label to be able to identify what she was wearing, it was more in the way they fit, the quality of the fabrics and the cut. On the other hand, he suspected that Julie would look equally stylish dressed in an old potato sack.

"Did she say anything about the baby's father?" Matt pressed.

Luke shook his head.

"Did you ask?"

"Of course not."

"Why not?"

"Because I figured if she wanted me to know, she'd tell me."

"Aren't you curious?"

"Sure," he admitted. "But it's really none of my business."

"She's living under your roof."

"She was stranded in a storm." Luke felt compelled to point out the obvious. "I haven't put her on the title to the property."

"I know," his brother admitted. "Just…be careful."

"Careful of what?"

"Falling for her—and her baby."

He snorted. "I'm not the falling type."

"There's a first time for everything," Matt warned.

"No need to worry," he assured his brother. "She's not going to be here long enough for me to even lose my balance."

"It doesn't take long."

Of course, Matt would know. Seven years earlier, he'd accepted the daddy role not just easily but eagerly when he'd learned his girlfriend was pregnant—only to find out, three years after their wedding, that the child she'd given birth to wasn't his. And yet, that experience hadn't prevented him from falling all over again—this time for a young widow and her three children. Thankfully, that story had a much happier ending.

"And I've seen the way you look at her," Matt added.

He frowned at that. "How do I look at her?"

"The same way you used to look at the green mountain bike in the window of Beckett's Sporting Goods store when you were a kid."

Luke remembered that bike—and the quick thrill that had gone through him when he'd seen it in the family room with a big bow on it the morning of his twelfth birthday. A thrill not unlike what he felt whenever Julie walked into the room.

"She's a beautiful woman," he said, careful to keep his tone light.

"She is that," his brother agreed. "But there's something about her—a vulnerability that reminds me too much of the wounded strays you were always bringing home."

"First a bike, then a puppy—I wonder if Julie would appreciate either of those comparisons."

"I'm not worried about her. I'm worried about you."

"I'm thirty-four years old," he reminded Matt.

"And starting to think that it's time to settle down and have a family?"

"No." Luke shook his head. He was happy for both of his brothers, pleased that they were happy, but he didn't want what they had. Marriage and kids? Not anywhere on his radar.

At least not before he'd heard Caden's first indignant cry and looked into those wide, curious eyes trying to focus on a whole new world. In that moment there had maybe—just maybe—been the tiniest blip on Luke's radar. Not that he would ever admit as much to his brother.

"Right now, the only thing I'm thinking about is hot chocolate," he said, and turned to follow the path his nephews had taken back into the house.

Chapter Seven

"I really like your brother's family," Julie said to Lukas after Matt and Georgia had packed up their kids and puppies and gone.

"He definitely lucked out when he bought the house next door to Georgia," Luke agreed. "She's one in a million."

"He must be one in a million, too—a man willing to take on the responsibility of her three kids."

"Not just willing but eager," he admitted, remembering how he and Jack had both worried about their big brother's single-minded pursuit of the widowed mother of three. "Of course, Matt's always wanted a big family. And he couldn't love those kids any more if they were his own."

"You can see it in the way they are together—like all of the pieces just fit." She sounded just a little bit wistful.

"They do fit," he agreed. "But that doesn't mean it was easy."

She looked down at her baby, snuggled contentedly in

her arms. "That's what I want for Caden," she told him. "A real family."

Luke waited for the warning bells to start clanging inside of his head, but nothing happened. Okay, so maybe he was overreacting. After all, she hadn't been looking at him when she'd said it, but at the baby. There was no reason—aside from a possibly overinflated ego—to think that she imagined him anywhere in the picture of that family she wanted.

In fact, it was entirely possible that she wasn't thinking about him at all but the man who was her baby's father. Which, recalling his brother's warnings, seemed the perfect opportunity to ask about him.

"Maybe Caden's father wants the same thing," he suggested.

"I told you—Caden doesn't have a father."

Of course, he knew that wasn't true. He also knew that whatever had happened between the man and Julie didn't negate his parental rights and responsibilities. But she obviously wasn't ready to tell him anything about that relationship. Maybe he'd cheated on her—or maybe he'd been cheating *with* her. If the man already had a family with someone else, he wouldn't be in a position to give Julie the family she wanted for her son.

"Well, I'd say he's off to a good start, because he's got a great mother, anyway," he told her.

Her lips curved, but the smile didn't reach her eyes, and he suspected that she didn't trust he was willing to drop the subject of Caden's father. "I'm flattered you think so," she said. "But the truth is, I have absolutely no idea what I'm doing."

"Fake it till you make it."

"That's interesting advice."

"I'm an interesting guy," he said immodestly.

She looked at him now, her gaze speculative. "And far too charming for your own good," she decided.

"Since when is an excess of charm a bad thing?"

"When it's part of a package that includes a too-handsome face and a smile that makes a woman's knees weak."

There was no way he could not smile in response to that. "You think I'm handsome?"

"It's not an opinion but a fact," she told him.

"Do I make your knees weak?"

"Right now, I'm weak from hunger," she told him. "Breakfast was a long time ago and that chili your sister-in-law brought over smells fabulous."

His teasing smile faded. He was accustomed to being on his own and not having to think about anyone else, and it was only now he realized they'd skipped lunch. Which wasn't unusual for him, but probably wasn't advisable for a nursing mother.

"You should have said that you were hungry," he admonished. Then he shook his head. "No, you don't have to tell me—just help yourself to anything you want. And if there's something that you want that I don't have, let me know so I can get it for you."

She touched a hand to his arm, silencing his rambling apology.

"I'm not really starving," she assured him. "But that chili does smell good."

"I'll dish it up."

Julie decided to try Caden in the car seat/carrier that Georgia had brought over. When he was buckled in, she sat him across from her at the table while Lukas sliced a loaf of crusty bread to accompany the chili.

Conversation throughout the meal was casual and easy, and Julie began to relax again. She'd enjoyed the teasing banter they'd exchanged earlier, had felt comfortable with Lukas. And then she'd touched him—just a casual brush of her fingertips to his sleeve—but the sparks that had flown from the contact had unnerved her.

"Fiction or nonfiction?" he asked, pushing aside his now empty bowl.

"Sorry?"

"What do you like to read?"

"Almost anything," she told him. "But I'm not a fan of the horror genre. What about you?"

"Mostly nonfiction," he said. "Rock or country?"

"Alternative."

His brows lifted at her response. "Me, too," he admitted. "Romantic comedies or action flicks?"

"Depends on my mood."

"What are you in the mood for tonight? There's a Sandra Bullock, Hugh Grant movie on TV or we can choose something from my James Bond collection."

"You don't have to entertain me," she told him.

"I don't see how sliding a DVD into a player qualifies as me entertaining you."

"I just figured you had better things to do than hang out with me."

"I can't imagine anything better than spending a few hours in the company of a beautiful woman," he countered.

Julie was flattered—and tempted. Because as tired as she was, she was even more tired of being alone. For the past seven months, she'd moved from city to city, gallery to gallery. Yes, she'd routinely been introduced to new people, but at the end of each day, she'd gone back to an empty hotel room alone. She'd kept in touch with her family and friends, but the distance had been lonely.

Now the show was over, Evangeline's collection had been carefully packed up and shipped back to The Grayson Gallery, and Julie was officially on the three-month maternity leave that she'd negotiated with her employer. She didn't have to be "on" anymore, she didn't have to present a polished and professional image. What Lukas was offering her right now—the chance to sit and relax and tuck her feet up beneath her on the sofa—sounded too good to refuse. And she wasn't going to.

"Despite the blatantly inaccurate but much appreciated compliment, I would enjoy watching a movie with you," she told him.

"So what will it be? Rom-com or double-oh-seven?"

"Double-oh-seven," she said without hesitation. "I'm still feeling a little emotional and I don't know you well enough to want to bawl my eyes out in front of you twice in one day."

"You didn't bawl earlier," he denied. "You were just a little teary."

"That doesn't make me feel better," she told him.

"Okay—any particular Bond flick you want to see?"

"Do you have the latest one?"

"Is it your favorite?"

"I haven't actually seen it yet."

"Then that's what we'll watch." He stood up to carry their bowls to the dishwasher. "Did you, uh, want to nurse the baby before we start the movie?"

She glanced at the slim, white-gold watch on her wrist. He noticed that the elegant oval was ringed with diamonds and the name on the face said Cartier. "I probably should," she said in response to his question.

"I'll tidy up in here and make popcorn while you're doing that," he said.

"Popcorn? We just finished dinner."

"There's always room for popcorn," he insisted.

She frowned. "Isn't that Jell-O?"

"Sorry, I don't have any Jell-O."

She was shaking her head when she carried Caden out to the family room.

Luke puttered around in the kitchen for a while, putting

away the leftovers, loading the dishwasher, checking that both Einstein and Daphne had water in their respective dishes. The popcorn would only take a few minutes in the microwave but it would take Julie longer than that to nurse Caden.

When the popcorn was popped, he dumped it into a bowl and carried it, along with a can of cola for himself and a glass of water for Julie, to the family room.

"Can I ask you a question?"

"Sure," he agreed easily.

"Does being around a nursing mother make you uncomfortable?"

"No," he immediately responded, though his gaze shifted away. "I think it's one of the most incredible and beautiful things I've ever seen."

"Then why do you jump up and leave the room every time you think Caden's hungry?"

"Because I thought you might be uncomfortable, nursing in front of a stranger."

She shrugged. "My body stopped being my own when I got pregnant. And considering that you helped deliver my baby, it seems pointless to be self-conscious about baring a breast when you've seen much more intimate parts of me."

"Okay, then," he said, because his brain suddenly seemed incapable of generating a more articulate response.

"And it's your house," she reminded him. "So if I'm uncomfortable, I can go to my room. And if you're uncomfortable, you can send me to my room."

"Seeing you nurse your baby doesn't make me uncomfortable," he assured her. "This conversation, on the other hand..."

She laughed. "Okay—conversation over."

"Thank you," he said, and picked up the remote.

Luke wasn't surprised that Julie fell asleep before the end of the movie. What did surprise him was that when she did succumb to slumber, her head tipped toward him, then nestled against his shoulder.

He could smell the scent of her shampoo, and it reminded him of fruity drinks and tropical beaches. Her hair was soft and shiny and a thousand different shades of gold. Her skin was flawless and pale, her cheekbones high, her lashes long and thick. Her lips were exquisitely shaped, and temptingly full.

He felt a stirring low in his belly, tried to ignore it. She was an attractive woman so it wasn't unexpected that he would be attracted to her. But under the circumstances, it would be completely *in*appropriate to act on that attraction.

So though he was tempted to dip his head, to brush his lips over the sweet, soft curve of hers and wake her with a long, lingering kiss, he knew that he couldn't. She wasn't *his* sleeping beauty and he wasn't anyone's prince.

Even if, for just a minute, he wanted to be.

Luke loved all of his nieces and nephews, and he got a kick out of hanging out with the kids, but that was good enough for him. He had no desire to tie himself to one woman—who would want that when there were so many fascinating and interesting women to choose from?—and no concern about carrying on the family name—and why would he, when his brothers already had that covered? In fact, he couldn't remember the last time he'd been involved in a relationship that had lasted even six months. And that was okay, because he'd never seen himself as the type to settle down with a wife and a couple of kids.

But his mind had started moving in a different direction when he'd helped deliver Julie Marlowe's baby. There was something about the little boy that had taken a firm hold on his heart. Maybe it was the fact that his hands had been the first to hold the newborn infant, but whatever the reason, he felt as if there was a real connection between them.

Unfortunately, he knew that when Julie decided to go back to Massachusetts he'd probably never see her or Caden again. The prospect left him feeling strangely empty inside.

And it wasn't just the little guy that he would miss. Though he'd barely known Julie for twenty-four hours, they'd been through a lot together in that short period of time. He didn't know her well, but he knew that she was smart and strong and brave and spunky, and he knew that he wanted some time to get to know her better.

Whether it was fate or providence or luck, she wasn't going anywhere for at least a few days. Not while the snow was still falling and her vehicle was at Bruce's Body Shop. And maybe, by the time the storm passed and her car was fixed, she would want to stay a little longer.

Or maybe by then he'd be ready for them to go.

Okay, so he didn't think *that* was a likely scenario, but living with a woman and her baby was completely outside of his realm of experience so he wasn't going to assume anything.

The end credits rolled, and still she didn't stir. With sincere reluctance, he finally nudged her gently with his shoulder.

"Come on," he said. "I don't want to sleep in a chair again tonight."

Her eyelids flickered, then slowly lifted. It took a moment for her soft blue-gray gaze to focus, but the moment that it did, she pulled away from him. "I fell asleep," she realized. "I'm so sorry."

"No need to apologize to me." He lifted the baby from her arms, then helped Julie to her feet. "Although Daniel Craig would probably be upset to know that he put you to sleep."

"I *wish* Daniel Craig was here to put me to sleep."

He sighed and shook his head. "Runner-up again."

"Actually, you're better than Daniel Craig," she told him. "He's just a fantasy, but you're real. And you saved my baby."

He wasn't comfortable being thrust into the role of a hero.

Especially when anyone else would have done the same thing under the circumstances. So he ignored the latter part of her comment and said, "Come on." He nudged her toward the stairs. "Let's get you up to a real bed."

When they reached the guest room, he turned on the bed-side lamp, then gently laid Caden down in the cradle.

"Do you have pajamas?" he asked Julie, who was already tugging back the covers on the bed.

"I'm too tired to get changed," she said.

He didn't argue with her. And when she'd crawled between the sheets, he moved over to the bed and dropped a chaste kiss on her forehead. "Sweet dreams."

"You, too," she said, her eyes already shut.

As Luke made his way to his own room down the hall, he suspected that he would be tossing and turning all night. Thinking about the woman down the hall, and wanting what he couldn't have.

When Julie awoke the next morning, she didn't remember if she'd dreamed, but she'd definitely slept better than the night before. She was still up countless times to nurse and change and cuddle with Caden, but she didn't have any trouble falling back to sleep in between. And Caden had slept well in the cradle—if not for any longer than three hours at a time.

After his morning feeding, Julie took another shower and changed into a clean pair of yoga pants and a wrap-style sweater. A quick glance at the clock revealed that it was after 8:00 a.m. She hadn't heard any activity from down the hall, and she wondered if Lukas was already up and about or if he was still sleeping.

As she started down the stairs, she noticed Einstein waiting for her at the bottom, dancing around in excited anticipation.

She bent to pat his head, and he fairly quivered with excitement. For an active and exuberant pup, he was surprisingly restrained around the baby, which she appreciated.

He raced down the hall, then back again. She didn't have any trouble interpreting his silent message, and she followed him to the kitchen.

"Pancakes okay?" Lukas said by way of greeting when she appeared in the doorway.

"Very okay," she said. "But you don't have to cook for me all the time."

He shrugged. "I was cooking for myself, anyway."

She settled Caden into his carrier as Lukas put a platter of food on the table. Along with a generous stack of fluffy pancakes was a pile of crisp bacon strips.

"You made bacon again?"

"You don't have to eat it if you don't want it," he told her.

"The problem is that I do want it," she admitted, and snagged a piece from the platter.

"Would you feel less guilty if I told you it was turkey bacon?"

"Yes." She bit into it. "Is it?"

"No, but I'll lie if it will make you feel better."

She took a couple more slices, then added a couple of pancakes to her plate. Lukas sat down with her and proceeded to slather his pancakes with butter and drench them with syrup.

They chatted while they ate. Lukas teased her with hints about what parts of the movie she'd missed when she'd fallen asleep the night before—although she was skeptical about his claim that James Bond had to battle a one-legged Gypsy bank robber and his buxom transgendered girlfriend. He made her smile and laugh, and he made her forget all the reasons that she'd run away from Springfield more than seven months earlier and appreciate the fact that she was with him here in Pinehurst now.

He was halfway through his stack of pancakes when a low hum sounded from across the room. "Sorry," he apologized, pushing his chair away from the table. "That's my pager."

He read the message on the display, then disappeared into his office, no doubt to make a call. Julie finished her breakfast, stealing another piece of bacon from the platter and chatted with Caden while she waited for Lukas to return.

When he came back to the table, he wasn't smiling. Without a word, he picked up his plate and scraped the contents into the garbage.

"Is everything okay?" she asked tentatively.

He shook his head. "No. I have to go see a patient."

"I didn't know vets made house calls."

"Sometimes." He grabbed his keys from the counter, and Einstein was immediately at his feet, tail wagging. Lukas shook his head. "Sorry, buddy. Not this time." When the puppy's ears dropped, he bent to give the dog a quick scratch.

"I'll be back soon," he said.

Julie wasn't sure if he was talking to her or the dog, and then he was gone.

Despite his promise to be back soon, Lukas was gone for most of the day. Julie wasn't concerned by his absence so much as she was concerned about him, because it was apparent that whatever had called him away from home on a Sunday morning had been serious.

Early afternoon, she made herself a peanut butter sandwich and washed it down with a glass of milk. After she'd fed and changed Caden, she sat him on her lap and read out loud to him from one of the picture books that Georgia had brought over.

The DVD was still in the player from the night before, so

Julie fast-forwarded to the part where she'd fallen asleep and watched the end of the movie.

When it was over, she fed Caden—again, and changed him—again. Then she laid him on a blanket on the floor for some "tummy time" because it was supposed to help develop upper body strength for crawling.

As soon as Einstein heard the key in the lock, he was racing toward the door, dancing and barking in excited anticipation of his master's return. Julie scooped Caden up from the floor and carried him to the hall to greet Lukas.

From the wide doorway, she could see that he was seated on the deacon's bench beside the closet, a takeout bag beside him and Einstein in his lap. His boots were still on his feet, there was a light dusting of fresh snow on his jacket, and though his eyes were closed, tension was evident in the clenched muscles of his jaw.

She took a quick step back, not wanting to intrude on what was obviously some private pain, and retreated to the family room again. She'd turned on the TV after the movie finished, more for the background noise than because she had any interest in the crime investigation show that was playing out on screen, but she settled back on the sofa now and feigned rapt attention.

A few minutes later, Lukas spoke from the doorway. "I picked up Chinese."

Caden, who had just started to drift off to sleep, woke up again. His eyes opened wide and immediately began searching for him. The realization that her son already recognized the man's voice was both startling and unnerving for Julie, but it was Lukas's avoidance of her gaze that worried her.

She followed him into the kitchen and put Caden in the portable car seat.

"I'm sorry," he said, still not looking at her. "I didn't think I'd be gone so long."

"I'm just a stranger passing through town," she reminded him lightly. "You don't have to clear your schedule with me."

He got plates from the cupboard, retrieved cutlery from the drawer. "I know. But I didn't even think about the fact that you were stranded here without a vehicle—"

"There wasn't anywhere I needed to go," she interjected gently.

He started to unpack the bag of food, still not looking at her. "I got spring rolls, chicken fried rice, orange beef—"

Julie deliberately stepped in front of him, so that he had no choice but to look at her. And when he did, the stark pain evident in his blue-green eyes hit her like a fist.

She took the foil container from his hands and set it aside. "Why don't you leave the food for a minute and tell me what happened?"

"It's not a story with a happy ending," he warned her.

"I kind of figured that."

He blew out a breath. "It was Mrs. Boychuk who called about her seven-year-old boxer." One side of his mouth kicked up in a half smile. "Sweet'ums.

"Even as a pup, the dog was built like a tank and with the proverbial face that only a mother could love, but to Mrs. Boychuk, he was Sweet'ums. Six months ago, he was diagnosed with osteosarcoma—bone cancer."

"What kind of treatment do you offer for that?"

"We don't have the ability to offer any treatment locally," he admitted. "So Mrs. Boychuk took him to a clinic in Syracuse for radiotherapy. The treatment seemed to be successful, at least initially, but a couple of months ago we found that the cancer had spread to his lungs."

And she could tell by the flat tone of his voice that there was nothing to be done at that point.

"She lost her husband to cancer three years ago—she didn't want to lose her companion, too. She refused to believe the diagnosis. But over the past couple of days, Sweet'ums really began to struggle with his breathing and yesterday he stopped showing any interest in food."

"She called you to put him down," Julie realized, her eyes filling with tears.

He nodded.

She swallowed around the lump in her throat. She wanted to say or do something to help ease his pain, but she felt completely helpless. He obviously cared about his animal patients and losing this one was tearing him up inside.

And although Julie didn't know Mrs. Boychuk or Sweet'ums, she felt as if she knew Lukas, and it hurt her to see him hurting. In the end, she went with her instincts, lifting her arms to wrap around his neck and holding him tight.

For a brief second, he went completely and utterly still, and she wondered if she'd overstepped the boundaries of their fledgling friendship. Then his arms came around her, too, and he hugged her tight. She felt a shudder run through him, an almost-physical release of the grief he was holding inside, and then the tension seemed to seep from his muscles.

After a long moment, he finally eased away.

"Are you okay now?" she asked gently.

"No," he admitted. "But I'm doing much better. Thanks."

And he impulsively touched his lips to hers.

She felt the jolt of the fleeting contact all the way down to her toes. And when he took a quick step back, she knew that he'd felt it, too.

She cleared her throat, focused her gaze on the takeout containers on the counter. "Orange beef?"

He nodded. "Are you hungry?"

"Always," she said, and forced a smile.

What she didn't admit was that she was suddenly craving something other than Chinese food. Because that teasing brush of his lips had triggered a hunger for more of Lukas Garrett's kisses.

Chapter Eight

Luke was at the clinic before eight o'clock Monday morning. Not surprisingly, Karen's vehicle was already in the parking lot. He hung his coat on a hook in the staff room/kitchenette, then traded his boots for shoes before heading out to the front to retrieve the files for his morning appointments.

When he opened the door to reception, he heard Karen lift the top off the jar of doggy treats that she kept on her desk. She frowned when he came around the corner and there was no dancing puppy at his feet.

"Where's Einstein?"

"He decided to stay at home today," Luke told her.

"*He* decided?"

"Yeah." He shook his head, still baffled by the animal's unusual behavior. "He seems to have assigned himself as the baby's protector and doesn't like to be too far away from him."

Her brows lifted. "Baby?"

"Sorry—I guess a lot of things happened on the weekend that you don't know about."

"I saw Sweet'ums's file on top of the stack this morning," she said, her voice quiet, her eyes filled with compassion.

He just nodded.

"But since that doesn't explain Einstein staying home with a baby, maybe you should fill me in."

He did—briefly summarizing the details of discovering Julie's car in the ditch and inviting the laboring mother into his house to help deliver her baby.

"That was Friday?" Karen asked.

He nodded.

"And this woman and her baby are still at your place?"

"Her car's at Bruce's shop," he pointed out. "What was I supposed to do—call a cab to take them to a bed-and-breakfast?"

"It sounds like you did more than enough," she told him. "I would have thought *she* might have called her baby's father to come and pick them up."

"I don't think he's in the picture," Lukas admitted.

Karen's brows rose again. "You don't *think?*"

"She hasn't volunteered very much information about her personal life."

"And that isn't waving an enormous red flag in your mind?"

Of course it was. Julie's reluctance to talk about Caden's father did give him cause for concern. But he wanted to give her the benefit of the doubt. He wanted to believe that she had legitimate reasons for the secrecy. And he hadn't demanded answers or explanations because he wanted her to trust him enough to tell him those reasons of her own volition.

If he thought about it, he might wonder why he wanted her to open up to him, why it mattered so much to him. He'd only known her for three days. He barely knew her at all. But there was something about her that made him want to know her a whole lot better.

Part of that was the immediate and undeniable physical attraction he felt toward her. An attraction that hadn't dimmed when he'd realized she was pregnant nor even through the experience of childbirth. But he'd managed to downplay it—to convince himself that it didn't need to be a factor.

Of course, that was before he'd kissed her. Not that it had been much of a kiss. In fact, he would have argued that the brief contact barely met the most conservative definition of a kiss, except that he'd felt the impact of it in every cell of his body.

And if that wasn't reason enough to be wary, Karen had pointed out another: there was too much about Julie that he didn't know. He wasn't sure what to think about the fact that she'd never told her parents about her pregnancy. If she'd hidden the existence of her baby from them, had she also hidden it from her baby's father? This disconcerting possibility inevitably made him think about Jack, who hadn't learned about his daughter's existence until Ava was twelve years old.

And the effortless way that Caden had completely taken hold of Luke's heart made him remember that Matt had raised another man's son as his own for three years—until the child's biological father came back into the picture. Which wasn't something he should be worrying about after only three days with Julie and her son, except that after only three days, he already knew that he would miss them when they were gone.

He pushed those concerns aside when Megan Richmond came through the front door with her eighteen-month-old chocolate Lab. He loved his job and the familiar routines of his work. Not that the work was ever routine, but there were certain patterns and rhythms to his days at the clinic. The needs of the pets and the concerns of their owners were always his primary focus, but several times throughout the day on Monday, he found his attention drifting. He called home three times, just to see if Julie and Caden were doing okay, to ensure that Einstein wasn't being a bother, to inquire if there was anything they needed.

And when the last patient was gone from the clinic at the end of the day, he was the first one to head out, even before Drew—the animal tech—had finished wiping down the exam rooms.

He could smell the rich, savory scents of basil and garlic as soon as he walked through the door. Einstein came running when he tossed his keys on the counter, reassuring Lukas that the pup still did know who was his master, even if he'd chosen a mistress for today.

Then Luke looked up and saw Julie standing at the stove, and he felt an instinctive hum through his veins.

He was a decent cook. He didn't live on fast food the way some of his single friends did, but he did eat a lot of grilled cheese sandwiches in the winter and hamburgers in the summer—usually because, by the time he got home at the end of the day, he didn't have the energy or the imagination to make anything else. It was a pleasant change to walk in the door and have a meal waiting. And an even more pleasant change to find a beautiful woman in his kitchen.

"I didn't know what your after-work routine was and I didn't want to overcook the pasta, so I haven't put it in yet," she said.

"My after-work routine is to look in the fridge, then look in the freezer, then open a bottle of beer while I try to figure out what I want to eat."

She went to the fridge and retrieved a bottle of beer, twisted off the cap and handed it to him. "Tonight you're having chicken parmigiana and spaghetti with green salad and garlic bread. It will be on the table in fifteen minutes."

He grinned. "You just fulfilled a fantasy I never even knew I harbored."

"Do I want to know?" she asked cautiously.

"A sexy woman offering me a home-cooked meal at the end of a long day." He tipped the bottle to his lips, drank deeply.

She laughed at that as she used her thumb and finger to measure the pasta, then dropped it into the pot of boiling water. "If you think I'm sexy, you need to seriously reevaluate your standards."

As he swallowed another mouthful of beer, he realized that she wasn't being coy or fishing for compliments—she honestly believed what she was saying. "You really don't see it, do you?"

"See what?"

"How incredibly attractive you are."

"I had a baby three days ago," she reminded him.

"Yeah, I think I remember hearing something about that," he said dryly, and turned his attention to the infant securely strapped in the carrier on top of the table, where Julie could keep an eye on him—and vice versa.

"How was the little guy today?" he asked, tweaking Caden's toes through the velour sleeper. The baby kicked his legs instinctively in response to the touch, making Luke smile.

"Hungry. Sleepy. The usual." She lifted the lid of another pot, stirred the sauce that was simmering.

"Did you manage to get any rest?"

"A little." She stirred the pasta. "What did your day entail?"

"Along with the usual checkups and vaccinations, there was a calico with a mild respiratory infection, a diabetic Doberman, a Saint Bernard with a urinary tract obstruction and a ten-month old kitten whose owner was convinced she had a tumor in her belly."

She held her breath. "Not a tumor?"

"Not a tumor," he confirmed. "Pregnant."

Her lips curved. "So a better day than yesterday?"

"A much better day," he agreed.

"I'm glad."

"I also talked to Bruce Conacher today. He didn't have a number for you, so he called me."

"Is my car fixed?" she asked hopefully.

Luke shook his head. "Unfortunately, it's going to be out of commission for at least a few more days."

"Why?"

"You snapped the right front drive axle and Bruce has to wait on delivery from an out-of-town supplier. He was apologetic, but he doesn't do a lot of work on imports so he didn't have the part in stock or easy access to one."

She sighed. "Are you willing to put up with us for a few more days?"

"I told you, you can stay as long as you want," he reminded her. "And the few more days will only make your car drivable. If you want the damaged bumper and fender repaired, it will be a little bit longer than that."

"I guess, since my car's already at his shop, Bruce might as well fix everything that needs to be fixed."

"I'll let him know," Luke said. "And I promise—you'll be pleased with the results. He does good work."

She nodded. "Okay. Now wash up so we can eat."

He fed the animals first, then scrubbed his hands at the sink while she served up the meal. His brows drew together as he looked at the plate she set in front of him.

"You don't like Italian food?"

"What?"

"You're frowning," she noted.

"I love Italian food," he assured her. "But when you asked

if pasta was okay for dinner, I thought you'd cook some spaghetti and top it with canned sauce."

"This is canned sauce," she admitted. "You didn't have all the ingredients to make fresh, but I doctored it up a little bit."

"It doesn't look anything like what comes out of the can."

"I'll take that as a compliment."

"It was intended as one," he assured her. "I really didn't expect anything like this. You didn't have to go to so much trouble."

"It wasn't any trouble. I like to cook."

"Well, that's convenient because I like to eat."

"Then dig in."

So he did, and his taste buds nearly wept with joy. "This is really good."

"You didn't believe me when I said I could cook, did you?"

Truthfully, the luxury car, the diamonds at her ears and designer labels on her clothes had made him suspect that she was more accustomed to having someone cook for her than vice versa. "I didn't think you could cook like *this*," he admitted.

She smiled, choosing to be pleased by his obvious enjoyment of the meal rather than insulted by his skepticism. "Carla, my parents' housekeeper, was originally from Tuscany—although she would be the first to renounce this meal as American Italian and not *real* Italian."

The revelation about the housekeeper confirmed his suspicion about her privileged upbringing. And yet, she seemed perfectly at ease in his humble home, more than capable of looking after herself—and perfectly content to do so. "What is real Italian?"

"Simple recipes with quality seasonal ingredients," she said, then shrugged. "But I've always been partial to a good red sauce."

"This is definitely that," he agreed. After a few more bites, he couldn't resist asking, "What else did Carla teach you to make?"

"You'll have to wait until dinner tomorrow to find out."

The next night Julie made stuffed pork chops with garlic mashed potatoes and green beans. The night after that was broccoli and beef stir-fry with wild rice. On Thursday, it was chicken in a cream sauce with new potatoes and baby carrots.

"Did you want any more chicken?" she asked, when he set his knife and fork down on his empty plate.

"No, thanks." He rubbed a hand over his flat belly. "I couldn't eat another bite."

"You have to have room for dessert," she told him. "Caden napped a little bit longer than usual today, so I had time to make apple crisp."

"One of my favorites," he told her.

"And you've got French vanilla ice cream in the freezer to go with it."

"We never had dessert on a weeknight."

"Never?"

"Well, maybe a slice of birthday cake, if it happened to be someone's birthday."

"When is your birthday?"

"June twenty-second."

"I guess I won't be making a birthday cake anytime soon," she noted.

"When's yours?"

"March fifth."

"How old are you going to be?"

"That was a smooth segue," she told him. "If not exactly subtle."

He shrugged. "I've been trying to guesstimate, but I can't figure out if you're older than you look or younger than you seem."

"I'll be twenty-four on my next birthday," she admitted.

Which meant that she was only twenty-three now, eleven years younger than him. But so what? There were no age taboos with respect to friendship. And he really felt as if he and Julie were becoming friends. Or they would be if he could continue to ignore the way his pulse pounded and his blood hummed whenever he was near her.

"Apple crisp?" she prompted.

"Why not?"

She cut a generous square of the still-warm dessert and topped it with a scoop of ice cream.

"I am feeling seriously spoiled," he confessed, lifting his spoon toward his mouth. "I don't think I've ever eaten as well as I've eaten this past week."

"If you want to continue eating, you're going to have to make a trip to the grocery store," she said. "Since I'm going to be here for a while, I could make a list of some things that will help with the menu planning."

"Why don't you make that list and we can go out tonight?"

She seemed startled by the suggestion. "Tonight?"

"Sure. I figured, since you haven't been out of the house since you got here, you might enjoy a quick outing."

Her face lit up as if he'd given her a precious gift. "I would *love* to go out."

Julie had been so excited about the opportunity to get out of the house for a little while that she hadn't thought about the repercussions of going out with Lukas. What was intended to be a quick trip to the store ended up being an hour-long parade up and down the aisles as the local vet seemed to be acquainted with everyone in town—and everyone was curious about the unknown woman and baby who were in his company.

He was always polite and made a point of introducing her

to everyone who stopped to chat, but he didn't divulge any information about her aside from her name. After the third introduction, Julie realized that he was being deliberately secretive. When he put his hand on her back to nudge her along after a brief exchange of pleasantries with a bubbly blonde he'd introduced as Missy Walsh, the pieces started to come together.

"Why do you want people to think that we're together?"

"We are together," he said, deliberately misunderstanding her question.

Her gaze narrowed. "You know what I mean."

Before he could reply—and undoubtedly deny any complicity—they turned up the next aisle and crossed paths with someone else he knew. It was another woman, this one stunningly beautiful with long dark hair, warm golden eyes and a wide smile.

"Hey, stranger," she said, and touched her lips to his cheek in a way that confirmed they were anything but strangers. Her gaze shifted to take in Julie and Caden, then moved back to Lukas again. "I heard whispered speculation in aisle four about whether or not it was 'his baby,'—now I know who they were talking about."

He just shrugged. "People are always going to find something to talk about."

The brunette moved to take a closer look at Caden, then shook her head. "No way. He's much too cute to be your kid." She offered her hand to Julie. "I'm Kelly Cooper."

"Jack's fiancée," Lukas added, in case she hadn't made the connection.

"And one of Lukas's oldest friends," Kelly told her.

"It's nice to meet you," Julie said.

"Who was in aisle four?" Lukas asked.

"Tara Gallagher and Missy Walsh."

"Is there anything I can bribe you with to go back there and tell them that the baby is mine?"

Kelly shook her head. "It wouldn't matter. Not to Missy, anyway. I could say that you had a dozen kids by a dozen different mothers, and she would take that as hope she might bear the thirteenth." Then she turned to Julie. "Missy's been in love with Lukas since tenth grade, but he never gave her the time of day."

"Julie isn't interested in ancient history," Lukas said.

"It doesn't sound ancient to me," she couldn't resist teasing.

Kelly laughed. "I've got a lot more stories I could tell."

"And we've got to get to the produce department," Lukas said pointedly.

His friend rolled her eyes. "You could at least pretend to be subtle."

"Why?"

"To make a good impression on your houseguest."

"I'm trying to make a good impression—which is why I don't want her hanging around here to talk to you."

She poked her tongue out at him. Lukas kissed her cheek then started to push the cart away. Since Caden's carrier was attached to the cart, Julie automatically fell into step beside him. "It was nice meeting you," she said to Kelly.

"We'll finish our conversation another time," the other woman promised.

"I'll look forward to it."

After Julie had selected the fruits, vegetables and fresh herbs she wanted, they made their way to the checkout line. She always liked to have a list when she went to the grocery store, but she invariably added to the list as she shopped. She hadn't realized how much she'd added until Lukas was unloading the cart onto the checkout belt.

She tried to move past him, closer to the register so that

she would be in position to pay, but he deliberately blocked her path.

"I want to get this—"

He put a hand over hers as she reached into her purse. "We'll discuss this later."

"But—"

He dipped his head closer, his mouth hovering just a few inches above hers. "The gossip from aisle four just moved her cart into line behind us."

She lifted a brow. "What does that have to do with the price of free range chicken at the Saver Mart?"

"Nothing," he admitted. "But I wouldn't mind adding fuel to the speculative fires."

"You think she'd really believe that we're together?"

"Why not?"

To an outsider, it probably did look as if they were having an intimate conversation. Their heads were close and their voices pitched low so that only Julie and Lukas could know that they were arguing about who should pay the grocery bill. "Because I drove into town less than a week ago."

"Eight months after the brief but blistering hot affair we had when I was in Boston for a veterinary rehabilitation symposium."

His lips brushed the shell of her ear as he spoke, making her blood heat and her heart pound. It was an effort to focus her attention on their conversation, and she had to moisten her lips with the tip of her tongue before she could respond. "Were you really in Boston eight months ago?"

"Actually it was Baltimore," he admitted. "But Missy never had an aptitude for geography."

The clerk announced the total of their order and Lukas drew away to pull out his wallet. Julie's fingers tightened on the handle of the buggy as she exhaled a long, shaky breath.

She wanted to believe the flood of heat that made every

inch of her skin itch was nothing more than postpartum hormonal overload, but the more time she spent with Lukas, the more she was beginning to suspect otherwise.

She secured Caden's car seat into the truck while he loaded the grocery bags.

"I'm writing you a check when we get back to your place," she said, when he slid behind the wheel.

"We'll talk about it then," he said agreeably.

But she wasn't fooled for a minute. And since she knew he was going to give her grief about paying for a few groceries—even though she would be eating the food—she decided to give him some grief, too.

"I'm a little surprised that you'd be resistant to such an attractive woman."

He turned the key in the ignition. "Who?"

"Missy Walsh."

He pulled out of the parking lot and onto the road. "You don't know anything about the situation."

"I know that you're apparently afraid of a five-foot-tall curvy blonde in pink spandex."

"With good reason," he told her. "She adopted a kitten last year just so that she could make regular appointments to come into my clinic."

"You don't think it's possible that she just wanted a pet?"

"Within six months, she gave it away because she was allergic. Then she tried a dog—same problem."

"Maybe she's just a lonely woman who wants some company," she suggested.

"I told her to try a goldfish."

"And?"

"She brought the bowl in when the fish went belly up."

Julie couldn't help but laugh. "You're kidding?"

"I wish I was."

"Okay, that is a little strange," she admitted.

"The biggest problem is that she's really sweet," Lukas admitted. "She just tries too hard. She actually dated one of my friends for a while, and he really liked her at first. He said she was fun and interesting to talk to. But the more time they spent together, the more she assimilated his ideas and opinions. She liked everything he liked, wanted to do whatever he wanted to do, agreed with everything he said."

"I would think that's the kind of woman every man would love."

"Maybe for five minutes," he acknowledged. "After that, it would get pretty boring."

"So you've never gone out with her?"

"No. And I've never given her the slightest bit of encouragement. But that hasn't stopped Missy." He shook his head, obviously frustrated by the situation. "She came into the clinic a couple of weeks ago—coincidentally only a few days after Jack and Kelly got engaged—to ask my opinion about geckos."

"With one brother recently married and the other engaged, it's understandable that she might think you're ready for a committed relationship," Julie pointed out to him. And then she couldn't resist asking, "So why are you still single?"

"Never met the right woman, I guess."

"Really? That's your answer?"

"Or maybe I'm just not the marrying kind."

"That sounds like the response of a man who's been burned by love."

"It's the truth."

"How old are you?"

"Thirty-four."

She shifted in her seat so that she could see him more clearly. "Are you honestly telling me that you've never known a woman who made you think in terms of forever?"

"Not really."

"What does that mean?"

"Well, I did propose to someone once," he confided. "But she turned me down."

Which confirmed her "burned by love" theory but still didn't quite add up. "And that was it? One heartbreak and you gave up?"

"I wouldn't even call it a heartbreak," he admitted, turning into his driveway. "In retrospect, I'm not even sure I was in love with her, but I could imagine sharing my life with her."

"Now that's the foundation of a really romantic proposal."

Her dry tone made him smile. "My proposal was motivated by more practical considerations."

"And you wonder why she turned you down?"

He just shrugged.

"So if you weren't wildly in love, why did you want to marry her?"

"Because she was pregnant."

Her jaw dropped. "You have a child?"

"No," he said quickly. "It wasn't my baby."

"Oh." She thought about that for a minute. "Have you always had a hero complex—a desire to save the damsel in distress?"

He scowled. "I don't have a hero complex. She was a friend, and the baby's father was out of the picture, and I knew she was terrified by the thought of going through pregnancy and childbirth on her own.

"And," he confessed with a small smile, "for the few minutes that she took to consider my offer, I was absolutely terrified that she would say yes."

"I can understand why she would have been tempted," Julie admitted.

"Because I'm so tempting?" he teased.

"Because having a baby without a father is a scary prospect—even when it's the right thing to do."

"Right for whom?"

She didn't say anything, was afraid that she'd already said too much.

"Who were you thinking about when you decided to have your baby on your own?" he pressed. "Yourself or Caden?"

"Both of us."

Then she unbuckled her belt and reached for the door handle, a clear signal that the conversation was over.

Chapter Nine

Kelly tried not to worry. She knew that Lukas was a grown man, capable of making his own decisions and accepting the consequences of those decisions. But he was also her best friend and, as such, she was entitled to pry—just a little.

And wasn't it a lucky coincidence that she had an appointment to take Puss and Boots—the pair of kittens her daughter had insisted on adopting from Lukas a few weeks earlier—to the clinic for their sixteen-week immunizations the following Tuesday morning?

The vet gave them a quick once over, nodded approvingly. "They're doing well. Thriving."

"Does that mean they're getting fat?" she asked. "Because every time I turn around, Ava's giving them treats."

"They're not getting fat. But as long as they're eating the right amount of food, treats should be reserved for special occasions."

"Tell your niece that."

"I will," he promised.

"She won't listen," Kelly warned. "I told her that they had to have their own bed—which they do. And they still sleep with her."

"So long as she has no allergies and they aren't interfering with her sleep, it shouldn't be a concern. In fact, for these two—because they were orphaned at such a young age—that close physical contact could be one of the reasons that they're thriving. Love is as necessary as food, water and shelter to living creatures."

"Even you?" she asked.

He glanced up at her, his brows raised. "Where did *that* come from?"

"It's a simple question," she told him. "I can't help but admire the life you've built for yourself. You have a successful veterinarian practice, a fabulous house—but no one to go home to at the end of the day."

"I have Einstein and Daphne," he reminded her.

"And now you have Julie and Caden."

"They're not mine."

"But you want them to be," she guessed.

"What are you talking about?"

"I'm talking about you playing house with a beautiful woman and her brand-new baby."

"I'm not playing house."

"And I'm concerned about you falling for her," Kelly admitted. "For both of them."

"I'm not falling for her," he said.

She didn't believe that claim for a second. "I don't want you to get hurt, Lukas."

"Don't you have more important things to worry about—like your wedding?" he said pointedly.

She shook her head. "Ava's taken care of every single detail—I don't have to do anything but show up."

"You're letting your twelve-year-old daughter plan your wedding?"

"She's almost thirteen," Kelly reminded him. "And she had very strong opinions about what she wanted. Since Jacks and I really just want to make it legal, we decided to put Ava in charge of the details."

"And is everything on schedule?"

"Almost everything." She let out a long sigh. "I still don't have a dress."

"You know that Jack will be happy to marry you if you show up at the church in old jeans and a T-shirt."

"Yeah," she said, and smiled because she did know it was true.

The smile slipped as her stomach pitched. She sucked in a lungful of air, trying to fight against the unexpected wave of nausea. *Not now. Please not now.* Unfortunately, her body refused to listen to the mental pleas, and she bolted out of the exam room and to the washroom.

After she'd expelled the meager contents of her stomach—and heaved a few more times just to make sure there was nothing left inside—she flushed the toilet. Her hands were shaking as she dampened some paper towels and wiped her face. When she was reasonably certain that her legs would support her, she returned to the exam room, where Lukas was waiting with the kittens.

He handed her a bottle of water. "Morning sickness?"

"I don't know." She lowered herself onto the stool beside the exam table and unscrewed the cap from the bottle. "It might just be a touch of a stomach bug that's going around. Ava was home from school two days last week."

"Do you have any other flulike symptoms? Fever? Chills?"

"No," she admitted. "Just the nausea."

"Then I'd guess *pregnant* over *flu.*"

Kelly lifted the bottle to her lips, took a long swallow of

water. "Jacks and I both wanted to have another baby, and Ava has been asking for a brother or a sister almost since she could talk. But a baby in the abstract is a lot different than a flesh-and-blood child."

"You're scared," he realized.

"I'm almost thirty-four years old," she said. "The last time I had a baby I was twenty-one—too young and stupid to know that I should have been terrified."

"You're not alone this time," he reminded her.

"I know. I mean—assuming that there is a 'this time.'" She sighed. "He said that this is what he wanted—but what if it isn't? I know Jackson still thinks about everything he missed out on when Ava was a baby, and I understand that. But I don't know that he's truly ready for the reality of a baby."

"Is any parent ever truly ready?"

"Good point," she admitted. "Okay, on the way home I'll stop at the pharmacy and pick up a pregnancy test."

Lukas settled the kittens back in their carrier. "And you'll let me know?"

"If there's anything to know," she told him. "You'll be the first—*after* Jackson this time."

He grinned. "I can live with that."

While Kelly was at Lukas's clinic, Julie was at Jackson's law office.

After an extended delay waiting for parts that had be ordered from an out-of-town supplier, Bruce had finished the repairs to her vehicle and delivered it to Lukas's driveway the previous afternoon. She'd been waiting to get her car back so she could continue her journey to Springfield, but with her parents out of the country, she wasn't really anxious to go home. Because going home meant facing Elliott, and she wasn't ready to do that just yet.

So when Lukas had assured her that she was welcome to

stay as long as she wanted, she found herself accepting his offer "for just a few more days." But she was grateful that having her car back afforded her the freedom to come and go as she pleased, because she was finally able to reschedule her appointment to see the lawyer.

She hadn't told Lukas about the appointment, although she couldn't have said why any more than she could have said why she felt as if she was going behind Lukas's back to meet with his brother. After all, Jackson Garrett was the reason she'd come to Pinehurst in the first place. It was just an odd twist of fate that his brother was the reason she'd stayed.

She was summoned into the office at precisely 11:15 a.m., and when she walked through the door, Jackson rose from the chair behind his desk.

"I've been trying to figure out why your name sounds familiar," he admitted, offering his hand. "But I don't think we've ever met."

"We haven't," she admitted. "I was looking for a family law attorney in the area and my brother, Dan, recommended you. He said you went to law school together."

"Dan Marlowe," he said, and smiled. "It is a small world, isn't it?"

"Smaller than I ever would have guessed," she agreed. "Because your brother Lukas delivered my baby."

"So this little guy is the one?" He crouched down to get a closer look at the sleeping infant. "Well, he doesn't look any the worse for wear."

"I feel very fortunate that your brother knew what he was doing—or at least how to fake it."

"Then you're not here to sue him for malpractice?" Jackson teased.

She managed a smile. "No. I just wanted some general information. At least, that's why I originally requested to see you."

"And now?"

"Now that Caden was born in New York State, I have some specific questions about registering his birth." She opened her purse, pulled out a checkbook. "How much do you need as a retainer?"

"I don't need a retainer at all if I'm only answering a few questions."

"I'd rather keep this official."

"The minute you walked through the door of my office, the rules governing solicitor-client privilege came into effect," he assured her. "I'm not going to repeat anything you say here to anyone—not even your brother or mine."

She dropped her gaze. "I feel a little disloyal," she admitted. "Talking to you instead of Lukas."

"If you need a rabies shot, my brother's your man. If you have legal questions, not so much."

She smiled again. "Fair enough. Okay, the first question is about the paperwork I have to fill out to register Caden's birth. Do I have to include his father's name?"

"Are you married to him?"

She shook her head. "No."

"Then there's no presumption of paternity," he told her. "He could sign an acknowledgment of paternity, in which case his personal information would be included on Caden's birth certificate, but if he isn't willing to do so, you would have to apply to the court to request a paternity test."

"What if I don't want him named on the birth certificate?"

He considered her question for a minute. "Your son's biological father has certain rights and responsibilities, regardless of what either of you wants," he finally said. "Has he indicated that he is unwilling to fulfill his responsibilities?"

She dropped her gaze to the sleeping baby. The beautiful baby who was the reason for everything she'd done since she'd learned of the tiny life growing inside her. The reason she was here now.

"He doesn't know about Caden," she admitted.

"I try not to make judgments," he told her. "Especially when I don't know the whole story."

"I appreciate that." And she knew it couldn't be easy for someone with his personal experience to remain objective. Lukas had told her about his fiancée keeping the existence of their child a secret for twelve years. But despite that history, they'd obviously worked things out and were together now.

Julie knew that she and Elliott would never work things out, because she would never forgive him for what he'd done—or herself for not taking control of her life sooner. And right now, she wanted to focus on her son, to be the best mother that she could be, and to keep him away from his father.

"But I can't give you legal advice specific to your situation if I don't know what that situation is," he told her. "So you're going to have to give me at least some of the details."

"I can do better than that." She reached into her purse again, this time pulling out a slim envelope of photographs. "I can show you."

When Julie looked at the calendar Saturday morning, she was surprised to realize it was the fifteenth of November. The month was already half over and her stay in Pinehurst had been extended from a few days to more than two weeks.

Even more surprising was the fact that she wasn't eager to leave. Part of her reluctance was because her parents were on the other side of the world, but another—maybe even bigger—part was that she enjoyed spending time with Lukas.

And she was starting to worry that she was enjoying this unexpected detour a little too much, and starting to seriously crush on the man who had delivered her baby. So when Lukas asked if she wanted to go over to Matt and Georgia's for a while after breakfast, she decided that was probably a good idea. Being around other people would help keep her focus off the man who occupied far too many of her thoughts.

She started questioning her decision when she stepped into the entranceway of Matt and Georgia's house and realized that the entire Garrett family was in attendance—adults, children and pets. Her reservations multiplied when Kelly said, "Don't take your coat off—we're kidnapping you."

Julie took an instinctive step back, holding Caden tight against her chest. "What?"

"Only for a couple of hours," Georgia said, her tone reassuring. "And you will thank us for it—I promise."

Her panicked gaze met Lukas's amused one. "Did you know about this?"

"Not until about two minutes ago," he assured her. "But I heartily approve of their plan."

"What is the plan?" she asked warily.

"A mini-spa retreat," Georgia said.

Wariness gave way to interest. "Really?"

Kelly grinned. "Massage, pedicure. A few hours of girl talk."

"No boys allowed," Jack's fiancée said firmly. "Not even baby boys."

"But—"

"No buts, either," Georgia said.

"I'm not sure about leaving Caden," Julie admitted. While she was undeniably tempted by the invitation, she couldn't help but think that abandoning her two-week-old baby into someone else's care made her a bad mother.

"Of course you're not," Georgia acknowledged. "It's the scariest thing in the world for a new mother to leave her baby for a few hours. But he'll be with Luke and Matt and Jack—they know what they're doing."

"Their hands will be full with the twins and two babies, three puppies and two kittens."

"Ava's here, too," Kelly reminded her.

Which made Julie feel a little better. Jackson and Kelly's daughter might be twelve, but she was mature for her age. She promised Julie that she had "tons of experience" looking after Pippa, and her easy confidence and obvious competence in handling the infant reassured the new mother.

But truthfully, Julie would never have even considered saying "yes" to the proposed outing if she didn't know that Lukas would be there, too. And she had pumped so that she'd have the option of giving Caden a bottle instead of nursing at Matt and Georgia's house, so she didn't have to worry about her baby going hungry if she wasn't around.

"You need this," Kelly told her. "And even if you don't think you do—*we* do."

Julie smiled at that.

"Everything is new and exciting now," Georgia told her. "But trust me, a few hours away from your baby to recharge your batteries will make you an even better mother."

"The new mother looked panicked at the thought of leaving her little guy for a couple of hours," Matt commented when the women had finally gone, leaving the men with the kids and a menagerie of pets.

"Maybe she was just panicked at the thought of leaving him with Lukas," Jack teased.

"I don't blame her," Luke said. "What do I know about babies?"

"A lot more now than a couple of weeks ago," Matt guessed.

"Which means you have more experience at this stage than I do," Jack admitted. "I never knew Ava when she was this young. In fact, I can't believe that she was ever this small."

"Next time around, you'll be there every step of the way," Matt said.

"The next time around is going to come sooner than either of us expected," Jack confided.

"Really?" Matt grinned. "Kelly's pregnant?"

"Due next summer—July twenty-seventh, to be exact."

"Congratulations," Luke said.

"It's hush-hush right now," Jack told them. "Because it's early days, but mostly because Kelly doesn't want to tell Ava until we're married."

"Yeah, you wouldn't want your twelve-year-old daughter to suspect you've had sex with her mother out of wedlock when your wedding isn't scheduled for another few weeks," Matt said dryly.

"We've had the talk," Jack said. "Ava knows all about the important role of the stork."

His brothers laughed.

"Seriously, though," Luke said. "You're good with Kelly's pregnancy?"

Jack nodded. "I'm thrilled. I think Kelly's a little apprehensive, because Ava's almost a teenager. But I know our daughter will be all for it. She desperately wants to be a big sister."

"She certainly enjoys being a big cousin," Matt commented. "She's great with the twins and Pippa. And she's jumped up to check on Caden every five minutes since he went down for his nap."

"Yeah—Luke's managed to limit his checks to every seven minutes," Jack said dryly.

He just shrugged.

"It's pretty obvious you've fallen for the kid," Matt said. "The question is—have you fallen for his mother, too?"

"I'm just helping her out," he said.

"By inviting her to move in with you?"

"She hasn't moved in," he denied. "She's only staying with me temporarily."

"Temporary is a couple of days," Jack said. "Julie's been sleeping in your bed for longer than that already."

"Jesus, Jack. She just had a baby two weeks ago—she's not sleeping in my bed."

His brother's brows lifted. "I was speaking figuratively. The house and everything in it is yours, including the guest room bed. Therefore, she's sleeping in your bed."

"But that was quite the vehement protest," Matt noted.

Luke glowered at him.

"She's a beautiful woman, you're both single and living in close quarters. You wouldn't be human if you hadn't thought about taking things to the next level."

"And what is the next level of friendship?"

Jack shook his head. "You can lie to yourself all you want, but you can't fool your brothers."

And, of course, they were right. Luke *was* attracted to Julie. But he had no intention of putting the moves on a woman who'd had a baby just two weeks earlier—he wasn't a completely insensitive idiot.

Unfortunately, her time in Pinehurst was limited. Exactly how limited, he wasn't sure. He'd half expected her to start packing up when she got her vehicle back, and the fact that her parents were away had obviously been a factor in her decision to stay in Pinehurst a little bit longer. But how much longer? And would she stay long enough for him to figure out if there was any fire to go with the sparks he felt whenever he was around her?

"You can't fool Missy Walsh, either," Matt interjected.

"What does any of this have to do with Missy?" Luke demanded.

"I heard she was absolutely distraught after seeing you cuddling up to Julie in the grocery store," Jack told him.

"I wasn't cuddling up to her," Luke denied.

"It's not like Missy to get her facts wrong. At least not where you're concerned."

"I was purposely flirting with Julie," he admitted.

"Is it possible to accidentally flirt with a woman?" Matt wondered.

"Actually it is," Jack told him. "If flirtation is perceived but not intended."

Matt turned back to Luke. "But you were purposely flirting with Julie."

"I just wanted to give Missy something to think about."

"How is Missy?" Jack teased. "Has she got a new pet yet?"

"I'm glad you think it's funny. But at least I haven't come home and found her in my bed," Luke retorted.

His middle brother winced at the memory of what a former client had done to try to win his affection. As if that scenario wasn't awkward enough, Kelly had been with him when they found the naked woman in his condo.

"Not yet," Matt warned.

"I can't imagine her trying to break in when she knows Julie and Caden are there."

"So it's the new mom-and-baby security system," Jack concluded.

"Which might work with respect to Missy but has to put a damper on the rest of your love life."

"It would if he had one," Jack scoffed. "He hasn't even dated anyone since Sydney Dawes—and how long ago was that?"

More than six months, but Luke wasn't going to admit that. Instead, he just shrugged. "I got tired of going through the same routine with different women, and I decided I wasn't going to do it anymore."

"You've given up dating?"

"I've given up dating for the sake of dating," he clarified.

"You've finally realized that all those meaningless relationships were…meaningless?" Matt teased.

"Just because I'm not looking to hook myself up 'till death do us part' like you guys doesn't mean I don't want to meet someone different, someone who matters."

"How can you possibly know if someone's different unless you get to know her—by dating her?" Jack demanded.

"You ask her to move in with you," Matt said, not entirely tongue-in-cheek.

"Julie and Caden are only staying at my place for the short term," Luke reminded his brothers.

"You just keep telling yourself that, and maybe you'll even start to believe it," Jack said.

"Or maybe," Matt suggested, "you'll figure out that a real relationship isn't such a bad deal, after all."

Chapter Ten

When the women arrived at Gia's Salon & Spa, they were escorted to individual treatment rooms. Julie enjoyed a head and neck massage with warm oils and scented wraps that worked out knots she hadn't even known existed. After that, she rejoined Georgia and Kelly in the pedicure area. It was set up like a private living room, with the chairs arranged in a semicircle facing the fireplace. Flames were flickering in the hearth and soft music was piped through speakers in the ceiling.

Totally relaxed now, they talked about everything and anything—from recent movies and favorite books to local events and sports legends—which, Julie learned, included the three Garrett brothers.

When their toenails were painted and they were sitting around waiting for the polish to dry, Kelly looked at Julie and huffed out a breath. "Dammit," she said. "I like you."

"Thank you," Julie said cautiously.

The other woman smiled. "I didn't want to like you," she admitted. "Because I know that Lukas is falling for you and I'm afraid that you're going to break his heart."

Julie felt a jolt of something—surprise? alarm? hope?—in her chest in response to Kelly's words, but she shook her head. She didn't believe it, couldn't let herself believe it.

She was just beginning to acknowledge to herself that she had feelings for Lukas. And under different circumstances, she knew that she could easily fall for him. But circumstances weren't different. Maybe he was the right man, but this was definitely the wrong time. Her life was simply too complicated right now to even consider a personal relationship, no matter how much she might wish otherwise.

"I think you're misreading the situation."

"I don't think so," Kelly denied.

"Lukas has been incredibly kind but—"

The other woman snorted.

"He *is* kind," Georgia confirmed, shooting a look at her soon-to-be sister-in-law. "But I think Kelly's suggesting that his motives aren't quite so altruistic where you're concerned."

Julie shook her head. "He knows that I'm not staying in Pinehurst, that my life's in Springfield."

"Is it?"

The question surprised Julie. But then she realized that Kelly was right to challenge her statement, because in the two weeks that she'd been in Pinehurst, she'd barely thought about her former life at all. She certainly didn't miss it.

Yes, she missed her family. But they were still her family and always would be, regardless of where she made her home. On the other hand, she had no reason to consider making her home in Pinehurst. Her growing feelings for a sweet and sexy veterinarian aside, there was nothing for her here.

"It used to be," she finally said. "Although the truth is, I've been on the road working for the past seven months."

"What do you do?"

"I'm a curator at The Grayson Gallery in Springfield, but I've been traveling with a private collection since April."

"You haven't been home in all that time?" Georgia asked.

Julie shook her head.

"I'm thinking there's a better reason than an art show to stay away for so long," Kelly mused.

"A lot of reasons," she agreed. "Although I fully intended to be home before my baby was born."

"Except that Caden had other ideas."

"Or maybe it was fated that you would get stuck in Pinehurst," Georgia suggested.

Kelly frowned, obviously not pleased to consider that stronger forces might have factored into setting up the current situation.

"It wasn't fate," Julie denied. "It was simply the combination of no snow tires and a freak blizzard."

"The snow melted last week," Kelly pointed out.

"I just got my car back from Bruce on Monday." Which even she knew was a lame explanation, considering that it was now Saturday and she was still there, still without any firm plans to leave or any set date to do so.

"Monday," Kelly echoed in a considering tone. "So maybe Lukas isn't the only one who's falling?"

Julie sighed. "I'm *not* falling. But I will say that Lukas is handsome and kind, sexy and sweet. He's smart, funny, warm, compassionate and probably the most incredible man I've ever met."

"She's definitely falling," Georgia confirmed. "Can you believe it—all of the Garrett brothers finding true love in the same calendar year?"

Kelly shook her head. "You read too many romance novels."

The mother of three shrugged, unapologetic. "I like happy endings."

"And you got your very own when you married Matt."

"Actually, I like to think of the day I married Matt as a happy beginning," her friend clarified. "And speaking of weddings…"

Kelly sighed. "I know—I need a dress."

"Not that you should rush into anything," Georgia said. "After all, you still have three whole weeks before the wedding."

Julie's jaw dropped. "You're getting married in three weeks and you don't have a dress?"

"I've got the groom," Kelly said, just a little smugly.

"And an appointment at Belinda's Bridal in Syracuse next Saturday," Georgia told her.

"Why do I have to go all the way to Syracuse to go shopping?"

"Because your daughter found a beautiful strapless satin Alfred Sung gown in stock and in your size, and she begged and pleaded and somehow convinced the manager to hold it until next weekend."

"She just wants me to go strapless so that she can go strapless," Kelly muttered.

"Possibly," Georgia admitted. "But she showed me a photo of the dress she picked for you, and it's gorgeous."

The bride-to-be still didn't look convinced. "Any dress looks good on an airbrushed model in a glossy magazine."

"Next Saturday," Georgia said firmly.

Kelly wiggled her painted toes, then looked at Julie. "Can we kidnap you again next Saturday?"

Julie grinned. "For shopping? Anytime."

Only later did she realize that none of them—herself included—had questioned the assumption that she would still be in Pinehurst a week later.

* * *

Julie enjoyed her visit to the spa with Kelly and Georgia, but by the time she slid her "Fabulous Fuchsia" painted toes into her shoes, she was anxious to get back to Caden and Lukas. Not that she would dare admit as much to either of the women in her company.

When they arrived at Matt and Georgia's house, they found a much quieter scene than the one they'd escaped from a few hours earlier. Lukas was in the living room with Caden in his lap, watching a football game and explaining the set plays and terminology to the baby. When there was a stoppage in play, he told them that Matt was in the basement playing video games with the twins, Pippa was napping in her crib upstairs and Jack was in the kitchen working on a science project with Ava.

As the other women went off to track down their respective partners, Julie crossed to the sofa and scooped her baby into her arms. She breathed in his sweet baby scent and noisily kissed both of his cheeks. "There's my big guy."

"And still in one piece," Lukas said proudly.

"If I hadn't been absolutely certain, I never would have left him with you."

"Did you leave him with me?" he asked. "Because Ava seemed to think she was in charge."

She smiled at that. "Kelly says she's desperate for a baby brother or sister of her own."

"And in the meantime, she's been practicing with Pippa— and now Caden."

"Did either you or Ava have any problems?"

Lukas shook his head. "Aside from the fact that he did *not* want to take the bottle you left for him."

"I wondered about that. The books warn that when nursing mothers attempt to bottle-feed, their babies can suffer from nipple confusion..." She let the explanation trail off as she felt her cheeks flush. "Sorry, I spent the last few hours with two women who have been through the same thing, I wasn't thinking about the fact that you probably don't need to hear those kinds of details."

He just shrugged. "He screamed for a while—and let me tell you, that boy has a very healthy set of lungs—but when you didn't miraculously appear to give him what he wanted, his hunger won out."

"I guess that's a good thing," she said. "But it almost makes me feel superfluous."

"It was one bottle—you're not superfluous."

"I know I'm being silly. It's just that I really missed him. I had a fabulous time, but I missed him."

"You look like you had a good time. In fact, you look…" He trailed off, as if not quite sure how to complete the sentence.

"Rested and refreshed?" she suggested. "Kelly promised that I would be both when Gia was finished with me, and that's definitely how I feel."

"I was going to say beautiful," he admitted.

"Oh." There was something about the way he was looking at her, the intensity in his eyes that started her heart pounding just a little bit faster again.

"But you're always beautiful," he continued. "Even the first time I saw you—through the foggy window of your car—you took my breath away."

"Of course, that was before I got out from behind the wheel and you saw me waddle like a penguin behind the belly of a whale," she teased.

"You never waddled," he denied.

"I was eight and a half months pregnant," she reminded him.

"And beautiful."

He brushed his knuckles down her cheek, but it was her knees that went weak.

"And I've been thinking about kissing you since that first day." His words were as seductive as his touch, and the heat in his gaze held her mesmerized as he lowered his head, inching closer and closer until his lips hovered above hers.

"You have the most tempting mouth." He traced the outline of her lips with his fingertip. "Soft. Shapely. Sexy."

"Are you still thinking about it?" she asked, the question barely more than a whisper. "Or are you actually going to kiss me?"

Luke breached the tiny bit of distance that separated their mouths and lightly rubbed his lips against hers.

They were even softer than he'd suspected.

Even sweeter.

He kissed her again, another gentle caress—a question more than a statement. She sighed softly, her eyes drifting shut—the answer that he'd been seeking.

He nibbled on her mouth, savoring her texture and flavor. Her response was unhesitating. Her lips yielded, then parted, and her tongue dallied with his. They were barely touching— it was only their mouths that were linked, and the taste of her made him crave more. He slid an arm around her waist, to draw her closer, and finally remembered that she had a baby in her arms. And that they were standing in the middle of his brother's living room.

With sincere reluctance, he eased his mouth from hers.

She looked up at him, her eyes clouded with desire and confusion.

"That wasn't an actual kiss," he told her.

She blinked. "Then what was it?"

He wasn't sure how to answer that honestly without scaring her off. Because the truth was, it had been just enough of a taste to make him realize that he was starving for her, and that he wanted to feast not just on her mouth but on all her delicious parts.

"Let's call it...a prelude to a kiss," he decided.

"So am I ever going to get a real kiss?"

It was reassuring to know that she was experiencing at least some of the same attraction that was churning him up inside. Unfortunately now wasn't the time or the place to figure out how much.

"Yeah," he promised. "But not when I have to worry that we might be interrupted by either of my brothers, their significant others, kids or animals, or any combination of the same."

When they were home and Caden was fed and settled down for a nap, Julie went to the laundry room to take the clothes out of the dryer. She carried the basket into the family room, intending to fold while she watched TV, and froze in the doorway when she saw Lukas was already there.

He was reading a veterinarian periodical and didn't even look up when she entered the room. She exhaled an unsteady breath and sat down on the edge of the sofa, with the basket on the coffee table in front of her.

At Jackson and Kelly's house, when Lukas had been looking at her and talking about kissing her, all she'd been able to think about was how much she wanted the same thing. Now that her mind wasn't clouded by his nearness and her hormones weren't clamoring for action, she was having second thoughts. Mostly because what he'd called a prelude to a kiss was actually one of the best kisses she'd ever experienced in her entire life.

"I'm not going to jump you, Julie."

But she jumped when his voice broke the silence, knocking the basket off the table and spilling its contents all over the floor.

He immediately crossed the room, dropping to his knees beside her to help gather up the laundry.

"I'm sorry," he said. "I didn't mean to make you nervous."

She wanted to say that she wasn't, but since it would obviously be a lie, she remained silent.

"Although I have to admit I'm a little curious about why you're suddenly so on edge," he continued. "Is it because you're afraid I'm going to really kiss you? Or disappointed that I haven't already?"

"I'm not sure," she admitted, picking up scattered baby socks. "Maybe a little of both."

His smile was wry. "At least you're honest."

She scooped up the last sleeper and dropped it into the basket.

"Your pulse is racing," Luke noted, and touched his fingertip to the side of her neck, just beneath her ear.

Her skin felt singed by the touch, and her throat went dry. She lifted her gaze to his, and saw the desire in his eyes. She hadn't seen it when he looked at her before. Maybe she hadn't wanted to see it. But there was no denying it was there now.

"It's the way you look at me," she admitted. "You make my heart pound."

He took her palm and laid it against his chest, so she could feel that his heart was pounding, too. And then his head lowered toward her, and her breath caught in her lungs.

"Can I kiss you now, Julie?"

She wanted him to kiss her. She wanted to feel his lips against hers so desperately she ached, but she also knew that if he kissed her, everything would change. And she wasn't sure she wanted anything to change.

She genuinely liked Lukas. She enjoyed spending time with him, talking to him. She even enjoyed being with him when they didn't have anything to talk about, because the silence was never awkward or uncomfortable. She didn't want things to get awkward between them.

But as his lips hovered above hers, she couldn't deny that she wanted his kiss a lot more than she wanted the status quo.

His hands—those wide-palmed, strong, capable hands—cradled her face gently. He tilted her head back, adjusting the angle to deepen the kiss. He touched his tongue to the center of her top lip, a light, testing stroke. She met it with her own, a response and an invitation. He dipped inside her mouth, and the sweep of his tongue sent shockwaves of pleasure shooting down her spine, leaving her weak and quivering with need.

After what seemed like an eternity—and yet somehow nearly not long enough—he finally eased his mouth from hers. "That was a kiss," he told her.

She made no attempt to move out of his arms, because she wasn't sure her legs would support her. "Maybe we should have stopped with the prelude," she said, when she'd managed to catch her breath.

"I don't think that would have been possible."

"I don't want to start something we can't finish. You know I'm only going to be in town for a few more weeks."

"How could I possibly forget when you keep reminding me every time I turn around?"

"I just don't want to give you mixed signals."

He tipped her chin up, forcing her to meet his gaze. "Are you attracted to me, Julie?"

"Do you really have to ask?"

He grinned. "Then I can be satisfied with that."

She eyed him doubtfully. "Really?"

"I'm not going to push for more than you're ready to give."

"I'm grateful for that," she told him.

"And until you trust me enough to talk to me, I can't see a few kisses leading to anything more."

"I do trust you."

"And yet you haven't said a single word to me about Caden's father."

Well, that was a complete mood killer. Except that she knew it wasn't unreasonable for Luke to want at least some of the details. "Not because I don't trust you," she told him. "But because I don't want to talk about him."

"As I said, I'm not going to push for more than you're ready to give."

She understood why he would have questions, and maybe it was time to give him some answers. She sat back on the sofa and drew in a deep breath. "His name is Elliott Davis Winchester III. He works in public relations at the Springfield Medical Center but has aspirations of a career in politics. I've known him for two years—well, I guess closer to three now, although I haven't seen him since I gave him back his ring seven and a half months ago."

Luke had been reluctant to push for answers—probably because he suspected he might not like what he learned. Her words confirmed it. "You were engaged to him?"

She nodded.

He wasn't really shocked by the revelation. Julie didn't seem the type of woman to get pregnant as a result of a one-night stand. But a relationship, however long-term, was different than an engagement. An engagement was a promise to marry, a plan for forever. If Julie had been engaged to Caden's father, she'd obviously been in love with him. Maybe she still was.

He cleared his throat. "What happened?"

"I realized he wasn't the man I thought he was—and he definitely wasn't a man I wanted to marry."

"Have you been in touch with him, to tell him that you had the baby?"

She shook her head.

"Don't you think he has a right to know?"

"Of course, the biological father has all kinds of rights, doesn't he?"

Something in her tone alerted him to the possibility that there was more to her situation than a jilted lover not wanting to fight over custody of her child. "Tell me what happened, Julie. Because I can't imagine that you went from making wedding plans one minute to hiding out with your baby the next without a pretty good reason."

His patient tone succeeded in dimming the fiery light in her eyes. "He hit me."

Luke hadn't seen that coming, and he almost felt as if he'd been punched.

"We'd been out to a political fundraiser and Elliott had been busy working the room, drinking and chatting with everyone who was anyone, telling jokes and laughing and drinking. When we got back to his place, he poured another drink and wanted to rehash every word of every conversation he'd had, but I was tired and just wanted to go to bed. He accused me of not being supportive, I said that he seemed more interested in Johnny Walker's company than mine, and he backhanded me.

"He only hit me once," she said, and touched a fingertip to her cheek where there was a tiny white scar he'd never before noticed. "But it was with the hand that proudly displayed the Yale class ring, and that was enough for me. I left.

"There was a pattern of escalating behavior, of course, that I only recognized after the fact. But the slap was—for me—the final straw."

"What else did he do?" Luke asked the question through gritted teeth.

"Does it matter? I left him. It's over. Now I just want to forget."

"Yes, it matters," he insisted. "Because unless you tell somebody about what he did, he gets away with it."

"Most of the time he was very courteous and considerate," she finally said. "But sometimes, when he was drinking, he would become impatient, angry, aggressive."

"What did he do?" he asked again.

"He'd berate my opinions, belittle my feelings. Outwardly, he would be attentive and affectionate, but he'd hold my hand a little too tight, or his fingers would bite into my skin when he took my arm."

"Did he leave bruises?"

"Not really. He never really hurt me before the night I left. But…"

"But what?" he prompted.

"I guess I knew it was escalating toward that," she admitted. "I wasn't really scared of him, but I was uneasy. I think that's one of the reasons that I didn't want to set a wedding date, because I was waiting for something like that to happen so I could leave him."

"Why did you need a reason to leave?"

"Because until he actually hit me, he seemed like the perfect man. My parents knew him, respected him. And for the first time in my life, they approved of a man I was dating. When we got engaged, they were thrilled."

"Do you think they would be thrilled to know that he'd hit you?"

"Of course not," she immediately denied. "Neither of them has any tolerance for domestic abuse."

Luke didn't, either. He'd never understood how anyone could hurt someone they claimed to love—spouse, child, parent or even pet. But he knew that it happened far too often.

"I understand now why you don't want him to be part of Caden's life, but I don't understand why you didn't immediately go to the police and press charges," he said.

"It was my first instinct," she confided. "My cheek was still burning when I reached for the phone. Elliott saw what I was doing, and there was a quick flare of panic in his eyes... and then he smiled.

"And he warned me that if I called the police—if I told anyone at all—he would destroy my father's career."

Chapter Eleven

Luke knew it didn't matter if the man had the ability to follow through on his threat, what mattered was that Julie obviously believed he did.

"How was he going to do that?" he asked her now.

"My father's a judge—a superior court judge, actually, with a reputation for being strict and unyielding. He built his career on a foundation of ensuring everyone had equal access to justice and was treated equally by the law."

"And it didn't occur to you that he might be a little bit upset that you gave in to your abusive fiancé's blackmail?"

"It occurred to me that he'd be devastated if his career was ended and I could have saved it."

"What do you think he did that you needed to save it?"

She picked up a sleeper out of the basket and carefully began to fold it. "Can I refuse to answer that question on the grounds that it may incriminate me?"

"This isn't a court of law," he reminded her. "You don't have to tell me anything that you don't want to."

"I don't want you to think badly of me," she admitted.

"I don't think I could."

She put the sleeper down, reached for another. "I had a very privileged upbringing," she confided. "I had the luxury of a stable home and a loving family, but I didn't always make smart choices.

"In my junior year of high school, a bunch of kids were planning to go to Mexico for spring break. My parents weren't thrilled with the idea, but they agreed that I could go if I paid for it. After Christmas, I went shopping with a few friends and there was this gorgeous Kate Spade handbag that I just couldn't resist. Except that, after buying the bag, I realized that I was almost two hundred dollars short for the trip and my parents refused to loan me the money."

"Which made you furious," he guessed.

She nodded and kept folding. "Because it wasn't that they didn't have the money—it was the principle, they said. They'd agreed that I could go if I paid for it, and I said that I would."

"So you didn't get to go on the spring break trip," he concluded.

"No—I went. When I told Tomas, my boyfriend at the time, that I didn't have the money, he said that he would loan it to me and let me pay him back in a few months. It seemed like the perfect solution to me, except that when we were ready to leave Mexico, Tomas wanted me to carry some souvenirs back for him as repayment for the loan."

He could see where she was going with this story and he really didn't want to hear anymore. But it was like passing the scene of a motor vehicle collision—he didn't want to see the carnage, but he couldn't seem to look away.

"I was young and naive, but I wasn't stupid," Julie continued. "I told him to carry his own drugs and I would reimburse him the cost of the ticket when we got home."

"Nothing about that sounds scandalous to me."

"No, that's just background—the first really bad choice that I made. Of course, I promised myself that I'd learned my lesson. Then, about six months later, I met Randy Cosgrove."

She'd finished with the sleepers and moved on to diaper shirts. "Randy was another bad boy. His father was a minister and Randy was the stereotypical preacher's kid who went in the opposite direction of everything his family believed. He was dark and brooding and sexy—the type of guy that all fathers warn their daughters about."

He wasn't sure how much more he wanted to hear about her relationship with Randy, but he wasn't willing to interrupt now that she was finally talking to him.

"My father warned me. My mother warned me. My brothers warned me. But I didn't listen. I was so sure they were wrong about him, and even if they weren't, I didn't care. Because I had fun with Randy—he was defiant, sexy and exciting, and I was totally infatuated with him.

"One night Randy came by to take me for a drive in a friend's car he'd borrowed. It was a candy-apple-red 1965 Ford Mustang convertible and it was a starry night, and we drove around for nearly an hour with the top down and the music blaring. And then the cops showed up and arrested both of us for stealing the car."

"How old were you?"

"Seventeen."

"That must have been a scary experience for you."

"I was terrified. I don't know how long I was at the police station before my parents came—probably not more than a few hours—but it felt like forever. Then my dad and the arresting officer were in conference for what seemed like several more hours, and when they finally came out, we went home."

"The way you told the story to me, you didn't even know the car was stolen."

"I didn't," she assured him. "But I didn't ask any questions, either. Not even the name of the friend Randy supposedly borrowed the car from. Randy did six months in juvie, and I walked away.

"Elliott told me that he could prove my dad had pulled strings and called in favors to keep me out of jail, that I wasn't charged because I got deferential treatment. If that's true, if he has proof, it will completely undermine my father's assertion that everyone is equal under the law."

"If you were never charged, what kind of proof could he have?"

"I don't know," she admitted.

"Then maybe you should consider that he manufactured whatever so-called evidence he has."

"I wish I could believe that was true, but I never told Elliott about that…incident. Which means that he must have gotten the details from someone else. Someone who was there, at the police station, and who knows what happened behind the scenes."

"Have you talked to your father about this?"

She shook her head.

"Why not?"

"I couldn't. At first, I couldn't because I didn't want to face my parents after what Elliott had done. And then—" she blew out an unsteady breath "—I was afraid to ask him about it."

"Afraid that it might be true?" he guessed.

She nodded. "I didn't want to believe it. At the time, I was so relieved that I didn't have to be photographed and fingerprinted and go to court, that I didn't even question it. But later, I started to wonder how I'd managed to slip out of that sticky situation so easily.

"Elliott's allegation that my father pulled strings and called in favors would certainly answer that question. And after everything my parents had done for me, there was no way I could do anything that would risk my dad's reputation and career."

"Instead, you let Elliott get away with what he did to you?"

She winced at his blunt assessment, though it was true. "I chose to end my relationship with Elliott and walk away. It seemed like the easiest solution at the time. Of course, that was before I knew I was pregnant."

"And now?"

"Now...I don't know," she admitted. "Elliott has political ambitions, and a strict timetable in which he wants things to happen. And I honestly don't know how he'll react to his ex-fiancée showing up with his out-of-wedlock child.

"I know I have to tell him about the baby, but one of the reasons I didn't tell him when I first discovered that I was pregnant was that I was worried he would try to force a reconciliation. He would say it was for the sake of our baby, but it would really be for the sake of his career. In politics, married men are viewed as more trustworthy and reliable than unmarried men—add a baby to the mix, and he'd be laughing."

"Do you think he'd still try to get you back?"

"I don't know," she admitted.

"Would you go back to him?"

"No." Her response was unequivocal and without hesitation.

"I'm sorry."

"For what?"

"Asking you to talk about this."

"You didn't push me for more than I was ready to give," she reminded him.

"Okay, then I'm sorry that talking about this undid all the good of Gia's massage."

She managed a smile. "Well, at least my toes still look good."

There was a definite chill in the air on Monday, so Julie decided to put a roast in the oven for dinner. She peeled carrots and potatoes to go with it, and figured she would try her hand at Yorkshire pudding, too.

Sunday had been a quiet day. Despite the passionate kisses she and Lukas had shared on Saturday night and her heart-wrenching confessions afterward, there was no lingering awkwardness between them.

There were also no more kisses, and although she was undeniably disappointed, the rational part of her brain reassured her that it was a good thing. It was scary to think about how much he meant to her already, how quickly he'd become not just a good friend but an important part of her world. And she knew that if there were more kisses, if they took their relationship to the next level, it would only be that much more difficult for her to leave.

After the basic prep for dinner was done, she spent some time playing with Caden—talking nonsense to him and showing him blocks and squeaky toys. Then they had a nap together, lying on a blanket on the floor with Einstein. When Julie woke up, she noticed that even Daphne had joined them. And when she reached a tentative hand out, the cat not only endured her gentle scratching but actually purred in appreciation.

She had just checked the potatoes when Lukas called to say that he was leaving the office. Caden wasn't on any kind of schedule yet, but she liked to nurse him before Lukas got home. Despite his claim that he was okay with the nursing thing, and although she knew her breasts were functional rather than sexual, the sizzle she felt around Lukas was so completely sexually charged that she'd decided it was best to keep her clothes on whenever he was around.

After Caden was fed and his diaper changed, Julie put him in a clean sleeper. She was just fastening the snaps when she heard the crash.

She raced down the stairs with the baby in her arms just as the back door opened and Lukas walked in.

They stood on opposite sides of the room, staring at the scene. The roasting pan had been upended in the middle of the kitchen floor, meat juices were spreading over the ceramic tiles and Einstein was in the middle of all of it, joyfully wolfing down prime rib.

It took Luke all of two seconds to accurately assess the situation. "Einstein!"

The dog cowered, his ears flat, his belly against the floor. Which meant that he was pretty much marinating himself in beef juice.

Julie was silent for a long minute, trying to comprehend the carnage, then her blue-gray eyes filled with tears.

Luke's first instinct was to go to her, to put his arms around her and reassure her that it wasn't a catastrophe of major proportions. But he knew that if he took a single step in her direction, Einstein would jump up, vying for his attention, and splashing in the au jus. Instead, he moved toward the dog, trying not to step in the gravy. He scooped him up and held him at arm's length.

"Let me get him cleaned up first, then I'll come back to deal with that," he told Julie, nodding toward the remains of Einstein's feast.

Of course, bathing a wriggling puppy who didn't like to be bathed wasn't an easy task. Einstein kept trying to jump out of the laundry tub, which meant that Luke ended up as wet as the puppy, and every time he plunked the animal back down in the water, he howled so desperately and pitifully that Luke started to feel guilty for forcing the bath.

When he finally drained the tub and rubbed the dog down, Julie had cleaned up the kitchen.

"I hope you're not hungry," she said, when he came out of the laundry room. "Because that was dinner."

"For what it's worth, it smelled really good."

"It would have been delicious." She glared at the dog. "He didn't even savor it—he scarfed it down like it was a bowl of three-dollar kibble rather than thirty dollars worth of prime rib."

Luke tried to look in the bright side. "I was kind of in the mood for pizza, anyway."

She just stared at him. "Pizza?"

"What's wrong with pizza?" Aside from the fact that it wasn't prime rib, of course. But he wasn't going to bring that up again.

"Nothing," she finally decided. "As long as we can get it with pineapple and black olives."

"I'll go along with the pineapple and black olives if I can add bacon."

"Are you that determined to clog your arteries before you're forty?"

"My doctor isn't worried."

"Fine. Pineapple, black olives and bacon," she agreed.

"Speaking of doctors," Lukas said. "Weren't you supposed to take Caden for a checkup soon?"

"We have an appointment with Dr. Turcotte on Thursday afternoon."

"What time?"

"Two o'clock."

"Do you want me to go with you?"

She lifted a brow. "You don't think I can manage to take the baby to a doctor's appointment on my own?"

"I'm sure you can," he agreed. "But I usually book surgeries on Tuesday and Thursday afternoons, and it just so happens that I don't have anything scheduled for this Thursday. Besides, I'm kind of curious to see how much the little guy has grown."

"You're not worried that going to see my baby's doctor with me might send the wrong message?"

"Cameron isn't the type to jump to conclusions," he assured her.

"I wasn't thinking about him so much as any other patients who might be in the waiting room—particularly those of the female variety."

"They can jump to all the conclusions they want."

She smiled. "So it's true."

"What's true? Who have you been talking to?"

"Maybe I'm just observant."

His gaze narrowed. "Kelly."

"Perhaps," she allowed.

"What else did she tell you?"

"I'm not dishing on our girl talk to you."

"Then I'll ask Kelly."

"You do that," she said, her tone reflecting certainty that Kelly would keep her confidence.

"We go back a long way," he reminded her.

"You were the first friend she had when she came to Pinehurst in fifth grade and still her best friend," she said, repeating what Jack's fiancée had obviously told her. "And the woman you once proposed to."

He winced. "Apparently she had no problem dishing to you."

"She wanted me to understand what kind of man you are,"

Julie explained. "But I already knew, and I'd already figured out that she was the woman you told me about."

"When she told me that she was pregnant—I knew she was terrified. And I didn't want her to think that she had to go through it on her own."

"And you were in love with her."

He frowned at the matter-of-fact tone of her statement. "Maybe I thought I was," he allowed.

"Of course you were," she continued. "And why wouldn't you be? She's a beautiful woman, you obviously shared a lot of common interests and history."

He was surprised—and a little unnerved—by the accuracy of her insights. No one else had ever known the true depth of his feelings for his best friend. No one had ever guessed that the real reason he'd never fallen in love with any other woman was that he was in love with Kelly.

Then he'd realized that she was in love with his brother— and that truth wasn't just a blow to his ego but a dagger through his heart. Until he'd seen them together and saw the way they looked at one another. Even when they were both still hurt and angry, there was no denying the love between them—and he knew they'd both tried.

And that was when Luke had finally let go. Because he knew that he could feel hurt and betrayed, but he couldn't continue to pretend that he and Kelly had ever been anything more than friends.

"We did share a lot of things," he admitted to Julie. "But never more than a single kiss when we were in seventh grade."

She held up her hands. "None of my business."

"I just want to make it clear that I didn't have any kind of romantic history with my brother's fiancée."

"Aside from the fact that you were in love with her."

"Infatuated," he clarified, because he understood now that unrequited love wasn't really love at all. He'd spent too many years comparing all the other woman he met to the ideal of the one he held in his heart, and now that he'd finally let go of that ideal, a different woman had taken up residence in his heart.

"To-may-to, to-mah-to," she countered.

He frowned, feigning confusion. "I thought you said bacon, pineapple and black olives?"

She rolled her eyes. "Why don't you actually order it so that we get to eat sometime tonight?"

So he did.

The pizza was delivered within twenty minutes, but even when the delivery boy rang the bell, Einstein didn't move from the corner to which he'd been banished. In fact, he even stayed there the whole time that Luke and Julie were eating.

But when the pizza box was empty and pushed aside, the pup slowly inched across the floor on his belly until he was beside her chair. Even when Einstein dropped his chin onto her foot, Julie pretended she didn't see him. Einstein, devastated by this rejection, licked her toes.

"He's trying to apologize," Luke pointed out to her.

"Well, I don't accept his apology," she said.

But in contradiction to the harsh words, one hand reached down to scratch the top of his head, and Einstein's tail thumped against the floor.

She had every right to be furious with the animal still, but her soft heart couldn't hold out against the obviously contrite puppy. It seemed to Luke further proof that she fit into every aspect of his life, and with each day that passed, he couldn't help wondering if she might change her mind about passing through.

He'd dated a lot of women in his thirty-four years, and he wasn't sure how to interpret his growing feelings for Julie. Was it just proximity? Was it the shared experience of Caden's birth that had forged a bond between them? Or was it because his brothers had both fallen in love so recently that he was looking to fill some void in his own life?

He knew that was a distinct possibility, except that he'd never felt as if there was a void in his life. He'd always been happy—he had a job he loved, good friends, close family and pets that lavished him with affection.

Okay, so that might be a bit of an exaggeration where Daphne was concerned, but he knew the cat loved him, too. Or at least appreciated being fed every day, having a warm bed to sleep in and a clean litter box at her disposal.

But with Julie and Caden under his roof, even though they'd been there only a few weeks, he felt as if they belonged. Which wasn't something he should be thinking when she was planning to go back to Springfield soon.

He didn't know exactly when, but he was hoping he could convince her to stay at least until her parents came back from Australia.

"Ava called me at the clinic today," he told her.

She was immediately concerned. "Is something wrong with Puss or Boots?"

"No. She just wanted to know if I'm bringing a date to the wedding. Apparently she's trying to finalize the seating plan for Jack and Kelly's wedding and the numbers would work better if I had 'plus one.'"

"I'm sure Missy Walsh would clear her schedule for you," Julie teased.

"I was actually hoping you might be available."

"You want me to go with you to your brother's wedding?"

"Sure."

She looked wary. "That's a pretty monumental occasion."

"The second wedding in five months for the Garrett brothers," he confirmed.

"That's why you want me there," she realized. "As a barrier against all of the single women in Pinehurst who will be looking at you and dreaming of orange blossoms."

"I've never understood the connection between weddings and orange blossoms."

"They've played a part in wedding traditions tracing back to the ancient Greeks and Romans."

"So they're just a myth?"

She rolled her eyes. "They're a symbol."

"Of what?"

"Of innocence, fertility and everlasting love."

"That's a weighty responsibility for one flower."

"And they smell nice," she told him.

"They don't have any mystical powers, do they? Because apparently I have to wear one in the lapel of my tux."

"No mystical powers," she assured him. "You don't need to be afraid that you'll fall in love with the third woman who crosses your path after the sun sets."

"I'm not afraid of falling in love," he denied.

"Says the only Garrett brother who's never sweated in a tux waiting for his bride to walk down the aisle."

"I never used to think that I wanted what my brothers have."

"Why not?" she challenged.

"Maybe I just never found the right woman," he said, his tone deliberately casual. "Until you."

Chapter Twelve

Julie's eyes went wide, wary. "You don't even know me."

"I know that my life is better—richer and fuller—since you and Caden have been part of it," Luke told her. "I know that I look forward to coming home at the end of each day because you're here. And I'm hoping that you'll stay in Pinehurst at least until the wedding."

She sighed. "Does anyone ever say 'no' to you?"

"Do you want to say 'no'?"

"No," she admitted. "And that's the problem."

"You're going to have to explain how that's a problem."

"Because you're a good man, Lukas Garrett, and I've never fallen for a good man before."

Although she hadn't come right out and said that she'd fallen for him, he was happy enough to accept the implication.

"In fact, I've always had notoriously bad taste in men," she continued. "I thought that had changed when I met Elliott, but even then, it turned out that he wasn't a good man—I only thought he was."

"And you're afraid that you might be wrong about me?" he guessed.

"I'm afraid that I'm totally wrong *for* you."

"You're not," he insisted.

"I'm a twenty-three-year-old single mother who ran away from home without even telling her parents that she was pregnant."

"You had a lot of reasons for running, but now you've stopped."

"Have I? Or is the fact that I'm still here and not in Springfield proof that I'm still running?"

It was a question that Julie spent a lot of time thinking about over the next few days, and still the answer continued to elude her.

As she kept reminding Lukas, her home was in Springfield. So why wasn't she any hurry to go home? Part of the reason for her reluctance was that if she went back to Massachusetts now, she'd be alone in the house she'd grown up in. Another part of the reason was apprehension. When she returned to Springfield, it was inevitable that she would cross paths with Elliott, and she wasn't yet ready for that to happen. She wasn't afraid of him—at least not physically. But she was afraid of what it would mean for Caden when Elliott learned that he had a child.

But the primary reason that she was still in Pinehurst was that it was where she wanted to be. Not just because it was a picturesque town in Upstate New York, but because it was where Lukas was.

Julie felt more comfortable in Lukas's home than she'd ever felt in Elliott's condo. Her former fiancé hadn't liked her to cook. He'd preferred that they go out to eat, to be seen at the best restaurants, to be seen with people who could advance his career ambitions.

She couldn't remember ever tucking her feet up beneath her on his couch and falling asleep while they watched TV. Because they didn't watch TV—they went to the theatre and museums and political fundraisers and charity events.

She hadn't realized how tiring it was to always be "on" until she finally had the opportunity to turn "off" and just relax. She could relax with Lukas—so long as she didn't think about the physical attraction that had her on edge.

His nearness made her weak, the slightest touch made her quiver, and even from across the room he could make her all hot and tingly with just a look. And the way he looked at her, she knew he felt the same way.

But he hadn't kissed her since that day she'd been kidnapped by Georgia and Kelly, and that was probably for the best. She was already more involved than was smart, and when she finally left Pinehurst, she knew that she'd be leaving a big part of her heart behind.

It was Sunday night, just four days before Thanksgiving, and Luke and Julie still hadn't reached a consensus with respect to their plans for the holiday.

"Kelly called today to tell me that she borrowed a highchair for Thanksgiving—one that has a reclining seat specifically designed for infants so that Caden can be at the table with everyone else."

"That was very thoughtful of her, but we're not going to be there for Thanksgiving."

"You and Caden were invited," he reminded her.

"Thanksgiving is a family holiday, and we're not family."

"Thanksgiving is a time to celebrate with those we care about," he countered. "Family *and* friends."

Apparently she didn't disagree with that, because she said nothing.

"And it's Caden's first Thanksgiving—so it should be special."

She lifted a brow. "Are you really using my child as a negotiating tool?"

He grinned. "Whatever works."

"Not that," she assured him.

"Okay, what if I said that my brothers and I haven't had a real Thanksgiving in a lot of years and I'd really like you and Caden to be there?"

"What do you mean, you haven't had a real Thanksgiving?"

"For the past few years, Matt, Jack and I have ordered pizza and chowed down on it while watching football on TV. This year, Georgia and Kelly have promised a traditional turkey dinner with all the trimmings," he explained. "And I'd really hate to miss out on that."

"There's no reason why you should," she assured him.

"I can't go if you don't go."

"Of course you can."

"And leave the two of you here?" He shook his head. "My mother raised me better than that."

The look she gave him confirmed that he'd finally played the trump card. But when she spoke, she said, "You often mention your parents in casual conversation, but you've never told me what happened to them."

"It's not a favorite topic of conversation," he admitted. "They were on a yacht that ran into a bad storm near Cape Horn. The boat capsized and everyone on board drowned."

"You lost them both at the same time?"

He nodded.

"I'm sorry," she said sincerely. "I can't even imagine how devastating that must have been."

"It was a shock for all of us," he agreed. "But I think it was the best way. Neither of them would have been happy without the other."

"They must have really loved one another."

"They did. They didn't always agree about everything, but there was never any doubt of their affection."

"Do you have any other family?"

"A couple of aunts and uncles and cousins on my father's side, but they're all in North Carolina, so we don't see them much."

"How long have your parents been gone?"

"Six years," he told her. "For the first three, I didn't make any changes around the house. I couldn't even rearrange the furniture. It was Jack who finally asked me one day if I was going to live in Mom and Dad's house forever.

"The house had been left to all three of us, but both Matt and Jack had already moved out, so I secured a mortgage on the property to buy them out. When I reminded my brother that it was my house now, Jack said he just wanted to be sure that *I* knew it, because every time he walked in the front door, he felt as if he was walking into their house still—right down to the ancient welcome mat inside the front door."

"Because part of you was still hoping they would come home," she guessed.

"That might have been a factor. And maybe I needed some time to accept that they wouldn't. But about six months after that conversation with Jack, I started a major renovation. It wasn't enough to tear down wallpaper and buy new towels for the bath—I knocked out walls, added another bathroom upstairs, updated the kitchen cabinets, refinished the hardwood."

"Converted the wood-burning fireplace to gas," she remembered.

He nodded. "Jack convinced me that the instant ambiance would help me get laid. And I can't believe I just said that out loud."

But she laughed. "I can't imagine you needed any help with that."

"That sounds like a compliment."

"A statement of fact," she noted. "You're an extremely handsome man—smart, sexy, charming. You've got a good heart, and a generous nature."

"And a soon-to-be sister-in-law who will give me no end of grief if I show up for Thanksgiving dinner without you and Caden."

Julie sighed. "You're also relentless."

"Does that mean you'll come for dinner?"

"If I do go, I can't go empty-handed," she protested. "I want to make a contribution to the meal."

"Kelly assured me that she and Georgia have everything covered."

"Even dessert?"

"Even dessert," he confirmed. "But if you want, we could take a couple bottles of wine."

"And flowers."

He wrinkled his nose. "For the main meal or dessert?"

She swatted his arm. "For the hostess."

"Okay," he relented. "We'll take wine and flowers."

He was right. Georgia and Kelly had everything covered. Roast turkey with pecan cornbread stuffing, buttermilk mashed potatoes, gravy, maple-glazed sweet potatoes, buttered corn, baby carrots, green beans with wild mushrooms, cauliflower gratin, tangy coleslaw and dinner rolls. Of course, everything looked so good that Julie couldn't let anything pass by without putting at least a small spoonful on her plate.

And everything was absolutely delicious. But even more than the meal, Julie found she genuinely enjoyed the interactions that took place around the table. There were often several conversations happening at the same time, bowls of food being passed in both directions and across the table, glasses clinking and cutlery clanging. It was, in her opinion, the most chaotic—and the most enjoyable—Thanksgiving dinner ever.

She was seated between Lukas and Caden and across from Quinn. The baby had sat contentedly in the borrowed highchair throughout most of the meal, but when Julie pushed her plate aside, she noticed that he was starting to fidget and rub his eyes. It was a sure sign that he was ready for a nap, and because he always fell asleep easier when he was being cuddled, she lifted him out of his chair.

Kelly and Georgia got up to start clearing away the leftovers and dishes to make room for dessert, so she passed the baby to Lukas in order to help.

She picked up the bowl that was mostly empty of buttermilk mashed potatoes and another with a few cauliflower florets and traces of cheese sauce, and headed toward the kitchen. But she couldn't resist turning back for one lingering look at the gorgeous man holding her baby. It wasn't just that he looked so comfortable with her son but that he looked so *right* with Caden in his arms.

Was it luck or fate that her car had slid into the ditch in front of his home? She didn't know, but she was grateful for whatever had brought him into her life. And she knew that her son was going to miss Lukas when she finally took him home to Springfield—maybe almost as much as she would.

Julie had just returned to the dining room when she heard Quinn say, "I was thinkin'."

The words made her smile, because the precocious twin had started a lot of conversations with the same preamble throughout the meal. Some of her favorite topics were the proposed marriage of his puppies, Finnigan and Frederick, with Ava's kittens, Puss and Boots, so that they could have "pup-tens"; having separate spaces for the boys and girls during carpet time at school so Shelby Baker couldn't sit beside him; and his confusion about why, if the glue at school was non-tot-sick (which Miss Lennon explained to him meant it wouldn't make kids sick) she worried about Cain eating it.

"What were you thinking?" Matt asked gamely.

As Julie gathered up a handful of cutlery, she waited to hear the child's response.

"There's lotsa mommies and daddies here."

"Sure," Matt agreed, a little cautiously.

"Me an' Shane an' Pippa have a mommy and daddy. And Uncle Jack and Auntie Kelly are Ava's mommy and daddy. But Caden only gots a mommy."

"Uncle Luke could be his daddy."

There was immediate and stunned silence, although Julie wasn't sure if it was the statement or the fact that Shane had spoken it that was the bigger surprise.

"Yeah," Quinn agreed, immediately onboard with that plan. "'Cuz he doesn't gots any kids."

"That's...an interesting idea," Lukas said. "But it isn't that simple."

"I know." Quinn nodded solemnly. "You'd hafta get married—like when Dr. Matt married Mommy so he could be our daddy."

"Yeah, it was all about you, kid," Jackson said dryly.

But Quinn's gaze was still focused on Lukas. "So—are you gonna do it?"

"I think we should focus on getting Uncle Jack to the altar before we start planning any more weddings," he replied cautiously.

"What's a altar?"

"It's where the wedding takes place," he explained.

"Uh-uh." Quinn shook his head. "Mommy and Daddy got married at the church."

As Lukas proceeded to explain that the altar was located inside the church, Julie felt a tug on her sleeve and saw Shane looking up at her. She was eager to make her escape to the kitchen, but she couldn't ignore the little boy's overture.

"Did you want something, sweetie?"

He shook his head. "We gots Legos."

She breathed a slow sigh of relief, confident this was a subject could handle. "I know. I saw you and Quinn playing with them earlier."

"When Caden gets big enuff, he can play Lego with us."

The offer, so unexpected and earnest, caused her throat to tighten. Or maybe it was regret that she knew they would be long gone from Pinehurst before her son was old enough to play anything with these adorable little boys.

"I know he would really like that," she said, because it was the truth.

"I like the blue blocks best," he told her.

"I like the yellow ones."

He offered her one of his shy smiles, and she made her escape with the handful of cutlery she held clutched tight in her fist and tears shimmering in her eyes.

Julie was quiet on the drive back to his house after dinner, and Luke didn't try to make conversation, either. He was thinking about the discussion Quinn and Shane had initiated, and wondering how it was that a couple of kids could so easily see what adults tried so hard to deny.

When they got home, Julie took Caden upstairs to feed and bathe him while Luke took care of feeding his pets.

Uncle Luke could be his daddy.

The words echoed in his head as he measured out food and filled bowls with water. They were words that, even a few weeks before, would have sent him into a panic. Because at that time, he hadn't been thinking about kids or a family.

But everything had changed when Julie and Caden came into his life. And now, instead of causing his chest to tighten with fear, those words filled his heart with hope.

He *could* be Caden's daddy. He *wanted* to be Caden's daddy. And he wanted Caden's mommy with a desperation that made him ache.

But over the past couple of weeks, he'd been careful to keep things light between them. He tried to remind himself that Julie was a guest in his home and he didn't want to make any overtures that might make her feel pressured or uncomfortable.

After the animals were fed, he went to the office to check his email. Then he played a few games of solitaire on the computer as he waited for Julie to come downstairs. Then he played a few more games and wondered if she'd fallen asleep with Caden or was avoiding him.

It was Einstein who alerted him to her arrival. The pup's keen sense of hearing always picked up the soft creak of the sixth step, and he raced out from under the desk to the bottom of the stairs.

"I thought maybe you'd fallen asleep," Luke said to her when she came into the family room.

She shook her head. "Unfortunately, Caden didn't want to, either. I think he was a little overstimulated today."

"Is this where I apologize for dragging you to the chaos that was Thanksgiving with the Garretts?"

"No. This is where I thank you for dragging us into the chaos." Then she touched her lips to his cheek. "Thank you."

"You really had a good time?"

"I really had a good time," she assured him. "Your family is wonderful."

He took her hand and led her over to the sofa, drawing her down beside him. "Even Quinn?"

"All of them," she confirmed with a smile.

"I wasn't sure if that was more awkward for you or for me," he admitted.

"I'd say for you—because I had an excuse to escape from the table."

And he suspected that she was thinking of making an escape now.

A suspicion that was confirmed when she said, "But his comment did make me wonder if we're giving people the wrong impression about us."

"What do you think is the wrong impression?"

"I think that the longer I stay the more awkward it's going to be when I go," she said, deliberately sidestepping his question.

"So what's your plan? Are you going to pack up now?"

"Do you want me to?"

He shook his head. "No. I don't want you to go," he said, and barely managed to hold back the word *ever*.

He let his fingertip follow the soft, full curve of her lower lip, felt it tremble in response to the slow caress, before he forced his hand to drop away.

The tip of her tongue swept along the same path as his finger, making her lip glisten temptingly. "Then we'll stay until December seventh, if you're sure it's okay."

December seventh was when her parents were due back from their cruise, and the date was now just a little more than two weeks away. It didn't seem like nearly enough time—but he would take whatever she was willing to give him.

"I'm sure. Besides, you promised to be my 'plus one' for the wedding," he reminded her.

"I know I did, but—"

"Ava's finished the seating plan," he said. "If you try to back out now, you'll have to face her wrath."

"I'm not backing out," she denied, though they both knew she'd been thinking about doing precisely that.

He tipped her chin up, forcing her to meet his gaze. "But you're still worried about 'people' getting the wrong impression."

She nodded.

"Then let's clarify the situation," he suggested, and covered her mouth with his.

It had been so long since he'd kissed her that Julie had forgotten how good he was at it. Of course, there didn't seem to be anything that Lukas Garrett wasn't good at, but kissing was definitely near the top of his list of talents.

He used just the right amount of pressure, so that his kiss was firm but not forceful. And he took his time. The man certainly knew how to draw out the pleasure until it seemed as if time was both endless and meaningless. His lips were masterful, his flavor potent, his kiss a leisurely and thorough seduction of all of her senses.

She was lost, drowning in sensation. He could have taken her anywhere, done anything, but he only continued to kiss her. In her admittedly limited experience, men raced around first base with their gaze already focused on second. Lukas didn't seem to be in a hurry to go anywhere.

And she didn't want to be anywhere but right where she was—in the moment with Lukas.

She lifted her arms to link them behind his neck, pressing closer to him. The soft curves of her body seemed to fit perfectly against the hard angles of his. He was so strong and solid, but when he was holding her, she didn't feel vulnerable, she felt…cherished.

His hands slid down her back, over her buttocks. He drew her closer, close enough that there was no doubt he was as thoroughly aroused as she was. Heat pulsed through her veins, pooled between her thighs. She wanted this man— she couldn't deny that any longer. But she couldn't afford to be reckless. She had a child to think about now—a four-week-old baby who had been fathered by another man. She had to be smart, rational, responsible. Unfortunately, that reprimand from her conscience did nothing to curb her desire.

Or was she just lonely? She'd been away from her family and her friends for so long, she wasn't sure how much of what she was feeling for Lukas was real and how much was simply a need for human contact. Except that being close to him now had her feeling all kinds of other things—none of which was lonely.

When he finally eased his mouth from hers, she touched her fingertips to lips still tingling from his kiss. "You're awfully good at that."

His lips curved in a slow, and undeniably smug, smile. "My father always told us that anything worth doing is worth doing right."

"Why do I think he probably wasn't expecting you would apply that advice to seducing women?"

"Do you think I could? Seduce you, I mean."

After that kiss, she didn't have the slightest doubt. "Just because you can doesn't mean you should."

"I realize that I'm probably a few steps ahead of you, that you probably haven't even thought about—"

"I've thought about it," she interrupted softly.

His gaze narrowed. "About what?"

"Making love with you."

He started to reach for her, then curled his fingers into his palms and thrust his hands into his pockets.

"You have?"

She nodded.

"So why are we talking instead of doing?"

"Because you scare me," she admitted.

He took an instinctive step back, his brow furrowed.

She immediately shook her head. "I'm not afraid that you'd

hurt me—not physically," she assured him. "But the way you make me feel—the intensity of it—absolutely terrifies me.

"When I'm with you, everything just seems right. But I don't understand how that's even possible. I've only known you a few weeks and there is nothing usual about the circumstances that brought us together. How can I trust that any of what I'm feeling is real?"

Luke didn't know how to respond, what to say to reassure her—or even if he should. She was right to be wary. He was wary, too. Neither of them could have anticipated what was happening between them. Neither could know where this path might lead. But he wanted to find out.

She'd been clear from the very beginning that she didn't plan on staying in Pinehurst beyond the short-term. Her family and her life were in Springfield. And even though he knew he could be setting himself up for heartbreak, he couldn't stop wanting to be with her, wanting to share every minute that she was in Pinehurst with her.

"I can't make you any promises or guarantees," he told her. "But I can tell you that the feelings you just described—I'm feeling them, too."

"You know I don't have a very good track record with men," she reminded him.

"It takes two people to make a relationship work."

"And I'm only going to be here another couple of weeks, so I can't let myself fall in love with you."

He wanted to smile at that. Though he was hardly an expert on the subject, he knew that falling in love wasn't a choice. He certainly hadn't chosen to fall in love with Julie, but he knew that he was more than halfway there.

Of course, admitting as much would only scare her more. So instead he said, "I'm not asking you to fall in love with me—just to let me make love with you."

She nibbled on her lower lip, something he'd realized that

she did when she was thinking. Unfortunately, the subconscious action deprived him of the ability to think. Instead, he wanted to cover her mouth with his own, to sink into the lush fullness of those lips again.

Then she drew in a deep breath and looked up at him, meeting his gaze evenly. "I guess those are terms I can live with."

His brows lifted. "You guess?"

She smiled. "Do you want to stand here and argue about my choice of words or do you want to take me upstairs?"

Before the words were completely out of her mouth, he swept her off her feet and into his arms.

Chapter Thirteen

Julie took a moment to glory in the thrill of being carried by a strong man. It was another new experience for her and a memory that she knew she would carry with her forever. As he made his way up the stairs, her heart pounded inside her chest and anticipation hummed in her veins. There wasn't any hesitation in her mind, no reservations in her heart.

But when he set her on her feet beside the bed, she felt the first subtle stirring of apprehension. When she realized that he'd already unfastened the buttons that ran down the front of her blouse—that he was undressing her—nerves jittered.

She hadn't thought about the "getting naked" part. It was a usual prerequisite to adult lovemaking, but it wasn't something that her lust-clouded mind had grasped when she'd suggested they come upstairs.

Then he pushed the blouse off of her shoulders and reached for the zipper at the back of her skirt. Except that there wasn't a zipper because it was a maternity skirt, complete with the stretchy panel in front because she wasn't yet able to squeeze into any of her pre-pregnancy clothes. But he quickly figured things out, and pushed the skirt over her hips until it pooled at her feet.

"My body isn't as toned or tight as it was a year ago," she said apologetically.

His hands skimmed from her shoulders to her knees, leisurely caressing her curves along the way. "You feel perfect to me."

She shook her head. "I'm not—"

"Shut up, Julie." The words were muttered against her mouth as he covered it with his own.

She wanted to make some sort of indignant reply, but she couldn't say anything while her lips were otherwise occupied kissing him back. And truthfully, kissing him was a much more pleasurable pastime than arguing with him. And when he kissed her and touched her, she couldn't think clearly enough to worry about the extra pounds. In fact, she couldn't think at all.

And when he pulled her closer, the turgid peaks of her nipples brushed against the hard wall of his chest, making her ache and yearn so that everything else was forgotten. His hands skimmed up her back, and down again. Lust surged through her veins, making her blood pound and her knees weak.

She slid her hands beneath the hem of his sweater, then upward, tracing over the ridges of his abdomen. His skin was warm and smooth, and his muscles quivered. The instinctive response emboldened her, and she let her hands explore further.

"Do you know what you're doing?" he asked, his voice strained.

"It's been a while," she admitted, with a small smile. "But I think I'm on the right track."

"You stay on that track and the train is going to start forging full-steam ahead."

She nibbled on his lower lip. "Is that a promise?"

"Yeah, it's a promise," he said. Then he captured her mouth, kissing her deeply, hungrily.

She pulled away from him to tug his sweater over his head, then reached for his belt. The rest of their clothes were dispensed with quickly, then he eased her back onto the bed. The press of his body against hers, the friction of bare skin against bare skin, was almost more than she could handle.

And then he cupped her breasts, his thumbs rubbing over the aching peaks, and she actually whimpered. When he replaced his hands with his mouth and laved her nipples with his tongue, she felt as if she might explode.

She arched beneath him, pressing closer so that his erection was nestled between her thighs.

"Somebody seems to be in a hurry," he mused.

"It's been a long time for me," she told him.

"Then let's not make you wait any longer."

"Condom?"

"Yeah, I'll take care of it," he assured her. "But first—I'm going to take care of you."

He kissed her then, deeply, hungrily and very thoroughly. Then his mouth moved across her jaw, down her throat. He nibbled her collarbone, licked the hollow between her breasts then kissed his way down to her navel, and lower. He nudged her thighs apart, and her breath backed up in her lungs.

Before she could decide if she wanted to say "Yes, please," or "No, thank you," his mouth was on her, stroking and sucking and licking, pushing her toward the highest pinnacle of pleasure. She fisted her hands in the sheets and bit down hard on her bottom lip as everything inside of her tightened, strained, and finally...shattered.

* * *

She was absolutely and stunningly beautiful.

Luke had meant it when he told her that he'd thought so from the very first, but never had Julie looked more beautiful than she did right now, with her cheeks flushed, her lips swollen from his kisses and those dreamy blue-gray eyes clouded with the aftereffects of passion.

But he wasn't nearly done with her yet.

He wanted to make love with her, slowly, patiently endlessly. And it would be making love. This wasn't sex—not on his part, anyway. Because he was in love with her. Not halfway in love or starting to fall, but one hundred percent head over heels. And for him, that changed everything.

Unfortunately, he knew it wasn't the same for her. She'd told him clearly and unequivocally that she wasn't going to fall in love with him. She was still intending to go back to Springfield on the seventh of December, with the expectation that he, of course, would stay in Pinehurst. Because this was where he lived, where his family, his career and his life were. But if she left—*when* she left—he knew that his heart would go with her.

And that was why this moment mattered so much. He wanted to touch her as no one had ever touched her before, so that when she was gone, she would always remember him. Their time together was already nearing its end, but he was determined to ensure that she enjoyed every minute of the two weeks that they had left together. Starting right now.

He worked his way back up her body, kissing and caressing every inch of her smooth, silky skin. He nipped her earlobe, nuzzled her throat, and his name slipped from her lips on a sigh. "Lukas."

He wanted to spend hours touching her, learning her pleasure points by listening to her soft gasps and throaty moans.

She had a lot of pleasure points, and discovering each and every one of them gave him an immense amount of pleasure.

But he was already rock-hard and aching for her. He sheathed himself with a condom and fought against the urge to lift up her hips and plunge into the sweet, wet heat at the apex of her thighs. Even if she hadn't warned him that it had been a long time for her, he knew it was her first time since giving birth, so he forced himself to go slow. He wasn't usually patient or restrained, but he focused his attention on both, easing into her a fraction of an inch at a time, giving her a chance to adjust and accept him.

Apparently he was taking too much time, because she suddenly planted her heels in the mattress and thrust her hips upward, taking him—all of him—fast and deep inside her. And that quickly, the last of his restraint snapped. She was so wet and tight around him, he feared for a minute that he would erupt like a teenager in the backseat at a drive-in.

But he drew in a deep breath and fisted his hands in the sheets, and when he had at least a semblance of control again, he began to move inside her. And she met him, stroke for stroke, in a synchronized rhythm that mated them together so perfectly he couldn't tell where he ended and she began.

Together they soared high and ever higher, until he captured her mouth and swallowed the cries that signaled her release even as his own rocketed through him.

Luke awoke alone in his bed. He'd heard Caden fussing in the night and then Julie had slipped out of his arms to attend to her child. He wasn't really surprised that she hadn't come back to his bed, but he was disappointed.

He grabbed a quick shower, shaved and headed down to the kitchen to make breakfast. To his surprise, Julie was already there, taking a pan of cinnamon buns out of the oven.

He crossed the room and nuzzled the back of her neck. "I'm not sure what smells better—you or breakfast."

"It's breakfast," she said, turning to face him. "And you have—"

"To kiss you," he said, and covered her mouth with his own.

Julie held herself immobile for the first three seconds, then her lips softened, and she responded to his kiss.

"Just because it's the morning after doesn't mean it has to be awkward," he said.

Her cheeks filled with color. "It's not the timing," she said quietly. "It's the fact that your brother's fiancée is sitting at the table."

He hadn't noticed Kelly when he walked in. He hadn't noticed anything but Julie. It didn't matter that they'd made love through the night—he only had to look at her to want her all over again.

"I brought over some leftovers from Thanksgiving dinner," Kelly said. "There's no way Jack and Ava and I will eat everything, and I'd hate to throw it out."

"Thanks," he said. "I'll think of you when I'm enjoying turkey sandwiches later. Now get out."

"Lukas!" Julie was shocked by his blunt—and undeniably rude—comment.

But his childhood friend simply pushed her chair away from the table and carried her empty coffee mug to the counter. "I'm going," she said. "I promised to take Ava shopping today, anyway."

But she looked worried as her gaze moved from Lukas to Julie and back again. Because he didn't want her expressing her concerns to Julie, who already had enough of her own, he kissed her cheek and steered her toward the door.

After he'd closed it behind Kelly, he turned to see Julie

spreading icing over the top of the warm pastry. "I kind of thought we would keep...this...between us," she said.

He went to the cupboard for a mug, poured himself a cup of the coffee she'd made. "I wasn't planning on any billboard advertising, but I don't keep secrets from my family."

She put two of the warm buns on a plate for him, took one for herself. She sat down beside Caden's carrier, tapped a fingertip to his nose, earning a wide, gummy smile.

"You're not worried that they'll disapprove?"

"No," he said simply. "I'm thirty-four years old—long past the age where I look to my big brothers for approval."

She poked at her cinnamon bun with a fork, peeling off layers of pastry. Luke had polished off one of the pastries and was halfway through the second before he realized that she hadn't taken a single bite.

"What else is on your mind?" he finally asked her.

She picked up her glass of juice, sipped. "Last night," she admitted. "It wasn't quite what I expected."

"Disappointed?" He didn't mind teasing her with the question because he knew very well that she had not been. "Because I promise you, I can do better."

"I wasn't disappointed," she said, and the color that flooded her cheeks confirmed it. "More like...overwhelmed."

"Why do you say that as if it's a bad thing?"

"Because I had no intention of getting involved with you. Because I thought—I'd hoped—the attraction was purely a hormonal thing."

"An itch that would go away once it was scratched?"

"I wouldn't have put it in such crude terms but, okay, yes."

"And now?"

She shook her head. "It's not just the way you made me feel last night. It's how you make me feel all the time. I've been happy here with you. Happier than I could have imagined."

He actually felt his heart swell inside his chest. "I'm glad," he said. "Because you make me happy, too. I care about you, Julie. You and Caden both."

Her eyes filled with tears. "I told you—I'm not going to let myself fall in love with you."

"I'm just asking you to give us a chance."

"A chance for what?"

He shrugged. "For whatever might happen."

"You make it sound so simple."

"I don't see any reason to complicate the situation unnecessarily."

"So you think we can keep this simple?" she asked hopefully.

"As simple as you want." He lied without compunction because he knew that the truth would send her back to Springfield before the words *I love you* were out of his mouth.

He couldn't have pinpointed when it happened. The revelation hadn't come to him like a bolt of lightning out of the sky, but he didn't doubt for a moment that it was true. What had started out as attraction had developed into affection that, over the past few weeks, had deepened and intensified. He loved her.

But he knew that even hinting at that would induce a panic. Instead, he gestured to her plate with his fork and said, "Are you going to eat that or dissect it?"

After breakfast, Lukas tidied up the kitchen while Julie nursed Caden and tried to convince herself that her relationship with the sexy veterinarian wasn't getting more complicated by the day.

When she'd put the baby down in the cradle, she checked her email and found a message from her parents. They'd been in regular contact over the past few weeks and their messages were always rich with details about excursions they'd taken, places they'd seen and people they'd met. In every word she read, Julie could tell that they were having a fabulous time, and she was happy for them. Because as much as she missed her family, she realized that she was happy, too. Being here with Lukas made her happy. Happier than she could ever remember being. So why did that scare her?

After things had gone so wrong with Elliott, she hadn't been able to imagine being with another man. How could she trust anyone when her judgment had been so wrong? Maybe she was confusing sex with love. Maybe her mind was still clouded from the incredible orgasms Lukas had given her the night before.

She wanted to believe that was the answer—that what she was feeling for him was lust and gratitude and nothing more. But she knew that what she was feeling was about so much more than the phenomenal lovemaking they'd shared. In fact, if she was being honest with herself, she would admit that she'd probably fallen in love with Lukas before he'd ever kissed her.

Yeah, she could tell him she wouldn't fall in love with him, but those words didn't actually give her power over her heart. And the fact was, she loved who he was and everything about him.

The past few weeks with him had been absolutely fabulous, but as much as she enjoyed being with him, she didn't belong here. She lived and worked in Springfield. And Evangeline was expecting her back at The Grayson Gallery at the beginning of February.

She didn't need to work, and she certainly wasn't working for the money. Being a part-time curator was never going to make her rich. True, there was a certain amount of prestige associated with her position, but that had never mattered to Julie. She'd taken the job because she'd needed the sense of purpose that it gave her, the independent identity. Something that separated her from Elliott, goals and ambitions that were entirely her own.

Except that, sometime during the past few months, those goals and ambitions had changed. Or maybe it was having Caden that changed everything. Now her career didn't matter to her nearly as much as being a good mother to her son. And she didn't want to go back to Springfield nearly as much as she wanted to stay with Lukas.

She'd never imagined herself living in a town like Pinehurst—but only because she'd never known that towns like it existed. She'd never thought of settling anywhere outside of Springfield because everything she needed and everyone she loved was there. Four years at college aside, she'd never lived anywhere else. She'd taken plenty of trips—educational jaunts to various destinations in Europe and Asia, vacations to sandy beaches in the Caribbean and exotic ports of call on the Mediterranean.

Her trip across the United States probably represented the most significant journey in her twenty-three years. Not just because she'd seen so much of the country and met so many interesting people, but because she'd learned so much about herself. And her favorite part of the journey was this unscheduled and extended layover in Pinehurst.

She felt as if she belonged here, in this town, with Lukas. She loved his house—the history and character of it; she adored Einstein—despite the prime rib incident; she was even starting to develop warm feelings toward Daphne—although she wasn't entirely sure the cat reciprocated. And she loved Lukas.

Her mind was still spinning with that realization when she walked into the bedroom and found him on her bed. He was lounging against a pile of pillows, reading a book. Or maybe just pretending to read while he waited for her, because as soon as she stepped through the doorway, he closed the cover and set the novel aside.

He rose to his feet and reached for her, drawing her into his arms and covering her lips in a slow, mind-numbing kiss.

"Are you okay? After last night, I mean."

Of course he would ask. And of course, the fact that he did made her heart go all soft and gooey. "Yes, I'm okay. Better than okay," she admitted.

"Good." He smiled and drew her closer.

"Lukas—" She tried to wriggle out of his embrace. "It's the middle of the day."

"And?"

"And I have to get dressed."

"Why would you bother putting clothes on when I'm just going to take them off of you again?" he asked logically.

Because she wasn't quite how to respond to that, she folded her arms over her chest. "Just because I let you seduce me last night, doesn't mean I'm going to get naked with you—"

With one quick tug, he had the belt of her robe unfastened. She sucked in a breath as the cool air caressed her bare skin, then released it on a sigh when he cupped her breasts in his palms.

"You were saying?" he prompted.

She didn't see any point in fighting with him when the truth was, she wanted the same thing he did. She reached for the hem of his sweatshirt. "I was saying that you have far too many clothes on."

"I can remedy that."

The night before Jack and Kelly's wedding, Matt and Luke decided to take their brother out for an impromptu bachelor party. In other words, wings and beer at DeMarco's.

"Tomorrow night's the big night," Matt said, pouring draught from the pitcher into three frosty mugs.

Jack's smile was wide as he accepted the first glass. "The biggest."

"Well, I guess I don't have to ask if you're having second thoughts."

"Not a one," his brother agreed.

"I'm glad," Lukas said. "Because I'm not sure whose side I'd be on if something went wrong."

"Nothing's going to go wrong," the groom-to-be said confidently. "In fact, for the first time in my life, I feel as if everything is exactly the way it should be."

"You're a lucky guy—she's an incredible woman."

"I know it."

"And though I wouldn't usually admit this, I think she's pretty lucky, too."

"Undoubtedly." Jack grinned again.

"It's a second trip down the aisle for Jack, and I've done it twice myself," Matt noted, turning to Luke. "When are you going to take your first?"

"When I find the woman who makes me believe that the first will also be the last," Lukas told them.

"You don't think you've already found her?" Jack prompted.

"Maybe I have."

"So why are you hesitating?"

"It's…complicated."

"It's always complicated," Jack noted.

"You mean because she has a child with another man?" Matt guessed.

"I don't want to go through what you went through," Lukas told him.

"It's not even close to being the same situation," his brother pointed out. "Lindsay lied to me. For three years, she let me believe that I was Liam's father. I don't think you're under any similar illusions about Caden."

He wasn't, of course. And the paternity of Julie's son wasn't an issue for him—except when he thought about what his brother had gone through. "And when Liam's father came back into the picture, you lost your wife and your child."

"Is that what you're afraid of?" Matt prompted. "That Julie will go back to Caden's father?"

"No. She's been clear about the fact that he's not part of her life anymore."

"But he could be part of Caden's," Jack reminded him.

Luke nodded.

"So what?" Matt challenged.

"So what?" he echoed.

"Maybe Caden's biological father will be part of his life," his brother acknowledged. "So what? I know it isn't an ideal situation, but at least you'd be with the woman you love."

"I never said I loved her," Luke said, just a little defensively.

"If you don't, then why are we even having this conversation?" Jack wanted to know.

"Okay—I do love Julie. And Caden. And the idea of being without either one of them..." He shook his head. "I don't even want to think about it."

Matt clapped a hand on his shoulder. "Then I guess you'd better convince her to stay."

Chapter Fourteen

While the Garrett brothers were drinking beer at DeMarco's, the women were eating chocolate fondue at Kelly's house. It was a girls' night in under the guise of a bachelorette party.

Ava hung out with them for a while, more for the chocolate than the conversation, and when she'd had her fill of both, she retreated to her room to study for a history test. Georgia had earlier sent the twins to the basement to play video games and since that was about as much privacy as they were going to get in a house full of kids, she took advantage of the moment to ask Julie, "So, how long have you been sleeping with Lukas?"

Julie paused with a chunk of chocolate-covered banana over her plate and glanced over at Jack's fiancée.

Kelly held up her hands. "I didn't tell her."

"She didn't tell me," Georgia confirmed, then turned to scowl at her soon-to-be sister-in-law. "You knew and didn't tell me?"

"Well, it's not as if I had a chance," Kelly admitted. "This is the first time I've seen you since Thanksgiving."

"So how did you know?" Julie asked Georgia.

"I'm not sure," the other woman admitted. "It wasn't anything obvious, but you seem…different. More relaxed and contented."

"One of the benefits of mind-blowing sex," Kelly agreed.

Georgia kept her gaze on Julie. "So…is it?"

She felt her cheeks flush, but she couldn't stop her lips from curving in a slow and very satisfied smile.

"That good, huh?"

"I don't know if it's hormones or Lukas," she admitted. "But I've never experienced anything like what I've experienced with him."

"So why are you not dancing on the ceiling?" Kelly asked.

"Because there are too many reasons why a relationship between us would never work."

"From where I'm sitting, I'd say that you already have a relationship," Georgia noted. "And it seems to be working just fine."

"I'm going back to Springfield after the wedding."

Kelly frowned. "Does Lukas know?"

"Of course he knows. We both knew, from the beginning, that this was only a temporary arrangement. My family, my job, my *life* are in Springfield." But the most important factor, from her perspective, was that Lukas hadn't asked her to stay.

"You're going back to work?" Georgia asked.

"I have to." Well, financially she didn't have to—she had a trust fund from her maternal grandmother and significant savings of her own that she didn't need to worry about where she'd find the money for rent, but she'd promised Evangeline that she would come back.

"When?" Kelly asked.

"In a couple of months."

"Who's going to look after Caden while you're working?"

"I haven't had a chance to make those arrangements just yet."

"When I was living in New York City, if you weren't on a waiting list before you were pregnant, you weren't going to get a spot in any reputable daycare before your child's third birthday," Georgia told her.

"Springfield isn't Manhattan."

"I did the single-working-mother thing," Kelly told her. "And I lucked out in finding an absolutely wonderful woman who looked after Ava while I was working. But I promise you, if I'd had any other choice, I would have done things differently, and I'd have spent every possible minute with my child."

"I don't have any other choice," Julie insisted.

The other woman's pithy one-word reply made her blink.

"If you think you don't have any other choice, it's because you don't want to see the opportunity that's right in front of you."

"Kelly," Georgia admonished. "Julie was always clear about her plans to go back to Springfield."

"Then she shouldn't have let Lukas fall in love with her."

"He's not in love with me," Julie denied.

Kelly scowled at her. "Do you really not see it?"

Julie refused to argue with the bride-to-be on the night before her wedding. "How did we get on this topic, anyway? Aren't we supposed to be celebrating one of your last nights as a single woman?"

Kelly stabbed a strawberry with her fondue fork, a little more viciously than necessary. "I just have one more question."

"Okay," Julie said cautiously.

"Do you feel *anything* for him?"

She couldn't lie, not to Kelly and Georgia, and not about this. "I feel *everything* for him."

Georgia's brows drew together. "Then why are you leaving?"

"Because he hasn't asked me to stay."

Kelly blew out a breath. "The man truly is an idiot."

"But even if he did," Julie said, "I wouldn't want to stay so that Lukas could take care of me and my son."

"No one's suggesting that," Georgia told her.

"You should stay here with Lukas because it's where you want to be," Kelly said. "Because he's who you want to be with."

Julie wondered if it could be that simple, because she had no doubt that it was true.

Later that night, when Julie and Lukas were snuggled together after lovemaking, he said, "I've been thinking about what Quinn said on Thanksgiving—about us getting married so that I can be Caden's father."

"He also said that Finn and Fred should marry Puss and Boots so that they could have 'pup-tens.'"

"I think the former idea is a little more valid and definitely worth considering," he insisted.

"I'm not surprised that you'd be thinking about marriage when your brother's getting married tomorrow. But to think about marrying a woman you've only known a few weeks is crazy."

"I am crazy about you, Julie."

Her heart felt as though it was going to leap right out of her chest. But someone needed to be rational, and it obviously wasn't going to be him. "This entire conversation is insane."

"I'm starting to get the hang of this daddy thing," he told her. "And if we got married, it would alleviate a lot of questions and speculation about Caden's paternity."

"Do you really think anyone would believe that story about the two of us having a torrid affair in the spring?"

He shrugged.

"And even if they did, that's hardly a valid reason to get married."

"Okay, how about the fact that I want to spend every day— and every night—for the rest of my life with you?"

Her heart leaped again, but she knew she couldn't accept his offer. He'd said that he was crazy about her, that he wanted to spend his life with her and be a father to her son, but he hadn't said anything about loving her.

"I'm flattered, Lukas," she said, because she was. "But when I gave Elliott back his ring, I promised myself that I wouldn't ever get married for the wrong reasons."

"And you don't think you could love me?" he guessed.

Julie didn't know how to answer that question. Because the truth was, it wasn't that she didn't think she could love him but that she already did.

Because Jackson had insisted on a short engagement and the church that Kelly wanted to get married in was booked for every Saturday into the following spring, they decided to have a midweek evening candlelight service. And when the bride and groom held hands and looked into one another's eyes to exchange their vows, it was one of the most beautiful and heartwarming ceremonies Julie had ever witnessed.

Of course, being at Jackson and Kelly's wedding got Julie thinking about her own aborted plans. She'd been so excited when Elliott proposed. As many young girls do, she'd dreamed about her wedding for a long time. She'd stockpiled bridal magazines, clipped out photos of dresses and flowers and cakes. Yet when Elliott put his ring on her finger, she'd never taken her planning to the next level. She hadn't gone dress shopping or visited floral shops or sampled wedding cakes.

And she had absolutely no regrets that the wedding had

never happened. Because even if Elliott had never raised a hand to her, he'd also never looked at her the way Jackson looked at Kelly. Or the way she looked right back at him.

Of course, Julie hadn't looked at Elliott that way, either. She'd loved who she thought he was and the life she'd envisioned for them together, but in the end, she'd had no difficulty walking away from him. There'd been no void in her life when she left him. In fact, she'd felt a sense of relief, a feeling of peace that she'd finally made the right choice. And that choice had, eventually, brought her to where she was today.

Glancing over at Lukas now, she saw that he was looking at her, and the warmth and affection in his gaze made her tingle all over. No one had ever looked at her the way he did; no one had ever made her feel the way he did.

But did he love her?

Despite Kelly's conviction that he did, Lukas had never said those words to Julie. And why would he put his heart on the line when she'd told him that she wasn't going to fall in love with him? Of course, she knew now that those words had been a lie even when she'd spoken them. But was she strong enough—brave enough—to trust in what they had together?

She thought about that question through the meal and the numerous toasts and speeches in honor of the happy couple. The first dance of the bride and groom was usually followed by the traditional father and bride dance. Instead, it was the groom who danced with his daughter. As they waltzed around the dance floor, Julie marveled at the fact that Jackson had only recently learned that he had a daughter—and now he was dancing with her at his wedding to her mother.

Her gaze shifted across the table to Lukas's other brother. Matt, always the doting father, was sitting beside Georgia with Pippa in his lap. Certainly no one would ever guess that he wasn't the biological father of the three kids he loved as if they were his own. Julie didn't have to wonder if Lukas could ever love Caden the same way—because she knew that he already did.

And it wasn't just Lukas—his whole family had accepted Julie and her son, easily and without question. Well, Kelly had had more than a few questions, but Julie understood that her inquiries were motivated by concern and affection. She was trying to protect Lukas, and Julie could appreciate and respect that kind of loyalty.

That was one of the reasons she could imagine herself living here, being part of this family, part of the community. Pinehurst would be a wonderful place to raise her son. In fact, Georgia had said one of the reasons she'd decided to move here with her family was to raise them in a smaller town with old-fashioned values. Looking at Georgia's adorable twins now, Julie remembered Shane's impulsive offer to share his building blocks with Caden, and she knew that she didn't want to take him away from here.

She wanted her son to know Quinn and Shane and Pippa. And although Ava was already mostly grown up, she absolutely adored Caden and Julie knew she wouldn't ever find a babysitter for him that she liked or trusted more. Maybe they wouldn't be related by blood, but spending time with Lukas's family had made her realize that family was about so much more than shared DNA. It was the bonds and connections that developed through mutual respect and affection, but the greatest connection was love.

Julie loved Lukas with her whole heart.

And that, she finally realized, was why she had to go back to Springfield.

When the dance floor was opened up to all of the other guests, Lukas came looking for her. The third song had barely begun when she saw him walking toward her, determination in every step. There was something incredibly sexy about a man with a purpose. Or maybe it was the glint in his eye that made everything inside her quiver.

He offered his hand to her. "Dance with me."

It was more of a demand than an invitation, but Julie didn't care. She just wanted to be in his arms. Ava, back at the table after her turn around the dance floor, willingly took Caden from her.

"Have I told you that you look absolutely spectacular tonight?" Lukas asked, as he drew her into his embrace.

She shook her head.

"Well, you do. When I saw you come down the stairs in that dress…you actually took my breath away."

She'd gone shopping for the occasion, because she knew she didn't have any appropriate wedding attire with her, and because she was always happy for an excuse to go shopping. The emerald-green wrap-style dress was both flattering and functional, with long, narrow sleeves and a full skirt that twirled above her knees.

He dipped his head and lowered his voice. "But as fabulous as you look in that dress, I can't wait to get you out of it."

The words sent a quick thrill through her veins. And as much as she wanted the same thing, she couldn't resist teasing, "You think you're going to get lucky tonight?"

He smiled, but his eyes were serious. "I think the luckiest day of my life was the day I met you."

"I feel the same way," she admitted.

"I realized something today, when Jack and Kelly exchanged their vows. For the first time in my life, I seriously envied my brother. And no—not because he was marrying Kelly, but because he was marrying the woman he loves. And because I know that they're going to be together forever, happily ever after.

"I want the same thing, Julie. I want to spend the rest of my life with you because you mean everything to me. But

I don't just want you—I want Caden, too. I want to be your husband and his father, and maybe, in the future, we could add another kid or two to the mix, but that doesn't matter to me nearly as much as being with you."

Her heart was pounding so hard inside her chest it actually ached. "Is that your idea of a proposal?"

"I've got the ring in my pocket," he told her. "And I'll get down on one knee right here and now if you want me to."

She shook her head. "No."

The last thing she wanted was the focus of all of Jack and Kelly's guests on them—especially when she couldn't give Lukas the answer he wanted.

"I'm hoping for a different response to the spending our lives together part," he prompted.

"I want to give you a different response," she admitted. "But I'm going back to Springfield. Tomorrow."

"What? Why?"

"To see Elliott."

Though the music continued, he stopped moving. "You're still in love with him."

"No." Her response was as vehement as it was immediate, because she didn't want Lukas to believe that for even half a second. "But I have to tell him about Caden. I've been putting it off, for reasons I'm not even sure I understand. But sometime during the past few days, I realized that I won't ever be able to move forward with my life until I know that the past is behind me." She held his gaze, not even trying to hide the depth of emotion she knew would be reflected in her eyes. "I want to move forward with my life—with you."

He took her hand and guided her off the dance floor. But instead of heading back toward their table, he turned in the opposite direction. He found a quiet corner, behind an enormous Christmas tree, and faced her. "So when are we leaving?"

She blinked. "What?"

"Do you really think I'm going to let you meet your former fiancé without backup?"

And that was just one of the reasons she loved him. But as much as she appreciated his protectiveness and willingness to rearrange his schedule to be there for her, she wasn't going to let him go all Neanderthal man on her.

"I'm meeting him for coffee at The Cobalt Room—a restaurant in the Courtland Hotel," she explained. "It's a public place, so there's no need to worry about backup."

"You don't want me to come with you?"

"I do want you to come to Springfield with me, but I need to meet with Elliott on my own. I need to stand up for myself. You don't have to like it," she told him. "But I hope you respect me enough to understand that this is something I have to do."

"I don't like it." He touched his lips to hers. "But I understand."

"Do you think you can clear your schedule so that we can stay in Springfield for the weekend?"

"Absolutely."

She took his hands, linked their fingers together. "Good. My parents will be home on Saturday and I'd really like them to meet the man I'm going to marry."

"Does that mean you accept my proposal?"

"It means that I'm hoping you'll ask me again after I've cleaned up the mess I've made of my life."

Julie was more worried about her meeting with her former fiancé than she'd been willing to admit to Lukas. Although she'd never loved Elliott with the same depth and intensity that she loved Lukas, she'd had genuine feelings for him. She didn't regret walking away. She would not be a victim and she would never forgive Elliott for what he'd done, but she still worried that seeing him again might stir up old feelings that she didn't want stirred.

"Mr. Winchester called to say that he would be a few minutes late, but his table is ready, if you'd like to be seated," the hostess told her.

"Yes, please."

She wished she'd accepted Lukas's offer to come with her. She'd wanted to do this on her own, to prove to herself that she could, but now she was regretting her decision. She wanted him there with her. She wanted the man she loved beside her, and she wanted the comforting weight of her baby in her arms. She felt so much braver and stronger when she was with Lukas, and she knew she was capable of doing anything to protect her son.

She ordered decaf coffee and was stirring cream into her cup when she spotted Elliott crossing the room.

She watched his approach, trying to view him through the eyes of an objective stranger. He moved with purpose and authority. He was a good-looking man, charming and charismatic, and he drew attention wherever he went.

She exhaled a grateful sigh at the realization that she honestly didn't feel anything for him anymore. Not even fear. And with that realization, a sense of peace settled over her, calming any residual nerves. He couldn't hurt her. She wouldn't let him. And she wouldn't let him hurt her son.

But could he hurt her father? That was the question that continued to nag at her.

He reached the table and leaned down to kiss her cheek, and though she stiffened, she didn't pull away. She'd wanted this meeting with Elliott to take place in a public venue for a number of reasons but causing a scene wasn't one of them. So she forced a smile and kept it on her face while he seated himself across from her.

"I'm so pleased you called," Elliott said.

"Are you?"

"Of course. I know the situation between us didn't exactly end on a positive note, but I hoped we could find our way back to being friends."

"Do you have a spin doctor on your political team now? Because 'didn't exactly end on a positive note' is an interesting interpretation of the fact that you slapped me around."

He winced at the bluntness of her assessment. "I'd had too much to drink. I lost my temper."

"That doesn't justify what you did."

"I'm not trying to justify it," he assured her. "I know the alcohol isn't an excuse, but it is part of the reason.

"When you left—when I realized what I'd done to make you leave—" he hastily amended "—I hit rock bottom. I finally accepted that I couldn't fix everything on my own. I went to an AA meeting, then I found a counselor who specializes in anger management, and I turned my life around."

"If that's true, I'm glad."

"It is true. But I couldn't have done any of it without Genevieve."

"Genevieve Durand?" She'd met the woman, whose family had been close friends of the Winchester family for years, on several occasions. But she'd never thought that Genevieve and Elliott were particularly friendly.

"Well, she's Genevieve Winchester now."

She just stared at him, still not comprehending.

Elliott's easy smile faded. "You didn't know?"

"Know what?"

"I got married. Four months ago."

"Oh. Well…congratulations."

"I'm sorry—I honestly thought you knew. The engagement announcement was in both the *Globe* and the *Herald*."

She shook her head. "I've been out of town. I didn't know."

If she had known, she might not have stressed for so long

about the possibility that he might want to reconcile for the sake of their child. The child who was, of course, the reason she'd needed to see him today.

"Does Genevieve know what happened between us?"

"I told her everything."

"Not quite everything," she countered.

Elliott's gaze narrowed. "What do you mean?"

She blew out a breath. "I had a child," she finally said. "He was born the first of November."

Chapter Fifteen

It went against every instinct Luke possessed to let Julie
meet with her former fiancé by herself. He understood why
she wanted to do so, but he didn't like it. And if she left that
meeting with even one hair on her head out of place, the as-
piring politician was going to be very sorry.

He'd been tempted to follow her, to lurk behind a potted
plant in the restaurant or hover at the wine bar. And maybe
she suspected that he would do something like that because
she'd left Caden in his care. Or maybe she just didn't want
the baby anywhere near his biological father.

Julie never referred to Elliott as Caden's father. As far as
she was concerned, he might have contributed to her son's
DNA but that didn't make him his father. Lukas agreed that
biology was only part of the equation, because while there
was absolutely no genetic link between him and the little boy,
there was an undeniable connection. And there wasn't anything he wouldn't do for the child—or his mother.

Which was undoubtedly why he ended up babysitting while Julie went to meet with the man she'd once planned to marry. The man who had used physical strength and threats to intimidate her.

Thankfully, she'd been strong enough to break away from Elliott. And while he understood that she wanted to prove that she could stand on her own two feet, he suspected that she'd also wanted to keep Luke a safe distance from her ex. Because if he came face-to-face with the man who had dared laid a hand on Julie, Luke knew it was entirely possible that he'd end up in jail on an assault charge.

Which reminded him of one more thing that he wanted to take care of while they were in town.

He'd dropped her off at the restaurant where she was meeting Elliott, and it turned out that the Courtland Hotel was conveniently located across the street from the DA's office. And by the time she called for him to pick her up, he'd made the necessary calls and contacts.

He very nearly forgot the plan when she came down the steps from the hotel lobby, her cheeks flushed, her eyes glowing. Just looking at her took his breath away. And when she planted her lips on his and kissed him, long and hard, right in the middle of the sidewalk, she took his breath away all over again.

"You look…happy."

"I am." She took Caden from his arms and held him close for a minute. "Thank you."

"For what?"

"For coming with me—and for staying away."

"You're welcome," he said dryly.

She grinned. "I've got something to show you."

"Here?" He looked pointedly at the pedestrians moving around them.

"Right here, right now," she said, and pulled a manila envelope out of her purse.

His curiosity undeniably piqued, Luke opened the flap and took out the papers inside. It was a formal legal document prepared, he noted, by Jackson Garrett. As he skimmed through the legalese, certain key phrases caught his attention, most notably "acknowledgment of paternity" and "voluntary relinquishment of parental rights." And it was duly signed and dated by Elliott Davis Winchester III.

"Why are you frowning?" Julie asked him.

He hadn't realized that he was, but he couldn't deny that he was a little perturbed by this unexpected turn of events. "I can't believe that he signed away his legal rights without ever seeing his child."

"I knew he'd be worried about the potential scandal of having an out-of-wedlock child. It turns out, that's only half of it."

"What's the other half?"

"His wife is pregnant."

"He's married?"

She nodded, apparently unfazed by the news. "They had a small, intimate ceremony in Boston four months ago."

"I guess it didn't take him long to get over his broken heart," he mused.

"I never thought I was the great love of his life, but I did think our relationship was about more than politics. But Elliott had a precise plan mapped out for his road to the House of Representatives, and finding a devoted wife was an important part of that plan—almost as important as his carefully documented ancestry and Ivy League education."

"Are you saying that when you left, he simply found an alternate bride?"

"And without much difficulty," she said. "Genevieve Durand's family and his have been close for a lot of years."

"Then I guess she knew what she was getting into."

She nodded.

"How do you feel about all of this?" he asked cautiously.

"Relieved. And ecstatic. My biggest worry was that he would try to make a claim on Caden—now I know that isn't a concern."

"What about his accusation against your father?"

"I didn't even think about that," she admitted. "And really, it doesn't matter anymore, because Elliott has nothing to gain by going public with his claim."

He stopped beside a two-story red brick building. "Don't you want to know if there's any truth to it?"

She looked at the writing on the glass door, then at him. "What are we doing here?"

"I thought, if you really wanted to put the past behind you, we should know exactly what's in that past."

"This is almost scarier than facing Elliott," she admitted.

He held out his hand.

After the briefest hesitation, she took it. And they walked into the DA's office together.

Nerves tangled in Julie's belly as Lukas chatted with the receptionist. After a few minutes, she led them down a long hallway to the conference room where Mr. Chasan was seated at the end of a long, glossy table, reviewing a file folder that was open in front of him.

He closed the cover when they entered and rose to his feet. "Harry Chasan," he said. "Former District Attorney, mostly retired now, but I hang around occasionally and consult on cases. I was hanging around today." He offered his hand to Lukas first, then to Julie, then smiled at Caden.

He gestured for them to sit, which they did. Julie didn't know what to say—she wasn't sure how Lukas had arranged this meeting or what information he'd given, so she let him take the lead.

"I was told that you were the prosecutor in the State of Massachusetts vs. Cosgrove case."

"I can't say the name rang any bells," Harry admitted. "But I pulled the file when your brother called to inquire about it, and sure enough, I was."

Julie looked at Lukas. Apparently he had no qualms about his brother pulling strings to help him get what he wanted. On the other hand, there was nothing unethical about one attorney contacting another for information about an old case.

"Do you remember it?"

"I do now." His gaze shifted from the file to Julie, and he nodded. "You've grown up, Miss Marlowe. I almost didn't recognize you."

She managed a smile. "It's been six years."

"A drop in the bucket when you get to be my age," he told her. "Can you tell me why you're digging into this now?"

"I just had some questions," she hedged.

"What kind of questions?"

"Mainly I wondered why I wasn't prosecuted."

"Insufficient evidence," he said bluntly.

"Who—" She swallowed. "Who made that decision?"

"I did."

"Did you, uh, consult with anyone about it?"

"Yeah, the idiot cop who arrested you."

She blinked at that.

"There wasn't any evidence to justify charges. You should have been released into your parents' custody as soon as you were brought in, but the arresting officer had a real hard-on about the fact that he'd busted a judge's kid." He shrugged apologetically. "Sorry, but there's no other way to describe it."

"So my father didn't pull any strings to get me released?"

Harry laughed at that. "Judge 'Morality' Marlowe? Not a chance."

"You didn't talk to him about the case at all?" she pressed.

"Sure I did. And Reg told me that I wasn't to do him any favors. If there was evidence to charge you, I should charge you.

"Between us now," he confided, "I think he was a little concerned about the path he could see you going down and thought a few hours in lockup might have done you some good. But I reviewed the evidence in this case the same way I would have any other, and the undisputed facts were that you went for a ride in a car that you didn't know was stolen. You made a bad choice, but you didn't commit a crime."

They shook hands with Harry again, thanked him for his time, and left the DA's office.

"I guess I owe you another thank-you," Julie said.

"Does that mean I get another kiss?"

"You're going to get a lot more kisses after we get back to my parents' place and get Caden settled down," she promised.

"When are your parents coming back?"

"Their flight is scheduled to get in to Boston at six-oh-five tomorrow morning, and it's about an hour and a half from the airport to our place." She glanced at her watch. "So we'll have the place to ourselves for about sixteen hours."

"Lead the way."

By the time they got back to the car, Caden was seriously fussing, so Julie fed and changed him before they started the drive to her parents. Sleepy and satisfied, the baby fell asleep within a few minutes. Fifteen minutes later, Luke pulled into the driveway of her parents' home.

He took Caden in his carrier while she gathered the diaper bag and her purse. Inside the door, he set down the carrier beside an antique chest so that he could take his shoes off. But he didn't get a chance before Julie pushed him back against the wall and started kissing him. A deep openmouthed kiss with full body contact. She teased him with her teeth and her tongue as she gyrated against him. And then, just as abruptly as she'd started, she stopped.

"That's just a prelude," she said, and turned away.

He snaked his arm around her waist and hauled her back against him.

"Two can play that game," he warned, and kissed her again, slowly and deeply, using his tongue in a teasing imitation of lovemaking until she moaned and shuddered against him.

"Julie?"

She jolted, dropping her hands from his shoulders and pushing him away. "Mom."

Luke closed his eyes and softly banged his forehead against the wall, cursing silently.

"I, uh, didn't think you were coming back until tomorrow," Julie said, crossing the room to embrace her mother.

The older woman's arms came around her daughter, and she held her close for a long moment. "We caught an earlier flight," she said. "And I'm so glad we did. I'm so glad you're home."

"It's good to see you, Mom. I missed you—so much."

Her mother blinked away the tears that had filled her eyes and turned her attention to Luke, who was hoping like hell she wouldn't notice that he was still partially aroused. Apparently being caught in an erotic lip-lock by a woman's mother wasn't quite humiliating enough to cool his ardor.

"And who is this?" she said, her tone decidedly less warm. "Is this the surprise you mentioned?"

"What? Oh, no. This is Lukas Garrett. Lukas, meet my mom, Lucinda Marlowe."

"I apologize, ma'am, for the, uh, situation you walked in on."

"I'm glad I wasn't ten minutes later." She took a few steps toward the staircase that led to the upper level. "Reginald—Julie's home."

"About that surprise," Julie began, just as her father came into the foyer.

There were more hugs and kisses and tears as Luke tried to blend into the elegant satin-striped wallpaper.

And then Caden woke up.

Several hours later, Julie took her overnight bag up to her childhood bedroom while Lukas was escorted by her father to the guest room on the opposite side and at the far end of the hall. After nursing Caden and settling him to sleep in his portable crib, she tiptoed down the hall in search of Lukas.

"I'm really sorry about this...arrangement," she told him.

"I'm not. In fact, I'm grateful they're not digging a hole in the backyard right now to bury my body."

"Maybe if it was the spring," she teased. "But this time of year, the ground's too hard for digging."

"Well, your brothers are supposed to be here en masse tomorrow. I'm sure between the three of them and your father, they'll figure something out."

She linked her arms behind his neck. "They'll figure out that I'm finally with the right man for me."

"Yeah, that's likely." His words dripped with sarcasm, but he wrapped his arms around her waist and drew her into his embrace.

"Seriously, I don't think either of my parents was as scandalized as you were," she teased.

"It's just that I'd hoped you'd have my ring on your finger instead of my tongue in your mouth when I met your parents for the first time."

"Actually, my dad was still upstairs when your tongue was in my mouth."

"Because that makes a lot of difference."

She laughed softly.

"I wanted to make a good impression."

"There's no doubt you made an impression," she assured him. "Now, about that ring you mentioned."

"You mean the ring you didn't want me to give you a few days ago?"

"If that's the same ring that I couldn't accept until I got my life in order, then yes."

"Are you saying you want it now?"

"I want the ring." She brushed her lips against his. "I want you."

"The ring's in my pocket," he told her.

"Really?" She immediately dropped her arms and began searching the pockets of his jeans, then she looked up at him and rolled her eyes. "It's *not* in your pocket."

"It's not? I was sure I put it there... Oh, right. It's in the pocket of my jacket."

She fisted her hands on her hips. "Are you going to give it to me—or have you changed your mind?"

He crossed to the wing chair in the corner, where he'd tossed his jacket, and retrieved the ring box from the pocket. "I haven't changed my mind," he assured her. "But I thought you might have reconsidered."

"Why would you think that?"

"Because Elliott is out of your life now, completely and forever. You don't have to worry about him making any claims on your baby, so you don't need a stand-in father for Caden."

"I never wanted a stand-in father for my son," she told him. "I want a real father for him. But that has nothing to do with my response to your proposal.

"I love my son, more than anything in this world. More than I ever thought it was possible to love another human being," she continued. "But I'm an old-fashioned girl at heart, Lukas. And I never would have agreed to marry you if I wasn't in love with you."

He felt as if an enormous weight had been lifted off of his

chest. "You told me you wouldn't fall in love with me," he reminded her.

"I didn't want to," she admitted. "But my heart had other plans."

He took the ring—a square cut diamond with smaller channel-set diamonds around the band—out of the box. "You really do love me?"

"I really do love you."

"And you want to marry me?"

She offered her left hand. "Yes, I want to marry you."

He slid the ring onto her finger, then dipped his head to kiss her.

There was no hesitation in her response, but when he eased his lips from hers, her brows drew together.

He rubbed a finger over the furrow. "Is something wrong?"

"Is something wrong?" she echoed. "Is that all you're going to say?"

One side of his mouth turned up, just a little. "What do you want me to say?"

"I'd kind of like to hear that you love me, too."

He skimmed his knuckles down her cheek. "Do you doubt it?"

"No," she admitted. "But it would still be nice to hear the words."

"I love you, Julie Marlowe." He brushed his lips against hers. Once. "With my whole heart—" twice "—for now and forever." And again.

She sighed happily. "Wow—that sounded even better than I expected."

"You'll probably get sick of hearing it," he warned. "Because I'm going to tell you every single day, for the rest of our lives."

"I'm looking forward to it." She snuggled closer to him. "It's hard to believe that only five weeks ago, I was stuck in my car in a ditch and thinking that things couldn't possibly get any worse. And then you tapped on my window, and changed everything."

"*You* changed everything for me," he told her. "You and Caden. Which reminds me—there was one more thing I wanted to ask you."

"What's that?"

"After we're married, will you let me adopt Caden so that I can be his father in every sense?"

Her eyes filled with tears. "You already are," she told him. "But yes, I would be thrilled if you adopted Caden."

"And maybe someday we could give him a little brother or sister?" Luke prompted.

She smiled, nodded. "I'd like that."

"But when we do start thinking about another child, could we try to plan it so that he or she will be due in the spring or summer?" he suggested.

"Why?"

"Because I don't want to chance you going into labor in the middle of another blizzard."

"You mean *you* don't want to have to deliver another baby," she accused.

"I'd rather not," he admitted.

She laughed. "I'll keep that in mind."

Epilogue

Julie stood at the window, her arms folded across her chest, watching the snow fall. Behind her, flames were flickering in the fireplace.

"I'm experiencing the oddest sense of déjà vu," she admitted to Lukas when he entered the family room.

"You said you wanted a white Christmas," he reminded her.

"I was hoping for a light dusting, just enough to make everything sparkly and pretty."

"Obviously Mother Nature had a different idea."

"So much for our plan to attend Christmas Eve church service," Julie noted.

He took her hand and drew her over to the sofa. Of course, Einstein tried to climb up, too, but settled when Julie reached down to scratch between his ears.

"Are you disappointed?" Lukas asked her.

"A little," she admitted. "It's one of my favorite Christmas traditions, and I wanted to share it with you and Caden."

"Next year," he promised. "And the year after that, and every year for the rest of our lives together."

"I like the sound of that."

"Me, too."

She settled into his arms. "I was thinking about a June wedding."

"June? That's six months away."

"A wedding takes time to plan."

"Ava managed to plan Jack and Kelly's wedding in a few weeks," he reminded her.

"And it was a beautiful wedding," Julie agreed. "But it's going to take some time for my mother to forgive me for not telling her that she was going to be a grandmother. I don't think she would ever forgive me if I deprived her of a proper wedding on top of that."

"I don't care about proper as long as it's legal. And my brother has connections at the courthouse—"

"No," she said firmly.

He sighed. "June? Really?"

"Maybe May."

"How about February?"

She shook her head. "Too soon, and the weather's too unpredictable." She tipped her head up to look at him. "Speaking of weather, I'm a little worried about my parents traveling through all this snow tomorrow."

"Your dad has an SUV with snow tires," he reminded her. "And as he assured you, no less than a dozen times, there's no way he and your mom are going to miss their first grandchild's first Christmas."

"I know they wanted us to spend the holiday in Springfield with them, but I wanted Caden's first Christmas to be here."

"No doubt it will be a Christmas to remember, with your parents and my brothers and their families all underfoot."

"It will be chaos tomorrow." And she was already looking forward to it. "But tonight—" she lifted her arms to link them around his neck "—it's just you and me."

"And Caden," he reminded her.

"Who has a full belly, a clean diaper and visions of sugar plums dancing in his head."

He dipped his head to nibble on her lips, and Julie's eyes started to close when she felt a swipe of tongue between her toes.

"And Einstein," she added, giggling when he licked her toes again.

Lukas went over to the Christmas tree and found a package with the dog's name on the tag. "Look, Einstein. Santa brought something for you, too."

He tore the paper off of the conical-shaped rubber toy that he'd prefilled with treats and offered it to him. Einstein raced across the room, his attention immediately and completely focused on the toy.

"That should keep him busy for a long time," Lukas said, returning to the sofa.

"And Caden will sleep for at least a couple of hours," Julie told him.

"If we have a couple of hours—" he brushed his lips over hers "—I have an idea."

His hands were already under her shirt, skimming over her skin, making her tremble.

"Am I going to like this idea?"

"I think so."

A long time later, snuggled in the warmth of his embrace, Julie knew that she had never been more blessed. Because she didn't just have their first Christmas as a real family to look forward to, but the rest of their lives together—and she knew the future was going to be a merry one.

* * * * *

A sneaky peek at next month...

Cherish™

ROMANCE TO MELT THE HEART EVERY TIME

My wish list for next month's titles...

In stores from 20th September 2013:

❑ The Christmas Baby Surprise – Shirley Jump

& A Weaver Beginning – Allison Leigh

❑ Single Dad's Christmas Miracle – Susan Meier

& Snowbound with the Soldier – Jennifer Faye

In stores from 4th October 2013:

❑ A Maverick for Christmas – Leanne Banks

& Her Montana Christmas Groom – Teresa Southwick

❑ The Redemption of Rico D'Angelo – Michelle Douglas

& The Rancher's Christmas Princess – Christine Rimmer

Available at WHSmith, Tesco, Asda, Eason, Amazon and Apple

Just can't wait?

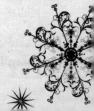

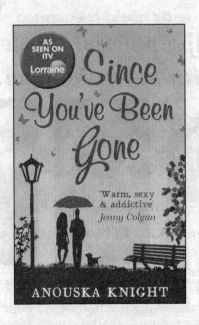

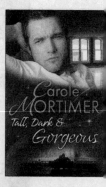

The World of Mills & Boon®

There's a Mills & Boon® series that's perfect for you. We publish ten series and, with new titles every month, you never have to wait long for your favourite to come along.

Blaze®
Scorching hot, sexy reads
4 new stories every month

By Request
Relive the romance with the best of the best
9 new stories every month

Cherish™
Romance to melt the heart every time
12 new stories every month

Desire™
Passionate and dramatic love stories
8 new stories every month